The blood of his ancestors recognized them . . .

The surface was a treasure trove, but he hated and feared it. Yet a man did what he had to do.

The sound of heavy boots on asphalt caught his attention. He turned.

Three strangers had appeared around the corner of the block. Their suits were covered with brown and green plastic plates like fish scales, a feature which he had never heard of and didn't understand. A long, sheathed cutter hung from each belt instead of the usual selection of tools.

He was surprised. The surface was a big place, and the odds were very high against two expeditions scavenging the same site at the same time. He switched to the common channel and spoke. "Welcome, gentlemen. I'm Hector Lopez, the chief scavenger of this Pemex Under expedition. And you are?"

The strangers didn't answer. They were ten feet away now, and it seemed to Hector that they were grinning. They pulled out their cutters, and the glistening strips of metal looked more like ancient weapons than scavenging tools.

Hector could make out the nature of their grins, the set of their eyes. He had never seen such expressions before, but the blood of his ancestors recognized them. . . . Too late.

ERIC VINICOFF

MAIDEN FLIGHT

BAEN BOOKS

MAIDEN FLIGHT

A Baen Books Original

Baen Publishing Enterprises
260 Fifth Avenue
New York, N.Y. 10001

First printing, December 1988

ISBN: 0-671-69795-1

Cover art by Alan Gutierrez.
Interior drawings by John McLaughlin.

Printed in the United States of America

Distributed by
SIMON & SCHUSTER
1230 Avenue of the Americas
New York, N.Y. 10020

To Mom

CHAPTER ONE

"ETA at target ten minutes, sir," the navigation officer reported.

The Operations/Control Center of the zep *Shenandoah* was a semicircle of aluminum and dark plastic, dimly lit to accentuate the glowing screens and displays. The officers leaned over their stations around the curved control console. Low voices broke through the muted growl of the motors.

Colonel McCrarey left his command chair in the middle of the OCC. He was a compact, muscular man nearing his fiftieth birthday. His face had been given a teak finish by the sun and creased by years of frowning. Those years had also cost him all but a fringe of close-cropped black hair. His Alpha uniform was perfectly tailored and immaculate.

"Any sign that we've been detected?" he asked the com officer.

"No, sir. The target hasn't transmitted since its last WeatherNet update. The next update is scheduled in three minutes. Stand by for EC."

Colonel McCrarey went over to the pilot. "Picking up any other traffic?"

"Nothing in radar range, sir."

Colonel McCrarey smiled inwardly. The *Shenandoah*

1

was about to engage the enemy. A helpless, pitiful enemy, true, but that was better than no enemy at all.

Peering out the bow windscreen, he saw blackness and a lot of stars. The *Shenandoah* was cruising through a moonless night thirteen thousand feet above the Pacific Ocean. Tokyo Four wasn't in sight yet.

He returned to his chair, and stabbed the com's all-ship channel. "Attention, this is Colonel McCrarey. We are about to go into action. I expect every one of you to do your duty and uphold the proud military tradition of Alpha. God bless you."

It was a strange sort of conflict. The windrider called Alpha had originally been a United States Air Force radar platform above the Beaufort Sea. Then the War had wiped out most of the human race, and rendered the Earth's surface uninhabitable. Remnants of civilization had survived by retreating in opposite directions. Alpha had survived too, thanks to a valiant defense and some very lucky breaks. As the new world of underground industrial enclaves and migratory windriders came into being, Alpha had chosen to remain a warrior rather than become a scavenger and tradesman.

So Alpha hid in the Arctic, where other windriders rarely came because there were no ruins to loot. Its two zeps flew sorties against the windrider towns. Alpha took what it needed, obeying the oldest law of all. And it zealously guarded the secret of its existence. The windrider towns were disgustingly non-violent, but they could pose a threat if aroused.

"Colonel, the target is sending the scheduled update," the com officer reported.

Colonel McCrarey nodded. "Proceed with EC."

"Yes, sir." The com officer's hands moved deftly across the electronic countermeasures board. Moments later he added, "Done, sir. The target's radio transmitter is burned out."

"Excellent." Colonel McCrarey swiveled the command chair to face the pilot. "Commence attack run."

"Yes, sir."

"ETA at target six minutes, sir," the navigation officer reported.

Colonel McCrarey watched the smooth functioning of the OCC's men and machines, and felt all the power of the mighty war zep focusing through him. It was what he lived for. Sex was highly orverrated by comparison.

He admired the *Shenandoah* in his mind's eye. It was a flattened torpedo thirteen hundred and sixty-five feet long, with a midsection diameter of two hundred and thirty-four feet. The four gigantic fins jutted rakishly astern, and the eight motor gondolas were side-mounted. The gas cells held over forty mission cubic feet of hydrogen. The hull was sheathed in a black coat of radar-absorbing ceramic honeycomb, except where solar cell panels ran along the top. The air-to-air missile racks were long gone, but the laser was still operational, and that was all the firepower it needed.

He raised the cargo bay. "Captain Patterson? Colonel McCrarey here."

"Sir." The gravelly reply came from the com speaker.

"We're starting the attack run. Are your men ready?"

"All set."

"Excellent. Make sure the camera ops are on the bounce. I want this to be a textbook mission."

"You'll enjoy the show, I promise."

"Good hunting, Captain. Out."

Colonel McCrarey thought about the doomed windrider out there in the night. Intelligence had done a typically thorough job. Tokyo Four had left its town to trade with the Aussieland enclave, so there weren't any other windriders around to witness the raid. It was carrying Tokyo-made electronic components and prime salvage from the corpse of Singapore.

"ETA at target three minutes, sir."

He felt the usual pre-engagement excitement: a tingling as if his blood had become carbonated, an inability to get enough air in his lungs. "Gunner, keep an eye on their blimp bay. If they try to launch one, burn it out of the sky."

"Yes, sir," the weapons officer acknowledged.

"Colonel, I have the target on the bow camera," the pilot reported.

Colonel McCrarey went over and looked at the pilot's

main screen. At maximum enhancement Tokyo Four stood
out from the darkness. Like all windriders it was a transparent ball five thousand feet in diameter. The lower third
was a checkerboard of lit and unlit rectangles which defined the public, residential and engineering levels. The
upper two-thirds was hollow, and interior lights created a
faint glow on the ball's shell.

Most of the rectangles were dark. Tokyo Four had gone
to bed for the night.

Well, he would soon be waking it up.

He stared at the tiny circle of light at the very bottom of
the shell, and wondered what the windrider's bridge crew
was doing. By now they knew something was wrong. Not
only was their transmitter out, but at this range the radar
cloak wasn't perfect.

"ETA at target one minute, sir."

The *Shenandoah* was moving toward the top of Tokyo
Four, slowing from its sixty-five MPH cruising speed. The
shell swelled until it looked like a planet seen from orbit.
The interior was dim and vague due to the shell's greenhouse tint.

"Stand by to set grapples," Colonel McCrarey told the
weapons officer.

"Yes, sir."

Colonel McCrarey was braced for the sharp deceleration
as the props reversed pitch. The *Shenandoah* was skimming across the top of the shell. The OCC jumped as the
zep struck and bounced. It dropped again, and slid with
slippery ease.

"Set grapples," he ordered.

There was a muffled crack as six hydraulic harpoons
were driven into the shell. The *Shenandoah* came to rest
with a shudder. The motors shut down.

"Set and secured, sir," the weapons officer reported.

Colonel McCrarey returned to his chair and raised Captain Patterson. "Commence boarding operation."

"Yes, sir. Out."

Swiveling so he could watch the monitor screens, Colonel McCrarey told the com officer to put up the cargo bay
camera. One screen filled with a starkly lit expanse of gray
deck.

Captain Patterson had his aircav company mustered by platoons. Black combat suits, parapacks and oxy-mask helmets made the sixty-four men look as robotic as Colonel McCrarey thought of them. The squad cameramen had their miked mini-cams in hand. All the aircavs wore scabbards belted at their sides. They didn't carry firearms, since using them in windriders and hydrogen zeps was too dangerous. Swords were sufficient against unarmed townsfolk.

The foreground was dominated by two points of brilliant light. The belly hatch was open, and a rubber gasket sealed the rim where the zep and windrider met. Two crewmen were using cutting torches to carve a hole in the shell. The half inch thickness of plastic composite melted easily, but the monomolecular filament cables which gave the shell its fantastic strength were slowing the crewmen down.

There were access air locks spaced across the shell, but they took too long to cycle. This was the quickest way in if you didn't care how much damage you did.

Finally a rough circle of shell fell away, revealing some of the solar cell panels which dangled in the top of the windrider. A catwalk hung almost under the hole. Emergency lights spread their meager illumination.

"By platoons!" Captain Patterson shouted to the aircavs, and Colonel McCrarey heard him over the com. "Move out!"

Eight more monitor screens began showing images as the cameramen went to work. Led by Captain Patterson the aircavs dropped onto the catwalk and fanned out through the gloomy ranks of solar cell panels.

"Status report," Colonel McCrarey rapped at the pilot. "All secure, sir."

"See that it stays that way." Colonel McCrarey's eyes returned to the screens.

C Platoon was the first unit to see action. It met six work crew personnel on their way to investigate and repair the shell damage. Their leader barely had time to shout, "Who are you?" in Japanese and English before C Platoon closed with them. Out came the long swords.

The work crew was wearing outside suits designed to provide air and warmth, not protection from carbon-steel

blades. Six swords chopped. Six heads flew from their
shoulders and fell toward the ground level thirty-four hundred feet below. The bodies followed as quickly as C
Platoon could kick them off the catwalk.

Colonel McCrarey nodded approvingly. The decapita-
tion stroke was the fastest, surest way to put an enemy out
of action.

Captain Patterson and A Platoon reached the end of a
radial catwalk, where it became an access belt following
the curve of the shell down to the ground level. The vast
upside-down bowl was empty, and dark except for tiny
lights at the bottom. Soon B, C and D Platoons reported
to Captain Patterson by com that they were in position on
the other radials.

"Stand by to jump!" Captain Patterson ordered over the
general channel. "Go!"

Colonel McCrarey had watched the jump drill from the
ground during exercises. It was an impressive sight: sixty-
five men leaving the catwalks as one, free-falling like giant
hawks to fifteen hundred feet, Captain Patterson's shout of
"Chutes!" followed by unfolding clouds of neosilk, and the
final gliding descent. He wished he could be watching it
from that vantage now. Instead he saw dizzying views of
swaying ground and vague aircav shapes.

One cameraman managed to get a relatively steady pan
of the ground level. Only a few of the pole lamps were lit,
standing guard duty over a shadowy landscape. Most of
the circular area was used for farming, but in the middle
he could make out the lake and other recreational facilities
of the park. Two tiny figures were running toward a black
hole that was an escalator entrance. Colonel McCrarey
stifled a laugh. Probably young lovers who had sneaked
topside for some privacy but found more than they expected.

Suddenly a loud siren reverberated throughout the shell.
The rest of the lamps came on, filling in the shadows.
Tokyo Four was catching on faster than the other windriders
he had raided. But that wouldn't matter. The crash siren
signaled the worst imaginable disaster, a breach in the
shell. The six hundred or so townsfolk, most of them
roused from sleep, would be rushing to their emergency
stations. Which was exactly where he wanted them.

The aircavs landed, shucked off their parapacks, and rendezvoused by the five escalators. Captain Patterson and A Platoon were at the park escalator. "Phase One objectives attained, Colonel," Captain Patterson reported. "No significant resistance. No casualties."

Thanks to the screens Colonel McCrarey almost felt he was with the aircavs rather than trapped in the OCC. "Very pretty so far, Captain. Carry on."

"Yes, sir. Out."

Two more work crews emerged from escalators on opposite sides of the ground level. They came warily, and they were holding cutters and wrenches like weapons. But B Platoon's first squad and C Platoon's second squad were laying for them. Before they realized they were in a fight, it was over. Eighteen work crew corpses were leaking blood into rice paddies.

"Begin Phase Two," Captain Patterson ordered his platoon lieutenants. "Move out by squads."

The aircavs started down the five escalators. They passed the deserted public levels, where the wide corridors led to businesses and town services. The townsfolk were either at their work stations in the engineering levels or waiting in their apartments for further instructions.

C and D Platoons deployed through the residential levels. Tokyo Four had gone to the usual pains to simulate its extinct homeland. The corridors tried to be stone walkways roaming through gardens and past cherry trees, while the apartment-fronts looked like feudal Japanese cottages. Almost everything that wasn't alive was plastic.

Colonel McCrarey watched the C and D Platoon screens closely to see how the greenies performed. The same scene repeated over and over. Two aircavs kicked open a flimsy 'lacquered wood' door and stormed an apartment. Inside they found all or part of a family sitting in an under-furnished 'lathe-and-rice-paper' living room. The startled townsfolk stared or screamed or tried to escape.

Nothing saved them. Men, children and most of the women were butchered out of hand. The best looking women were taken to an improvised detention area.

Two D Platoon aircavs were mysteriously slow delivering a prisoner. Colonel McCrarey felt momentary nostalgia for his own aircav days, and made a mental note to go easy on the discipline.

He expected B Platoon and A Platoon's second squad to have a harder time taking the engineering levels, which was why they were all blooded veterans. He was right. About sixty townsfolk armed with makeshift spears and clubs ambushed them in the noisy jungle of air circulation pumps and pipes. It was a hot ten minutes, and the aircavs suffered their first casualties. But they held. They flanked the ambushers, then turned the white plastic floor into a killing ground. A scouting sweep showed that the ambushers had made the elementary tactical mistake of putting all their eggs in one basket.

Colonel McCrarey hated losing good men, but the ambush had resulted in a faster wrap-up than he had anticipated. Guts plus military training beat plain guts every time.

Meanwhile Captain Patterson and A Platoon's first squad went straight to the bridge at the bottom of Tokyo Four. The engineers in the windrider's control room, frantically trying to make sense of the incomprehensible, could do no more than attempt to stop sword cuts with their hands. They died quickly.

"Phase Two objectives attained, Colonel," Captain Patterson reported. His combat suit was splattered with Tokyo Four blood, and he stood calmly over a decapitated corpse. "Four dead, five seriously wounded."

"Well done, Captain." Colonel McCrarey felt somewhat of a letdown now that the fighting was over. "Get the casualties ready for evac. Is the dock operational?"

"Yes, sir."

"We're on our way. Stand by to receive us. Out."

Captain Patterson switched to the platoon lieutenants channel. "Begin Phase Three. Get your evacs to the blimp bay on the bounce."

Colonel McCrarey turned to the pilot. "Have you spotted any traffic?"

"Nothing in radar range, sir."

"Take us down to the dock."

"Yes, sir."

Colonel McCrarey glanced at the cargo bay screen. The

crewmen had fitted a patch over the hole in the shell, so Tokyo Four wouldn't deflate permaturely, and sealed the belly hatch. The *Shenandoah*'s motors woke. The OCC vibrated as the grapples retracted, then the zep climbed away from the shell. It maneuvered toward the bottom of the windrider.

Colonel McCrarey split his attention between the OCC operations and the screens. Phase Three was the point of the entire mission.

Over two dozen woman lay or sat in stunned listlessness on the floor of a laundry room. Non-whites weren't suitable for wives, of course, but they would do as camp followers. He watched approvingly while Lieutenant Ryan chose fourteen to fill the requisition and had the rest executed. Then D Platoon marched the prisoners down to the blimp bay.

Meanwhile C Platoon took its requisition list to the food warehouse and the businesses in the public levels. B Platoon visited the library, the hospital and the engineering supply center. A Platoon's second squad retrieved the company's parapacks from the ground level, then stood by to load the electronic components which were conveniently stored in the blimp bay.

Tokyo Four's blimp bay was big enough to hold a pair of six hundred and nineteen foot long semi-rigid airships, as well as their support equipment. Its two docking hatches straddled the bridge. But what interested Colonel McCrarey about the giant hangar was the aircavs arriving in commandeered carts with tons of supplies. This mission was going to look damned good on his record.

The pilot eased the *Shenandoah* toward the windrider's zep dock, an aluminum girder framework reaching below the shell from the blimp bay. It was well lit by floodlights. The pilot gently guided the *Shenandoah*'s broad back into it, orienting the zep's topside hatch with the dock entryway.

Captain Patterson and A Platoon's first squad were still in the bridge. Colonel McCrarey saw the squad's tech sergeant trigger the magnetic clamps and attach the entryway. Seconds later the liberated supplies and the aircav casualties were being transferred to the zep.

It took twenty-six minutes to load the cargo, and Colonel McCrarey was acutely aware of each one. Finally Captain Patterson mustered his company in the overcrowded cargo bay. "Phase Three objectives attained, Colonel," Captain Patterson reported. "All secure."

"Excellent," Colonel McCrarey said, and he meant it. "Convey my appreciation for a job well done to your men. Out."

Colonel McCrarey swiveled to face the pilot. "Take us out, and stand off at one thousand yards."

"Yes, sir."

The motors revved. The *Shenandoah* pulled free of the dock, then backed slowly away from Tokyo Four. Colonel McCrarey stared out the bow windscreen at the night sky. Less than two hours had elapsed since the beginning of the attack run, so dawn was still over an hour away.

Soon the *Shenandoah* was floating one thousand yards from Tokyo Four's equator. The windrider looked the same, but he could sense the aura of death around it. Now for the climax.

"Gunner," he said to the weapons officer, "our batteries are low, and they have to last until morning. I don't want to waste current on a second shot."

The weapons officer grinned. "You won't have to, sir."

"In that case you may fire at will."

The weapons officer typed instructions into his keyboard. Then he touched the red-rimmed button.

The pencil-thin pulse from the free electron laser traced a tight circle during its momentary existence. It was invisible, but its effect wasn't. A piece of the shell blew out in a puff of vaporized plastic composite.

Colonel McCrarey knew that air was rushing out a hole twenty feet across, creating a mild windstorm inside Tokyo Four. Windriders were super-pressure aerostats, highly evolved hot air balloons. They floated because the shell's greenhouse effect kept the air inside warmer and lighter than the air outside. Now Tokyo Four was a hot air balloon with a leak in it.

"Excellent shot, Gunner," Colonel McCrarey admitted.

"Thank you, sir."

Tokyo Four was losing altitude. The air pressure inside was dropping, and the shell was deforming from the windrider's weight. In a few minutes it would start to break up. What finally fell into the ocean would sink.

Colonel McCrarey felt pleasantly drained. Destroying a windrider was the greatest act of negative creation left in the world. At a moment like this he could almost envision the ultimate nihilism of the War.

"Set course for Alpha," he ordered the pilot.

CHAPTER TWO

"Anyone want more orange juice?" Linda Calhoun asked from the kitchen doorway.

Jack Grigg, her husband of seventeen years, lowered his newspaper enough to make eye contact. "Yes, thanks."

Linda brought the pitcher to the dining room table. She looked five years younger than her thirty-eight thanks to a trim figure and clear unwrinkled skin. Her wavy golden hair was cut short for easy tending, and her hazel eyes seemed large amid the fine bones of her face. She went about her breakfast routine in a yellow sun dress. Every day was summer inside a windrider.

She filled Jack's glass and her own. "How about you, dear?" she asked Wanda.

"No, thanks, Mom." Fourteen year old Wanda Grigg was busy shoving dollar pancakes into her mouth, while squirming to look at the newspaper over her father's arm. She was well on her way to being a taller, more statuesque clone of Linda. Hair cascaded below her shoulders, and white shorts and a halter top showed off her tan.

Jack grinned down at her. "Newspapers are designed to be read by one person at a time." He was big and pleasantly rough-hewn, with bushy light brown hair and an even bushier beard. He slouched comfortably in shorts and a T-shirt.

"Looks like we're going to be climbing in a few days," he said to Linda. "We need to tack east, otherwise we'll end up over the South Pacific instead of Brazil. Chris showed me the latest WeatherNet forecast, and the best wind we can hope for is a prevailing westerly at thirty-one thousand feet."

"Oh, splash!" Wanda swore. "Thin air and no flying."

"Maybe we won't have to climb," Jack countered dryly, "if you'll go outside and push."

Linda's mind automatically filled in the details behind Jack's prediction. The operational ceiling for a windrider was thirty-five thousand feet. There wasn't any floor; a windrider could descend all the way to sea level if the air temperature outside was at least forty-two degrees Fahrenheit lower than inside. But because of the radiation killzone and the quick temperature changes near the surface, windriders rarely went below ten thousand feet.

The air pressure and density inside a windrider varied with its altitude. The pressure was always a bit higher than outside to keep the shell rigid, the density a bit lower to create lift. At ten thousand feet the atmospheric pressure was three-quarters of what it was at sea level, about as thin as humans could breathe over the long term without ill effects. When sailing at higher altitudes the air inside a windrider was enriched with extra oxygen as well as carbon dioxide for the crops. The oxygen came from a fractional distillation plant, while the townsfolk and livestock generated the carbon dioxide. Calgary Three was currently at nineteen thousand feet, so the air Linda was breathing was seven point two PSI with thirty percent oxygen and point zero six percent carbon dioxide.

Linda shared her daughter's opinion of the climb. Twelve thousand feet would exceed the fractional distillation plant's capacity, meaning they were in for a few short-breath days.

She returned to her chair, and delved unenthusiastically into her cottage cheese. Watching Wanda eat she felt a twinge of nostalgia. Her ears were cocked in the direction of eighteen month old Cheryl's bedroom. Cheryl was still asleep after a rough night, but that blissful condition could change at a moment's notice.

"Any other interesting news today?" she asked Jack.

"You mean besides the Twelfth Level Stompers winning their third straight match?"

"Yes, anything not related to balls being bounced off heads and kicked into goals." It was old repartee, but after seventeen years most of what they said to each other was old. Linda showed the smile that made her urchin face beautiful, while inside she was frowning.

"Well, a Japanese windrider dropped out of communications the night before last." Jack glanced at the flatscreen in his hands, which was displaying the *Calgary Chronicle*'s front page. "Tokyo Four. It missed its three AM WeatherNet update, and it hasn't answered any calls since. An Aussieland zep is heading for the last known position to investigate."

Linda felt a cold wind blowing through her mind. She had been a windrider engineer long enough to know how many things could go wrong with one. If communications hadn't been restored by now, they probably wouldn't be. RIP. "Maybe it's just radio trouble," she suggested because Wanda was listening.

"Could be," Jack replied for the same reason, and the subject was dropped.

Since Jack was one of Calgary Three's chief engineers, they rated a rim apartment. The dining room was spacious and sunshine-bright. (There was plenty of living space in a windrider, since the population was limited to the number of townsfolk the farm could feed.) Linda had picked a Hawaiian motif: a simulated teak floor, simulated frond thatch for the ceiling and three of the walls, and wall torch lamps. The plumeria shrubs in floor planters by the window wall bore yellow flowers that gave off a sweet fragrance.

The window wall was actually a section of Calgary Three's shell. Quarter and one-sixteenth inch reinforcing cables cross-hatched the clear plastic composite. Moisture from the air formed a damp mist on the inside, but nothing else hinted that beyond the shell the temperature was a brisk twelve degrees. The plastic composite was the best insulator possible, to increase the efficiency of the greenhouse effect. The temperature inside a windrider was normally kept around eighty degrees. A heat-exchange system with the air outside prevented it from getting too warm, while electric heaters offset the nightly cooling.

Linda stared out the window wall. The view was one of the few things in her life that hadn't lost its ability to stir her. It was magnificent. Miles below the Caribbean Sea was sparkling blue in the fresh morning light. Dozens of islands were scattered across it, irregular dark green and tan shapes. Some cottonball clouds were drifting between the windrider and the water.

Calgary Three was riding a trade wind southwest for winter scavenging in South America. She could see One and Four a few miles away, twin soap bubbles glistening with reflected sunlight. Two must have been on the blind side of the shell.

"I'm finished," Wanda announced, and took her dishes into the kitchen. When she returned she asked, "May I be excused, Mom? I'm supposed to meet Lori and Jan to go flying."

"You've pre-flighted your glider and suit?"

"Yes."

"No dareflying."

"I promise."

"Okay. Have a good time, dear."

"Thanks. Wide sky." Wanda kissed Linda and Jack, then disappeared into her room.

"Your meeting with Mayor Keith is at eleven, isn't it?" Jack asked.

Linda braced herself for serious talk. "Yes."

"Have you made up your mind yet about the supply run?"

She had, but it wouldn't do to just blurt out that she wanted to get away from everything. Including him. "It would be fun—I've never been to Pemex Under. I could learn some things at their windrider yard that haven't made the journals yet. And the extra income wouldn't hurt."

"But?"

"The usual but," she replied. "You and Wanda can take care of yourselves, but I'm not sure leaving Cheryl is a good idea."

"Wouldn't your sister be willing to look after her?"

"Sure. You know Margot—the more the merrier. But Cheryl might miss me."

"It's only for a week. She can survive. The important question is what do you want to do?"

She wanted to scream at him, "Don't be so damned reasonable!" But that wasn't fair. He was the same gentle, empathic man she had fallen in love with and married. She was the one who had changed. "You have some say in the matter too, you know." Sharpness seeped into her voice.

"I'd like to have you around all the time, hon. But you're a person with your own life to live. Anyway, you know what they say about absence."

Somehow the family that once meant so much to her had become just a comfortable arrangement, an anesthetizing prison of routine. She still loved Jack, Wanda and Cheryl, and what the four of them were to each other. But she was terribly, unbearably bored. She needed to escape from the sensory deprivation tank.

"I'm going to take the job," she said.

"Good for you. Too bad I can't get away, or we could make a family vacation out of it." His attention slid back to the newspaper.

She cleared the table and cleaned up, while he took over monitoring Cheryl with the unspoken efficiency of a veteran parent. Then she showered, put on a skirt/blouse/bow outfit suitable for business, ran a brush through her hair, and applied the pale pink lipstick which was all the makeup she ever wore. She stuck her head into Cheryl's bedroom. Cheryl was a small peacefully sleeping lump under the blanket. What showed gave promise that she would grow into another blonde fair-skinned Grigg.

Linda found Jack on the living room sofa enjoying his Saturday off. His next bridge shift wasn't until Sunday night. He peered over the top of the newspaper. "You look like you're running for Mayor instead of meeting one. Don't worry about Cheryl—I'll feed her when she wakes up."

"Did Wanda get off okay?"

"Off and soaring by now."

Linda leaned over him for a perfunctory goodbye kiss,

said, "I'll be back as soon as I can," and headed for the door.

The circum corridor looked like a plank road between rows of bark-shingled houses. The ceiling glow panels were set for imitation sunlight, nourishing the potted pine trees as well as the souls of the townsfolk. She strolled toward the radial corridor leading to the nearest escalator.

She and Jack had been apprentice engineers when they married. She had served two years in a blimp crew, then quit to have Wanda. After Wanda started school she had gone back to engineering part-time. Four years ago she had finally made chief engineer. Then she had felt the yearning again, and broke up Calgary's first husband and wife bridge crew team to have Cheryl.

At the escalator she ran into some neighbors. She had things on her mind, so her good mornings were automatic. She two-stepped onto the up ramp.

Even in her present massive ennui she didn't regret her choice. The blimp crew had been exciting, especially the scavenging expeditions, and as a chief engineer she had reached the summit of a demanding, important profession. But nothing was more exciting, demanding or important than creating a baby and raising it to become a good person. Wanda was already exceeding her expectations, and she had high hopes for Cheryl.

She just needed some time off.

She deboarded at the fifth level, which held the school and the town offices. Her heels clicked hollowly on the textured plastic as she walked down an empty corridor. School was out for quarter break, and civic services were at a minimum on weekends.

Suddenly she wondered about the timing of the meeting. Mayor Keith's secretary had called yesterday afternoon to set it up. If the Mayor had started putting in overtime, it was a very recent development. What was the rush?

The clear sliding door of the Mayor's office was closed; the reception room beyond looked dark and deserted. There was no sign of the secretary. Linda tapped on the door, asking herself if she could have gotten the time wrong. But the inner door opened, and Mayor Keith emerged from his private office.

"Welcome, Linda," the Mayor said as he let her in. He looked distinguished and well-fed in one of his trademark three-piece suits. "It's good to see you again. How are Jack and the little ones?"

"Fine, thank you," she said vaguely. Now she was really puzzled. Town Hall was in One; this was just a branch which Mayor Keith rarely visited outside of his scheduled days. Why had he come over on the shuttle blimp for the meeting? "I hope you're expecting me?"

"Of course. I'm grateful you could attend on such short notice. This way, please." He guided her into the private office.

It was a dim and cozy sanctum, thickly carpeted and paneled in imitation oak. The furniture was made out of real wood. One wall held the telescreen which Mayor Keith used to conduct business from One.

A pale woman Linda's age sat in one of the chairs. "Morning, Linda," she said in a hard-edged voice.

"Good morning, Edie." Edie Jackson was Jack's boss, the head of the engineering department. This wasn't the first time Linda had been lured from retirement to make a supply run. But none of the other times had involved a face-to-face meeting with the two most important people in Calgary.

"Please have a seat," Mayor Keith said to Linda. She sat next to Edie, while he settled into the big chair behind his desk.

"I suppose this is beginning to seem a bit odd to you," he went on, radiating the charm that had helped him win four straight terms.

"Now that you mention it, yes."

"Unfortunately there's a very good reason. We want to attract as little attention as possible. You'll understand why in a minute."

Linda glanced at Edie's grim expression, and laughed. "A secret meeting? Good heavens. I've read about this sort of thing in pre-War literature, but I thought we'd outgrown it."

"So did I," Mayor Keith replied. "Which is why we

aren't particularly good at it. I'm not going to try to swear you to silence or whatever. The people who know about this matter realize making it public at this time would cause more harm than good. I'm sure you'll agree."

Linda leaned forward in her chair. This was getting very interesting.

"By now you've figured out we're not talking about a supply run," Edie said. "That's just going to be our cover story."

"Covering what?"

Edie had a small control unit in her hand. She touched a button, and an outline map of the world appeared on the telescreen.

"A student in Two had a rather bizarre notion for his senior thesis," Mayor Keith explained. "Under other circumstances I would be worrying about his antisocial attitude. The subject of his thesis was unexplained windrider losses."

So far Linda didn't see anything bizarre. It was an overworked topic in engineering circles. Like the weather, everybody talked about it but nobody could do anything about it.

Edie touched the button again, and a cloud of red dots woke across the map. "The student did a scholarly job of research," Mayor Keith continued. "His teacher gave him a top mark, then brought the matter to my attention. These lights represent the known or estimated last positions of the ninety-four windriders lost since the War. As you can see, the distribution is random.

"Now we remove those for which we know or have a fair notion what went wrong—breaches, BW plagues and so on." Most of the red dots disappeared. "These are the unexplained losses. Do you see any pattern?"

Linda stared at the familiar twenty-six dots scattered from the North Sea to the Pacific Ocean. Besides the fact that they were all over water (which didn't mean much, since most of the surface was water) no one had ever spotted a pattern. "No, I don't."

"There isn't any significant correlation by position. Or age, construction yard, nationality, town business, activity when lost, or any other factor which might indicate a common type of accident. But the student suggested a possibility we hadn't ever seriously considered before. Deliberate hostile action."

Linda's first reaction was to laugh again. "You think something is eating windriders? Fireballs, maybe? How about giant mutant sparrows?"

Edie wasn't amused. "Fireballs have never shown any inclination to attack windriders. But something definitely has. Look."

A chronological graph appeared in the telescreen. "This is where the kid hit prime salvage. Drop those three losses out—unexplained accidents do happen—and you have a clear pattern. Twenty-three losses spaced over sixty-two years. One every two point seven years, plus or minus a few months to hide the pattern."

"You can find a pattern anywhere if you ignore the non-conforming data," Linda objected. "Your almost-correlation had been reported before. It's a tease. It has to be a coincidence, since it doesn't make any sense."

"Coincidence, bullshit!" Edie erupted. "It makes sense one way. Somebody is doing it on a schedule."

Linda didn't want to believe it. She didn't even want to think about it. Twenty-three windriders. Over fourteen thousand men, women and children. "You must be wrong!"

"We aren't," Mayor Keith said sympathetically. "I know how you feel, but the proof was damnably convincing."

"Proof?"

"You do recall the scientific method, don't you?" Edie asked dryly. "What validates a theory?"

"Its ability to predict. . . ." Linda's voice trailed off.

"The thesis ended with a calculation of the next unexplained loss window." A graph showing a bell curve filled the telescreen. "As you can see, we're now in the peak probability period. Yesterday it happened."

Linda's stomach turned to lead. "Tokyo Four," she said weakly. "But . . . why?"

"That is what we would very much like to know." Mayor Keith rarely let his hard core show through his amiable facade, but it was showing now. "To borrow your analogy, something is eating windriders. It brings down its prey without warning, and it doesn't leave any tracks. We haven't a notion what it might be."

"Who it might be," Edie corrected the Mayor. "Let's not get carried away with poetry."

Linda tried to envision people who could kill windriders, but she couldn't. That sort of mentality hadn't existed since the War. "You shouldn't jump to conclusions, Edie. We've been aloft less than a century. Fireballs may not be the only inhabitants."

"Monsters from the stratosphere! Vid crap."

"Whoever or whatever," Mayor Keith broke in, "the losses obviously must be stopped. First we need to identify the hostile force. Unfortunately it could be almost anyone—an enclave, a windrider town, even your monsters."

"Which is the main reason for the secrecy you find so amusing," Edie snapped. "Surprise is about the only advantage we have."

"And publicizing such a terrible danger while we're helpless would cause a panic," Mayor Keith added.

Linda wanted to flee back to her apartment and forget everything. Instead she asked, "Where do I come into this?"

"The Pemex Under zep *Mayan Princess* is scheduled to stop here in two days," Edie explained. "We want you to go to Pemex Under supposedly on a buying trip. You'll do some buying, but your real job is to meet with their CEO and bring him up to speed on this. We need their help."

"How do you know they aren't the ones responsible for the losses?" Linda was amazed at how fast her fear had generated suspicion.

"We made damned sure none of their zeps were anywhere near Tokyo Four. That's no absolute guarantee, of course, but we've done a lot of business with them and know them pretty well."

"Ernesto Gutierrez would never be party to such a thing," Mayor Keith insisted.

"What sort of help am I supposed to ask for?"

"Two sorts," Mayor Keith replied. "First, information. They have many sources which we don't. Maybe they can furnish some clue to the identity of the hostile force. As for the second. . . ."

He paused, then started again uncomfortably. "Our civilization is ill-equipped to deal with enemies other than nature. Every windrider town and enclave is politically independent, and of course we don't have any weapons—"

"We want to hire Pemex Under to build us some lasers like the ones used against missiles and aircraft during the War," Edie said crisply. "Calgary isn't going to provide the next victim."

Linda hadn't thought it could get any worse, but she had been wrong. Weapons were a myth from the evil past. The survivors of the War, sickened by its devastation and too busy staying alive to fight, had institutionalized their rejection of violence. But now Calgary was going to rearm. Her meager breakfast threatened to rise.

"Why me?" she asked.

"You're well qualified for both the cover and the real tasks," Mayor Keith answered. "And you're not a town official, so your trip won't attract any public interest. Which brings us to the question. Will you do it?"

She hated the thought of being involved with any part of this insanity. But she hated the thought of Jack, Wanda and Cheryl being killed even more.

"I will."

CHAPTER THREE

The work platform was a forty-foot-wide, twelve-foot-deep shelf on the inside of Calgary Three's shell at its equator. An access belt rose past the platform on its way from the ground level to the catwalks. The platform had been designed as a staging area for repair jobs, which explained the tools and materials stored there. But the townsfolk had discovered another use for the platform and belt.

Wanda waited at the back of the platform while Jan took off. Wanda was all zipped up in the orange flying outfit which Mom had made her from an old outside suit, and hated it. But the Council in its infinite wisdom had decided that fliers needed protection. All the metalized plastic and insulation made her feel like she was at the focal point of a solar furnace. She wiped a sheet of sweat from her forehead.

Nine hundred feet down some townsfolk were taking their turns at farm chores, while others were enjoying themselves in the park. The noise from the coops and stock pens was faint by the time it reached her. Several hang gliders were soaring against the shades of blue beyond the shell. She spotted Lori's tiger-striped wing over the park, and Jan gliding toward it. A bright crimson paraglider wheeled gracefully near the top of the shell. Mom had taken her catwalk skydiving a few times. She couldn't wait until she was old enough to solo.

The mandatory minute between launches had passed; the next flier on the belt was almost up to the platform. Wanda checked the aluminum frame and sheer yellow neosilk of her hang glider, and squeezed into the harness. Then she waddled over to the gap in the platform's railing.

The sight of that long step down to the ground level had made her wet her panties the first time. But she was used to it now.

She took a last swipe across her forehead before putting on the bowl helmet. Her gloved hands curled confidently around the control bar. She could feel her heart drumming under her ribs, and her breathing had become quick shallow gasps. She was ready.

She flexed her knees and leaned forward. Shouting, "Geronimo!" she dived off the platform.

She went into a steep glide to clear the downdraft near the shell. Air rushed past her, cooling her off a bit. The neosilk hummed. Dark green and brown ground jumped up to swat her. Occasionally it got a careless or unlucky flier, but it wouldn't get her.

She pulled out. The harness distributed her weight comfortably as she balanced on it. She skimmed fast over the blurred rows of fruit trees, corn, lettuce and other crops. The shrieking wind swallowed all the distant noises. A farmer waved, and she waved back.

The cold air outside the shell created the peripheral downdraft and central updraft which circulated the topside air, and incidently provided great hang gliding. She sailed over the park and started to climb. The ground level shrank into a plate surrounded by the ocean and islands of the fantasy world under the sky. Straight down she could see the lake and the park lawn.

She loved flying. She gloried in the swift motion, the spectacular view, and best of all the freedom. Up here she wasn't the peckee in the pecking order. She could do anything she wanted to. Almost.

She soared. She glided. She banked and looked. She played some tag with Jan and Lori. An older boy she knew vaguely buzzed her, then headed for the top of the shell.

She ignored the invitation/challenge. The top was officially off-limits due to the dangerous obstructions, she had promised Mom, and dodging through the solar cell panels and catwalks was a stupid game anyway.

Jan got tired first, as usual. Wanda and Lori followed her as she spiraled down to the park.

A strip of lawn was marked off for fliers. Wanda saw Jan and Lori make nice running landings while she circled. Then she went down.

She flew low over ground that was being plowed for a new planting. Other fliers were watching, so she decided to try something fancy. She dropped fast. Just as she was about to do some plowing of her own, she lifted the nose and stalled hard. The frame groaned, and the harness squeezed her lungs flat. But she didn't hear any tearing neosilk.

Her forward speed gone, she landed on the trimmed grass without falling over. Her bent legs soaked up the shock.

She shed the harness and helmet, took a deep breath of fresh air, and ran over to her friends. "An ultra flight!" she gasped. "Did you see my landing?"

Jan's eyes were wide. "You're lucky your folks didn't."

"Who was that boy who tried to get you dareflying?" Lori wanted to know.

"I couldn't care less."

"She's saving herself for Jeff," Jan giggled.

"Go take a stroll outside the shell."

They broke down their hang gliders, and walked over to where the lawn served as a beach along the lake. They had a lot of company. Some boys yelled to them, but they showed the proper cool indifference. They staked out a patch of grass.

"Let's get wet," Lori said. "I'm broiling."

They stripped off their flying outfits for their usual post-flight swim. Wanda had managed to sneak out wearing the swimsuit she had bought with her own money and definitely without Mom's permission. The lime-green string bikini hid little of her rich tan or what was developing into a prime shape. The shell screened out enough UV so you could sunbathe without risking a dangerous burn or skin cancer.

Jan was small, intensely freckled, and wore a modest pink one-piece swimsuit. Lori was a tall brunette, and her violet swimsuit looked like a tube on her skinny body. The three of them ran to the lake. Wanda was aware of admiring male eyes, liked the feeling, but made very sure it didn't show.

They jumped in. The water was wonderfully cool, washing the sticky sweat from Wanda's skin. She splashed out to the middle and floated on her back.

The lake was a shallow oval a bit bigger than the soccer field. She usually thought of it as a swimming hole, but it was also part of Calgary Three's ecology. Water vapor in the air condensed on the shell, ran down, was channeled by grooves in the plastic composite, and ended up in the irrigation ditches which meandered through the farm to the lake. The lake was the windrider's reservoir. It fed the tap water and trim systems, and was in turn fed by the waste water recycling plant. It also evaporated to keep the cycle going.

After the swim they sprawled on the lawn like accident victims, drying off under the noon sun. The solar cell panels intercepted some of the rays, a giant parasol which kept the sunshine from getting too bright. The lawn was crowded with sunbathers, family picnics, beached swimmers and a pickup volleyball game. Wanda wished she could feel this good all the time.

"I hear Jeff took Adrienne Maisel to the pubvid Thursday night," Lori said casually.

Lori and Jan were her best friends, but they could also be cow dung at times. She had been engaged in a year-long campaign to make Jeff Lewis see her as more than one of the gang. She had tried just about everything that wouldn't get her a reputation. So far the results were zero squared.

"It won't last," she predicted with more confidence than she felt. "He'll lose interest as soon as he tries to talk to her about anything but her."

"Boys don't care about our brains," Jan said. She considered herself an expert on boys, although she never put her knowledge to practical use. "They just want to mess around with the parts lower down."

"Do you think Jeff and Adrienne did the dirty deed?" Lori asked in an awed whisper.

Jan giggled.

Wanda wondered rather desperately about that too. Despite all of Mom's explanations and advice, life had become very confusing when her body changed. Sometimes she would look at Jeff and want him so much that she got dizzy.

"I'm not going to fight fire with fire, if that's what you're suggesting," she said sharply.

"Me?" Lori looked innocent. "I'm not suggesting a thing. Why not?"

"Because Mom says you can't catch a boy that way. It's something two people do when they already love each other."

Mom had taken her to the hospital for her first birth control shot when puberty struck; strict population control was part of windrider life. So accidental pregnancy wasn't a problem. But feeling right about sex definitely was.

"Then what you are going to do about Adrienne?" Jan asked.

"I'm going to sleep in late, go flying, watch lots of vid, get my hair cut, shop, play with Puff, and otherwise enjoy the quarter break. When Jeff realizes Adrienne's mind doesn't cast a shadow, I'll be around."

"If you don't really go after him, you haven't got a chance," Jan insisted.

"Look who's—"

A buzz from Wanda's wrist com interrupted her hot reply. She touched the switch on the imitation ivory band, wondering what Mom wanted.

Only it wasn't Mom. Teacher Ware's voice came from the tiny speaker. "Sorry to intrude on your vacation, Wanda, but it's important."

"That's okay."

"I'm in the lab. Do you think you could come down here right now?"

"I suppose so," Wanda said reluctantly. The extra class credit was nice, but she was beginning to regret agreeing to help Teacher Ware with his research project. Didn't he realize she had a life to live? "What's up?"

"According to the scanner a fireball is heading in our direction. The EM signature indicates it's your pet."

She closed her eyes for a few seconds, concentrating on the sense no one really believed she had except her parents and Teacher Ware. It was like hearing feelings instead of sounds. Or like touching. Usually it was quiet/empty. But now she could hear/feel Puff's voice/presence, faint and far away. "It's Puff, all right," she said happily.

"Good. Can you come down now?" Teacher Ware asked.

"Are you going to wire me into your tronics again?"

"I'm afraid so."

Wanda sighed. "Okay. I'm on my way."

"Thanks." The com clicked off.

Wanda started getting back into her flying outfit. "You heard," she said to Jan and Lori. "I have to go. I'll call you after dinner."

"You and your fireball," Jan giggled. "You better get some medical help before you hear clouds talking to you too."

"Wide sky," Lori said, looking down.

Wanda trudged to the park escalator with her rolled up hang glider under one arm and her helmet under the other. She was used to not being believed about Puff; it didn't bother her anymore. Much.

She rode down to the school level. It seemed gloomy after the sunny topside, and she had the radial corridor mostly to herself. She was heat-swollen and weighted down by all the cargo. But her stride was almost a prance, because she could hear/feel Puff coming to play with her.

The corridor ended at the door reading ELECTRONICS LAB. She knocked, and Teacher Ware's muffled voice yelled, "Come on in!" She did.

She dumped her stuff by the door. The lab was big, but work tables and equipment filled it up. The far wall was a window like the ones in her apartment's dining and living rooms. A metal plate set in the clear shell held instruments for outside experiments. Mainly it was a school lab, but some teachers used it for their own research.

She looked for Puff, but all she could see above Calgary Three was sky.

"I'm glad you could make it, Wanda," Teacher Ware said. He was standing beside his desk near the window wall, and there was a stranger with him.

"No problem," she lied politely as she maneuvered through the tables.

Teacher Ware was old, almost forty, but his lean body, curly brown hair and blue eyes could make you forget his age. "Wanda, this is Teacher Becker," he said. "He's a physicist from Four. I invited him over to see you in action."

"I'm pleased to meet you, Teacher." She shook Teacher Becker's offered hand. His bulging muscles and dark leathery skin made him look more like a farmer than a scientist.

"Teacher Becker is interested in fireballs too," Teacher Ware explained. "He's firmly in the phenomenon camp, but I hope we can enlighten him."

Teacher Becker grinned. "I prefer to think I have an open mind. Unlike my friend here, though, I base my theories on data rather than imagination."

"Compared to a head of lettuce maybe you have an open mind," Teacher Ware grumbled.

Historical sightings of fireballs near the surface went back way before the War. They had been variously identified as ball lightning, Saint Elmo's fire, "foo fighters," UFO's and religious visions. Radar probes by windriders' scientists had discovered thousands of them roaming the ionosphere, from which they descended to the windriders and more rarely to the surface. Ranging from ping-pong-ball size to big ones like Puff who was sixteen feet across, they could glow any color or be invisible. They traveled alone and in groups. The scientists agreed that they were complex self-maintaining fields of force, probably solar-powered. But they argued over everything else.

Mostly they argued over whether fireballs were an atmospheric phenomenon or a new form of life. According to the life-form proponents, fireballs were a race perhaps as old as humanity or older, the product of a separate evolution. They had little interest in the surface or its inhabitants, but showed more curiosity about the windriders

dwelling in their aerial domain. The phenomenon proponents, on the other hand, insisted that they were no more
than a sophisticated cousin of lightning and the northern
lights.

To Wanda the debate was all too familiar, and pretty
stupid. She didn't see how there could be any doubt. Puff
was as alive in her own way as Mom or Dad or anyone.

"Wanda is one on the most impressive rapport subjects
I've ever heard of," Teacher Ware said to Teacher Becker.
"She has adopted a particular fireball, who frequently
comes here to visit her."

"Her name is Puff," Wanda contributed.

"Puff?" Teacher Becker asked.

"After Puff, the magic dragon. From an old song."

Teacher Ware's work table was buried under scanning
equipment wired to outside antennae, as well as an EEG
and a computer. He gestured to a chair next to the table.
"Wanda, please show this poor-man's Einstein how you
communicate with Puff."

"Okay." She perched on the uncomfortably hard plastic,
and tried to ignore Teacher Becker's grin while Teacher
Ware attached the EEG electrodes to her head and fussed
with the equipment.

"Ready at my end," Teacher Ware said to her. He and
Teacher Becker were looking at the collection of screens
and displays. "Can you tell where Puff is?"

"Of course," Wanda sniffed, and listened/felt. "She's
pretty close. I think she's teasing me by hiding on the
blind side."

"It doesn't seem to be telepathy," Teacher Ward explained to Teacher Becker. "More likely fireballs are sensitive to the electrical activity in certain human brains.
Watch the EEG while Wanda is in rapport. The information exchange is limited to emotions and vague impressions—maybe because fireballs are so different from us, or
because they aren't very intelligent."

Wanda couldn't let the insult pass. "Puff isn't stupid!"

"I apologize," Teacher Ware said to her. "Maybe we're
the stupid ones. Can you coax Puff into visual range?"

"I'll try." She would show them.

She called/reached out, wanting to see Puff as hard as

she could. Moments later she heard/felt an echo. It was
strong, and getting stronger. "She's coming."

Both teachers were staring at the scanner screens. The
computer's memory unit hummed faintly.

"Hi, Puff!" Wanda waved at the window wall.

Puff swooped down from the top of the shell, and hovered about thirty yards from the window wall. She looked
like a ball of rippling pale blue flame. You could see right
through her. Wanda could tell she was excited, so excited
that she was going to put on a show.

Now the teachers were staring at Puff. "I've never been
this close to one," Teacher Becker said in a soft voice.

"She won't come any closer," Wanda explained. "She's
afraid to."

"The reinforcing cables could affect her, I suppose,"
Teacher Ware whispered. "We know so damned little
about fireballs. If only we could get a probe into one."

"You aren't going to do anything to hurt Puff!" Wanda
snapped. Puff fidgeted, and green splotches erupted inside her. "If you try, I'll send her far away and you'll never
see her again!"

"I promise I won't do any experiment which might
injure her," Teacher Ware said soothingly. "I couldn't
even if I wanted to—fireballs are too good at avoiding us."

Wanda calmed down, and so did Puff. Soon Puff's blue
radiance turned pure white. Yellow streaks poured from
the center, swelling until they filled the whole ball. Then
Puff became an orange jewel throwing out more and more
light. Finally a flash of brilliant crimson flooded the lab.
When Wanda's eyes cleared, Puff was pale blue again.

Wanda applauded. "Was that a light show or what!" Puff
was the most wonderful pet anyone ever had, and Wanda
loved her.

Puff spiraled out about a hundred yards, then went into
a series of maneuvers which put Wanda's flying to shame.
Wanda heard/felt Puff's happiness. It had been several
long weeks since Puff's last visit. When Wanda became a
windrider engineer like Mom and Dad, she was going to
follow Puff somehow and find out what Puff did in the
ionosphere.

"Now tell me fireballs aren't living beings, and rather

intelligent ones at that," Teacher Ware said to Teacher Becker.

Teacher Becker looked less smug than he had. "The fireball's behavior is certainly unusual. But there are other possible explanations."

"Go on," Teacher Ware snorted. "This should be good."

"Maybe Wanda and the other so-called rapport subjects have some psi ability which enables them to unconsciously manipulate fireballs. Maybe the fireball was reacting to environmental factors we don't understand yet. Maybe it was a coincidence."

Teacher Ware shook his head. "Wake up and smell the coffee, will you? Look at these EEG and emission graphs." They leaned over the computer, typing on the keyboard and shouting at each other.

Wanda watched Puff soar over One and disappear into the sky. Puff sounded/felt hungry. The show had drained her, and she was going away to eat some sunshine. But she would be back.

"Excuse me, Teacher Ware," Wanda interrupted the argument. "Are you done with me?"

"Huh? Oh, sure." He quickly removed the electrodes. "Thanks for your help."

The teachers went back to their yelling. She could have answered a lot of their questions for them, but she was just a kid. Kids didn't exist when adults were busy with adult business.

She picked up her stuff and headed home.

CHAPTER FOUR

Back in the apartment Wanda put away the hang glider, changed into her regular clothes, and wondered what to do with the rest of the afternoon. It was too late to go topside and synch with Jan and Lori, but too early to get ready for dinner. Mom was out somewhere, while Dad was playing with Cheryl in her room. Reluctantly Wanda decided to catch up on her household chores.

She got the battered old vac from the hall closet and coaxed it into action. It started growling across the fake grass carpet, usually avoiding the fake rattan furniture. She jumped around in its wake to catch and steady small items endangered by its erratic proximity sensors. When was Dad going to admit it was beyond the home repair stage, and let the salvagers have it for the down payment on a new one?

She was dusting when Mom returned. They exchanged hellos, then Mom went into Cheryl's room. Minutes later she and Dad came out, herding Cheryl between them.

"Please keep an eye on your sister for awhile," Mom said to her.

"Okay."

Mom and Dad disappeared into the den for one of their private adult talks, while Wanda turned her full attention to the task of keeping Cheryl entertained and restrained.

Wanda thought Cheryl was just about the cutest thing in
the sky. When Wanda grew up, she definitely wanted to
have babies of her own to raise and love. (Along with a
successful career as a windrider engineer, of course, like
Mom.)

The parental meeting eventually broke up. No storm
clouds drifted in Wanda's direction, so she didn't wonder
about the topic. Dad took Cheryl back to her room; Mom
headed for the kitchen to start dinner.

Wanda finished dusting, then went to her room to watch
some vid. She really liked her room. Because it *was* hers:
her comfortable place, her private place. Like most teen-
ers she frequently took her furniture plus her wall and
floor panels to the motif shop for reforming. Currently she
was living in a crystal cavern veined with gold and silver.
The furniture looked like giant uncut jewels. She had her
own com, and a new vid that had been a present from
Grandma and Grandpa Calhoun. Every flat surface in the
room was crowded with stuff.

She watched part of a zock concert from the Varig
enclave. Then it was time to clean up and dress for dinner.
She had asked Mom once why Calgary townsfolk wore
suits and dresses to dinner. Why not just come in whatever you had on? Mom had explained that civilized manners made it easier for people to get along with each
other, which was important in the confined environment
of a windrider. Wanda wasn't convinced. She suspected
adults just liked having things they had to do.

At six o'clock Mom rang the dinner bell. Wanda was the
first one to the table, as usual. Dad brought Cheryl in, and
installed her in her high chair. Mom served the first
course. When she sat down, that was the signal to dig in.

The sun was dropping out of the sky in the west, and
the dining room was filled with reddish-golden light from
the fiery sunset. Dad said the red horizons in the morning
and evening were caused by dust blasted into the upper
atmosphere during the War. There had been a lot more of
it right after the War, cutting off so much sunshine that
temperatures around the world dropped for over a decade.

Wanda unleashed the hearty appetite that she always
had after flying. The barbequed chicken was a year-round

dish, while the salad, onion soup, baked potatoes and apple pie were dictated by the crop schedules. Everything tasted great, also as usual.

She was concentrating so much on the meal that it took her awhile to notice something was wrong with Mom. Mom wasn't eating much, and she looked thoughtful. The few times she joined in the conversation, her comments were the sort people made when they weren't really listening. Wanda wondered what was up.

She found out after dessert. Mom and Dad were sipping their coffee, Cheryl had fallen asleep in her chair, and Wanda was about to ask to be excused.

"Wanda," Mom said, "I'm going on a business trip to the Pemex Under enclave. I'll be leaving the day after tomorrow, and I'll be away for about a week. Cheryl will be staying with Aunt Margot. You'll be the chief household engineer while I'm away—I'm counting on you to keep everything in trim."

"Uh . . . okay," Wanda answered automatically. Her mind was erupting with wonderful images conjured by the name Pemex Under. She had never been to an enclave, but she had heard so much about them. They were real cities. Popular culture, art, science, technology, you name it: the enclaves were the hub from which everything new spread out second-hand to the windrider towns. The activities that filled her days suddenly seemed few and unsophisticated.

"I have some more news which might interest you." Mom smiled slightly. "The zep taking me to Pemex Under is the *Mayan Princess*, still commanded by Captain Ramirez. I imagine you'll be glad to see him again."

Miguel! Wanda could feel the blush rushing into her cheeks. Six months ago she had managed to get the handsome, charming zep captain to escort her to the big end-of-quarter dance. It had been one of her schemes to attract Jeff's attention. As a jealousy generator it had failed completely, but she still remembered Miguel in her dreams.

Moments ago she had wished she could visit Pemex Under with Mom. Now she *had* to go.

"Mom," she said as nicely as possible.

"Yes?"

"Please take me with you to Pemex Under."

The request stunned Mom and Dad for a moment. Wanda launched her arguments as fast as she could, hoping to get all of them in before opposition could solidify. "I'm on quarter break for twelve more days, so I won't miss any school. You said I could visit an enclave someday—this is the perfect chance. It'll be tremendously educational. I—"

"Peace!" Dad cut her off with a good-natured roar. "Quit trying to steamroll us."

Wanda didn't know what steamrolling was, but she knew when to drop a bad tactic. "I'm sorry."

"I'd like to have you come along, dear," Mom said, "but I don't think it would be a good idea. Not this time."

"Why not?"

Mom looked like she was thinking fast. "Well, I'll be too busy to spend much time sightseeing."

"I can help you, so you'll get your work done quicker and have more time. I just want to *go*! Please!"

"I'm sorry, dear, but we can't afford it. Round-trip zep fare, a hotel room, meals at enclave prices—do you have any idea how much all that would cost?"

"I don't know, hon," Dad cut in. "The fact that you took the job on such short notice should put you in a strong bargaining position. I bet if you ask the mayor, he'll authorize Wanda's expenses."

Wanda felt like jumping into Dad's lap and hugging him. Mom turned to him and said, "I just don't think it would be a good idea."

"I don't understand." Dad was frowning. "Is there something about the trip—"

"No, of course not." Mom paused, then turned back to Wanda. "I'll talk to the mayor tomorrow morning. If he agrees to the town picking up your tab, you can come." The corners of her mouth rose. "We'll manage to fit some fun in."

"Ultra!" Wanda yelped. "Thanks, Mom. We'll have a great time. Thanks too, Dad."

Dad shook his head. "All my ladies are abandoning me. How will I survive on my own for a week?"

"You can go back to your old sinful bachelor ways," Mom suggested.

"I've been married too long. I've forgotten them."

Wanda listened with all the patience she could muster, while Mom and Dad told her about enclaves they had visited. Then she helped Dad with the dishes. Finally she was able to escape to her room.

She sat cross-legged on her bed facing the com screen. It took her over two hours to share the incredible news with Jan, Lori and her other friends. She just finished before bedtime caught up with her.

The next morning she stayed in Mom's shadow, until Mom went into the den to call the mayor. When Mom finally came out she said, "Good news, dear. The town is going to pay your way. Mayor Keith says to have a good time. You should write him a thank-you note before we leave."

"I will, I promise!" Wanda wanted to jump up and down and shout for joy, but she had some serious business to transact. "Thanks again, Mom."

Mom hugged her. "I really am looking forward to taking you with me. If it didn't seem that way last night, it's because I . . . had something on my mind."

"That's okay. But what about my clothes?"

"What about them?"

"I don't have *anything* to wear in an enclave. Can we go shopping after lunch?"

"No, we can't. You have plenty of nice things."

"But, Mom, I'll look like a hick canuck!"

"You can buy anything you want with your own money—like that bikini I'm not supposed to know about."

Wanda was crushed, but she bounced back when Lori and Jan came over to help her prepare for the trip. They visited the shops on the mall level, even though she had decided to save her meager bank balance for Pemex Under. After lunch Mom took her to the hospital for some shots; enclaves had a wider variety of germs than windriders. Then Mom went off to the mayor's office for awhile. Wanda returned to the apartment to take over the Cheryl-watch from Dad, who left for his bridge shift.

Assorted relatives and friends dropped by after dinner.

Mom served refreshments, and the impromptu bon-voyage party became pretty noisy. Wanda was flying higher than the moon, glorying in the envy of her peers. Eventually everybody left, so she and Mom could finish their packing.

Early the next morning Aunt Margot came over to pick up Cheryl and her auxiliary gear. Wanda kept staring out the window wall during breakfast, hoping to spot either Puff or the arriving *Mayan Princess*. She hadn't sensed Puff's presence since the show for Teacher Ware, and she felt bad about leaving without saying goodbye. But except for Two and some clouds the sky was empty.

At nine thirty A.M. Mom, Dad and Wanda left the apartment. Dress-wise Wanda had edged as close to urban sophistication as Mom would let her: a lavender jumpsuit, a wide black leather belt, a matching purse and a gold chain. The silly windrider objection to makeup (skin as well as eco-system pollution) had kept her from putting on one of the currently fashionable enclave faces. Mom had done her hair in a single French braid down the back. Even so she looked enviously at the grown-up style of Mom's white linen suit, kelly-green blouse, small purse and strand of pearls. Mom was carrying her own suitcases, while Dad, bleary-eyed from being up all night, took Wanda's.

They followed the radial corridor to the middle of the level, and stepped onto the downward moving stairs. The park escalator was the only one that went down into engineering country. At this early hour there weren't many other riders. Mom and Dad talked to each other, while Wanda stared around in fascination. The engineering levels kept Calgary Three aloft and its townsfolk alive.

Transformers hummed and relays clicked amid the blockish machines on the power level, where electricity generated by the topside solar cells was stored and distributed. The water level was a weird jumble of heating, pumping, sewage processing and trim equipment. Cold winds from the fractional distillation plant moaned through the air level. The work level was divided into four pie-slice sections: work crew, salvage processing, electronics and supply center. All the levels were well lit by glow panels plus

window walls. Lots of townsfolk were at work, mostly
wearing coveralls for protection.

The escalator ramps ended in the middle of the blimp
bay. The acres of floor, encircling window wall, graceful
pillars and the hundred-and-sixty-foot-high ceiling always
made Wanda feel uncomfortably insignificant. The two
deflated blimps on either side of the escalator looked like
. . . deflated blimps. Towering helium tanks and other
auxiliary equipment surrounded the blimps. The air current carried hard-edged sounds of activity and hints of a
dozen smells.

Mom, Dad and Wanda set out across the aluminum
grating toward the dock entryway, which was near the
stairway leading down to the bridge. Cargo carts were
moving between the freight elevator and the entryway.
Men in brown uniforms were helping the bay crew carry
crated salvage, leather goods and frozen sides of beef from
the carts into the entryway.

In addition to scavenging, windrider towns usually had
an export business or two. Calgary kept the pre-War tradition of its namesake alive by raising cattle. Most towns
only kept dairy cattle, since cattle were an inefficient
source of meat. So Calgary beef was an expensive delicacy.
The first level of each Calgary windrider was a ranch, with
a ring of outside mirrors reflecting sunshine onto feed
algae trays, and hundreds of bulls/cows/steers/calves wandering around pens. Wanda didn't like Calgary Three's
first level. It stank.

She stared hopefully out the window wall at the circle of
sky, but the *Mayan Princess* was hidden below the floor.

A man left the group at the entryway, and walked over
to them. Wanda's heart tried to jump out of her mouth as
she recognized Captain Miguel Ramirez.

"It's very good to see you again, my friends!" He had to
shout to make himself heard above all the noise. He spoke
English, the worldwide trade language, with only a slight
accent.

He was slim and a few inches shorter than Dad, but
sleek muscles showed below his short sleeves. His skin
was the color of coffee with cream. Locks of thick black
hair stuck out from under a brown Air Service cap with

silver bars. His lean face was dominated by deep, dark eyes and a wide mustache. It could have been a cruel face, but a merry grin made its power joyful. Memories of his musky after-shave and strong arms pushed everything else out of Wanda's mind.

"Welcome to Calgary, Captain," Dad said. "I wish there was time to show you proper hospitality—we still owe you a tremendous debt." He put down Wanda's suitcases, and shook Miguel's hand. Mom put her suitcases down too.

"I only did what anyone in my place would have done, Señor Grigg. As for the hospitality, I take the thought for the deed." Miguel shook Mom's hand. "Señorita Calhoun, I'm looking forward to the pleasure of your company on our homeward flight." Then he bowed crisply over Wanda's hand, and kissed it. "Señorita Grigg, I don't understand how it's possible, but you're even lovelier than when I had the honor of escorting you to your school dance."

A lightning bolt ran from Wanda's knuckles along her arm to her brain. She managed to mumble, "Thanks, Captain Ramirez."

"My special friends call me Miguel, remember?" He turned back to Mom. "Your cargo is being safely tucked away in the *Princess*'s hold. I've already settled the bill of lading with your business manager. Would you care to inspect the hold?"

Mom shook her head. "You know your job best, Captain. Of course I'll have to do an inventory when the cargo is off-loaded."

"Of course." Miguel's grin widened. "I'll try to avoid using your cargo as ballast."

"If you do toss it over the side, please toss me too. Better that than having to explain to the mayor."

Miguel laughed, then glanced over his shoulder. Empty carts were backing away from the entryway. The *Mayan Princess* crewmen were disappearing into the dimly lit mouth, while the bay crew prepared to seal it. "The time has come to go," he said. Then he shouted something in Spanish to the last two crewmen. They came over, took the suitcases, and headed for the entryway.

Wanda hugged Dad, feeling a sudden rush of fright.

Homesickness? It couldn't be, especially in front of Miguel. She struggled to hold back tears, while Mom kissed Dad goodbye.

Dad waved as Mom and she followed Miguel onto the entryway's moving belt. Dad looked sad standing all alone in the middle of the blimp bay, retreating until he was out of sight.

The thirty-degree slope of the belt made standing tricky, but Wanda managed not to embarrass herself. The entryway angled down to the *Mayan Princess*'s topside hatch. From there they rode a small elevator platform to the cargo hold in the zep's belly. The hold was crowded with trade goods and crewmen.

Miguel spoke into his wrist com, then offered Mom and Wanda sticks of gum. "An undignified habit, but it helps your inner ears adjust while the hold is being repressurized."

Soon everyone was chewing. Mom, Miguel and the crewmen talked about adult things. Wanda was worrying about what heavy air would feel like. She thought she was hiding it well, but Mom squeezed her hand and whispered, "It'll be all right, dear."

Unlike windriders the enclave zeps kept their air at surface pressure. To take the Calgary cargo aboard, the *Mayan Princess*'s hold had been depressurized and oxygen-enriched. Now it was being flushed and repressurized with regular air. Except for popping ears Wanda didn't notice any difference.

A few minutes later the lights over the forward and aft doors turned from red to green. "Enough of this sitting and scratching on company time!" Miguel shouted cheerfully at the crewmen. "It makes your captain look bad in front of these lovely ladies. To your stations."

They filed out the doors amid loud laughter and a few rude-sounding comments in Spanish aimed at Miguel.

Miguel held the forward door open. "This way, ladies, please."

The hold was in the zep's midsection. The main passageway ran aft through the engineering section, and forward past the living quarters to the bridge. The three of them followed the narrow white corridor for what seemed to

Wanda like a long time. They passed a few crewmen and passengers, and a lot of doors.

Finally Miguel stopped in front of one of the doors. "Your cabin—7B, the finest the *Princess* has to offer. If your bags aren't inside, I'll have Diego and Jorge keelhauled. The cabin is conveniently close to the dining room, the lounge, the communal shower—"

"You mean everybody shares one shower?" Wanda asked, startled.

Miguel's voice became apologetic. "Unfortunately we've had to make some sacrifices to the god of aeronautical efficiency."

"Sacrifice is a relative term," Mom said. "In a blimp on a scavenging expedition the only option is sponge baths. Cold ones."

"A comforting point," Miguel replied, laughing. "I must hurry off to the bridge—duty calls. But if you ladies wish, you may come along and watch our departure."

"Can we, Mom?" Wanda asked urgently. The great zeps held the world together, going everywhere, outracing the wind. She had been aboard the *Mayan Princess* once before, but only briefly. This time she intended to see everything. Plus she wanted to stay close to Miguel; her hand still tingled from the kiss. "Please!"

"I'd like that too," Mom said, and smiled at Miguel. "Thank you, Captain."

"You're most welcome."

They continued forward, until the passageway ended at a door. Wanda was glad to stop walking. She felt a bit dizzy, and figured it had to do with the thick air. Miguel pressed his thumb against an identiplate next to the door. The door hissed open. With a flourish Miguel ushered Mom and her into the *Mayan Princess*'s bridge.

CHAPTER FIVE

The bridge spread like a fan from the door which was in its aft bulkhead. The curved windscreen fit flush with the underside of the zep's nose, revealing a panoramic view of sky and ocean. Below the windscreen four chairs were spaced around the control console; three were occupied. The low ceiling had glow panels in the middle as well as more controls and displays where it angled down over the console. Wanda thought all the aluminum and gray plastic made the place look very serious.

"Ladies," Miguel said, "may I present the bridge's day watch. Elena Guzman, our pilot. Jose DeAlcuaz, our navigator. And Teresa Sandovar, our radioman. Shipmates, may I present Señora Linda Calhoun and Señorita Wanda Grigg of Calgary."

Jose DeAlcuaz was hunched over a computer screen staring at what looked like a weather map. He waved absently. Teresa Sandovar was busy talking softly into her headset mike. But Elena Guzman, a dark-haired young woman with big eyes and a toothy grin, spun her chair around. "Welcome aboard, Señora and Señorita. Wanda, I remember your other visit. I'm glad you came aboard the regular way this time." Her English was thick and awkward.

Wanda blushed, like she always did when reminded of the crazy day she had met Miguel.

"Captain," Elena said, "all stations have reported ready for departure."

"Elena, you're a model of efficiency. How much current was Calgary Three able to spare us?"

"Our batteries are fully charged."

"Good. We'll have use for the extra current very soon."

Wanda was busy staring around the bridge. It was like a blimp's bridge, only bigger and much more complicated. She pointed to the empty chair. "Is that where you sit?" she asked Miguel.

He nodded, and stepped over to the console in front of the chair. "This is the *Princess*'s brain, the master board at which I work my magic." He started gesturing. "The manual flight controls—rudders, elevators, motors, ballast, valving and trim. The auto-con. Radar. Radio and com. Monitor screens to keep me informed. All very simple, really—the *Princess* almost flies herself."

"Someone has to," Elena said pointedly.

"What are the rest of those for?" Wanda asked, looking at dozens of controls and displays Miguel hadn't indicated.

Miguel frowned and scratched his head. "You know, I've always wondered about that myself."

Mom smiled, so Wanda realized it was a joke and laughed.

Miguel unfolded a pair of observation seats from the aft bulkhead. "Ladies, as my pretty pilot has so tactfully reminded me, it's time to fly. If you'll please be seated and strap in, I can get to work without worrying about your safety."

"Thank you, Captain," Mom said as she sat and pulled the strap around. Miguel helped Wanda with her strap, which she didn't mind at all.

"Now I must apologize for an unavoidable rudeness," he said to them. "Flight operations must be carried out in our mother tongue for safety's sake. I hope you understand."

"Of course," Mom replied. "SOP. As it happens, I know some Spanish. I can explain what is going on to Wanda."

Wanda wasn't thrilled at the prospect of getting her audio input second-hand. She wished she had picked Spanish instead of French for her foreign language class.

"I'm glad." Miguel slid into his chair, strapped in, and put on a headset like Teresa's. Then he touched a com button. "Your attention, please, all passengers and crew. This is Captain Ramirez. We're about to bid a fond farewell to Calgary Three. Brace for maneuvering. You've been warned."

Wanda started to ask Miguel where else he had been on this cruise, but Mom put a finger to her lips.

Miguel glanced at a row of monitor screens above the windscreen between Elena and him, showing wide-angle views of sky, ocean, the zep's outside and Calgary Three's bottom. Then he checked the radar screens on his board. Elena, Jose and Teresa were also at work. Hands moved quickly, and clipped Spanish flew around the bridge.

Wanda stopped herself from giggling. Spanish sounded silly, full of bubbling and popping.

Miguel talked briefly with Jose, then turned to Mom and Wanda. "There is a storm front moving in from the southeast. Calgary will climb above it, but the *Princess* will show it her heels." Swiveling back to the console, he said something to Elena.

Wanda felt as well as heard the growling as Elena revved the motors one by one.

"*Mayan Princess,* Calgary Three here," a voice came from the bulkhead speaker. It sounded like Chris Fricken, one of Mom's and Dad's bridge-crew friends. "All clear at our end. Entryway retracted. Have a good flight, and take care of our people."

Miguel nodded to Teresa, who tapped a couple of buttons on her board. "Calgary Three, *Mayan Princess* here," he said into his headset mike. "As to the last, you may depend on it. Topside hatch sealed. Stand by to cut clamps on my five count."

"Standing by."

The flow of Spanish increased, and Wanda could tell they were about to leave. A commanding tone replaced the humor in Miguel's voice. It made her nerves tingle.

Miguel's left hand took the wheel, while his right darted here and there over his board. His black boots found the floor pedals. "Here we go," he said into his mike. Monitor screens showed the motor gondolas angling downward. "Five . . . four . . . three . . . two . . . one . . . cut!"

The motors growled together. The *Mayan Princess* dropped ever so gently. Then, as the enclosed props came back up, the zep stopped descending and started moving forward. It gradually built up speed.

"We're away clean," Mom whispered in Wanda's ear. "Next we'll be coming onto our course."

Miguel worked his controls, and the *Mayan Princess* began a sweeping turn to starboard. His attention jumped back and forth between the windscreen and his board. A few minutes later the zep straightened out and followed the sun west.

The growling softened a bit as the *Mayan Princess* reached cruising speed, becoming a monotonous part of the background. The zep didn't jump at every gust of wind like the shuttle blimps Wanda had ridden, but it wasn't as steady as home either. She didn't like the slight pitches and rolls.

"Take the con," Miguel told Elena in English. "Show your captain and his guests that you've learned something from him."

"Have your five minutes of piloting exhausted you, great hawk of the sky?" she asked merrily as she reached for her set of controls. "Maybe you should go take a nap, rest your creaking old bones."

Miguel, whom Wanda figured was about thirty, bristled dramatically. Turning to Mom and Wanda he said, "I took this young lady under my wing because of her soulful eyes, and what do I get? Abuse. Ignore her. Wave goodbye to your home instead."

Holding back giggles, Wanda looked where he was pointing.

Calgary Three was gliding by, a few miles to starboard and a few hundred feet higher. It was an awesome sight. It looked like a gigantic jewel, a diamond or a clear pearl set in the sky. The mirrors around the ranch level were the setting. The levels were in shadow, but swirls of reflected sunshine brightened the upper shell. Four was barely visible in the distance.

Wanda knew that a lot of townsfolk were at window walls, watching the *Mayan Princess*'s departure. Dad, of course. Jan and Lori, plus other friends and relatives. Maybe even Jeff. She felt another, worse attack of homesickness. But she wouldn't let herself give in to it. She planned to see some of the world, like Mom and Dad. She took a few deep breaths, and felt better.

Calgary Three slipped slowly astern, out of sight.

Theresa said something to Miguel, and they talked briefly. "Calgary has cleared us from its airspace," Mom whispered. "Captain Ramirez is telling her to raise Pemex Under, so he can report that we're safely underway."

"When will we reach Pemex Under?" Wanda asked just as softly.

"ETA is nine o'clock tomorrow morning. This is the last leg of the cruise."

Miguel talked over the com with the flight engineer, making sure (according to Mom) everything was working right. Then he talked to Jose about the zep's course. By the time he started his report to Pemex Under, Wanda had lost interest and was enjoying the scenery beyond the windscreen.

Solitary clouds drifted like fairy castles from her childhood bookdisks. White crests moved across the turquoise ocean, heading for a long island surrounded by over a dozen tiny satellites. The main island had a few patches of green, but mostly it was white around the edge and brown inside. The surface looked so strange and beautiful. She wondered what it would be like to swim in that water or walk on that beach.

Of course she would never know.

Suddenly she noticed that the *Mayan Princess* was much closer to the waves than it had been. Dangerously close. She turned back into the bridge chatter.

"—for maneuvering," Miguel was saying into his com. "We're descending into the killzone—radiation drill is now in effect. Enjoy the view."

Wanda tried to hide her fright. All her life she had heard stories about the belt of fallout, poisons and biobugs from the War which still kept people from living on the surface. She knew that the *Mayan Princess* was airtight and radtight, but the thought of being just inches away from a gruesome death made her stomach churn.

"Are we . . . landing?" she asked in a squeaky voice.

"I sincerely hope not," Miguel laughed, but his eyes looked serious. "We're going to come very close, though. Pickup is a delicate maneuver, so you must be as quiet as a mouse while I attend to it. Unless my pretty but cocky pilot wishes to take the con?"

Elena shook her head vigorously. "I'm here to learn, remember?"

The *Mayan Princess* kept angling downward, until it was only a few hundred feet above the waves. At close range they seemed less beautiful and more deadly, hills of water eager to hit, crush. The zep leveled off, then started to ease lower on an even keel.

"What's going on?" Wanda whispered in Mom's ear.

"Captain Ramirez is picking up water to replace dropped ballast, and to break out hydrogen to replace leakage and valving losses in the cells."

Wanda was shocked. "Water from the killzone?"

"Filtered ocean water is safe for those uses, if it isn't taken from the very top. Convection currents dilute the fallout and poisons."

"But why pick up hydrogen for lift *and* ballast to weight us down?"

Mom paused thoughtfully before she answered. "Zeps use hydrogen and ballast for descending and climbing. The *Mayan Princess*'s cells were probably somewhat deflated when it docked, and almost all of its ballast must have been dropped when our cargo came aboard. Now Captain Ramirez is going to take on more of both."

Wanda thought it sounded awfully complicated, like so many adult things.

She watched the bridge activity. Miguel, Elena and Jose were hard at work. She could feel the growing tension, worse than during the departure. Miguel looked as if he had been cast in bronze. The muscles in the back of his neck stood out like reinforcing cables. Sweat made his skin glisten, but his hands and voice were steady.

Wanda glanced out the windscreen, and gulped. The waves almost seemed high enough to crash into the bridge. The zep had slowed way down, but it was still moving too fast for her.

"I don't like this," she whispered to Mom.

Mom touched her hand. "Try not to worry, dear. Pick-ups are a normal part of long zep cruises. Captain Ramirez knows what he's doing."

The *Mayan Princess* came to a stop, floating about fifty feet above the wave crests. Miguel spoke into his com, and seconds later Wanda felt a new vibration. The keel monitor screen showed a long flexible tube with evenly spaced bulges and a doughnut-like ring about a hundred feet from the bottom being lowered into the restless ocean. When it stopped, the ring was riding the waves up and down. Wanda figured the tube was a siphon and the bulges were booster pumps.

The com spouted more Spanish. "The flight engineer reported that the pickup is underway," Mom whispered to Wanda. "Captain Ramirez is using the motors to hold our position."

"Why doesn't he just let the auto-con do it?"

"A zep exposes so much surface area to the wind. In a maneuver this tight, even electronic reactions can be too slow. But Captain Ramirez can use his experience to out-guess the wind."

"Did you ever do anything like this when you flew the blimps?" Wanda asked.

"Not as well as Captain Ramirez. He's a master pilot."

"What would happen to us if we splashed?"

Mom was quiet for a moment. "Zeps aren't built to ride ocean swells. But everything is going to be fine. Captain Ramirez has done this many times—trust him."

Minutes crept by. Each time the bridge shifted slightly, Wanda flinched. She didn't look at the waves, but at Miguel. She realized that there was a lot more to him than charm and heartblasting good looks. He was smart, skilled and totally sure of himself. A wonderful man. Her worry faded.

Finally the flight engineer reported again. "The ballast tanks are full," Mom whispered, "and the hydrogen cells have been fully inflated." Wanda watched the siphon rise back into the *Mayan Princess*'s belly.

Miguel rapped out a flurry of orders, and the bridge crew became even busier. The gondolas angled upward, growling loudly. Some of the freshly acquired ballast was dropped in wind-scattered streams. The deck gradually tilted as the *Mayan Princess* climbed away from the waves.

Mom was translating Elena's altitude reports. When she got to one thousand feet, the tension in the bridge broke. Miguel swiveled to Mom and Wanda. "Did you enjoy our little show?" he asked. His casual cheerfulness was back.

"Very impressive," Mom said. Wanda nodded.

Miguel switched his com to the all-ship channel. "Your attention, please, all passengers and crew. This is Captain Ramirez. Our surface maneuver has been completed. Radiation drill will continue until we clear five thousand feet."

Miguel gave some more orders. Elena took over the piloting; Teresa started tapping buttons on the radio board. Miguel shed his headset, unstrapped and walked over to Mom and Wanda. "That concludes all the excitement—I hope—until we land. Now I have to attend to some pesky details which would bore you to tears."

Mom and Wanda unstrapped, and stood somewhat unsteadily on the sloping deck. "We should get settled in our cabin," Mom said. "We've imposed on your hospitality too long already. But thank you for a fascinating and educational experience."

"Yes, thanks," Wanda added. She wanted to say something clever, but when she looked at him she could barely talk. "Wide sky."

After a bunch of good-byes, Miguel escorted Mom and Wanda to the door. "If I can be of any service, please don't hesitate to call," he told them.

They walked carefully back to their cabin. It had bunk beds, built-in furniture, a tiny bathroom and an even tinier closet. A round port let in the sunny afternoon. The bulkheads were ivory plastic, and the carpet was short-cropped. A painting of a pre-War airplane hung over the fold-out table. Wanda thought the cubicle was too small for one person, let alone two.

They maneuvered around each other, and managed to get unpacked. Watching Mom move, Wanda realized there were many advantages to being compact and graceful. Her headache, forgotten in the excitement of visiting the bridge, returned squared.

Mom fetched two pills from a vial in her purse, took one herself, and handed the other to Wanda.

"What's this for?" Wanda asked.

"Your headache. If you don't have one, you adjust to thick air faster than anyone I know."

"Thanks, Mom." Wanda swallowed the pill with the help of a cup of water from the bathroom.

They washed up, then went to the dining room for lunch. Mom explained that the galley was always open; except for the formal dinners you could just walk in and eat. They shared a table plus a boring adult conversation with two crewmen and a medical student from Tivoli Two on her way to Pemex Under University. The once-again-level deck made eating easier than it might have been, but the food wasn't very good.

After lunch they returned to the cabin. Wanda wanted to go exploring, but Mom insisted that they get some rest first to digest and unwind. Twenty minutes into the enforced down time Wanda was rescued by a com call from Miguel.

"It's our custom to offer a tour of the *Princess* to all passengers," he told Mom. "Usually I delegate this task to junior crewmen, but RHIP. Would you lovely ladies care to see more of the ship?"

Wanda felt warm and strange inside. Miguel wouldn't leave his important duties to be a tour guide unless . . . No, that was crazy. He must have had his choice of beautiful women his own age. But why then was he being so nice to her? Could he actually be interested?

Mom was looking at her. She nodded as hard as she could, and Mom said into the com, "We would like that very much, Captain."

"Good. I'm on my way."

Wanda barely had time to fix herself up in the miniature bathroom, before Miguel arrived. She and Mom joined him in the passageway.

"I'm relieved to find you've survived the worst danger of our flight," he said.

"Huh?" Wanda asked brilliantly.

"Our galley. Be brave, and look forward to the justly famous restaurants of Pemex Under. But now for the tour. We'll work our way aft. You've already seen the bridge, so if you'll come with me . . ."

The first part of the tour, the living quarters, wasn't very interesting. The dining room she had already been to. The galley, sickbay and laundry were small but otherwise pretty ordinary. The lounge had a vid, an auto-bar and a long port. Being the zep's social center, it was crowded with passengers and off-duty crewmen. Mom and Miguel were sucked into more adult chatter. Wanda stared through the plastic composite at the distant coastline of what someone had called the Yucatan Peninsula.

But things picked up aft of the cargo hold. Miguel took them into the dimly lit monitor room where the flight engineer and his team watched banks of screens and displays.

"Only the *Princess*'s keel region is pressurized and heated." Miguel spoke softly to avoid disturbing the crewmen. "These screens are the most convenient way to see the rest of the ship, unless you wish to put on outside suits and scramble around like monkeys."

"No, thank you," Mom laughed. "Wanda is too young, and I'm too old."

"You defame yourself unjustly, my dear lady."

The watched the changing images in the screens, while Miguel narrated. Wanda saw the long cell bays with their rows of hydrogen cells, bulging translucent shapes wrapped in network cording. She saw the zep's framework: deep ring main frames, transversed girders and bracing wires. She saw the ladders and catwalks which crewmen used to do maintenance. She saw the gigantic tail fins, the motor gondolas mounted laterally on ball socket supports, and the solar cell panels covering most of the utter hull.

"You should recognize much of this," Miguel said. "The hollow aluminum composite girders and the silicon/germanium solar cells, for example, are also used in windriders."

Wanda had been wondering about something since the water pickup. "Why do you use hydrogen as your lifting gas? We use helium in our blimps, which is a lot safer."

"For our long voyages we need an easily obtainable gas, and what is more common than sea water? As to safety, we treat our hydrogen with all the respect a highly flammable gas deserves."

"Hydrogen is also less expensive," Mom pointed out. "We get our helium from the Alberta enclave's natural gas wells, and pay a pretty penny for it."

They continued aft. Miguel showed them one of the battery rooms, filled with gray cannisters which were glass conductor superbatteries. They passed through a big compartment devoted to life-support machinery, and an even bigger one housing the trim, ballast and hydrogen generating systems. Then came several smaller compartments: electronics, workshops and stores. Finally the passageway ended at the aft observation room.

"So, my dear ladies, what do you think of the *Princess*?" Miguel asked as they looked back along the zep's course.

"It's ultra!" Wanda enthused. "I bet you could even follow Puff, my pet fireball, into the ionosphere to find out what she does there."

Miguel shook his head. "Modern zeps are lighter and stronger than their ancestors, thanks to improved technology. They can fly higher and carry more cargo. But there are still limits. We're presently cruising at sixteen thousand feet, which is close to our ceiling with a full load. Your windrider had to descend a few thousand feet so we could rendezvous. But I don't doubt that you'll find a way to accomplish your goal."

"You run a very trim ship," Mom told him.

"The crew does the work, and I take the credit. A fine arrangement for a captain, no?"

The tour over, he took them back to their cabin. "Now I must reluctantly part company with you until dinner. I have to return to the bridge before my ambitious pilot declares a mutiny."

"I can't recall when I've had a more enjoyable tour or tour guide, Captain," Mom said.

"Uh . . . thanks, Miguel." Wanda figured she might as well have her tongue amputated, if it wasn't going to be more helpful. "Wide sky."

"Wide sky, my lovely ladies." Miguel bowed, and headed forward.

Dinner wasn't until eight, so Mom and Wanda had some time on their hands. Mom studied her purchase lists and market reports at the table. Wanda sprawled on her bunk, thinking about becoming a zep captain instead of a windrider engineer, and about Miguel. She watched the blue outside the port turn into gold, red, then black with stars. Finally Mom put away her flatscreen, and announced that it was time to get ready.

That took a lot longer than usual, due to the tight quarters and Wanda's determination to look perfect for Miguel. She had brought along the off-the-shoulder pink organza dress, white stole and locket that she had worn when he escorted her to the dance. Mom put on her midnight-blue dress, and pinned a white neosilk flower above her left ear. Then they joined the flow of passengers and crew in the passageway.

The dining room tables had been pushed together into one long one, covered with a lace tablecloth, candles in fancy holders, china, crystal and silver. The ceiling glow panels imitated the candlelight, warming the burgundy carpet and the fake wood bulkheads. Wanda was surprised at how much nicer the room looked than it had at lunch.

A steward led them to their places and seated them. As the chairs filled up, Wanda noticed that passengers and crew were interspersed around the table. She spotted Elena, Jose and Teresa, and guessed that the whole crew except for the night watch was here. They were in their dress uniforms, brown with silver trim, while the passengers wore the formal fashions of a half-dozen towns.

When everyone was seated (nineteen crewmen and twenty-six passengers by Wanda's count), Miguel rose from his chair at the head of the table and tapped his wine glass with his knife for attention. "Good evening, my friends. Before we dine, I wish to introduce our newest guests. I give you Señora Linda Calhoun and her daughter, Señorita Wanda Grigg, from Calgary." Miguel gestured to them, and led the polite applause. Mom smiled and nodded, so Wanda did too.

"Señora Calhoun is traveling to Pemex Under on business, while Señorita Grigg is on holiday." Miguel winked at Wanda, then went on. "Señorita Grigg is a dear friend of mine, having literally dropped into my life a few months ago. Some of you may already be familiar with her courageous deed, but such tales bear repeating."

Wanda felt her cheeks getting warm, and regretted that she had so much blushing skin on display.

"A meteorite holed Calgary Three, and almost sent it crashing into the sea. But Señorita Grigg, like the legendary Dutch boy at the dike, patched the hole, thus saving over six hundred lives. Then a second disaster struck—she slid off the windrider's shell into the sky. Fortunately she was wearing an outside suit. Popping the paraglider, she showed great skill and bravery in soaring above the killzone until rescue could reach her."

The stewards had poured wine for the adults and grape juice for Wanda. Miguel raised his glass. "A toast, my friends, to a true heroine."

Everyone drank, and there was another round of applause. Wanda stared at her plate. The story always embarrassed her. She had just done what she was supposed to do, and she wouldn't have fallen if she hadn't gotten careless. As far as she was concerned, the only special thing about that day was meeting Miguel. But listening to his praise had made her feel the way drinking wine was supposed to.

Mom stood up. "Captain Ramirez neglects to mention that it was the *Mayan Princess* which rescued her. He went out on the hull, risking his own life to pluck her out of midair. A toast to Captain Ramirez and his crew."

Everyone drank and clapped again. Mom and Miguel sat down, conversations spread around the table, and the stewards started serving food.

Wanda didn't have much to contribute to the adult chatter. She told the whole meteorite story at the insistence of the crewman sitting next to her, and answered questions politely. But mostly she watched the yellow light dancing in Miguel's face.

After the dessert plates were cleared, people started

leaving for the lounge. Miguel invited Mom and Wanda to come along, but Mom said it was already past their bedtime. They returned to the cabin.

Wanda was soon tucked snugly in her bunk, but she had trouble falling asleep. Partly because of the zep's motion, and partly because of her heart.

She was in love with Miguel. It felt just like it had with Jeff, only stronger. She knew they couldn't get married, have children and be a family; the age difference was too big for such a fantasy. But she could give him her most precious gift. She had always wanted her first time to be ultra special, a perfect memory for the rest of her life. With Miguel it would be.

She drifted joyously through possible scenarios until sleep came.

CHAPTER SIX

"One . . . two . . . three . . . jump! One . . . two . . . three . . . jump!"

Linda's voice was a faint ragged gasp as she neared the end of her workout. She wished she had a musical beat to lose herself in, but she was disturbing the *Mayan Princess*'s early morning peace enough as it was. Sweat flew from her gyrating body. Her black and yellow exercise outfit cast a smear of reflection in the dark port.

"Up . . . back! Up . . . back!"

She had dragged herself out of bed early so she could have the lounge to herself. One hour of exercise, three times a week, and no excuses. She hated every minute of it. But the torture sessions were essential to maintain the health and figure she had once taken for granted. This one was also loosening the knots she had been tied in ever since the meeting in the mayor's office.

"Up . . . back . . . and done!" She stopped, swaying on jellied knees, breathing hard and fast. Free for another two days.

Soft clapping startled her. She whirled and saw Captain Ramirez standing in the doorway. Her first instinct was to cover herself. She tried to ignore it. "Why, good morning, Captain."

"Good morning, my dear lady."

"I hope I wasn't disturbing anyone."

"Over the motors that's not likely," he said. "I just happened by and heard familiar sounds of suffering."

"You work out too?"

"These rugged good looks aren't entirely due to my wise choice of parents. The crew exercises regularly to fight the sedentary effects of our long voyages." He picked up her towel from a table and handed it to her.

"Thank you." Linda wiped the sweat from her face, then draped the towel shawl-like over her shoulders. The zep's air was about ten degrees cooler than she was used to.

Captain Ramirez's eyes wandered lazily from her calves up her legs, over her stomach, her arms and chest, then back to her face. She *felt* them. She should have been insulted, but there was something disarming about his unabashed admiration.

"Your labor bears lovely fruit," he said.

"With my bulges bulging and hair sticking to my face? You flatter me."

She knew she should excuse herself and return to the cabin. Before letting Captain Ramirez take Wanda to the dance, she had had a talk with him. He hadn't been hard to size up. He was a textbook example of a traveling man, a confirmed bachelor who loved passionately but briefly and then moved on. A principled rogue who wouldn't take advantage of a fourteen-year-old child, but a rogue nonetheless.

Instead she went over to the port. The first reddened light of sunrise revealed a strange world over which the *Mayan Princess* was flying low. The zep was crossing a coastline of wide beaches, sandbars and mangrove swamps. In the northern distance she could make out the ruins of a city.

"It was called Tampico." Captain Ramirez had materialized at her elbow. "Full of life and beauty before the War, they say. Now the scavengers gnaw at its bones."

Linda had to admit that she was enjoying his campaign to seduce her. It was reassuring to find that she could still inspire such interest. Besides, she admired expertise in any field. A mother traveling with her daughter was a difficult romantic target. But he was meeting the challenge cleverly, ostensibly treating them like sisters while subtly tightening his orbit around her.

The vegetation below was thickening into a tropical forest. Evergreen giants supported a somber roof of branches and vines, but there were also smaller trees and patches of bamboo. Breezes moved the treetops. A muddy river wound through the forest toward the coast.

"It's lovely," Linda said softly.

Captain Ramirez sighed. "It's a shadow. Once monkeys ran along those branches, jaguars stalked, parrots flew. But they're gone forever."

Linda nodded. Brimming with life though it seemed, it was in the killzone. A closer view would have revealed the twisting, sickness and death. She remembered them all too well from her scavenging days.

Yet she remembered something else too, and she could see it in the areas of struggling new growth. "The surface is healing itself. It won't be the same as it was before, but in a few hundred years folks will be able to live there again."

"Unfortunately that's a point of only academic interest to us."

She could feel the warmth of his arm as it brushed hers. She didn't need his reflection in the port to remind her that he was extremely handsome, a tiger where Jack was a bear. His casual attitude hid a surprising amount of ability and strength. Her reaction to him had a flavor of girlish uncertainty which worried her. This man was dangerous.

His hand slid with silky gentleness down her arm, leaving a tingling in its wake, and curled around her hand. "I noticed that your flower was pinned behind your left ear last night," he said. "An old Hawaiian custom meaning the wahini isn't available, no?"

"Much like the wedding band on my finger." She pulled her hand free.

"I see it there, but not where it should be, in your eyes and heart. They're empty. That's a very sad thing."

"You're only seeing what you would like to see."

Captain Ramirez shook his head. "When it comes to the needs of a lovely woman, I'm very empathic."

Adultery was a rare thing in windrider towns, probably because secrets were so hard to keep in small close-knit communities. She wasn't used to such pursuit, or to the growing treason of her own body. She decided to counter his directness with directness.

"I still owe you a debt for saving Wanda's life," she said levelly. "If you want to make love to me, I'll come to your cabin now. But you understand it'll mean nothing to me. Less than nothing."

Captain Ramirez sighed. "How can one as sincere as I be so misunderstood? Obligation is a bitter spice. I only want a woman who wants me, and gives herself freely."

"Then you'll have to look elsewhere. If you'll excuse me, Captain, I have to go. Don't let me keep you from your duties."

"You remind me that I was on my way to the bridge, before your beauty distracted me. Wide sky." He bowed smartly and left.

Linda took a deep breath, letting it out slowly. Her escape had been a narrow one, and only temporary.

Wanda was in her gradual process of waking up, when Linda entered the cabin. Linda accelerated the pace with some judicious tickling. She introduced Wanda to the etiquette of a communal shower, then they dressed for an active day. The dining room was crowded with passengers and crewmen squeezing in breakfast before the landing. Linda and Wanda found adjoining chairs at a table, and ate quickly. The breakfast conversations were for the most part about Pemex Under.

They went back to the cabin, packed, and put their suitcases outside the door. Then Linda glanced out the port at the surface which was now even closer. "We're in the final approach," she told Wanda. "We can watch it from here, but the lounge has the best view."

"Can't we go visit Miguel in the bridge?"

"Since he hasn't invited us, no. Yesterday was a very special honor—passengers aren't usually allowed in a zep's bridge during flight. Let's go to the lounge."

Passengers traditionally watched launchings and landings from the lounge, and it seemed to Linda that the turnout for this one was a hundred percent. She and

Wanda sat where they could see the port as well as the vid's nose-camera view. There was a low rumble of nervous talk. Launchings and landings were the riskiest parts of a cruise.

"Your attention, please, all passengers and crew. This is Captain Ramirez." His voice came boldly from a bulkhead speaker. "We're about to land at Pemex Under. Brace for maneuvering, or on your own heads be it."

The big screen showed rounded foothills climbing toward the distant Sierra Madre Oriental mountain range. They were barren except for patches of grass and some stunted trees. Linda spotted the ruins of several villages, overgrown fields and what had once been a road. Here, where civilization had done little, nature was quickest in undoing it. But eventually even the cities would crumble and be covered by new life. Folks would return to an again-virgin surface, and hopefully treat it more kindly this time.

A dreary gray morning was sandwiched between the hills and a thick cloud cover. All that dark, massive water vapor hanging overhead made Linda uncomfortable; she preferred the white fluffy view from above. Tricky surface winds were moving the *Mayan Princess* around, making the pitches and rolls more noticeable.

She found Wanda's hand in hers and squeezed it. "Don't worry, dear. Zeps are built to ride air rougher than this. It isn't as bad as it seems—you just aren't used to surface weather."

Wanda didn't say anything. She was staring at the screen, some of the color gone from her face.

The *Mayan Princess* was approaching a low mesa-like spur of the range. On the rocky plateau Linda could make out a wide white dome and some much smaller structures. "That's Pemex Under," she told Wanda.

"I thought it was underground."

"It is, almost a mile. But some facilities have to be on the surface. The dome is the windrider yard's launch portal. There are also antennae, vents, air locks, the zep field, the train portal—"

"They have trains? Like in the old vids? I didn't think anyone could live on the surface."

"In airtight/radtight cars you can, for a limited time.

The lines run to the other Mexican enclaves, the oil fields and some old cities which are being scavenged. I hoped we might see a train coming or going, but no such luck."

The *Mayan Princess* moved over the plateau, less than a thousand feet above the gray plain and descending steadily. It was also shedding its forward speed. A few miles short of the dome Linda spotted the zep field, a wide deep trench with a flat bottom. The zep was maneuvering toward it. "That's where we're going to land," she told Wanda.

Its size became apparent as the *Mayan Princess* hovered over it. The tarmac-paved bottom covered with a pattern of guidelines was big enough to hold the zep and then some. The zep descended toward the center lines, the motors countering irregular breezes until it was safely below the rim of the trench.

Linda unconsciously tensed with the other passengers as the tarmac reared up. But when the *Mayan Princess*'s landing pads settled on the field, she barely felt it. The motors shut down.

"Even with laser guidance," she said to herself as well as Wanda, "that was a neat piece of piloting."

"Now what?" Wanda asked eagerly.

"Now we get towed inside for decon."

The sheer end of the trench beyond the *Mayan Princess*'s nose held a portal big enough to accommodate the zep. The two doors swung open ponderously, revealing a dim cavernous space beyond. Four box-like carts emerged and went to the zep's corners. Waldos wielding magnetic clamps locked onto hull plates. Soon the carts were carrying the zep inside.

"How can those four little things lift the whole zep?" Wanda asked.

"Its buoyancy is still almost neutral. Its mass makes moving it tricky, but it only weighs a few hundred pounds."

The carts stopped and the portal closed, sealing the *Mayan Princess* in a cylindrical chamber just barely bigger than the zep. When Linda's eyes adjusted to the less-bright artificial light, she saw bumpers, catwalks, pipes and some miscellaneous machinery clinging to the steel walls.

"Your attention, please, all passengers and crew. This is

Captain Ramirez. As you may have noticed, we're landed at Pemex Under. Deboarding will begin in approximately twenty minutes. My crew and I wish you well."

The stress level in the lounge dropped back to normal. Conversations were enthusiastic, and the auto-bar started doing a brisk business. Wanda was staring raptly at the activity beyond the port.

A wind was blowing past the *Mayan Princess*, nose to tail, strong enough to make the catwalks sway. Black disks at the ends of more waldos were moving over the hull.

"Those are ultrasonic scrubbers," Linda explained, "like the ones we use to decon the shell. Meanwhile the blowers are removing the contaminated air."

The scrubbers finished their sweeps and pulled back. Rad-suited folks with equipment slung on their backs appeared on the catwalks. They waved radmeters around, and every now and then sprayed decon foam at the hull. "Their job is to clean up any residual hot spots."

Finally they left, and the wind died. Another portal in front of the *Mayan Princess* opened. The carts resumed towing the zep forward.

It entered a tunnel much like the decon chamber. The portal sealed behind it. The image of a zep crawling along a hole in the ground like a gopher made Linda smile. The tunnel angled downward slightly for several minutes, then it leveled off and widened into a vast well-lit zep bay.

Six ribbed cradles were arranged in a row under the high vaulted ceiling; two held zeps like the *Mayan Princess*. Beyond them the cranes of a construction cradle towered over a partially completed zep framework. Machinery, supplies and building-fronts defined the bay's walls. The scale became awesomely clear when Linda recognized the bugs scurrying across the gray tarmac as cargo carts and people.

The *Mayan Princess* was towed into an empty cradle. It settled, there was a slight jar, and moments later the four carts drove away.

The passengers started drifting out of the lounge. Linda tapped Wanda on the shoulder, and Wanda reluctantly turned away from the port. "Time to deboard," Linda told her.

"Ultra! Can we explore around here before we go to the hotel? It makes our blimp bay look like nothing!"

"Business before tourism." Linda smiled at Wanda's enthusiasm, remembering her own first visit to an enclave. "I have to see to the unloading of our cargo, and you're going to help like you promised."

They went back to the cabin. The suitcases were gone, hopefully on their way to the hotel. They made a last sweep for any forgotten items, then joined the flow of passengers toward the cargo hold.

A section of the starboard bulkhead had folded out and down, forming a ramp to the zep bay's floor. Passengers were walking down to a row of waiting taxis. Soon the only ones left were Linda, Wanda and reps from two other towns with cargos in the hold.

Unloading proved to be the usual frustrating experience, taking the rest of the morning and much of the afternoon. They had to wait for the Pemex Under buyer to arrive with his fleet of cargo carts. *Mayan Princess* crewmen transferred the cargo, a tricky job since the zep's buoyancy and trim had to be constantly adjusted. There was some confusion sorting out the three shipments. Linda inspected the Calgary goods for damage, while Wanda checked them against the manifest. At lunchtime a steward brought out sandwiches and drinks, and everyone took a break. The inevitable arguments over quality and quantity arose when it came time for the buyer to accept delivery.

But finally the buyer and his carts were on their way to the company warehouses. A taxi came humming across the tarmac to pick up the four townsfolk. Linda was proud of Wanda; she had been helpful and only minimally restive during the tiresome process.

"Aren't we going to say goodbye to Miguel?" Wanda asked with some urgency in her voice.

Linda had been half expecting him to put in an appearance, and she was relieved (she thought) that he hadn't. "He's very busy right now. But I'm sure we'll be seeing him again while we're here."

The four townsfolk climbed into the open electric cart. Pushing her money card in the dashboard slot before the other reps, Linda said, "Casa Encantada, please."

"As you wish," the pseudovoice of the taxi's computer responded. The taxi accelerated toward the dark half-circle in a wall which was a tunnel/street entrance.

"How do these carts know where to go without drivers?" Wanda asked.

"They follow a network of guidance cables laid in the streets throughout the enclave. We don't use the system in windriders, since we have so few carts."

The tunnel/street carried cart traffic moving both ways. It slanted downward at a moderate angle, and seemed to go on forever. Linda talked market prices with the Tivoli and Niger reps, while Wanda stared curiously at the colorful wall murals.

Finally the tunnel/street came to an end at a circular intersection with a statue fountain in the middle. The taxi orbited, then turned into another tunnel/street. After a few hundred feet the walls and ceiling disappeared. Wanda gasped.

The dome was smaller than a windrider's topside, only fourteen hundred feet across and four hundred feet high, but it was much more crowded. Buildings lined three concentrically circular streets, while the street they were on ran radially to a small park in the middle. An array of graceful steel pillars rose to help support the dome's ceiling. It was also steel, but blue paint and clever lighting almost made it look like an afternoon sky.

As the taxi moved slowly through heavy traffic, Linda tried to adjust to the sudden sensory assault. This was the business dome; the sights and sounds of prosperous commerce were everywhere. The sidewalks were crowded with folks "talking" at the top of their lungs. Children and dogs ran wild, adding to the noise as well as the sense of confusion. Sidewalk vendors competed with the stores and restaurants. The suits, print dresses, bright shirts, embroidered blouses, jeans and skirts of the Pemex Under stockholders dominated, but saris, dashikis, kimonos, Eurosuits and other styles upheld the enclave's reputation as a global crossroads. There were trees and grass to help with the oxygen/CO_2 balance, but local decorative taste ran more to carved stone and dancing water. The air system somehow endured an overwhelming collection of smells. She even saw folks smoking tobacco, a vice which hadn't gone aloft with windriders.

Linda's other visits had been to the rather straitlaced Canadian enclaves. This was . . . different. Inefficient and undignified, but brimming with life. She understood Captain Ramirez a little better.

"Look at all those folks!" Wanda exclaimed.

"This is just one of eleven domes. The stockholder population passed thirty thousand a few months ago." Linda had read up on Pemex Under, but dry statistics hadn't conveyed its spirit.

The Casa Encantada was a white terraced pyramid which rose almost to the dome's ceiling. The taxi stopped in front, and the townsfolk entered the elegant lobby to register. Soon Linda and Wanda were following a bellboy Wanda's age to their rooms.

They had adjoining singles on an upper floor. The decor was in keeping with the hotel's jungle temple theme: blockish mahogany furniture, stone tile walls, hand-woven tapestries and gold fixtures. Linda opened the connecting door, so they could talk while they unpacked. Wanda was bubbling over about everything she had seen.

"Can we go shopping now?" she asked after they finished unpacking.

"We'll have plenty of opportunity for that later, dear. It's getting close to dinner time. I suggest we take it easy until then, let our eyeballs cool off."

Wanda settled for exploring the local vid channels. Linda sat on the edge of her bed. During the cruise she had been able to play tourist and almost forget the reason for the trip. But now she had to carry out her ugly errand.

Sighing, she called the office of Pemex Under's Chief Executive Officer. Thanks to her status as a town rep, she was able to make an appointment with his secretary to see him at ten thirty the next morning.

She was lying on the bed trying to unwind when the door chime rang. It was the bellboy bearing a dozen red roses. "For Señora Calhoun and Señorita Grigg," he said in halting English, "from Captain Ramirez. He requests the pleasure of your company for dinner this evening."

"Can we, Mom? Please?" Wanda begged from behind her.

A dinner for three seemed safe enough, and Captain Ramirez was certainly an entertaining companion. "Please tell him we happily accept." She took the roses.

"He'll call for you at seven." The bellboy bowed and left.

The invitation launched Wanda into frenzied preparations, while Linda dressed with practiced ease. Linda took care to look good but not too good. When the dust settled in Wanda's room, she came out and admired herself in Linda's mirror.

"I wish I had perfume to wear," Wanda sighed. "Can I buy some while we're here?"

"If you're only going to use it here, yes." Townsfolk didn't wear scents for the same reason they bathed regularly; air quality in a windrider was a social issue as well as an engineering problem.

Captain Ramirez arrived promptly at seven. He was in his dress uniform, a gaudy but impressive sight. "My lovely ladies, your radiance is almost too much to bear!" He kissed Linda's hand, then Wanda's.

"Hi, Miguel," Wanda said, her face almost matching the pink bows in her hair. "I wanted to see you today, but Mom said you were too busy."

"Your mother was right. But now I'm off duty for a few days, and I hope to make it up to you. I imagine your mother will be spending tomorrow with dull businessmen. Would you like to see Pemex Under as only I can show it to you?"

"I sure would!" Wanda looked hopefully at Linda.

Linda nodded. "I wish I could join you, but Captain Ramirez has described my fate tomorrow all too well." Then she locked eyes with Captain Ramirez. "You're very kind, for this as well as the roses and dinner. But you mustn't keep putting yourself out for us."

"I assure you it's no trouble at all. I happen to stay here myself between voyages. My room is just down the hall—number 116."

Linda's eyebrows rose ever so slightly. "My, that is a coincidence."

"Where are we going for dinner?" Wanda asked, her shining eyes looking up at Captain Ramirez.

"To the finest of our many fine restaurants. I hope you like Mexican cuisine."

They went down to the lobby. The doorman summoned a taxi, and Captain Ramirez told it to take them to the Zocalo. The dome's lights had been dimmed and angled downward to simulate the real night a mile above. The "sky" was black except for a false moon and stars. A blower-generated breeze stirred the cool air.

The taxi drove through streets which were less busy but more festive now that the work day was over. The Zocalo turned out to be an outdoor restaurant on top of the Banking Building. It was very impressive, with fountains, potted palm trees, hanging lamps and a panoramic view of the dome. It was also crowded with diners, but Captain Ramirez discreetly handed something to the maitre d', and they were immediately shown to a good table.

"Did you bribe him?" Wanda asked in a shocked tone.

Captain Ramirez grinned at her. "The bite, as we call it, isn't illegal or immoral. It's part of our economy."

The food was fiery but fascinating, and two margueritas relaxed Linda considerably. Captain Ramirez was in fine form, telling amusing stories from his years in the Zep Service. Wanda was listening avidly, but Linda's attention drifted in and out of the monologue.

She was trying to understand what was happening to her. It seemed as if the real Linda Calhoun had been left behind in Calgary Three. She was someone else, a stranger playing a role out of a spy bookdisk. The bizarre sensation made her feel frightened and freed at the same time.

She wanted Captain Ramirez. She might as well admit it to herself, if no one else. He reached deep inside her, touching the place Jack hadn't for so long. The real Linda Calhoun would have been shocked at the thought of having an affair; she savored it. She might actually have considered going to bed with him, except for Wanda's presence. Wanda was one responsibility she hadn't left behind.

She didn't have much to say during dinner, or on the ride back to the hotel. But she had plenty to think about as she tossed restlessly in her big lonely bed.

CHAPTER SEVEN

Waking unrefreshed, Linda went to the window to look at the new day. The business dome was already as active as it had been the previous afternoon. The ceiling gave a fair imitation of a morning sky, but she found it as unsatisfying as a picture of a meal. She missed the nourishment of actual sunshine. The weight of uncounted tons of rock pressed down on her.

Or was it the weight of the upcoming meeting with the CEO? She was terribly afraid of the windrider eater. But she was also afraid of what using evil to fight evil would do to her home, her family . . . and her. Already it had driven a secret between her and Jack and Wanda, made her lie to them.

Shrugging, she roused Wanda and began putting herself together. She dressed with an eye toward making the proper impression at the meeting. The two of them had breakfast in the hotel's restaurant, then Wanda hurried off to tour the enclave with Captain Ramirez.

Linda took a taxi to the public services dome. The Pemex Corporation Building was a steel and glass tower overlooking the central park, and a very busy place. She rode an elevator up to the top floor. Outside the door of the CEO's office she paused, resisted an urge to turn and run. But that wouldn't solve anything. She took a deep breath and went in.

The outer office was every bit as stylish as she had expected. A young lady behind a reception desk was talking to a computer terminal. She looked up at Linda, smiling. "Good morning. You're Señora Calhoun, no?" she asked in English.

"I am. I have an appointment with Señor Gutierrez."

The receptionist spoke softly into her com, listened to her earpiece, then got up and walked around the desk. "Come this way, please."

She ushered Linda into the CEO's private office. It was bigger and more impressive than the mayor's office in One. Three of the walls were intricately worked walnut, while the fourth was a window looking down on the park. The furniture pieces were also walnut, actual pre-War antiques. A pole bearing the red, white and green Mexican flag stood beside the broad desk.

The man seated behind the desk rose as Linda entered. "Welcome to Pemex Under, Señora Calhoun," he said warmly in English. They shook hands. "I am Ernesto Gutierrez."

The Chief Executive Officer of the Pemex Corporation resembled an elderly Spanish grandee from an earlier century. He was slim, with erect posture despite his years, and his seamed face radiated strength of will. A gold tie clip, watch chain and cuff links glittered against the white backdrop of his suit.

"Thank you," she said in her rusty Spanish. "It's good of you to see me. But since I'm the visitor here, I don't want to impose my language on you."

"If all travelers were as thoughtful, the world would be a more civilized place." He gestured to a comfortable chair across the desk from his. "Please be seated. May I have Rosita bring you something to drink?"

"No, thank you." They sat down.

"How is my friend, Mayor Keith?" Señor Gutierrez asked.

"He's fine. He sends his regards."

Señor Gutierrez leaned forward. "Please forgive my directness, but I don't think you are here to exchange social graces. This office isn't involved in purchasing cargos."

Reaching into her purse, Linda brought out the vid disk

the Mayor had given her. She handed it to Señor Gutierrez.
"Mayor Keith asked me to deliver this to you. It's very
important." The disk had been preying on her mind for
three days; she was glad to be rid of it.

Señor Gutierrez looked at the label. "A zock concert?
Samuel must be mad to send me such noise."

"It's . . . something else disguised as a zock concert."

He was quiet for a few moments, then he stood up.
"Would you mind waiting outside while I view this?"

"Not at all."

He showed her out. The receptionist, Rosita Salsido,
made her coffee. They had a pleasant chat comparing
enclave and windrider lifestyles, until Señor Gutierrez
emerged from his office.

He looked somewhat ill. With good cause, Linda thought.
The disk was a copy of what she had seen and heard in the
mayor's office.

"Señora Calhoun, could you return here at two o'clock
this afternoon? I need some time to look into this matter."

"Certainly."

She decided to put the time to good use. Going down
six floors to the purchasing department, she managed to
see her buyer without an appointment by casually men-
tioning whom she had just been talking to. Negotiating a
price for the Calgary cargo took over two hours. The buyer
had a volatile style, and Linda released some stress by
matching him decibel for decibel. But when the credit was
transferred to Calgary's bank account, the buyer changed
from lion to lamb and took her out to lunch.

At two P.M. she returned to the CEO's office. Rosita told
her to go right into the inner sanctum.

Señor Gutierrez and three other stockholders rose to
welcome her. "Señora Calhoun," Señor Gutierrez said,
"may I present my associates. Señor Uribe runs our Zep
Service. Señor Portilla is the director of our scientific
research department. Señor Cardenas coordinates all of
our information services. Gentlemen, this is Señora Calhoun from Calgary."

All three of them were men, which didn't surprise Linda.
Enclaves were only beginning to emerge from male domi-
nation. When she was younger that had angered her, but

now she knew the world was too complex for dogmatic judgments. Small endangered communities couldn't afford to lose child-bearers, so women were protected. Sexism had never been a problem in windrider towns, because in *very* small technology-dependent communities the worst danger was not using every bit of ability available.

Linda shook hands and exchanged greetings with the three shockholders. Señor Uribe had too much paunch and too little hair to be impressive in his elaborate uniform. Señor Portilla was the youngest of the three, though still older than she. Señor Cardenas looked like a perpetual worrier.

He probably had plenty to worry about. She knew that the euphemism "information services" included, among the more innocuous functions like publicity, spying. Enclaves might be non-violent, but industrial espionage was a thriving part of their economic competition.

Everyone sat down. "The news you have brought us is very disturbing," Señor Gutierrez said to her. "Even though this hostile force doesn't seem to be interested in enclaves, I speak for Pemex Under when I say we will do anything we can to help. Mankind is slowly, painfully crawling away from the very brink of extinction. Enclaves and windriders are interdependent, so that a threat to one is a threat to both."

"Then . . . you believe it?" Part of Linda had been hoping the Pemex Under experts would find some flaw in the analysis, pop the nightmare bubble which had engulfed her.

"We have verified both the data and the calculations. Moreover we have uncovered additional facts which support the theory."

"It occurred to us to run a similar analysis of all the unexplained zep losses since the War," Señor Uribe said. "The number has always been higher than our computer models can account for. We found a slight but definite time/position correlation between the zep and windrider losses." He paused. "The hostile force is also hostile to zeps."

"Maybe those zeps happened upon something they weren't supposed to witness," Señor Cardenas suggested. He had a flat, emotionless voice.

"So you see the danger is indeed ours as well as yours." Señor Gutierrez shrugged. "Unfortunately we are as mystified as you concerning the nature and identity of the hostile force."

"We thoroughly researched our information files," Señor Cardenas elaborated, "but found nothing. Our sources are widespread and, shall we say, well informed. This leads me to think the hostile force isn't an enclave or a windrider town."

"What else is there?" Señor Portilla asked dubiously.

"I don't know, but I intend to find out."

"We have made identifying the hostile force a number-one priority for our, ah, information services," Señor Gutierrez said to Linda. "I am confident that we will succeed, but such things take time. Which brings us to your major's second request.

"He wishes us to build laser weapons for Calgary. I understand the need, but this particular cure could prove more disastrous than the disease. One of the few good things to come from the War was the elimination of conflict. People who live in glass houses don't dare throw sticks. How would the other enclaves and towns react to the news that we are rearming? What would they feel compelled to do to defend themselves?

"Of course we would do everything we could to keep this secret—I agree with your mayor's reasoning. Hopefully we would succeed well enough to put an end to the hostile force. But eventually the truth would come out, and our hiding it would make it look all the worse."

Linda was afraid of the same thing, but she had been sent here to obtain protection for her home. "We aren't going to use the lasers against anyone except the windrider eater. When it's gone, I'm sure we'll get rid of them."

Señor Gutierrez sighed. "If history is correct, that is how it begins."

"How what begins?"

"War."

The word hit her like a spray of liquid oxygen. "So you won't build the lasers for us?" she almost gasped.

"You misunderstand me, Señora. I merely wish to make clear the possible consequences of such action. The windrider eater, as you so cleverly name it, must be stopped. We will build the lasers for you, and also install them aboard our zeps. If we can. For even that presents a problem."

Señor Portilla coughed before speaking. "There are many different types of lasers. The one used as a weapon is called the free electron laser. Its advantages are that it can be operated at high energy levels, and its frequency can be tuned to minimize atmospheric dissipation. But all we know about it is the general theory. The details of how to construct one were a military secret, and didn't survive the War."

"Can you reinvent it?" Señor Uribe asked him.

"Eventually, yes. But that could take years."

"I am trying to find some of the lost knowledge for you," Señor Cardenas said. "I have enlisted the assistance of the University's top expert on the War, Professor Fuentes."

Señor Uribe shook his head at the name, while Señor Gutierrez and Señor Portilla smiled.

Señor Cardenas turned to the CEO. "Shall we see whether Professor Fuentes has learned anything yet?"

Señor Gutierrez nodded, and his hand moved over controls built into the desk. Part of a wall slid up, revealing a telescreen. It flickered to life.

It showed a cramped room lined with so many shelves that no walls were visible. The shelves held hundreds of books, hand weapons and other military items. The grim utility of the weapons made Linda somewhat queasy. An ancient troll-like man sat hunched over a cluttered desk, studying a document.

He glared impatiently at his com's camera. "Well, well, who is it?" he demanded in a voice like tearing aluminum. "I'm busy!"

"Professor, this is Juan Cardenas. I called you earlier, remember?"

Professor Fuentes pushed his thick glasses higher on his nose. "Remember! Yes, I remember! I'm not senile, despite what you may have heard from idiotic students and jealous faculty. I remember you wasting my time with your ridiculous problem."

Linda was shocked, but Señor Cardenas ignored the

fiery rudeness. The Pemex Under leaders actually seemed to be enjoying it, comic relief from their serious business.

"Are you alone?" Señor Cardenas asked patiently.

"Yes, yes, I'm alone! My office is my refuge from the fools with whom I'm forced to associate. Or it would be, but for this infernal communications device."

"I apologize for interrupting your studies again, but the question I asked you is extremely important."

"Important to you, no doubt, but just a flyspeck on the tapestry of history. Can you comprehend that? Of course not! So, to put an end to your pestering, I searched my files.

"Military lasers. Young weapons, virtually devoid of historical character. Very dull. You want to know how they worked? Unfortunately they are all slagged or rusting scrap now. The factories, research facilities and databanks are craters."

"Then you weren't able to learn anything?"

Professor Fuentes looked even more angry, if that was possible. "Did I say that? No, I didn't! Military lasers are as extinct as dinosaurs, but a military laser by any other name would burn as hot."

Señor Portilla rubbed his chin. "I beg your pardon?" Señor Cardenas asked, echoing Linda's confusion.

"I came across a curious reference in my salvaged pre-War records. The company which built laser satellites for the United States Air Force also built one for the Department of Agriculture for a Project Rainmaker. Something to do with weather modification experiments. The project was based at the University of California in Davis, a small town in northern California. Since Davis didn't have any military significance, it wasn't attacked during the War. You might find the information you're looking for there."

"Thank you, Professor," Señor Cardenas said. "You have been most helpful. Please send a full report of your findings to the Chief Executive Officer and myself."

"You can show your appreciation by not bothering me again!"

"As you wish. I trust you will remember not to discuss this with anyone."

"I wouldn't waste my breath. Good day." The telescreen went dark.

The stockholders broke into controlled laughter, and Linda joined in despite herself. Professor Fuentes reminded her of a bantam rooster.

Señor Gutierrez stared at his hands for several seconds, then looked up. "I believe this possibility is worth pursuing. Your opinions, gentlemen?"

Señor Portilla was excited. "By all means! It could save us a great deal of time and effort. Just think, an entire lost technology rediscovered. There would certainly be non-military applications—"

"I don't wish to cool your enthusiasm," Señor Cardenas cut in, "but a civilian project is unlikely to have technical specifications for a top-secret weapon."

"Perhaps not, but it will at least have some sort of operating manual. Give us that, give us any clues at all, and our R-and-D time will be shortened."

Señor Cardenas nodded to Señor Gutierrez. "In that case I also agree."

Señor Uribe looked dubious. "It seems a very slim hope. *If* Professor Fuentes is correct, *if* the project's records haven't been destroyed, and *if* they include any useful data, it night be worthwhile to retrieve them. Meanwhile I need all of my zeps to meet schedules."

"Thank you, gentlemen." Señor Gutierrez paused. "We will send an expedition to Davis, California as soon as possible. Señor Uribe, I regret upsetting your schedules, but our need is urgent. Can you have a zep outfitted in two days?"

Frowning, Señor Uribe brought out a hand computer, tapped keys and peered at the tiny screen. "The *Mayan Princess* is due for port maintenance, but that can be deferred. I can reassign it to special operations. It can be ready to sail in forty-two hours."

"Please see to it. Ostensibly the expedition will be for the purpose of scavenging—the actual goal should be known to as few people as possible."

"Our competitors will wonder why we are scavenging in a small town," Señor Cardenas pointed out, "so I suggest we adopt a secondary cover story. The University of California at Davis was a center for agricultural research. We could let out a hint that our real interest is in, say, genetic engineering techniques."

Señor Gutierrez nodded, then turned back to Señor Uribe. "Is the *Mayan Princess*'s captain the man for such a delicate mission?"

The meeting had taken Linda so far away from herself that she was startled to realize they were talking about Captain Ramirez. Her ears perked up.

"Captain Ramirez is one of our best zep commanders. He is very responsible for one so young, and he has quite a bit of scavenging experience. I recommend him unconditionally."

"He will be in charge of the expedition. Please brief him as soon as possible."

Then Señor Gutierrez spoke to Linda. "Señor Cardenas tells me you were once a scavenger. Since you are already privy to our plot, would you be willing to accompany the expedition and seek out the information we need?"

Linda was stunned. She didn't know what to say or think. An overwhelming urge to go rose inside her. It would be wonderful to ply her trade again, turn back the calendar to when she was young and free. But she wasn't either. She was a mother with a daughter in tow. "I'm flattered, Señor Gutierrez. But I'm just here as a messenger. My daughter and I will be returning to Calgary in a few days."

The CEO looked distressed. "I hope you will reconsider. We are undertaking this expedition for Calgary's benefit as well as our own. Calgary should be represented. In fact, without such representation, I would be very reluctant to proceed."

"Because if this first step toward rearming should raise the ire of other enclaves and towns," Señor Cardenas added, "we don't wish to face it alone."

They were valid points. And Wanda was old enough to travel home on her own, with appropriate safeguards. Linda took a deep breath, then said, "You've talked me into it."

She told herself she was doing what she had to do to protect her home and family. The choice for the expedition's commander had nothing to do with her decision.

CHAPTER EIGHT

Wanda touched the door chime button outside Miguel's room. Her breath was coming fast, and she felt hot. A whole day with Miguel! Taking his invitation as a sign, she had decided that today was the day to give herself to him. All she needed was the right moment.

She wiped her sweaty palms on her skirt.

The door opened, and Miguel stepped out into the hallway. He was wearing his short-sleeved flight uniform. She had hoped/feared that he would invite her into his room, but he was too much of a gentleman to do that.

"Welcome, my dear lady. How are you this morning?"

"I'm fine, thanks. Uh . . . you still want to show me Pemex Under, don't you?"

"But of course. Which of our many wonders would you like to see?"

She had given that question long thought. Shopping was high on her list, but she could do that with Mom. Dragging Miguel to the arcade, the zoo and the vid studio would make her look like a child. "I want to see how Pemex Under works, the machines and all. And of course the windrider yard."

"So be it. The Ramirez Tour Service promises complete satisfaction."

They went down to the lobby and outside. But instead

of asking the doorman to call for a taxi, Miguel led her to a strip of yellow-painted curb.

"What are we doing here?" Wanda asked.

"Waiting for a tram. Poor zepmen can't afford to take taxis everywhere."

"Couldn't we walk?"

Miguel shook his head. "An enclave isn't as compact as a windrider. Your pretty legs will get plenty of exercise as is."

A few minutes later the tram arrived, stopping in front of them. The driverless vehicle looked like four cargo carts linked end to end. It was crowded, but Miguel found seats for them. A warning chime sounded, then the tram lurched into the flow of traffic.

"The trams follow routes through the domes and the other facilities," Miguel explained over traffic noises and Spanish chatter. "They're slow and less than comfortable, but they have the virtue of being free."

The tram left the business dome, passed through a short tunnel/street lined with murals, and entered another dome. "This is the life support dome," Miguel said, "the pulsating heart of Pemex Under." They got off at the first stop.

They walked to the fenced edge of what he told her was an oil refinery. "Most enclaves resort to solar cell farms for power, but we pump in oil from the Tampico field. We know oil well. Pemex was originally an oil company."

The refinery, a weird jumble of tanks, pipes and machines, dwarfed everything else in the dome. Miguel pointed out the pipes carrying fuel to the power plant and petrochemicals to the plastics factory.

The power plant was next to the refinery. Wanda felt very small as Miguel led her between the huge turbines and generators. The harsh whining made her ears hurt. "We use a separate air system to fire the turbines," Miguel explained, "pumping down surface air and venting the exhaust. Otherwise the air we breathe would smell even richer than it does."

Wanda wrinkled her nose. "It is pretty bad."

"One learns to live with it."

The air and water machinery looked like Calgary Three's, but built by giants. "Where do you get uncontaminated air and water?" she asked. "Or are your recycling systems one hundred percent efficient?"

Miguel shook his head. "Hardly. For one thing, we lose quite a bit of both every time we launch a windrider. Our air comes from the same place as yours, above the killzone. We pipe it in from the top of a nearby mountain. After decon it's safe to breathe. As for water, one of the reasons this site was chosen for the enclave is because it's close to a reservoir of ground water. Fossil water protected from contamination by solid rock, enough to meet our needs for centuries."

"You're lucky. When we need more water, we have to send a blimp to mine glacier ice from before the War."

They jumped aboard another tram. As it rumbled through a tunnel/street Miguel said, "The domes are arranged like a wheel. The life support dome is the hub, surrounded by a rim of six domes, which in turn is surrounded by the first four domes of what will eventually be a wider rim. The zep bay, windrider yard and so on are beyond the wheel."

Wanda pointed to sets of gasketed steel doors positioned so they could close the ends of the tunnel/street. "What are those for?"

A frown passed over his face like the shadow of a cloud. "An anti-rad precaution. In the event of a leak, any dome can be isolated."

When she figured out what he meant, she decided that she didn't want to think about it.

Their next stop was the food dome. She was surprised to see no farm, just ugly block-like buildings. Miguel took her inside one, to a big room with warm moist air. Her eyes blinked in the painfully bright light. Workers in plastic coveralls moved between rows of shallow liquid-filled trays.

"To feed so many hungry mouths, we can't wait for nature to take its course," Miguel explained. "Instead of raising whole plants or animals, we only culture the parts that we eat."

He pointed to a tray from which two workers were skimming tiny yellow things. "Those, for example, are juice sacs from the orange, on their way to be squeezed. Cultured food is as nutritious as natural food, but the taste is inferior, as I'm sure you've noticed. Some natural food is imported at great expense, mostly for restaurants."

Wanda felt a bit sick in the stomach as they left the building.

But she quickly got over it. In the manufacturing domes she saw the salvage decon plant, the foundry, the chemical plant, and factories making everything from kitchenware to structural members for a new windrider. In a residential dome she saw apartment buildings styled like pre-War Mexican villas, and courtyards full of children at play. Spectators weren't allowed in the new dome being excavated, but from the tunnel/street she saw giant laser and sonic digging machines at work.

"If you've recovered from the food dome," Miguel said, "maybe you would like to make lunch our next stop?"

"Yes, please. Can we have more Mexican food?"

"Of course." He laughed. "You're learning fast. Salsa, tabasco and chilis help to hide the taste of cultured food."

They rode a tram back to the business dome, and ate at a busy sidewalk restaurant. Wanda listened to Miguel's funny stories, while mostly she stared at him. Her love rushed back from where the morning's wonders had pushed it. She wanted him so much; she was almost bursting from her need to tell him. But not here, with so many people around to overhear. She would have to wait for some privacy.

Meanwhile she might as well get more questions answered. "What are stockholders?"

"I beg your pardon?"

"Mom called the people here stockholders. What did she mean?"

Miguel looked thoughtful. "That's a simple question requiring a not-so-simple answer. Like many enclaves, Pemex Under is a corporate state with some private enterprise. At birth each citizen receives a non-transferable share of Pemex Corporation stock, which entitles him or her to basic services and to vote for officers. In prosperous quarters we receive a dividend."

Wanda was vague on some of the ideas, but she understood enough to be confused. "You're a company? Why?"

"My, you're the curious one. How much do you know about the War?"

"Not a whole lot. They say we won't study it for a few more years."

"That's wise. The history of that time is very dark, not for innocent young ears. I'll try to answer your question without outraging your sensibilities.

"The great pre-War nations created atomic, biological and chemical weapons, and laser satellites to defend against them. In their false sense of security they let a minor dispute grow into the War. The weapons worked very well, the satellites less well. The opponents destroyed each other. Winds carried the fallout and poisons across borders, while refugees carried the diseases. The world started to die.

"Fortunately the Collapse, as we call that period, took several months. Most of the fallout was blown high in the atmosphere, from which it settled slowly. But the world knew that it was under a death sentence. Even in the countries untouched by the War civilization fell apart. Governments, armies, religions crumbled. Commerce stopped, money became worthless. Hopeless, terrified people fought over scraps.

"Yet the worst of times seem to bring out the greatness in mankind. Around the world groups tried to build habitats in which people could survive. Many of these efforts fell victim to the shortness of time and the general chaos. But some succeeded. A few, like Montreal and Toronto, were founded by local governments where suitable underground facilities already existed. But the majority were founded by companies.

"Many big pre-War companies, forseeing the possibility of war, had built refuges to save their records and important personnel. The Pemex Corporation refuge was located where our zep bay is today. In the midst of the Collapse it managed to make itself a self-sustaining community. The early years of Pemex Under were by all accounts Spartan and dangerous. But we've applied ourselves, and conditions are better today, though still far from idyllic.

"Now you know why Pemex Under is a company."

The story made Wanda uncomfortable. Her world was a

familiar, safe place. She didn't like thinking about how it had once been so strange and terrible. Maybe it was still like that, only she couldn't tell.

She wondered how the towns had happened despite all that disaster. "What about windriders? Where did they come from?"

"Your mother could probably tell you more about that than I. But I'll share what little I know. Windriders were invented before the War by a company called Goodyear in the United States. The first ones were built for the military, but soon there were yards around the world producing the habitat type. The War destroyed most of those windriders and yards. But the remaining yards became enclaves, building windriders in exchange for needed goods. That's how the trade between enclaves and windrider towns began. Other enclaves bought the technology and set up their own yards."

"Is that what you did?"

Miguel shook his head. "Our yard exists thanks to a glorious adventure. Before the War there was a yard near the city of Brownsville, Texas, a few hundred miles to the north. It escaped destruction, but local conditions were so grim that it had to be shut down. Some of its personnel and their families made their way here with a mutually beneficial proposal. The yard was the price of their admission to our enclave. Transporting its elements here by rail through the killzone took almost a decade. You'll hear some Texican names when we visit the yard this afternoon, but most of the gringos went aloft in the first Pemex Under-built windriders."

Wanda felt a strange thrill. History wasn't all bad; it could make you see how you were part of the great things that people did long ago.

"So, what do you think of Pemex Under thus far?" Miguel asked her.

"It's ultra! Really and truly! Only . . ." Her voice trailed off. She didn't want to be impolite.

"Only what?"

"Everything is so . . . crowded, closed in. There isn't any outside. Doesn't that bother you? It would me, if I had to live here all the time."

"The word you're looking for is claustrophobic. Most stockholders don't miss what they've never known, so they're content. But some do feel enclosed. We tend to become zepmen."

He put down his coffee cup. "If you're finished, the windrider yard awaits. Shall we?"

"Yes, please!"

This time the tram left the domes completely. It drove around the circle which Wanda remembered from the day before, and entered a long descending tunnel/street.

A few minutes later the tunnel/street ended in a huge cavern crowded with all sorts of machinery and supplies. Dozens of people were busy building things and loading cargo carts. "This is the staging area," Miguel explained. "At the moment final preparations are underway for the launching of a new windrider. I believe it goes aloft tomorrow morning."

Beyond the staging area the tram joined cargo carts and strange-looking vehicles in an upward-spiraling tunnel/street. Each time around a straight tunnel/street branched away from the staging area.

"The staging area is on the bottom level of the yard. This corkscrew climbs all the way to the top, more than a mile."

The tram picked up and dropped off people at some of the branch tunnel/streets. After a lot of spiraling it stopped at a particularly busy one. Miguel and Wanda deboarded with many other riders. They followed the branch's sidewalk, until they came to what looked at first like an intersecting tunnel/street curving away from them in both directions.

The far wall was clear plastic composite, part of the shell of a windrider.

Wanda stared. She was across from the windrider's ground level, and despite the greenhouse tint dimness she could make out the lake, the escalators, and the farm and park structures. But no plants or animals, just a plain of raw dirt. Cargo carts were going in and out through the four big topside air locks as fast as they could cycle.

"I'll bring you back here after the launch, if possible," Miguel said, "and show you the assembly and work areas as they should be seen. At the moment there's a windrider in the way. Maybe I can describe what you can't see, namely how they're arranged.

"The assembly area is a hole in the ground a mile in diameter and over a mile deep. The bottom half mile is shaped like a bowl, an egg cup in which the windrider sits. The top is covered by an anti-rad dome. Work areas like this one wrap around the assembly area from top to bottom."

Wanda had known about windrider yards, but now that she was actually here she was finding them unexpectedly hard to believe in. Windriders were what you lived inside. To see a windrider inside something else was mind-boggling.

But boggled or not, she wanted to learn as much as she could. "How do you build windriders?"

"I'll have to do my homework before I serve as your guide again," Miguel laughed. "Again I only know the things everybody knows. The framework for the levels is assembled first, then the big equipment is installed. Forms extend from the work areas to create the spherical mold. The shell has to be cast as a single piece, because of the reinforcing cables. It's kept rigid by increased air pressure after the forms are removed. The rest of the equipment is installed, the supplies are taken aboard, and you have a windrider."

Wanda wanted to ask a few thousand more questions on the subject, but she decided Mom would be a better source. Or maybe a bookdisk. "Can we go inside the windrider?"

"Unfortunately, no. It's off-limits to unauthorized personnel. We've come this far unchallenged thanks to my silver bars, but it's a privilege which won't stretch beyond the air locks."

She didn't really mind. It probably looked a lot like home. The yard was what she had come to see.

"There's a visitor center by the staging area," Miguel said, "with vids, holos and tons of information. But I knew you would rather see the real thing."

He led her to a walkway which followed the rim of the work area, and they set out to the left. The windrider was swarming with last-minute activity, inside and outside.

Sounds rang off the metal work area surfaces. The air smelled like machinery.

Wanda saw water being pumped into the lake, a test run of an access belt, techs wiring sections of shell into the sensor web, a mech checking the greenhouse tint, plus some things which she didn't recognize. But even more impressive were the monstrous machines sitting in the shadows at the back of the work area: wall-like forms, cranes, plastic composite mixers, pumps and empty cable spools twice her height. She wished she could have come a few weeks earlier, when the shell was being cast.

"Howdy, folks! You all don't look like workers, so you must be admiring our new home too."

The male drawl startled her, and yanked her attention back toward the shell. A man and woman were standing near it. They were both long, lean and tanned, with vid character good looks. She guessed they were in their middle twenties. The man was wearing a buckskin shirt and pants with plenty of fringe, tall alligator boots and a big brown cowboy hat. The woman was strikingly red from her curly auburn hair to her scarlet cotton frock.

"Good day," Miguel said cheerfully as he and Wanda detoured to join them. "I'm Captain Miguel Ramirez of the Pemex Under Zep Service. This lovely young lady is Señorita Wanda Grigg, on holiday from Calgary. I'm showing her some of the local sights."

"Well, you all have come to the right place," the man told them. "Tomorrow morning Lone Star Five here is going to soar like an eagle."

"Howdy, Captain, Wanda." The woman's drawl was softer. "I'm Delia Polk, but everyone calls me Dede. The dude in the buffalo hunter outfit is my husband, Jim Polk."

"Hello, Dede. Hello, Jim," Wanda said, figuring first names were okay. There was a round of handshaking, then she added, "Is that your windrider?"

"It surely is," Jim answered. He and his wife looked excited. "We hail from Lone Star Two. We're part of Five's shakedown crew, and when she's proved we'll be a founding family."

"I haven't docked at Lone Star in some time," Miguel

said to Dede. "But if I'd known it held one so beautiful, the wide sky wouldn't have kept me away."

"Why, you flatterer! Jim used to talk like that before he got all married and overconfident. Thanks for brightening my day."

"You're most welcome."

"What are you two going to do on the shakedown cruise?" Wanda asked. "Are you engineers like my Mom and Dad?"

Jim grinned. "Nothing so fancy. Dede is a tronics tech—just made journeyman—and I'm an aggie."

"Aggie?"

"An old-fashioned Texas dirt farmer."

"Oh." Farming was important, but not very interesting.

Miguel glanced at his wristwatch. "Much as I dislike cutting a merry meeting short, it's time Wanda and I started back." He turned to her. "We don't want your mother to worry."

Wanda didn't want to go, but she didn't want to argue with him either. "Okay. It was nice meeting you, Dede, Jim. Wide sky."

"Same here," Jim drawled. "You all be sure to come watch the launch. Should be mighty pretty."

Miguel nodded. "I hope to bring Wanda and her mother to the launching fiesta. May you and your windrider both fare very well."

"If you all ever get over Lone Star way," Dede said, "be sure to look us up."

Miguel and Wanda walked back toward the tram stop. Wanda glanced over her shoulder, and saw the two townsfolk standing hand-in-hand, gazing raptly at their new home.

CHAPTER NINE

It was late in the afternoon, so Miguel and Wanda had to squeeze into a tram crowded with yard workers going off-shift. The noise level discouraged any conversation between them. But Wanda didn't mind. She had a lot to think about.

The yard was fantastic. She knew she had toured only a tiny part of it, but she hoped to come back and see everything. She was soaring high despite a pair of aching feet. She liked learning things (a trait she had picked up from Mom and Dad), and she had learned more today than she could have in a quarter of school.

Gradually the images of giant machines faded. She became more aware of Miguel sitting next to her, his firm thigh pressed against hers, his aftershave cutting through the bad air. Her precious day alone with him was almost over. Mom was probably back at the hotel, and they would be a threesome again.

She would have to act now. Thanks to her long thinking about the subject of sex, she knew when to make her move and how to do it. The decision sent something like electricity racing along her nerves. All the sights and sounds around her pushed in, making her feel naked, obvious.

They deboarded in front of the hotel. Her pace slowed

as they crossed the lobby. "Did we do too much walking today?" Miguel asked sympathetically. "If so, I apologize. Soon you'll be able to soak your lovely legs in a nice hot tub."

"I'm okay," she said in a high forced voice. It seemed like she was outside her body, watching programmed actions.

They rode up alone in an elevator. She wanted to blurt everything out, get it over with. But the setting wasn't very romantic. She made herself stick to the plan. The electricity had concentrated in certain parts of her body; her swollen nipples were almost painfully sensitive. She was having trouble breathing.

Getting off at their floor, they started along the fancy hallway toward her room. That was out of the question, of course. Mom might be next door. Fortunately Miguel's room was on the way. They could slip inside unseen, and make love. Then she could go on to her room with nothing more to explain than overdoing the tour. Mom would never know.

That was important. Not just because it would upset Mom, but because it was ultimately special and private.

When they came to Miguel's room, Wanda stopped. Miguel turned and looked at her curiously.

His gaze knocked the carefully prepared words right out of her head. She knew what she wanted to say, *had* to say. But someone had poured super-adhesive on her vocal cords.

"Is something wrong?" Miguel asked her. "Surely you can manage a few more steps."

"Uh . . . . no, nothing is wrong."

"In case you've forgotten, this is my room, not yours."

"I know. I, uh . . . want to talk to you."

"I'm listening."

Her head jerked from side to side as she made sure the hallway was empty. It was, but she still couldn't tell him. What if he didn't take her seriously? What if he rejected her?

What if he didn't?

His hand moved toward the door's ident-plate. "Would it be easier to talk in private?"

Suddenly her thoughts flashed to what awaited her beyond

the door. She saw a room like hers but filled with a man's things, a big bed . . . and her electricity shorted out. Fright took its place. All she wanted to do was get away, back to the safety of her own room. "No! That's okay. I just, uh . . . wanted to thank you for showing me around. I had an ultra time."

"You're most welcome, my dear lady. Your charming company made the day a memorable one for me too."

"Wide sky," she said quickly. "You don't have to walk me to my room."

"As you wish. Until later, then."

She wanted to run, but she made herself walk to her room. The fright didn't go away until the door closed behind her.

Throwing herself on the bed, she wiped a few hot tears away with her hands. Everything had been so perfect: the right man, the right place, the right moment. But she had turned yellow from head to toe. For all her bold talk, she was just as scared of sex as Jan and Lori.

She wallowed in self-pity for awhile, then she started thinking more constructively. Okay, she had missed a chance. But there would be others. She would be ready for the next one.

She undressed, went into the bathroom, and took a wonderfully relaxing bubble bath. She was sprawled on the bed again, watching vid and feeling better, when she heard Mom's door. Moments later came the expected knocking on the connecting door.

"I'm here, Mom," she said. "Come in."

The door slid aside, and Mom leaned in. "Sorry I'm so late, dear. My business took longer than I thought it would." She looked like she was still thinking about it.

"Miguel and I just got back awhile ago." Wanda tried to remember the good parts of the day, not how it had ended. "We saw food growing in nutrient trays, lasers carving out a new dome, the windrider yard—so many incredible things!"

"I want to hear all the details over dinner. Speaking of which, we should invite Captain Ramirez to be our guest tonight, to thank him for last night. How does that sound?"

Wanda's first reaction was a flash of embarrassment. But

she had run away before Miguel could suspect her of anything more than stupidity. Dinner would be a good way to get her campaign moving in the right direction again. "It sounds like fun."

"Fine. I'll call and invite him." Mom stepped back into her room, and closed the door. Wanda worried about that for a moment. Did Mom suspect? Was the call to check up on her? No, that was just her prematurely guilty conscience talking. Most likely Mom didn't want to be distracted by the vid.

Wanda turned back to the adventure show she had been watching. It had an English track, and it was pretty good. But the local computer live-animation wasn't up to Canadian or Japanese standards. As the faint mumbling of Mom's voice beyond the door went on and on, Wanda started to worry again. What could Mom and Miguel be talking about for so long?

Finally Mom hung up and opened the connecting door again. "Captain Ramirez has accepted our invitation. We're taking him to a nice French restaurant where I had lunch today. He'll be by at seven thirty. If you're tired after all your running around, you have time for a nap."

A nap! How old would she have to be before Mom stopped treating her like a child? "I'm not tired. My feet hurt, but I took a bath and they feel better."

Mom brought out a small gift-wrapped box which she had been hiding behind her back. "I bought you a present, dear. I hope you like it."

Inside the box Wanda found a beautiful cut-crystal bottle of perfume. The scent reminded her of flowers, but stronger. "I love it!" she yelped. "Thanks a lot, Mom!"

"You may wear some to dinner if you like," Mom suggested. "But remember that very little goes a long way."

"I will, I promise!" It was just what she needed to show Miguel that she was a woman.

Mom went back to her room. Wanda half-watched the rest of the vid show, thinking about what she would wear and how she would act to impress Miguel. Outside the window "dusk" settled over the business dome.

It was a relief to be alone for awhile. All the folks, noise and things going on had given her a case of sensory over-

load. Pemex Under was a wonderful place to visit, but
how anyone could live here without getting shredded nerves
was beyond her.

She spent twice as long as usual dressing for dinner, and
still wasn't happy with the results. She was learning the
limitations of a travel wardrobe. Touches of the perfume
on her wrists and throat finished her preparations.

"Are you ready, dear?" Mom asked when Wanda went
into her room.

"Yes. I think. I didn't overdo the perfume, did I?"

Mom sniffed. "Well, if you sit at the next table . . ."

Wanda was panic-stricken. "Do I have time to wash?"

"I was just joking," Mom laughed. "It's fine."

Then her smile faded, and the thoughtful look came
back. Probably some business problem, Wanda figured.

The door chime rang promptly at seven thirty. Miguel,
a prime heartblaster in his dress uniform, presented them
with another dozen red roses. "Good evening, my lovely
ladies. It's most generous of you to treat a poor zepman to
a free meal."

"Good evening, Miguel," Wanda replied in her best
adult manner. "Mom bought me some perfume. Do you
like it?"

"It becomes you, and that's the highest praise I can
imagine."

Wanda blushed. Mom said, "Thank you for the roses.
But if you didn't spend so much money on us, you wouldn't
be a poor zepman."

"Money is an abstraction. I prefer the joyful light that
my presents bring to your faces."

"Your presents, or your presence?"

"Both, I hope."

Mom and Miguel laughed. A look passed between them
that Wanda didn't understand, or like.

They took a taxi to a restaurant called La Mirage. It was
very fancy, with paintings and other antiques scavenged
from what had once been France. When dinner was served,
Wanda vividly remembered the trays in the food dome
building. But the meal tasted wonderful, and she quickly
got over her squeamishness.

She did most of the talking, since Mom encouraged her

to tell all about the tour. Miguel only added an occasional comment, and Mom didn't say much about her day. But Wanda kept noticing that strange look passing between them. By dessert she identified it as one that Mom and Dad sometimes exchanged. Mom and Miguel had a secret, one they weren't going to let her in on.

She had no idea what it might be. Some boring adult thing. But she was annoyed that they were hiding it from her. She couldn't dig for it now; making a scene in front of Miguel would be bad strategy. But later, when she could get Mom alone . . .

It was close to bedtime when they returned to the hotel. Miguel said his good nights outside Mom's door, then left for his own room. Mom and Wanda went inside. Letting out the yawn she had been fighting, Wanda headed for the connecting door. The mystery could wait until after she got some sleep.

"Wait a minute, dear," Mom said in her serious voice. "I want to talk to you."

Wanda turned, wondering if she could be in any trouble. Except for Miguel her conscience was pretty clear.

"Please sit down." Mom pointed to one of the room's chairs. Wanda sat, suddenly not a bit sleepy.

"Something has come up," Mom went on, "and unfortunately it's going to change our plans. The day after tomorrow the *Mayan Princess* will be leaving on a scavenging expedition. I'll be going along. A very nice young lady named Rosita Salsido will look after you, until the *Toltec Princess* sails. I'm counting on you to take care of yourself on the trip home. I'll be back in about three weeks."

Wanda felt like someone had yanked the floor out from under her. Mom going away! Miguel going away! What in the sky was happening?

"I hate to just leave you here, but the expedition is very important." Mom looked like she was trying not to show how upset she was.

As the initial shock faded, Wanda thought fast. Mom used to tell her exciting bedtime stories about scavenging, and she had planned to include some in her own career. This would be the perfect time. She could serve under

Miguel, impressing him with her ability while pursuing her romantic campaign.

"You don't have to leave me," she said eagerly, hoping to use Mom's worry as a lever. "Take me with you. I'll work hard and—"

"I'm sorry, but that is out of the question. Scavenging is too dangerous for the untrained and underaged. Besides, I don't have any say in picking the personnel. Pemex Under is sending the expedition—I'm just a guest."

"But Mom—"

"Don't waste your creative energy." Mom smiled sadly. "I have to go, and you have to stay behind. That is the way it is."

Wanda recognized finality when she heard it. She lapsed into sullenness. "What's so important about this scavenging expedition anyway?"

"I'm not supposed to tell anyone. When I can, I promise I'll tell you first." Mom took a deep breath. "You better get some sleep now."

Wanda felt frustration burning inside her. She started to storm past Mom without a good night kiss. Suddenly she found herself in Mom's arms, and tears of impending abandonment flowed. "Please don't leave me here alone, Mom!"

"I'm sorry, dear," Mom whispered as she stroked Wanda's hair. "So sorry. But it won't be for long—you'll be just fine."

Wanda pulled herself together, kissed Mom good night, and went into her room. She undressed automatically. Her thoughts were broken fragments, the wreckage of her beautiful dream. She felt numb. Climbing into bed, she turned off the lights. Darkness wrapped comfortingly around her.

It was so splashing unfair! Tomorrow Miguel would be busy getting ready for the expedition, too busy to spare any time for her. The next day he would be gone. Gone! She had had her chance, and had thrown it away. How long would she have to wait before the *Mayan Princess* docked at Calgary Three again? Months? Years?

Despair tormented her. Now she knew for sure that she loved Miguel, and being parted from him was more than she could bear. She imagined his mouth kissing hers, his hands stroking her skin, his passion overwhelming her. But her imagination was all she would ever have. Because in real life she was a failure as a woman.

She tried to sleep. She wanted to stop thinking, stop suffering. But the harder she tried, the more awake and miserable she became. She tossed and turned in the big bed.

The notion came into being as a wisp of semi-conscious fantasy. It cheered her, so she dwelled on it, added to it. Gradually excitement pushed despair aside. She was wide awake now, shivering with delicious thrills as she realized that it didn't have to be a fantasy. She could really make it happen.

She listened hard, but heard only silence from the other room. Mom had turned in. She could get started right away.

Turning the lights back on, Wanda eased out of bed very quietly. She tiptoed into the bathroom. It was sound-proofed, so she took a shower, scrubbing thoroughly with her body soap. The warm water lulled her into a heavy-lidded languor, as her lust became a dream-like inevitability. After the blow-dry she rubbed baby powder all over.

Leaving the bathroom, she considered her meager selection of bedclothes. Pajamas were out of the question. She wished she had a sexy nightgown like Mom's, but she wasn't old enough. Her pink-with-white-lace baby doll would have to do. She put it on, and added her black high heels for effect.

She brushed her hair until it shone like spun gold. Deciding against jewelry, she dabbed on what she hoped was a subtle amount of the perfume. When she finished, the mirror showed her a beautiful young lady ready to become a woman.

She started for the door, then stopped. She couldn't walk the hallways of the hotel in a baby doll; even this late someone might see her. She put on her bathrobe. It wasn't really proper dress either, but it would do. And she could shed it in a hurry.

The sensible voice inside her head had given up telling her she was being crazy. She knew it, and didn't care.

This time she wasn't afraid. She was serenely, unquestioningly confident.

Mom's room was still quiet. Wanda turned off the lights, and stepped cautiously into the hallway. It was empty. She felt like she was floating, not walking, toward Miguel's room.

She stopped in front of his door, on the very threshold of the adult world. She was ready to cross over. She knew that he was on the other side of the door in bed, maybe kept awake by a mysterious restlessness. Waiting for her.

She turned the doorknob. The door was unlocked, as she had known it would be. She quietly pushed it open a crack.

Miguel's room was deep in shadow. Only the glow panels in the middle of the ceiling were giving off a soft yellow light. Miguel was standing in the light, his back to the door.

He wasn't alone.

Wanda's dream castle shattered, became a rain of crystal shards slashing at her heart. She wanted to flee, but she couldn't stop staring.

They were much too busy to notice her. Miguel had his arms around the woman's waist, while her hands rested on his bare shoulders. His uniform shirt and her dress were strewn on the carpeting at their feet. The woman whispered something. He laughed and bent to kiss her. A long, total kiss.

An eternity later they parted. The camisole-clad woman moved out from behind Miguel, and Wanda got a clear look at her.

At Mom.

CHAPTER TEN

Wanda's hand closed the door as quietly as possible. It was acting on its own, out of instinctive horror and/or shame, because her mind had gone totally blank.

The thickness of fake wood helped a bit. She could still see Mom and Miguel; the image had been laser-etched in her eyes. But thoughts started to form again.

Once she had walked in on Mom and Dad, when they had forgotten to lock their bedroom door. So she knew what Mom and Miguel were doing. She desperately tried to come up with another explanation, any other explanation. But she couldn't.

All the ugliness hit her. She had never felt so bad. Miguel's betrayal hurt terribly, but it was nothing next to Mom's. The hallway was wobbling, and she hunched forward from the pain in her stomach. Yet the worst thing was being so scared and alone. Nothing made sense, nothing was right. She wanted to be dead. Or better yet, never to have been at all.

Awareness of where she was returned. She didn't want anyone to see her here, especially Mom or Miguel. She started back to her room. Her attempt at a composed walk turned into a staggering half-run. Whimpers escaped from between her clenched teeth.

She all but slammed the door shut behind her, and

97

lurched into the bathroom. She was just barely in time. Falling to her knees, she lost her dinner—the hateful food she had eaten with Mom and Miguel—into the toilet. She clung weakly to the cold porcelain, unable to move, utterly sick and miserable.

All the time Miguel had been pretending to like her, he and Mom had been . . . How could she have ever loved such a monster? He probably thought her play-acting at being a woman was funny, if he had even noticed it. And Mom! Wanda had heard stories about folks who broke their marriage vows. But Mom and Dad *loved* each other, as much as they loved her. Or so she had believed. If she was wrong about one, she could be wrong about the other. About everything.

She decided that she hated Mom and Miguel. Especially Mom.

She never wanted to see either of them again. She had to get away. Before Mom came knocking on her door in the morning, acting like nothing had happened.

She got up and washed her face. There wasn't time to take a shower, but she managed to scrub away most of the perfume. Hate gave her the strength to stand, to ignore her cramping stomach, to do what had to be done.

Going back into her room, she put an ear against the connecting door. Mom's room was still quiet. Her mind shied away from thinking about where Mom was and what she was doing right then.

Instead Wanda prepared to run away. She figured that she had better work fast, since she had no idea how soon Mom would . . . finish and return to her room. She dressed for comfort for a change: white shorts (even though Pemex Under was cooler than home), a pullover cotton shirt, sandals, and an elastic band to ponytail her hair. The few things she really needed from her purse she stuck in her pockets. Fetching her small suitcase, the best one for traveling light and fast, she filled it with her regular clothes and personal items. There wasn't any room for her dress-up stuff, which was okay since she never wanted to wear it again anyway.

She opened the hallway door a crack, and peeked both ways to make sure the hallway was empty. This was the riskiest 'part of her escape. If Mom left Miguel's room while she was on her way to the elevators, they would run right into each other. The thought made her shiver.

The alternative was to turn around, slip back into bed, and try to forget what she had seen.

Opening the door the rest of the way, she went out into the hallway and walked along it quickly but quietly. She looked straight ahead. The knot in her middle pulled tighter and tighter as she neared Miguel's door, and unconsciously she held her breath. Every second she expected the door to open and Mom to step out. She passed the door. But the tension didn't let up; it just refocused on the back of her neck.

Only when the elevator door hissed shut behind her did she feel safe. She slapped the lobby button, and the elevator started down.

Her stomach slowly unknotted, but she felt even more alone and scared. She had no idea where to run. She was on her own with a vengeance, in a very strange place. She had no home, no friends, and not much money. There was also the problem of avoiding being picked up by the proctors and returned to Mom. The more' she thought about it, the bleaker her future looked. But she wasn't going back. Not ever!

She straightened her back, squared her shoulders, and marched through the lobby like an adult on an important errand. Her act worked. The desk clerk ignored her, and the doorman wished her a good night as he ushered her out.

She followed the sidewalk away from the brightly lit area in front of the hotel, then stopped and put her suitcase down. She had to catch her breath, let her pounding heart calm down.

Fake stars shone in the black "sky." The night wasn't very dark, about like a full moon back home. A cool breeze woke her all the way up. The business dome was a wonderland of lights: colorful neon signs, street lamps, lit building windows and cart headlights. According to her watch it was almost eleven, but there were still plenty of folks on the sidewalks and carts in the street. Miguel had told her that Pemex Under worked twenty-four hours a

day to get the most out of its facilities. The activity was
reassuring, since she planned to disappear into it.

Then what? Home had always been the center of her
world, where Mom and Dad took care of her. That was all
over now. She thought about asking Grandma and Grandpa
Calhoun to take her in. But even if she could get a zep
ride to One, they would want to know why she couldn't go
home. No, she was stuck in Pemex Under. The air was too
thick, the sky wasn't real, most of the folks didn't speak
English, and it was 'way too big. But somehow she had to
make it her new home.

Some of the folks passing her on the sidewalk smiled
and nodded, but most ignored her. Their Spanish chatter
set up a wall between them and her. She felt a bit unreal,
like a lonely ghost. There wasn't anyone she could turn to
for help.

Suddenly she noticed somebody noticing her. A proctor
was walking casually in her direction. She recognized him
by his powder-blue uniform and the stunrod slapping against
his thigh. (She had seen them in vids; Calgary proctors
wore regular clothes and hardly ever carried stunrods.)
Apparently he was on patrol, since he was looking around
and pausing to talk to folks. But his eyes kept coming back
to her.

Trying to hide a sharp rush of guilt, Wanda smiled at him.
Had Mom already discovered she was missing and reported
her? Not likely. Probably her standing on the sidewalk
doing nothing had attracted his attention. So, to look like
she was doing something, she picked up her suitcase and
walked with forced calmness to the tram stop. She felt his
gaze following her. But when she reached the stop and
sneaked a peek over her shoulder, he had passed her.

She decided she had better keep moving. She could
ride a tram around the enclave, checking the possibilities
while figuring out her next step. She spotted some kids
her own age window shopping; fortunately there wasn't
any curfew here.

After awhile a tram showed up. The Spanish destination
sign meant nothing to her, but she jumped on and found a
seat. The tram lurched along the streets of the business dome,
then through a tunnel/street to the public services dome.

But her thinking about her future wasn't going anywhere. Fantasies were easy, but real actions needed to be based on facts. One day of touring hadn't shown her how to get a job, rent an apartment, or any of the other things she had to do. Her shopping money wouldn't last long.

The tram stopped in front of a strange little building. The one-story box of white fake adobe sat primly in the middle of a well-kept lawn. It had an A-shaped roof and a bell tower. It didn't look very important, huddled at the feet of the University blocks. Vague memories from history class and pre-War vids came back to her. The building had to be a church, and churches were supposed to help folks. Maybe this one would help her.

She got off the tram, and walked over to the tall double doors. They daunted her for a moment. Then, taking a deep breath, she went inside.

She found herself in the back of a hall which took up most of the building. Rows of long wooden benches faced an equally old-fashioned altar. Dozens of candles cast an uneven yellow light, too dim for her to make out the pictures in the stained glass windows. She was alone. Not knowing how to go about attracting some attention, she perched on the end of a bench. All the tiredness that adrenalin had been holding back crept into her. She sagged, and might have fallen asleep except for the hardness of the bench. Her mind drifted like a cloud.

A soft, questioning voice snapped her back to reality. She looked up. An old man wearing a dark robe and a skullcap was standing in front of her. He repeated the question.

"I'm . . . I'm sorry," she said uncertainly. "I don't speak Spanish."

"Then you must be a visitor to Pemex Under." His English was more accented than Miguel's, but she could understand him. "Don't be afraid—you're welcome in God's house. My name is Father Reyes."

"I'm Wanda. Wanda Grigg, from Calgary."

"Ah, yes, the windrider town. It must be a remarkable thing to live in the sky. I apologize if I interrupted you at your prayer."

"I wasn't praying," Wanda admitted. "I'm not . . . religious. We're learning scientism in school."

Father Reyes sighed. "As are the children even here, in what was once a great Catholic nation. Only a handful still believe. Mankind has turned away from God because of the War. And how shall I blame the faithless, when it must seem that God has turned away from us? Who can find a divine purpose in utter devastation, or will worship so pitiless a Lord? I have no answers. All I have is my faith."

Wanda didn't understand much of what he was saying, but he seemed to be talking mostly to himself. She decided scientism was a lot simpler than religion. The universe and the natural laws that ran it had been created by something probably beyond human understanding. The only hope of understanding the creator was to learn all about the creation. Meanwhile folks should love the universe for its wonders, and make the most of their time in it by living good lives.

"But I shouldn't be bothering you with my own troubles," Father Reyes said, sounding a bit embarrassed. "If you haven't come to pray, may I ask what brings you here at this late hour?"

"I . . . I need help. But since I'm not a . . . Catholic, maybe I better leave."

Father Reyes smiled reassuringly. "We're all His children, and your soul doesn't seem so black that I can't hold hope for your salvation. What kind of help do you need? I'll gladly do what I can."

But suddenly Wanda was afraid to tell him. If she admitted that she was running away, he might turn her over to the proctors.

He seemed to read the fear in her face. "I'm obligated to keep secret anything you tell me in confidence. We priests are counselors, but we can't counsel if people are reluctant to talk to us."

She believed him, and the words came spilling out. "I'm sort of running away from home. I want to stay here in Pemex Under. But I'm not a stockholder, and I don't have a lot of money. I don't know what to do."

Father Reyes stared at her for a long time before he spoke. "I see. A very serious matter, running away. I would take you in here, if it were possible. In the old days the Church ran schools and orphanages, but no more. Perhaps the civil authorities can do something."

"No! Please! They would just send me home."

"Would that be such a bad thing?" Father Reyes asked softly. "I'm sure that you have a good reason for running away, but there may be a less drastic solution to whatever is troubling you. Would you care to talk about it?"

She wanted to desperately, but she couldn't make the words come out. She stared at the fake hardwood floor.

"I see. Perhaps later, after you've had some time for reflection."

"But I need help right now. I need some sort of job, so I can pay for food, an apartment—"

Father Reyes shook his head. "To be hired for any work, you must have an identification number. I assume that you don't. If you give a false one, you will be found out. All identities are confirmed by fingerprints."

"Then what can I do?" Wanda felt like the walls of the church were closing in on her.

He paused again, looking thoughtful. "Perhaps you're considering the problem in the wrong way. What do you *want* to do?"

"Huh?"

"Put your troubles aside for a moment. Close your eyes, let your thoughts travel through the realm of possibilities. Seek out where your heart would lead you."

Leaning back, Wanda stopped holding her eyelids up. At first she was too aware of Father Reyes to relax. But he started chanting softly in a melodious language that wasn't English or Spanish, and soon she was floating out of herself. She left her tired body, the church, the whole hateful enclave behind as she climbed into the real night sky. Above the clouds she saw her destination, the only one that could ever really be home. A windrider.

But not just any windrider. A new one, without ugliness and betrayal, where she could live a new life.

Her eyes flew open. "You were right! I know what to do now."

He looked at her intently. "I believe you do. Well, I won't pry. I'm sure He gave you better advice than I could."

"Thanks a lot, Father. I have to get going—I don't have much time." She grabbed her suitcase, curtsied, then headed for the doors.

"If you find that you need further assistance, I'm here most of the time."

"Wide sky," she said over her shoulder.

"God go with you."

Wanda almost ran back to the tram stop, where she waited impatiently. She kept glancing at the church. It didn't look small or unimportant now. She still didn't believe in God, but she believed in Father Reyes. Maybe that was what religion was really about.

She didn't remember how the destination sign on the tram to the windrider yard had looked. So she boarded the first tram that came along, and embarrassed herself a few times until she found a rider who knew English and the tram routes. She transferred to another tram in a residential dome. It was filled with folks in work clothes; she had to stand holding an overhead rail as it entered the long tunnel/street to the yard.

How could she sneak into Lone Star Five? This time she wouldn't have Miguel to get her past the yard workers and the proctors. She was too young to pretend to be a worker, and Miguel had said an unescorted tourist couldn't get near the windrider. She might not even be allowed in the yard this late at night or this close to the launch. She was already getting some curious looks from the other riders.

The staging area was still daytime-bright, and even busier than it had been that afternoon. The light and noise plucked at her nerves. The tram stopped, letting a lot of folks off and on. Wanda had a hunch that if she tried to ride up the spiral to the work areas, someone would ask her where she was going and why. She got off the tram in the thick of the crowd.

She moved along with it past the tram stop benches, and came to a low wall holding a row of time clocks. Workers were milling around, putting their hands on the ident-plates to clock in and out. She kept going.

She was quickly surrounded by impressions of activity on a scale too big for her to take in. Cargo carts rumbled this way and that. Piles of supplies shrank. Sparks and

dust flew from machine tools. Everywhere folks were working, driving, running, gesturing.

She wanted to stare at everything, but she didn't dare look like a tourist. She hoped to pass as the daughter of a worker or maybe a student on a field trip. Finding a roadway that ran toward the spiral, she set out on the sidewalk as inconspicuously as possible.

Her half-formed plan was to walk up the spiral unnoticed. But as she got close to the far wall of the staging area, she spotted a ceiling-mounted vid camera sweeping the place where the roadway entered the spiral. A monitor, she figured, probably linked to a proctor station somewhere in the yard. She couldn't go that way.

Her sudden turn attracted some attention from the folks around her on the sidewalk. One of them asked her something in Spanish. She tried her smile again, and kept walking. He didn't say anything else, or come after her, so it must have worked.

She needed a new plan. Lone Star Five would be going aloft in a few hours; there wasn't time for anything fancy. Could she disguise herself like a worker to get past the monitor? No, she didn't have the skill or the props. Was there some other way to reach the windrider? Probably, but she didn't know where, and anyway it would have a monitor too.

She had stopped noticing the cargo carts going by, but now she stared at one. Of course! She could ride into Lone Star Five in style.

She looked around the staging area, hunting for the right sort of transportation. A translucent green building to her right seemed to be a nursery. A cargo cart was backed up to its entrance. She headed for it, nervously watching for monitors, proctors . . . anything. She half-expected each of the workers she passed to stop her. But they were all busy, and didn't have time for anything more than curious glances.

Even so, the feeling grew inside Wanda that everyone knew what she was doing. They were playing a big game, letting her think she was getting away with it, until just the right moment.

Reaching the nursery, she strolled by the cargo cart.

The open bed was partly filled with girl-high rolls of grass destined for Lone Star Five's park. Four workers were loudly struggling to lift another roll into the back.

She circled the nursery, checking where the folks were who could see her and what they were doing. She decided her best chance would come just after walking past the front of the cargo cart. The cart and the nursery would screen out most of the staging area, the workers cutting sheet plastic across the roadway were concentrating on their job, and the grass rolls would be between her and the loading crew. If none of that changed, she might be able to bring it off.

She closed in on the cart. Her heart was going like a power hammer, and the starch had disappeared from her knees. She was going to need a few seconds of very good luck.

She crossed the blunt front end of the cart, and walked back along the side. The cart bounced as another roll went in. She reached the bed. After looking around quickly, she pushed her suitcase onto the bed, grabbed the side railing, and swung up after it. Then she scurried like a gerbil into the darkness between two rolls, pushing the suitcase in front of her. All as quietly as she could manage.

The fit was tight, but she squeezed through to the middle of the bed and lay very still. The smell of dirt and sweet grass reminded her of better times. She listened hard for noises over her half-stifled gasps for air.

Things sounded muffled and far away because of the rolls, but she didn't hear any shouts or approaching footsteps that would have meant she had been spotted. The heavy thud of a roll hitting the bed sent her heart up into her throat. She tried to calm down. She was going to be here awhile, if all went well.

She heard and felt two more thuds, the clang of the back gate being closed, then the hum of the cart's motor. The rolls shifted a bit as the cart accelerated. For a moment she was afraid she would be crushed, but they only moved a few inches.

Traffic noises reached her. Soon the bed tilted back, shifting the rolls again. That and the endless right turn told her the cart was climbing the spiral. She had gotten by the monitor without being caught. So far so good.

The bed came level again, and the cart speeded up. Wanda figured it was entering the same work area she had visited earlier. A windrider's topside airlocks were the only ones big enough to hold a cart. She was bruised and cramped, and the air was getting close. But she was too excited to be uncomfortable.

The cart stopped, crawled forward, then stopped again. A hatch hissed. Most of the distant noises disappeared; all she could hear were the motor and the driver's whistling. Her ears popped. She was inside the airlock. Inside Lone Star Five!

Another hatch hissed, and the cart started forward again. It all seemed so easy. She wondered why there weren't more anti-stowaway precautions. Maybe enclave folks felt the same way about living in the sky as she did about living under the surface.

Wanda nerved herself up for the riskiest part. She figured the cart was going to stop somewhere in the park to unload; she had to get away before that. Crawling to the end of the two rolls, she peered out.

Lone Star Five's ground level looked naked, a plain of brown dirt where there should have been greenery. The lake, the escalator entrances, the pole lamps, and the farm and park structures stood out unnaturally. She had been worried about workers spotting her, but there wasn't anybody in sight. The cart was following a well-worn path across the farm-to-be, to the white box that was the freight elevator entrance.

She didn't have time to wonder why the grass was being taken below. This was probably the best chance she would have to escape unnoticed. Another cart rumbled by on its way to the air lock; the drivers waved and shouted to each other. As the carts moved apart, she got ready to jump.

Her cart wasn't going very fast, but she still tumbled when she hit the ground. She scraped her hands and knees, and knocked the wind out of her lungs. Other than that she felt okay. The cart went on. As she had hoped, its noise had kept the driver from hearing her fall.

She wanted to lie there and catch her breath for a few

minutes, but she had to get going before another cart showed up. She didn't dare stand up, because the folks in the work areas beyond the shell might spot her, so she started crawling toward the nearest escalator. Crossing hard dusty ground while dragging a suitcase wasn't easy.

The escalator wasn't moving. A slab of clear plastic cut to fit the entrance lay next to it, probably something to do with the launch. She ran down the ribbed steps.

She slowed as she descended into almost-night. Only a few of the glow panels were on, saving power where no work was being done. She could hear heavy machinery noises far below. She was glad she had dressed lightly; after her time in the enclave Lone Star Five felt way too warm. Sweat and dust mixed uncomfortably on her skin.

Wanda figured most of the last-minute activity was in the engineering levels, so she got off the escalator at the mall level. Creeping along a wide circum corridor, she kept her eyes and ears open, but she was alone. The gloom and silence closed in on her. The shop-fronts with their big empty display windows looked forlorn. It was spooky, walking in a windrider that hadn't been born yet.

She needed a hidey hole, in case any workers or shake-down crew members came to the mall level before the launch. She also needed to get some sleep. Her excitement was fading, and she could barely hold her eyelids up. Vaguely wondering why all the doors were open, she picked one at random and went in.

The darkness inside the shop was total. She felt her way into the back room and found some sort of closet. The floor was just long enough for her to stretch out on. Taking off her clothes and using them as a pillow, she tried to pretend the thin carpet was a bed.

She had made it. She should have felt wonderful, but her mind kept dragging her back to the sight of Mom and Miguel in his room. Her thoughts were bitter until sleep came.

CHAPTER ELEVEN

Fernando Uribe closed the door of his townhouse like a man putting a barrier between himself and a feared enemy.

He crossed the spacious living room to one of the floor-to-ceiling windows. The homes of Pemex Under's elite ran along the rim of the residential domes. He looked out at the apartment blocks, children at play, and evening shift-change traffic: the symbols of the common stockholder. Usually such reminders of what he had risen above refreshed his spirits, but tonight he was too deeply troubled. He pulled the silver-embroidered drapes shut.

Several mistresses of increasingly sophisticated taste had turned the townhouse into a showplace. Hidden lights played the colors of a desert sunset over the ersatz adobe walls and neo-modern furniture. A scavenged piece of a Rivera mural was the centerpiece of his art collection. He poured himself a tall glass of tequila at the bar, then dropped into his favorite chair.

The alcohol started to ease his tiredness and aching muscles. The meeting with the CEO and the woman from Calgary had turned his day into one of frantic activity. Organizing a zep expedition on such short notice, with a minimum of disruption to regular operations, had required every iota of his managerial skill. But the gears were in motion. Even as he sipped his drink, subordinates were attending to dozens of details. The *Mayan Princess* would sail before noon the day after tomorrow.

Yet that was just a wearying distraction from the fear which had been devouring his soul ever since the meeting. The lie at the core of his existence had caught up with him at last.

He stared into the distorting depths of his glass. Sixteen years ago, upon leaving the fleet for his first minor administrative post, a stranger had contacted him. After very cautiously sounding him out the stranger had offered him, not money which would have been noticed, but information to help advance his career. In exchange the stranger had also wanted information. Fernando had seen the hand of destiny held out to him, and he had grasped it.

The ongoing arrangement had served him well through the years. At times he had felt some guilt, but the information that he had passed on—zep technology, shipping records and general news—hadn't seemed likely to cause Pemex Under any serious harm. He had always assumed that his mysterious benefactor had been a spy for another enclave.

Until today.

Fernando had no proof, but he knew in his heart that he had been dealing with the hostile force behind the zep and windrider losses. The blood of the dead was on his hands too. No Pemex Under zep had been victimized, but that wouldn't let him sleep any easier.

A half-dozen times that afternoon he had decided to go to the CEO and tell what he knew. But he couldn't. He couldn't face the thought of falling from his high place. He would lose everything, be mean and common again, perhaps even suffer the humiliation of penal labor. Then there was the question of how the murderers of thousands would repay his betrayal.

Besides, he had no information that would help locate or even identify the hostile force. The means by which he sent and received his reports made certain of that.

He gulped down the last of the tequila. He had sown, and now he would reap. Hopefully the crisis would pass without destroying him. But even if he was doomed, that just made each remaining day, each minute more precious. He would do what he had to do.

He walked back to the study and locked the door behind him. In all these years he hadn't become comfortable with the actual processes of espionage. He nervously checked the room for signs of observation, feeling the usual embarrassment at such paranoid excess. Reassured of his solitude, he sat down at the antique roll-top desk and touched three hard-to-reach places in quick succession. An oiled oak panel between two shelves clicked. He pulled it open, revealing the more modern panel of a radio transceiver.

He didn't bother with the headset, since he would only be reporting. He clipped on the mike, thumbed the power switch, and took slow measured breaths to compose himself while waiting. He had already distilled the meeting and the resultant activity into a few concise sentences. Half a minute later the ready light turned green.

Fernando's mind wandered as he recited the memorized report. In the early days he had actually made the difficult and dangerous trip to the surface, but after acquiring the townhouse he had installed this more convenient arrangement. The risk that someone might discover his unauthorized com line was slight; the trips had been much riskier.

He followed his words up the obsolete conduit to the surface, through the cable buried under the plateau's rocky soil, to the small cave excavated and concealed by his mysterious benefactor. The laser transceiver consisted of three mottled green metal boxes, one with a moving dish antenna on top. According to the stencils on the boxes the transceiver was United States Air Force equipment, but anyone could have scavenged it. His report was recorded, compressed and hurtled skyward in a single pulse.

He had always assumed that the destination was a zep or perhaps a windrider, but he was wrong. As he was closing his secret radio panel, the pulse arrived at a satellite in a geosynchronous orbit above the Atlantic Ocean.

The only United States military communications satellite to have survived the War and the intervening years, it was just barely operational. Its orbit had decayed, one of its solar collectors had been disabled by a micrometeoroid, and it had acquired a slow roll because its attitude rockets were exhausted. Its traffic capacity was reduced almost to zero. But it managed to pick up the pulse, clean and amplify it, and relay it toward the Arctic.

Twenty-nine thousand feet above the ice pack and storm-troubled ocean Alpha hung in the northern twilight. Alpha was old, a first-generation windrider. It was heavier than a modern one, and it couldn't climb as high. From the outside it looked the same, except that the dock was simpler. (The *Shenandoah* and the *Valley Forge* were on training cruises, until weather conditions allowed Alpha to descend below their flight ceiling.)

The major differences were inside. Alpha had been built to be a military base, not a self-sustaining habitat. There were fewer levels and more open topside. The air in the levels was pressurized rather than enriched, while topside was a dead volume of unbreathably thin air. After the War the first level had been converted into a farm, its sunshine coming through the transparent ceiling.

The pulse passed an antenna on top of the shell, leaving part of itself behind. As electrical impulses it ran down a cable to the radio room. Soon the duty officer was scanning a soft copy of Fernando Uribe's report, one of several from friendlies to arrive that night. He decided that it was important enough to be routed directly to General Armbruster's office. Keying the instruction into his console, he moved on to the next incoming message.

General Armbruster happened to be topside at the time. He was standing on an observation platform with Academy Commandant Stoddard and a half dozen other officers, watching a cadet field exercise. Figures in black combat suits were stalking each other through a fake power level set up over an acre of deck. Steel rang against steel, a faraway sound in the thin air, and cadets dropped as drill swords scored electronically simulated kills. Blood-red light from outside the shell lit the scene as if from God's own battle lamp.

General Armbruster liked the simile. He stood as smartly as he expected his men to, ignoring the sweaty heat and other discomforts of his combat suit. Orders and reports crackled from the helmet's com speaker over the hiss of the air system. He was present to make certain that these newest Alpha warriors would uphold their proud heritage; despite some rough edges he was satisfied.

He glanced down through the transparent deck, at the old bent woman in tattered clothes who was watering a plot of wheat. Alpha only took female slaves. When they were no longer of use in the brothels, they were assigned to the farm or other scutwork.

The sight led him to reflect on how Alpha had achieved harmony with the true nature of the human animal. All the pseudo-intellectual garbage which weakened and degraded had been scrapped. Alpha had returned to the purity of the tribe. Its men were providers/protectors; even the techs, medics and teachers were warriors. Its women were mothers/homemakers, the nurturers of the future. Its slaves carried out the menial functions. Iron discipline held all the elements in place.

But discipline was more than a tool. General Armbruster had lived his life immersed in it, had studied it, and only now felt that he really understood it. It created order, the enemy of chaos. It made civilization possible. It was mankind's defense against a hostile universe.

A beep cut through the com voices, interrupting his thoughts. He switched to his private channel and growled, "General Armbruster here."

"Sorry to intrude, General, but something has come up that I think you'll want to know about right away." Colonel Fry, his Chief of Staff, owned a voice which always reminded him of the wife's canary. "An incoming report from one of our friendlies."

An early escape from the discomfort of his combat suit appealed to him, so he withheld the caustic comment about delegated authority which came to mind. "I'll be right down. Out."

Switching to the officers channel, he spoke to Commandant Stoddard. "Nice-looking crop, Harry. A real credit to their families and the Academy. I hate to miss the rest of the show, but I have to go below."

"I'll let you know who wins," Commandant Stoddard replied without looking away from the exercise.

"Thanks." General Armbruster returned the salutes of the officers, then went down the stairs at the back of the platform. His boots clicked on the plastic as he walked over to the mushroom-shaped air lock/elevator entrance. The car descended to the second level, building up air pressure on the way.

His aide was waiting in the suit room. The lieutenant helped him struggle out of the combat suit, then checklisted it and hung it up while he dressed. A blunt, massive man in a uniform with silver stars glared back at him from the lavatory mirror. He paused briefly to admire the full head of brown hair, the hard flat stomach, the aura of physical as well as mental toughness. Not bad for a buzzard pushing sixty-five. Then he headed for his office with the lieutenant at heel.

He walked through gray corridors and down gray stairways lined with doors, conduits and stenciled signs. Everything was in perfect condition, and he didn't see so much as a speck of dust. The air was fresh except for a hint of honest sweat. Every man he passed looked sharp from the polished boots to the crisp salute. He was pleased. To borrow an expression from an extinct sister service, he ran a very taut ship.

He took the long way around through the cheerfully decorated PX level, so he could enjoy the sight of wives and daughters shopping for the Fall Cotillion. All the lovely ladies in their pink and white finery brightened his day. He tipped his cap to Santees, Montanas, McCrareys, Stoddards, Frys, Rhines, Dowlings: the first families of Alpha, which had produced so many distinguished military men. Families made careers, and careers made families.

Arriving at the Office of the Base Commander, he strode past busy staff officers in the outer room and went into his private office. The lieutenant stayed outside.

General Armbruster had gone to a great deal of trouble to make his office a reflection of himself. Besides being comfortable, it imposed his personality on visitors. The massive furniture, gleaming brass lamps, raid souvenirs and photos from his career set a mood of confidently wielded authority. A window in the somber walnut paneling revealed clear shell and the night sky. A squadron of polychromatic lights raced through the darkness, fireballs playing their silly games. He sat in the tall straight-backed chair behind his desk, and waited impatiently for the desktop com to buzz.

His wait ended seconds later. Slapping the talk button he said, "Send the colonel in."

Colonel Fry was slight and balding. He had worked his way up through Logistics, and had the fussy manner of an old supply sergeant. His abilities complemented those of General Armbruster, while his utter lack of imagination kept him from posing a threat. "Good evening, General," he said in that damnable chirping voice.

"Evening, Jerry. Have a seat," General Armbruster pointed to a chair facing the desk, "and tell me what's so hellaciously important."

Colonel Fry settled nervously on the front edge of the chair. "Maybe you ought to look at the report yourself—it's in your incoming file. A situation alert from one Fernando Uribe, our friendly in the Pemex Under enclave."

"How does Intelligence rate him?"

"A reliable source. And well informed—he's the top man in their zep service."

"He's a damned traitor," General Armbruster growled, "but everything has a use." He typed on the desk's flip-up computer terminal, and Fernando Uribe's report appeared on the screen.

He read it twice, making notes the second time. He called up library information about laser satellites, Pemex Under, Calgary and the surface town Davis. Then he sat back, closed his eyes, tuned out all distractions, and thought. The situation was serious, very much so. But it could still be handled by taking bold, decisive action. The world shrank to a playing board in front of his mind's eye, its pieces awaiting his hand. He felt totally alive.

When he opened his eyes, Colonel Fry was staring at him. "You did the right thing in calling me," he said. "We have to get moving on this at once."

"May I ask what we're going to do?"

General Armbruster grinned. "How would you handle it?"

"I, ah . . . well, I would start by burning Calgary out of the sky."

"You would. But now that rumor of our existence has spread to Pemex Under and God knows where else, you would just be confirming their suspicions. No, we'll let them wonder and hunt snipe. They haven't a clue as to who or where we are. And if we stay on the bounce they won't ever find out, because we control all the contacts."

"Then we'll continue to follow SOP?"

"Except in one particular." General Armbruster frowned. "This expedition to Davis. I doubt it'll find anything, but the possibility does exist. If the enemy were to develop a laser capability, our sorties and even Alpha itself would be endangered. I don't intend to allow that. Which zep is on top of the ready board?"

Colonel Fry didn't have to consult his pocket computer terminal. "The *Shenandoah*."

"I'm going to send it to Davis ASAP. See that it gets servicing priority when it docks."

"I will. May I ask what the mission objectives will be?"

"Search and destroy, in the literal sense. Secure any laser data with military value, and arrange a fatal accident for the Pemex Under zep."

CHAPTER TWELVE

Linda sat down at the dressing table, the first step in getting ready for bed. But instead of reaching for her earrings, she just looked at herself in the light-encircled mirror. Her exhaustion was more emotional than physical. It had been a long difficult day, from the meeting with Señor Gutierrez to breaking the news about the scavenging expedition to Wanda.

She felt like a particularly poor excuse for a mother. Step by step, problem by problem, she had been twisted until she found herself doing things which would have been totally unimaginable a week ago. The fear of abandonment she had seen in Wanda's eyes had cut her like a laser torch. Her guilt was all the worse for coming on top of growing excitement. She wanted to go on the expedition more than she had wanted anything in a long time, for reasons which didn't bear close scrutiny.

The door chime sounded loud and obtrusive in the night stillness. It should have startled her, but it didn't. She had almost been expecting it. Waiting for it. Instinctively she ran the tip of her tongue across her lips, patted a few stray hairs back in place. Then she went to the door.

She opened it a few inches. Captain Ramirez had left his cap behind, but otherwise he was still crisply attired in the dress uniform from dinner. "I timed my arrival for the

117

window between Wanda's bedtime and your own," he said. "I'm pleased to see my calculation was correct."

"You do have a gift for timing. But isn't it a bit late for a social call?"

"Actually I'm here in my official capacity, on a matter of business."

"Funny business, more likely." She kept her expression serious. "Can't we take it up in the morning?"

"I apologize for imposing," Captain Ramirez said in an earnest voice, "but tomorrow is going to be somewhat hectic. I would like to talk to you privately about this unusual expedition."

Well, he did have a legitimate reason. They hadn't risked discussing the actual purpose of the expedition on the com that afternoon. She would just have to make sure his mind stayed on business. Opening the door the rest of the way, she said, "Please come in."

His aftershave preceded him into the room. He sat on the edge of the bed, leaving a space beside him which she ignored. "I've known from the first that you were a remarkable woman, but I never suspected you were a secret agent. I'm certainly impressed."

Linda couldn't help laughing; the image was ludicrous. "I wish I were a spy. Then maybe I would know how to cope with all this."

"Have you told Wanda about the expedition?"

"Yes. She took it as well as I could hope."

Captain Ramirez nodded sympathetically. "It's a hard thing, but you're doing it for her welfare as well as so many others. Think how proud of you she'll be when she learns the whole story."

Linda was standing in front of him, just beyond arm's reach. The knot in her heart which had formed during the talk with Wanda loosened. "How is it you know just the right things to say to a woman?" she asked.

"Empathy and dedicated research, my dear lady."

The silence which followed became long and uncomfortable. "You said you wanted to discuss some business, Captain?"

"Captain sounds so formal—I wish you would call me Miguel. I'm here to inform you of the security arrange-

ments for the expedition. Officially it'll be a regular scavenging run, but Señor Cardenas is spreading a rumor that
we're actually seeking agricultural genetic engineering information. Only three of us will know the true goal—you,
myself and the university's laser expert. I dislike lying to
my crew, but I understand why it's necessary."

"Do you believe there is a windrider—and zep—eater?"
Linda asked anxiously. "It's such an incredible notion, and
we don't have any hard evidence."

"I don't know," Captain Ramirez admitted. "I've heard
some strange zepman legends in my time. Ghost zeps,
crazed fireballs, that sort of thing. The hostile force would
explain a lot. And if it does exist, I want a laser weapon
aboard the *Princess* in case our paths ever cross."

She stared at him, shocked. "Would you really fire it at
someone? To kill?"

Something grim crept into Captain Ramirez's smile.
"I'm not a violent man. But I am a man. If necessary, I
would kill to defend the *Princess*, Pemex Under—or you."

She should have been disgusted, but instead a delicious
thrill ran through her. Captain Ramirez was a throwback
to the pre-War mentality which she had read about. She
felt the power inside him, capable of being unleashed as
physical violence or . . .

"I think you better leave now," she said unevenly. "As
you said, tomorrow is going to be a full day for both of us."

The room was suddenly much too small. Despite her
best efforts her body was beginning to respond to him
again. His knowing look added to her unease.

He stood up, deftly insinuating himself just a few inches
in front of her. His presence wrapped around her. He took
her hands, helpless prey, in his. "I love you, Linda Calhoun. I want you, and I can tell you want me."

"I'm a married woman," she said, but whether to him or
herself she didn't know. "I have a husband, two daughters—"

"Not tonight," he whispered in a way which caressed
like fur. "Tonight you're the only woman in the world, and
I'm the only man."

He kissed each hand, then released them and slid his
arms around her waist. A distant part of her was admiring
his technique. He spoke to her innermost needs. His

touch was firm but not confining. He didn't move too fast, yet he was relentless, leaving her no time to gather her resistance. The sum was a sense of seamless inevitability.

"Please don't," she begged softly.

"Please don't make love to you, or please don't stop?" His dark eyes were engulfing her. He tilted her head up, and kissed her. Her mouth melted open under his. The kiss spread through her, tingling from scalp to toes.

She was outnumbered two to one, so she gave up. She stopped thinking about who she was and how wrong this was. She stopped thinking. Her arms went around him, and she kissed back.

But when he turned her toward the bed, she pulled back. "Wanda is next door. We might wake her."

"We can't have that," Captain Ramirez agreed. "We'll go to my room."

She couldn't put her weakness and shame into words, so she nodded. Taking her by the hand, he led her out of the room and along the empty hallway. His grip was a focal point for her intense physical awareness of him.

A solitary glow panel created a puddle of soft light in the middle of Captain Ramirez's room. It set exactly the right mood: an unthreatening space in which to nurture intimacy, while the bed and other jarring realities were cloaked in shadow. Dark night for dark deeds. Even so, she could sense unfamiliar male possessions around her, reminding her that she was in the domain of a man who wasn't Jack.

He took her into the light, and pulled her close to him. "Welcome to my home away from home," he breathed in her ear.

"Do you . . . really live here?" She was having trouble concentrating. His body was hard and hot. "Or did you arrange this . . . for my benefit?"

"A man will do mad things for a truly special woman."

Captain Ramirez didn't attempt the juvenile, mood-breaking tactic of undressing her. Instead he unbuttoned and removed his shirt as calmly as if he were alone. His chest was smooth, like burnished bronze. Slowly, in a dream-like state, she reached back to unhook the catch on her dress. She shrugged, and the dress slid down to the thick carpeting. She stepped out of it and her high heels, into his arms.

The kiss was longer, deeper, more passionate than she had ever thought possible. He let her up for air barely in time. "You've done this before . . . haven't you?" she gasped.

He laughed. Then he kissed her again. When he paused, she backed away and walked around him in an effort to regain some composure.

He gathered her in his arms. "Now, my dear lady." He lifted her the same way she lifted Cheryl, and carried her to the bed.

Being held in strong arms brought back echoes of childhood dependency. He laid her gently on the woolen bedspread, and stretched out beside her. The darkness made a private place for them. His hand moved caressingly up her right thigh, over the sheer lace of her camisole to her breast. She was ready. More than ready.

Then she noticed the equations which were taking shape in the back of her mind.

The association with lifting Cheryl had started it; tactile memories were powerful and enduring. Linda plus Jack equaled Cheryl. Linda plus Jack equaled Wanda. Linda plus Jack/Cheryl/Wanda, times seventeen years, equaled a family.

Linda didn't move or make a sound, but Captain Ramirez stopped his rhythmic kneading. "Is something wrong?" he whispered.

She still hungered for him, almost unbearably. But she removed his hand and sat up. "I . . . can't," she managed to reply.

He was quiet for several seconds, and she was glad that she couldn't see his face in the shadows. "Is it something I did? Or didn't do?"

"No, it isn't anything . . . to do with you. You're perfect. It's me. I just . . . can't."

"Surely you aren't troubled by guilt? No one else will ever know, and you aren't the sort to punish yourself where no harm has been done. Marriage vows aren't chains. Let your heart guide you—we can make each other very happy."

She tried to find the right words to explain what she only half understood herself. The way her concentration

wavered each time his leg brushed against hers made it
even harder. "I'm sorry. It's just that . . . this isn't me. I
wish it could be, more than you can possibly imagine. But
if I went to bed with you, I . . . wouldn't know who I am
anymore."

"You would be even more wonderful."

"Not to me, I'm afraid. It would cost me too many
things that are important to me." She struggled to her
feet. "I better go back to my own room. I hope you
understand."

Captain Ramirez chuckled. "Not really. But for now I
bow regretfully to the inevitable. Man proposes, woman
disposes according to her will." He rose from the bed,
picked up her dress and shoes, and handed them to her.

She dressed in awkward haste, all too aware of her
semi-nakedness. Even in defeat Captain Ramirez's style
was flawless. She saw disappointment in his face, but no
anger or self-pity. Her resolve teetered. If he took her by
force, he would get very little resistance. Did he sense
that? She thought so.

Instead he took her by the arm, and escorted her to the
door. His grin was as sincere as if he had achieved his
goal. "I love you still and totally," he said, kissing her
hand.

She gave him a safe peck on the cheek. "Strange as it
may seem, I'll always remember this night fondly."

"And I. Good night, my dear lady."

Linda trudged back to her room, too tired to care if
anyone saw her. But thanks to the late hour she had the
hallway to herself. Shame, worry and undissipated passion
tugged at the edges of her mind, but she had used up all
of her emotional energy.

Closing the door quietly behind her, she put an ear to
the connecting door to make sure Wanda was still asleep.
Her pre-bed preparations used up the last of her strength.
She crawled between the cold sheets, and closed her eyes.
Lingering traces of Captain Ramirez's aftershave haunted
her dreams.

When the travel alarm shocked Linda awake the next
morning, it took her a few moments to sort out reality
from fantasy. Then that reality sank in.

She couldn't believe the thing that she had almost done. What had she been thinking, wanting to trade her self-respect for a night of sex? Great sex, maybe, but still just sex. She shivered at the memory of how close she had come. And it wasn't over; Captain Ramirez had made that clear enough. She would have to be very careful around him from now on.

She made her aerobic workout a form of self-punishment, pushing herself so hard that her lungs burned and her muscles screamed. After showering and dressing she knocked on the connecting door to rouse Wanda.

There was no response.

She knocked again. More silence. Envying the deep sleep of the innocent, she opened the door.

Wanda wasn't in her bed. Nor was she anywhere else in the room, or in the bathroom. Both rooms were a mess: clothes hanging out of open drawers, a pile of belongings on the unmade bed, Wanda's pink baby doll wadded on the bathroom floor. Linda's irritation at such sloppiness turned into concern. Why had Wanda done it? Where was she?

Linda checked the com, but Wanda hadn't left a message for her. A call to the lobby also yielded negative results; the doorman had been on duty since midnight, but he hadn't seen Wanda.

It wasn't like Wanda to be so irresponsible as to go somewhere without leaving word. A terrible thought came unbidden into Linda's mind. She checked the closet, and found that Wanda's small suitcase was gone. Trying not to jump to conclusions, she went through Wanda's belongings to see what else was missing.

When she finished, she sagged into a chair, absently holding the perfume bottle which she had found in the bathroom wastebasket. Wanda had run away. And Linda didn't have to think hard to figure out why. Her eyesight misted. She felt the crushing weight of what a religious person would have called divine justice. Cruel, Old-Testament justice. She had sinned, and this was her punishment.

She had to find Wanda! Jumping to her feet, she ran back to her room to get her purse.

The door chime triggered an instant of ecstatic relief. Then it died; Wanda wouldn't need to ring. Linda yanked the door open impatiently.

Captain Ramirez had a cheerful greeting on his lips, but the moment he saw her expression he turned serious. "What's wrong?" he asked.

Any embarrassment which she might have felt about facing him after last night was smothered by fear for Wanda's safety. She stepped back to let him in, then closed the door. "Wanda is gone," she said dully.

"I beg your pardon?"

"She ran away. Packed a few things in a suitcase, no note, no clue to where she went, just . . . gone."

"Why?"

"Because of last night!" Her fear became white-hot rage. "Because you had to play your macho game, and I was too weak to tell you to go to hell! Somehow she must have seen or heard us! Now she's out there somewhere, alone, afraid, maybe in trouble! She must hate me!"

The fire died down as quickly as it had ignited, leaving ashes of embarrassment at her outburst. "I'm sorry," she said out of politeness. "I . . . I have to go now." She started for the door.

Captain Ramirez stopped her by stepping into her path. He looked concerned rather than offended. "Where are you going?" he asked calmly.

"To search for her."

"Pemex Under is substantially bigger than a windrider. You aren't likely to find her by wandering the streets, particularly if she doesn't wish to be found."

"I have to do something!"

"You will. Our proctors are very good at finding stray children. They have the resources for it, and they know where to look." He gestured to the com. "May I?"

She ached to be in motion, actively searching for Wanda. But she knew that he was right. She nodded.

He called proctor headquarters, talking so fast that she couldn't follow his Spanish. Then he let her take his place in front of the com.

She found herself talking to Proctor-in-chief Guerrero, a sober-looking older man. He was sympathic yet very professional. She felt like a computer memory unit as he skillfully extracted a complete description of Wanda, the clothes she had taken with her, her activities since arriving in Pemex Under, and her personality profile and interests. He tactfully didn't ask why she had run away, and Linda didn't volunteer the information.

"Try not to worry too much," Señor Guerrero told her. "I'm sure your daughter is in no danger. Pemex Under is very safe, and children are looked after. We'll find her. But it may take some time, so you must be patient."

"I'll try to be."

"You'll be notified immediately when we have any word of her. Good day, Señora."

"Thank you very much."

The com's screen went dark, and Linda stared at Captain Ramirez across a painful silence. She felt stretched taut; her bodily engine was racing with nothing to do. Guilt and helplessness tore at her. She was as alone as Wanda, in a strange environment far from home. It all seemed too much to bear. Feeling tears welling up, she fled to the bathroom and let them flow.

After she washed her face, she returned to the room. Captain Ramirez smiled at her. "Do you feel better?" he asked.

"Somewhat."

"I hope you realize that if I had thought there was the slightest risk of Wanda being hurt, I would never have come here last night."

The sincerity in his voice was unmistakable. She could condemn him for reckless amorality, but not for intentional harm. "I do."

"If you're up to it, we should be going. We both have a great deal to do before the *Princess* sails. I came over to invite you two to join me for a quick breakfast. I imagine you aren't very hungry, but you should keep up your strength."

She stared at him incredulously. "I can't possibly go on the expedition now. I have to be here when the proctors find Wanda."

Captain Ramirez shook his head. "The reasons why you must go haven't changed since yesterday. As for Wanda, she's a clever and determined young lady. I doubt she'll be found before we return. If she is, the proctors will take good care of her."

"But I have to explain to her . . . about last night. I can imagine what she thinks happened, but she has to know it wasn't . . . I didn't . . ."

"All the more reason to come. She'll need some time to cool down, before you can hope to talk sense to her." He took her hand. "Shall we go to breakfast?"

She pulled her hand free. She wasn't used to being led; decision-making with Jack had always been a joint effort. But despite the offensive manner in which they had been presented, Captain Ramirez's points were valid. She had to remember all of her responsibilities.

"You're right," she admitted in a strained voice. "About the expedition and breakfast."

"Welcome back aboard, my dear lady. We'll stop at the front desk and get you a wrist com, so the proctors can reach you anywhere today. Then to breakfast."

They ate in the hotel's restaurant. Captain Ramirez kept up a cheerful monologue, while she said little and ate automatically. Her thoughts were full of her missing daughter. After the meal Captain Ramirez regretfully hurried off to the zep bay.

Linda went about the chores which she had set for herself the day before. At first she suffered from an irrational feeling that everyone she encountered knew about Wanda and what a terrible mother she was. But having work to do kept her from dwelling on it, and gradually it passed. Her worry receded to a bearable level. Yet no matter what she was doing, she yearned to hear the buzz of the silver band on her wrist.

A buzz which didn't come.

She spent the morning making purchases for Calgary, which would be shipped in the *Toltec Princess*. They were miscellaneous items, since Calgary had traded with Montreal and Toronto less than a month ago. She bought fertilizer for the farm, replacement parts and plastics for the engineering department, a new helium pump for One's blimp bay, bookdisks for the library, medical supplies, and a variety of imported goods for the mall shops.

Pemex Under seemed half deserted; many stockholders and visitors had flocked to the windrider launching fiesta. Under other circumstances she would have eagerly fit it into her schedule. As it was, her only reaction was gratitude for being spared the usual crowds.

At the Bank of Montreal office she made arrangements for the remaining credit from the cargo sale. Most of it was used to pay the current installment on the bill for Calgary Four; the rest went into an account which in six more years would become the down payment for a new Two.

Her supply-run work done, she spent the afternoon preparing for the expedition. She did some library research, met again with Señor Gutierrez, and went shopping to outfit a proper kit.

Finally, because she couldn't put it off any longer, she visited the telecom office and sat down in one of the booths. For almost an hour she tried to compose an explanatory gram to Jack. Giving up, she just typed that her and Wanda's return would be delayed and she would explain when they got back. The booth accepted her money card, and told her that the gram would be relayed to Calgary before morning.

Returning to the hotel, she ate a lonely dinner in her room. She used her flatscreen to study maps and summaries until bedtime. By focusing her mind on the expedition every second, she managed to avoid spiraling into despair.

She was about to turn in, when Captain Ramirez came calling. Despite some misgivings she was glad to see him. A rogue and a cad he might be, but he was also the closest thing to a friend that she had here.

"What a day," he sighed as she let him in. His uniform was somewhat wilted, but the spring in his step and the light in his eyes were still strong. "I yelled, I pleaded, I ran myself ragged, and I worked like a beast of burden. Truly a madhouse cubed. But the *Princess* and her sturdy crew have once again risen to the occasion. We sail at eleven tomorrow morning, weather permitting—which apparently it will." His humorous expression turned serious. "How are you holding up?"

"As well as can be expected. My business went well, and I'm ready to go."

"Any news concerning Wanda?"

"Nothing."

Captain Ramirez stepped close, and put a hand on her arm. "Be brave. The Proctor-in-chief was right—Wanda is perfectly safe."

Linda's fear came rushing back. "But I can't *see* her! I can't visualize where she might be, what she might be doing. I've lost her."

His arm had eased around her waist. "You need some relief from your cares. Come over to the bed, and I'll rub those knots out of your muscles."

It sounded good. She started to move under his gentle guidance. Then the chilling realization of what he was up to came to her, and she jerked free. "Don't you ever stop?" She was as amazed as she was angry. "Is this all Wanda's running away means to you—an opportunity to catch me in a pliant mood?"

The light in Captain Ramirez's eyes dimmed. "You wound me. I care very much for Wanda, and I would put the *Princess* to the torch if it would bring the two of you happily together again. I didn't come here to trick you. For us to make love would give me pleasure, true. But it would also give you comfort, which you could very much use tonight. I'm sorry you find the notion distasteful."

She had to admit that by his twisted standards he wasn't acting dishonorably. But the thing he called comfort would destroy her. "What we both need is a good night's sleep," she told him, "in separate beds."

Captain Ramirez bowed, then went to the door. On the way out he paused, smiling. "Tomorrow is another day. Until then my dear lady, I bid you good night."

She locked the door behind him. Sagging against it, she took a deep breath and tried to will away the fluttery feeling inside her. Ten days with him in the close quarters of the *Mayan Princess*. She would have to be very careful indeed.

CHAPTER THIRTEEN

Wanda writhed in a land of fire, like the religious hell she had read about and heard adults swear by. The flames seared her, charred her skin to a black crisp. Her screams filled the smoky air. She ran, but there was no escape. Huge red shapes wearing the leering faces of Mom and Miguel stabbed at her with burning pitchforks. Far away she thought she could hear Father Reyes's voice praying futilely for her.

She wished she could die. Instead she burned and screamed and suffered . . . .

She woke up suddenly in total darkness. The silence was also total, except for her hard breathing and the terrified drumming of her heart. Her momentary confusion passed; she remembered where she was and why she had come here.

But one part of the nightmare had followed her. She was *hot*! Despite being naked (she must have shed her clothes during the restless night) the closet was an oven. She felt like a roasting chicken basted in sweat. She could hardly breathe.

Modesty kept her from just jumping outside. There shouldn't have been anybody in the shop, but you never knew. So she fumbled into her clothes by touch as fast as she could. Then she carefully opened the door and crept out.

The back room was just as dark as, and if anything, even hotter than the closet. She guessed it was over a hundred degrees. She was really thirsty.

But she was even more worried. Why was it so hot? Could Lone Star Five have caught on fire? She had heard gruesome stories about fires, but there wasn't any bite of melted plastic in the air. Could the heat have something to do with the launch? She figured it was early morning, just a few hours before the windrider was scheduled to go aloft.

Stinging sweat ran into her eyes; she wiped it away. She couldn't take much more of this.

The explanation came to her in a brilliant flash of amazement at her own stupidity. The launch! Somehow the air was being heated to create lift. Why hadn't she ever wondered how windriders went aloft? Probably because she was too used to thinking windriders just *were*. She knew they floated because the air inside them was warmer and lighter than the air outside, but her imagination hadn't taken the next step until now. Too late.

How hot was it going to get? Wanda remembered that neutral buoyancy for a windrider at sea level was supposed to take a temperature differential of about forty degrees. Lone Star Five would need a higher differential than that to climb; how much higher she wasn't sure. The temperature on the surface would probably be about seventy degrees at launch, so she guessed the inside temperature would have to be at least a hundred and thirty degrees.

Judging from how she felt already, she didn't think she could take over a hundred and thirty degrees for very long.

There were some insulated places in a windrider where she could hide from the heat: refrigerators, electronics compartments, fractional distillation tanks and so on. But suffocating to death wasn't much of an alternative.

She fought off a wave of dizziness. The air seemed to be getting hotter. That could have been her imagination, but she wasn't about to bet her life on it. Her hope of stowing away wilted. Just surviving would be hard enough.

She had to get out. Feeling her way to the door, she quickly crossed the shop's customer area to the entrance. But there she stopped. She didn't know where to go.

The bridge and the air locks would all be sealed. The coms, like every other non-essential system, would be shut down. She could go topside, try to attract somebody's attention. But the yard's work areas would probably be evacuated by now, Lone Star Five's monitor cameras would be looking outward, and it would be even hotter up there.

Wanda was having trouble concentrating, but she kept dragging her mind back when it wandered. The heat couldn't be everywhere. The shakedown crew had to be in a safe place. Where? A big place, obviously. The blimp bay had the most cubic. It was over the bridge which also needed to be kept livable, and it held helium tanks that could blow if they were overheated.

She doubted she would last long enough to try more than one place. The blimp bay was her best guess.

She lurched into the corridor. All the overhead glow panels were off; fortunately a little work area light reached in from a window wall at the radial's outer end, just enough to show her surroundings as different shades of gray gloom. Combined with the heat, the unnatural version of familiar things reminded her of her nightmare. She didn't like it.

"Help!" she yelled. "Can anybody hear me?" She listened hard, but only silence came back. No, that wasn't totally true. A scorching wind whistled along the corridor. The mix of hot and cold had to be creating air currents all over the levels.

Wanda ran toward the park escalator, sandals slapping, shouting as she went. She couldn't help feeling embarrassed at making so much noise. She knew she would have a lot to explain to anybody who found her, but at least she would be alive to explain.

The escalator wasn't running, of course. She hurried down the ramps, taking the wide steps two at a time. Some light came down the well from the topside entrance. She slid her palms along the handrails for guidance and support; she was gasping from her effort as well as the heat. Her head swam, and her strength was pouring out of her along with the sweat. She staggered, almost falling a few times.

The public levels became residential levels, and then engineering levels. Wanda vaguely noticed stacked supplies, unfinished construction and other signs of how much work was left for the shakedown crew. The heat was now like an invisible fire all around her. It burned her throat and chest, and the handrails were painfully hot to touch.

Coming to the work level, relief swept through her as she found she had guessed right. Where the escalator continued down into the blimp bay, a big hatch sealed off the well. It was normally used to keep the windrider from deflating when blimps were being launched and docked.

No time for dignity. She could feel herself slipping away. She dropped to her knees on the hatch and started banging on it, screaming, "Help!" over and over until her voice gave out. Her hands and knees were in agony, but she kept banging.

Nothing happened.

She managed to hold her ear against the hatch for a moment, but didn't hear a thing. Total silence, even though the blimp bay had to be the scene of a lot of noisy activity. So the crew members on the other side couldn't hear her either.

Safety was just inches away. Wanda looked around frantically for a hatch control, a com: any way out of the trap. But she couldn't find anything. Nobody was supposed to be out here now. There had to be some emergency precautions, but she didn't know what or where they were.

She got up to ease the pain in her hands and knees, and stared at the hatch, defeated. Now she understood why there weren't more anti-stowaway measures in the yard. Everybody knew better than to try. Everybody except her.

She sagged against the side of the escalator. The gloom was spinning around her, and she could barely stay on her feet. She was terribly tired. Sliding down to the floor, she found she didn't care much about the scorching plastic. Or anything. She just wanted to sleep.

No! It would be the sleep you never woke up from, and she wasn't anywhere near ready for that. She had hardly started living yet. A rush of adrenalin drove her back to her feet, swaying but filled with the energy of fear.

What would Mom do? Mom always had the answer to any problem: scraped knees, tough homework problems, stomach aches, the ways of the world. So Wanda tried to think like Mom, calmly, analytically. She needed an insulated place with air she could breathe. Starting at the bottom and working up, she visualized every part of a windrider as fast as she could. The bridge, out. The blimp bay, likewise. Salvage processing, no help. The supply center, likewise. Electronics, insulated but no air. The work crew station—

The work crew station!

Hope put some starch back in her legs. She shook her head to get it working better, then tried to figure out which way to go. She knew she was on the work level, but there wasn't enough light to read the signs. The circle of radial corridor entrances stared at her. Which one?

Was Lone Star Five laid out like Calgary Three? Back home the corridor to your right as you got on the blimp bay escalator ramp led to the work crew station. Wanda staggered into that dark hole before she could have any second thoughts.

She half ran, half slid along the left wall, grateful for even the searingly hot support. The darkness thickened as she headed toward the rim. For awhile she was afraid her aching eyes were going blind. Then the corridor started to brighten again thanks to a window wall at the far end.

Suddenly the wall she was leaning on disappeared. She fell sideways onto the hard floor, and raised blisters on her arms and legs before she could scramble to her feet. That used up the last of her adrenalin-given strength. She looked around, disoriented. Black unconsciousness was closing in on her. She almost fell again.

After a few seconds the shapes around her started to make sense to the still-functioning part of her mind. Tall walls wrapping around a big, cluttered room. Tables, cabinets, racks and shelves. Boxes, bottles, tanks, replacement parts, machinery and tools. She had made it to the work crew station.

She was too numb to feel any happiness or relief; the

heat had burned her down to almost nothing. Only a vaguely remembered purpose kept her going. She dragged herself around the station, through a nightfall that had nothing to do with night. She peered at shelves, pried back corners of boxes, yanked open cabinets. Tiny whimpers of frustration escaped from her raw throat.

She almost didn't believe it when she found the outside suits hanging in a wall alcove. She grabbed the nearest one. It was too big, of course, but it would have to do. Dropping to the floor, she squirmed into it. Outside suits were *always* supposed to be ready for use. If this one wasn't, she was dead.

She managed to put on the helmet. Her fingers weren't doing what they were told very well, so she slapped her whole hand across the wrist buttons. Air, wonderfully cold air, came hissing out of the neck vents. The cooling system (which she had often wished she had in the obsolete suit she used for flying) kicked in automatically. She heard the compressor throbbing and refrigerant flowing through the suit.

But it was too late. The blackness swallowed her and took her away.

CHAPTER FOURTEEN

The bridge of Lone Star Five was a circular room thirty feet across. The curved console, divided into nine stations, ran around the wall except where the stairway descended from the blimp bay. The transparent floor revealed a gray surface below the bottom of the shell. The rim of the ceiling slanted down over the stations, holding more controls and screens. White plastic, overhead glow panels and colorful displays created a bright, optimistic setting. Nine men and women in hot-weather clothes sat working at the stations.

Vic Jarman glanced up at a screen which showed a wedge of the deserted bottom work area. With everything portable removed to simplify the post-launch decon, it looked empty and forlorn. Vic was a few inches shy of six feet—short for Lone Star—with prematurely thinning black hair and a poker face. Being the runt of the litter had pushed him from childhood to do the best he could at everything. It had pushed him all the way to the chief engineer's station for the shakedown cruise of Lone Star Five. If the cruise went well, he expected to get the job permanently.

But right now he was wondering why he hankered after the grief.

"Mean interior temperature one hundred and forty point

nine degrees," Catlin Rogers reported from the environment station. "Black-line in four minutes."

"Wind nine MPH from one four oh." Frank McCullough's raspy voice came from the weather station. "The short-rango forecast gives us a probable window in the first nine minutes of black-line."

Usually forecasts came from WeatherNet, the pooling and analysis of weather data from hundreds of windriders around the world. But Lone Star Five wasn't on line yet. Even though Vic knew that Pemex Under's weather service was reliable for local conditions, he couldn't help wishing that they had access to WeatherNet's more comprehensive picture.

"Shell stress, temperature and integrity readings are nominal," Lefty Adams reported from systems station two. The data flashing on his displays came from the shell's sensor web. Thousands of microchips on the reinforcing cables enabled the computer to maintain a detailed real-time model of the shell. Experience did much the same for Vic; he could almost feel the tortures being inflicted on the skin of their new home.

For the past thirty-six hours a ring of giant microwave generators on the work area surrounding Lone Star Five's equator had been heating the air inside the windrider. Almost three hundred thousand tons of heat-expanded air had been vented into yard storage for use in the decon. Thanks to the extensive use of lightweight materials Lone Star Five weighed just shy of one hundred and ten thousand tons. So the windrider was straining to escape into the sky with a will that gave him the inside shakes every time he thought about it.

He used the bright yellow bandana around his neck to wipe his forehead. "How's the rest of the crew holding up?" he asked Gray Tanner at the com station.

She broke off her low-voiced headset conversation. "Hot, sweaty and fit to be tied—otherwise okay. They'd kind of like us to hurry things along."

"Tell them I said to put a hitch in it."

She chuckled, then added, "Swede thought he heard some buckling in the escalator well above the hatch a while back, but the seal is still tight."

"Log it low priority for the work crew post-launch."

"On it."

Vic felt a twinge of sympathy for the seventy-one folks jammed into the blimp bay along with everything else which couldn't stand the heat. Despite the insulation in the bay's ceiling, the temperature in the bridge was crawling up toward ninety-five degrees. He knew it was even worse upstairs.

From the bridge Lone Star Five seemed to be an isolated and forgotten place, but Vic knew that it was actually the focus of a tremendous amount of interest. Yard camera images of it were being shown on giant telescreens set up in the staging area. Vendors, performers and thousands of celebrants were gathered there for the traditional launching fiesta. He briefly wished that he was one of those watching the show, preferably with a cold beer in his hand, instead of being the show.

"Mean interior temperature black-lining at one hundred and forty-one degrees," Catlin reported. The tension in the bridge, already substantial, jumped another quantum.

"Confirm it with Yard Operations," Vic rapped at Gray.

"On it."

If Operations was paying attention, it would already be scaling back the microwave output to maintenance level. Launches were a major drain on Pemex Under's electrical power generating capacity.

"Confirmed, Vic. Operations says to stand by for release on a thirty-second count."

Now they were into gut-shredding time, waiting for the wind to drop. The tremendous lift which had been built up was needed to overcome inertia and kick Lone Star Five out of the yard pronto. Even so, because it had so much surface area, it couldn't be safely launched unless the wind was under four MPH. Otherwise it might be pushed into the yard's rim with catastrophic results.

Vic activated the blimp bay channel on his com. "Jarman here. We're black-lined and holding on the thirty-second count. All systems are nominal. If you all aren't sitting down and braced, I surely recommend it. This bronc is about to buck."

A quick glance at the overhead view in one of his

screens (the chief engineer's station was mostly monitors) reassured him that the launching path was clear. The dome, a strong but lightweight metallized plastic, had been retracted in pie-slice sections. He saw a sunny autumn morning with cirrus streaks against the bright blue. The real sky was a welcome sight after weeks of pre-launch preparations in the burrows of Pemex Under.

It almost made him forget that the air outside Lone Star Five was now killzone air, sure death for the careless and unlucky. As soon as the windrider was aloft, the dome would be put back. The cradle and work areas would be deconned, the doors sealing them off from the rest of the yard during the launch would be reopened, and construction would begin on a new windrider.

Vic's announcement had been the signal for a strained silence in the bridge. Eyes watched displays, hands moved over controls, but only emergency situations would be reported. Vic wiped more sweat from his face. He hated the feeling of impotence. Not that he disagreed with Operations' insistence on running launches; they had primary access to the systems involved. He just didn't like it.

Of course he wasn't a total spectator. Without looking away from the go light on his console, he activated the abort switch. If something went seriously wrong during the first few minutes of the launch, he could use it. An explosive charge would blow a hole in the top of the shell. In theory Lone Star Five would deflate slowly, and make a reasonably soft landing. The shakedown crew could then return to Pemex Under in their outside suits.

As for the chief engineer who had wrecked Lone Star's new windrider, he could pick a direction and start walking.

Vic's thoughts came back to the force which was trying to tear Lone Star Five free of the cradle's anchoring bolts. The shell was tough, but the stress readings were almost twice normal operating max. It couldn't take that for long. His nerves were stretched as tight as the reinforcing cables, screaming for release.

The go light turned green.

"Thirty," Gray began the countdown for the bridge and the blimp bay. "Twenty-nine . . . twenty-eight . . ."

As soon as Vic's heart started beating again, he moved

his hand closer to the abort switch. Everything on his monitors looked good. He twisted around in his chair to get maximum support.

"Seventeen . . . sixteen . . . fifteen . . ."

"Brace for release," Vic reminded the others. There wasn't anything else to say. They knew what to do, and were busy doing it.

"Eight . . . seven . . . six . . ."

Vic had to go to the bathroom. Badly.

"Three . . . two . . . one . . . release!"

The bridge shuddered as dozens of explosive bolts blew simultaneously. If one or two bolts failed, they were sheared by main force. The microwave output readings dropped to zero. Lone Star Five groaned, a vast hollow sound, and began to climb like a pre-War rocket. Vic was shoved down into his chair. He had known what to expect, but it still scared him spitless.

The gray below the floor dropped away, becoming the shallow steel bowl that was the cradle. The equator camera screens showed work areas descending faster and faster. Vic watched the yard's rim in the trajectory display, his hand poised to slap the abort switch, his body tensed for the feared impact.

It didn't come. Lone Star Five sprang into the sky, undamaged, free.

"YAHOOO!" Lefty yelled, voicing the excitement which swept through the bridge. Vic felt like yelling too, but he had work to do. First and foremost, he carefully deactivated the abort switch. Voices behind him rapped out reports, while Gray fed a running account of the launch to the blimp bay. The rocket-like sensation slacked off.

Vic felt the slight tremor of the air pumps kicking in, so he didn't need Lefty's report, "Venting and heat-exchange on line," to tell him what was happening. As Lone Star Five climbed, the outside air density and temperature dropped. To keep climbing at a steadily decreasing rate which would bring the windrider to neutral buoyancy at ten thousand feet, some inside air had to be vented and the rest had to be cooled. The cooling job was 'way beyond the capacity of the heat-exchange system. So, as soon

as the windrider cleared the killzone, cold outside air
would be pumped into the windrider.

"Two thousand feet," Sara Jane Austin reported from
the flight station. "Rate of climb grooved."

Vic glanced down through the floor. The yard was a
dark hole surrounded by the enclave's surface structures
and barren brown mesa. A few stunted trees and patches
of summer-burnt grass were the only signs of life. It was
an ugly, disturbing sight; he quickly turned his attention
back to his station.

"Four thousand feet. Rate of climb grooved."

"Operations reports everything green at their end," Gray
told him. "They wish us a long and joyous flight."

"Thank them for us, for all of Lone Star. Tell them Lone
Star Five is a thoroughbred."

"On it." She spoke softly into her mike.

"Six thousand feet. Rate of climb grooved."

Vic punched up a topside camera view. It was a sight to
rend a windrider engineer's heart. The massive commin-
gling of hot and cold air had created a windstorm, rocking
the catwalks and solar cell panels, whipping up dust dev-
ils, and raising whitecaps across the lake. He was glad the
camera didn't have a sound pickup.

"There surely ought to be a better way," he whispered
to himself.

"Doppler radar shows a minor turbulence layer at seventy-
one hundred feet," Frank rasped nervously. "ETA one
minute forty seconds."

"Hang onto your hats, pardners!" Lefty yelled. Vic thought
evil thoughts about weather.

Lone Star Five climbed into the turbulence. The rough
air didn't move the windrider's one hundred and ten thousand tons around much, but it added considerably to the
stress on the shell. Vic almost groaned in harmony with
the deep, terrible sounds of flexing plastic composite. The
trim system wasn't operational yet; the windrider picked
up a few degrees of rock. The unsteady floor added to his
shakes.

None too soon Lone Star Five cleared the turbulence.
Lefty's shell stress reports lost their anxious edge.

"Eight thousand feet. Rate of climb grooved."

The venting was being steadily decreased, and Catlin's temperature reports dropped under a hundred degrees. Now Vic would find out whether the greenhouse effect worked. If it didn't, Lone Star Five's flight would be a mighty short one.

Despite the sweat running down his face, Vic looked fondly at the clear blue sky in his screens. Windriders were always launched in the morning, so they would have plenty of sun to work with before their first night.

He checked the topside screen again. The storm had all but died away, leaving a hellacious mess but no major damage that he could see.

"Nine thousand feet. Rate of climb grooved. Coming onto course two nine oh, airspeed six MPH."

"We have AOS from WeatherNet," Gray reported. "Plus a message from the relaying windrider, Dublin Two. Quote. Acknowledging transponder, Lone Star Five. We've been expecting you. Wide sky, and the luck of the Irish to you. Unquote."

Vic let out a quick bark of laughter. "Ask them to pass the word to Lone Star that our launching went well—details to follow. And tell them the eyes of Texas are upon them."

"Droll. Very droll."

A few minutes later Sara Jane said, "Ten thousand feet and holding."

"Catlin, how does the inside temperature look?" Vic asked.

She checked her console, then leaned back, smiling. "Mean interior temperature steady at eight-two degrees. No fires or hot spots. Pumps and vents shut down, heat-exchange in maintenance mode. The greenhouse effect is green."

Someone threw a plastic water cup at her, and the tension in the bridge collapsed. Vic joined enthusiastically in the hand slapping, shoulder punching and reb yelling. Gray was shouting into her mike, her news undoubtedly triggering the same thing on a bigger scale in the blimp bay. Vic was damned proud of his shakedown crew: all hand-picked for steadiness as well as skill, the core of what was going to be the trimmest windrider in the sky.

Lone Star Five was aloft!

The bridge crew wrapped up their celebrating before Vic had to step in. Everyone got back to work, albeit in a more relaxed mood. Vic called the blimp bay. "Yo, Swede. Can you hear me?"

The growling voice of Swede Hansen, the work crew chief, penetrated what was either a wild party or a cattle stampede. "I'm here, Vic. What's the word?"

"Time for you and your gang of deadheads to start earning your keep."

"Deadheads! You chair jockeys ought to try doing some real work for a change. Can we crack the hatch?"

"Do it," Vic replied, "and get busy. You know the drill. Add the solar cell panels to the priority inspection schedule. Get the fractional distillation plant on line pronto—we need a few more thousand feet under us before sundown. And *please* toss the abort bomb over the side, so I can breathe easy again."

"I'll take care of that last item personally." The com clicked off.

Vic's ears popped, a reminder of how refreshing it was to breathe normal air again instead of Pemex Under's soup.

"Got a mid-range forecast yet?" he asked Frank.

Frank didn't look up from his map screen. "Almost."

"You reckon it's safe to hold our course for two, three hours? I want the preliminary inspection reports before we do any climbing."

"Sure—you knew that before the launching. The tropical disturbance off Yucatan will mosey east of us, and the sky up ahead is downright dull. Ask me a hard one."

"Okay. Find us a roughly northbound wind between fifteen and thirty thousand feet, preferably one that won't turn us inside out."

"I'll see what's blowing."

Vic looked down at the raw surface terrain, and thought ahead. Lone Star One through Four were over old Wyoming, scavenging oil from a field which had survived the War. Petrochemical products were Lone Star's export business. The shakedown cruise would take Lone Star Five northwest to join them, while the crew put her through her paces on the way.

Vic was walking around the bridge, collecting data and opinions, when his com beeped. He was there in three long strides, slapping the button. "Jarman here."

"I'm in the hospital," Swede growled. "Better get up here pronto."

"What is it?" Vic demanded.

"A stowaway."

Silence came crashing down on the bridge. Vic felt the eyes of the others on the back of his neck as he digested Swede's message. A stowaway! Every Pemex Under stockholder had it drummed into his head that a hundred and forty degrees of moist heat was sure death. Yet there always seemed to be some idiot who didn't reckon natural laws applied to him. Vic's gut twisted. Any death was a tragedy in itself, but when it christened a new windrider it was the worst possible omen.

"Shit!" he muttered. "Can you identify the body? I'll have to report this to Pemex Under ASAP, and I'm surely not looking forward to it."

"The stowaway isn't dead."

"Huh?" Vic heard sharp intakes of air behind him.

"We found her in the work crew station, zipped up in an outside suit. Its air and cooling systems saved her life. She's unconscious, but Doc says she'll be okay."

"I'm on my way," Vic rapped. "I'm mighty glad she survived—so I can light into her for stowing away!"

He turned the bridge over to Sara Jane, then took the stairway three steps at a time. The blimp bay was jammed like a pack rat's nest, but deserted except for a gang loading cargo carts. The air held a lingering reminder of plenty of sweaty folks.

Swede had the park escalator going. Vic started up the ramps running, then reconsidered when his gasps began sounding like one of the air pumps, and let the motors do the work. Windriders hadn't been aloft long enough for townsfolk to evolve the Himalayan Sherpa's resistance to hypoxia. They lived with thin air by not overexerting themselves, but sometimes Vic forgot.

The glow panels in the levels were on. The escalator

well hatch had been swung open; he didn't see any buckling above it. Everything he passed looked brand spanking new and generic, awaiting the personal touches which would make Lone Star Five unique. He spotted crew members on inspection tours and hurrying to work stations. Normally he would have been pleased by the way they were putting the spurs to themselves, but he had the stowaway on his mind.

He got off on the fifth level, and took the east radial corridor to the second circum. Air started hissing softly from the grated wall vents. System by system, Lone Star Five was coming to life around him.

The hospital was drawing a crowd. Vic wasn't surprised; news traveled fast by com, and even busy crew members could find a few minutes to indulge their curiosity. He decided to let it be unless it got out of hand. He pushed through the reception area, into the examining room where Doc Starnes had set up temporary shop.

He ignored the gawkers whispering to each other near the doorway. The brightly lit white room with its glistening aluminum fixtures hadn't yet acquired the traditional alcohol smell. Some of the supply boxes had been opened, and medical gear was scattered haphazardly on a tabletop. Doc was treating someone sitting up on the examination table in the middle of the room, while Swede watched anxiously over Doc's shoulder. Doc looked as cool and sleek as usual in the white shirt and slacks of her profession. Swede, big and bluff, was wearing his grubby old lucky coveralls.

As Vic joined them, he realized that the stowaway was a girl.

About fourteen or fifteen, he reckoned. Pretty, too, despite matted hair and sweat-stained clothes. Her fair skin, blond hair and windrider style outfit suggested that she wasn't from Pemex Under. She was well enough to be gulping water from a cup and giving Doc a hard time.

"Please take it," Doc wheedled in her best bedside manner, holding out a tablet. "It's just salt. You lost plenty in your sweat, and you need to replace it."

The girl stared dubiously at the tablet awhile, then she finally picked it up and swallowed it with some water.

"How is she, Doc?" Vic demanded. He was hot and tired, and he didn't like surprises which complicated his job.

"And good morning to you too, Vic. She'll be fine. A touch of heat stroke and dehydration, some minor burns on her hands, elbows and knees, is all. I've patched her up. Plenty of rest and fluids, and she'll be good as new."

"Maybe." Vic swung around to face the girl. "Now, young'un, you have some tall explaining to do. I'm Vic Jarman, the ramrod of this outfit. What's your handle?"

"My name, sir?" Her voice was pinched tight. "I, uh, can't tell you."

"The hell you can't! I'm in no mood for games. Talk."

She met his angry gaze steadily, her expression a mix of worry and stubbornness. "I'm sorry, but I just can't."

"Can you tell me where you're from?"

"No, sir."

Vic took a deep breath, trying to calm down. "Why not?"

"Because you'll make me go back."

"Damned right I will!" Vic glanced at Swede and Doc. "Did you check her for ID?"

"When I got her here," Swede growled. "Nothing on her."

"The labels in her clothes read New Hong Kong," Doc contributed. "Of course NHK sells to half the windriders aloft."

"Do you have any idea how stupid it was to stow away?" Vic asked the girl. "You could have been killed."

"I know now. But I had to get away. I want to live here, be a citizen of Lone Star Five. I'll work really hard—"

"Forget it," he cut in. "I don't know what kind of hare-brained notions you have, but you aren't staying. You belong back home with your own folks, and that's just where you're going as soon as we ID you."

The girl looked as if she was about to cry. "There, there," Doc soothed, stroking her arm. "Don't mind that old buzzard—he sounds meaner than he is. How about telling me why you had to run away?"

The girl smiled wanly at Doc, but shook her head.

"We're all out of time to waste," Vic said crisply. "Swede,

get back to work, and take all these gawkers with you. This isn't a football game. As for you, young'un, I'm going to send a description of you to Pemex Under. I reckon the proctors will have a handle to go along in two shakes. Then we'll see about getting you back where you belong."

"Excuse me, Vic?" a woman's voice came from behind him.

He turned his head, and saw Dede Polk standing in the doorway with her husband. They were looking at the girl. She let out a small muffled gasp when she saw them, but they grinned reassuringly.

"What is it?" Vic sighed.

"Somebody is going to have to look after the poor child while she's here," Dede said, moving aside to let Swede and the others out. "Jim and I would like to volunteer."

Vic wondered if he was missing something, but the Polks were steady, reliable folks. "Doc, can she check out of your hotel?"

"Any time."

"Then she's all yours for as long as she's with us," he told Dede, "which hopefully won't be long."

The Polks' grins widened, and the girl's mood seemed to improve. "Thanks, Vic," Dede said.

Vic nodded. As he headed for the door, his thoughts returned gratefully to the kind of problems he had been taught to handle.

CHAPTER FIFTEEN

Wanda jumped down off the table as soon as Mister Jarman left. She felt a lot better than she had when she woke up. The anesthetic in the spray-on bandages had numbed her burns, cups of water had taken care of her thirst, and normal air was soothing her raw throat. But she was too busy worrying about her future to appreciate being alive or the medical care she had gotten.

"Can we take her with us now?" Dede asked Doctor Starnes. Dede was wearing tight denim shorts and a maroon blouse that was unbuttoned to a startling depth.

The doctor looked at Wanda. "How do you feel?"

"I'm okay," she said firmly.

"Then mosey." Doctor Starnes turned to Dede. "See she gets plenty of rest and fluids, and call me pronto if she starts feeling poorly." Dede nodded.

"Thanks, Doctor," Wanda said. "Wide sky." She walked warily over to the Polks, trying not to look like she knew them.

The Polks fell in on either side of her. "Come along, young'un," Jim said, winking at her. He looked like a cowboy today: leather boots, jeans, a tan shirt and a bright red bandana. "We'll head down to the residential levels and find a new place to bunk—our one-bedroom apartment won't do now. But there are plenty of two-bedrooms to pick from."

When the three of them were alone in the corridor, Wanda asked the question that she had almost burst from holding in. "Why didn't you tell them who I am?" she whispered urgently.

Jim and Dede looked at each other, then Jim answered. "We both took to you right off yesterday. In Lone Star we don't tell tales on our friends, at least not without hearing them out first."

"Thanks," she said sincerely. Mom's betrayal was too fresh in her mind for her to be looking for new parents, but she was glad to have some friends in Lone Star Five. Now she didn't feel so alone.

"Honey," Dede said, taking Wanda's hand carefully so she didn't touch the burns, "can you tell *us* why you lit out?"

Wanda shook her head. She couldn't tell anybody, ever, about the terrible thing Mom had done.

"We'd keep that secret too," Jim promised.

"I know. It's just . . . I can't . . ."

"It isn't too late to change your mind," Jim told her. "Running off is a mighty poor way to solve your problems. Better to face them, work them out. Your kin must be worried sick about you. You really want it that way?"

Wanda's heart ached when she thought about Dad, but she didn't say anything.

"That bad, huh?" Dede asked softly. "Maybe we can help. Or maybe just talking about it will help."

Wanda wished she could tell them. They were adults; maybe they could explain why Mom had done what she had. But it was just too disgusting and shameful to put into words.

"Okay, honey, we won't pry. If you change your mind about the help, feel free to bend our ears any time."

"I will." Wanda's voice broke. "It's really nice of you two to take me in. I'm sorry for the trouble I'm putting you to."

"We're doing it as much for ourselves as for you," Jim said. "Dede and I have only been hitched for a couple of years. We don't have any young'uns yet, but we reckon to pretty soon. This way we get to practice on you."

"Speaking of which," Dede added, "you're going to need something to use for a handle. Suppose we call you Wanda, but tell everybody we picked it since you wouldn't 'fess up?"

"Okay."

Dede's expression turned serious. "We'll keep your secret, honey, but even so it won't last long. Most likely your folks have already reported you missing to the Pemex Under proctors. When Vic sends them your description, they'll make the connection and have the nearest Pemex Under zep dock here to pick you up. Odds are you'll only be with us a few days. But we'll make the most of them."

Wanda didn't say anything. The talk with Mister Jarman had discouraged her, but she wasn't giving up. She would never go back to Mom! She had a few days to convince Lone Star Five to let her stay. If that didn't work . . . well, a windrider was a big place, and she knew some really good hidey holes.

They rode an escalator down to the ninth level, and walked out to the rim. The escalator well and the corridors were mostly plain white plastic, without any of the styling Wanda was used to. Now she knew why all the doors were open: to make air circulation easier during the launch.

"We want an outside apartment, naturally," Jim said. "Nothing but the best for the shakedown crew. Until the end of the cruise, that is. Then RHIP again."

"This is where we were going to stay." Dede pointed to an apartment-front. "Our bags are inside. Did you bring anything with you, honey?"

"My stuff is in a back-room closet up in the mall level," Wanda replied. "Good thing I left my wallet there, or Mister Jarman would know who I am and where I'm from."

Jim pointed to another apartment-front. "How's this for a place to hang our hats gals?"

Wanda followed Dede in. There was some lingering heat, so Jim left the door open. The two-bedroom apartment had the usual layout and features. The unstyled white surfaces, carpeting and furniture seemed naked, but the window wall looked out on a bright blue sky with clouds thickening in the distance. She stared at the beautiful sight, and pure joy spread through her. She had escaped from Pemex Under. No more underground holes, no more thick air and headaches. She was home.

Dede's arm draped over her shoulders. "I know just how you feel, honey." To Jim she said, "How about fetching our bags—and Wanda's things, if you can find them— while I put her to bed?"

"I'd be delighted." Jim gave Dede a big kiss, then he hurried off.

"Now you just come over here and stretch out," Dede told Wanda, patting the back of the living room sofa.

"I'm not sleepy," Wanda replied sharply. She had things to do, and no time to waste.

"I know, I know. But I promised Doc. So let's put one over on her."

"Huh?"

"Just pretend to sleep for a few minutes, say until Jim gets back. Then you can be up and about. Okay?"

"Okay."

Wanda took off her sandals, and curled up on the warm, soft upholstery. Dede sang softly about a baby falling out of a tree. Wanda counted seconds . . .

She vaguely remembered waking halfway up, drinking a cup of water, strong arms carrying her, gentle hands undressing her and putting her to bed.

She woke up to a wonderful aroma. Opening her eyes, she saw she was in a plain white bedroom. She had been tucked into a made bed, and her suitcase sat in front of the closet. Dede was putting a bowl and a cup on the bedside stand.

Wanda yawned and stretched. "I guess I was a bit sleepy after all. What time is it?"

"Just shy of four in the P.M. How are you feeling?"

"Really good." The aroma coming from the bowl was making her hungry.

"Better eat your soup before it gets cold," Dede told her. As she started spooning up the thick vegetable soup, Dede went on. "I've been homemaking. I fetched what we needed from stores, and got started on the unpacking and setting up. Soon as I had the pressure boiler working, I whipped up some soup for us. Freeze-dried travel rations concocted from what Pemex Under calls food." Dede made a face.

Wanda giggled, then said, "It tastes okay. Where's Jim? I want to thank him for getting my stuff."

"He's topside with the other aggies, getting started on the farm. That's another reason why I woke you up. He said we should mosey up soon, if we want to see something that only happens once in the life of a windrider."

Wanda was mystified. "What is it?"

"He wouldn't tell me, the ornery polecat. Just grinned and promised we'd kick ourselves from here to there if we missed it. You up to a quick trip?"

"You bet." Wanda's curiosity was aroused, pushing her troubles into the background.

"Finish up your soup, get dressed, and we'll go see." Dede kissed her on the forehead, then left.

Wanda was happy to find that the bathroom plumbing was working. She showered, scrubbing off a crust of dried sweat and shampooing her matted hair. After combing it out, she put on fresh clothes from her suitcase.

She took her dishes into the kitchen, and washed them. Dede was putting things away. When they were both done, they headed topside.

They passed some other crew members on the way. Dede seemed to know and like everybody, and vice versa. Wanda attracted a lot of attention. She was polite, but she didn't talk about herself.

As the two of them rode up the last escalator ramp, Wanda saw the top was covered. The sheet of plastic she had noticed last night was fitted over the entrance. Dede pushed up one side, and they crawled out.

Wanda almost slipped as she stood up; the dusty dirt had turned into mud, and slopped onto the walkways. She looked around. The golden light of the late afternoon sun showed the topside she remembered, a big empty field with the lake and the farm and park buildings clustered in the middle, covered by a bowl of hard-to-see shell. But something had really messed it up. There was mud in the irrigation ditches (which were starting to fill up with wa-

ter), on the sides of the buildings, even on the lowest part
of the shell. The lake looked browner than usual, and the
ground around it had been worn away. Lone Star Five's
launching must have been pretty rough. Even so, she was
sorry she had slept through it.

She noticed wet drops falling on her head and arms.
They were coming down all around, slanted by the rim
breeze. They looked, felt and tasted like water. She glanced
up at the top of the shell. The grid of solar cell panels and
catwalks was all but hidden by a dark gray mistiness she
had never seen before.

The cool spray was refreshing, but its mysterious origin
worried her. "Is there a leak in a pipe or something?" she
asked Dede.

"It's *rain!*" Dede laughed. "So that's what he meant!"
She faced the breeze and spread her arms.

Wanda had studied rain in class, had even watched
storms from above. But *inside* a windrider? "Isn't that
impossible?"

"Usually, yep. But plenty of lake water evaporated in
the heat of the launching, enough to make a genuine
cloud. When the temperature came down, so did the rain.
Jim was right—it won't ever happen again."

Wanda decided she liked rain, but the mud underfoot
was a bother. The escalator entrances must have been
covered to keep the rain out of the wells.

Wanda and Dede weren't alone topside. Some crew
members had come to get a quick look at the rain, while
others were working on the ground level and riding the
access belts up to the top of the shell. Jim was one of a
group at the freight elevator entrance unloading potted
saplings. Dede yelled, "Yo, Jim!" and he waved the cowboy hat he was now wearing.

"Can we go over there?" Wanda asked Dede.

"Best not to—he looks busy. But he'll be done for the
day pretty soon."

They enjoyed the rain awhile longer, then returned to
the apartment. Their clothes weren't wet enough to need
changing. They did what they could for each other's hair,
then Wanda helped Dede turn a pile of ration pacs into
dinner.

Jim came stomping in as the last of the sunset faded outside the window wall, his coveralls and work boots caked with mud. He tried to kiss Dede, but she shooed him into the bathroom. Soon, scrubbed clean and back in the outfit he had been wearing earlier, he got to kiss Dede and Wanda too.

Dinner was like the ones back home, only different. Nobody had to dress; Dede explained that the shakedown crew had too much to do to bother with such things. Wanda liked the idea of a vacation from fancy clothes, particularly since she hadn't brought any. The dinnertime conversation was casual and noisy. Wanda felt free to say anything she wanted to, the way she did with Jan and Lori.

They all did the dishes. Then Jim checked his watch and said, "Time to mosey, gals. The campfire ought to be starting pretty soon."

"What's a campfire?" Wanda didn't recognize the word, except that fire was part of it. That was enough to make her nervous.

"You've never been to one? Well, you're in for a treat. Ready, Dede?"

"Coming." Dede stuck a few things from the kitchen in a shoulder bag, and rejoined them.

They headed topside. They weren't the only ones; by the time they reached the park escalator, they were part of a chatting, happy group. Stepping out onto the ground level, Wanda was disappointed to find that the rain had stopped. The air smelled fresh and clean. The night sky was a jet-black canopy with hundreds of diamond-bright stars and a full moon rising. Some of the pole lamps were lit, spreading a shadowy twilight over the ground level.

By staying on the walkways they mostly avoided the mud. Next to the lake they came to a wide circle of dry dirt, with rolled tarps around the rim suggesting how it had been kept dry. In the middle there was a slab of what looked like clay set in the dirt. Real wood logs were stacked on it in an adult-high pyramid. A lot of crew members were already standing in the circle or sitting on the rolls, and more were coming.

"That's a campfire," Jim told Wanda proudly.

"You're going to *burn* those logs? Right here in the open?" Wanda asked unbelievingly. Lighting an uncontrolled fire was like breaching the shell; you just didn't do it.

"Don't you fret," Dede said, patting her arm. "It's safe enough. The fireplace keeps the heat and flames where they belong. Campfires are a Lone Star tradition, and we've never had an accident yet."

"As for fouling the air," Jim added, "we use a flue to vent the smoke. Haven't set it up yet, because the engineers want to test the air scrubbers. Makes the campfire more natural, too."

"But burning wood seems so . . . so wasteful."

"It surely does cost," Jim admitted. "We get the logs from enclaves—they grow them the same shortcut way they grow food, mostly for furniture. But we don't mind paying, at least not much."

"Why not?"

"It's our favorite sort of get-together. Like tonight, we're celebrating being aloft. Don't you—whoa, looks like Swede is about to light the fire. Let's pull up a rock and set a spell."

The three of them found an unoccupied tarp roll. Looking around, Wanda figured just about everybody was here except the night shift. She saw Doctor Starnes but no Mister Jarman, and was happy on both counts.

The bear-like man she remembered from the hospital was standing by the stacked logs. "You all know why we're here," he growled. "You all know what we've done so far, what we still have to do, and what it means. I reckon you don't need to hear any fancy words—"

"First you'd have to learn some, Swede!" somebody yelled. Everybody laughed, including the speaker.

"So let's kick our heels together and whoop it up!" he finished, and touched something on the edge of the fireplace. For a few seconds nothing happened. Then smoke started to rise from the wood, and it burst into flame.

"Microwave induction," Dede told Wanda. "Handy way to light a fire."

The crew members let out a loud, ragged cheer. Wanda was staring at the fire, something she had only seen in smaller and safer forms. (Puff wasn't really made out of fire, so she didn't count.) The orange-yellow flames climbed ten, twelve feet in the air before giving way to others. Reds and purples played among the logs. Sparks flew skyward like swarms of reversed shooting stars. The soft flickering light was reflected in the faces of the crew members.

"It's beautiful," Wanda sighed to herself. But Dede heard her and said, "It surely is." Dede was sitting between Jim and her, with an arm around each.

The heat reached Wanda. For a scary moment it reminded her of the launching. Then she relaxed, and basked in the cozy warmth. She gradually became aware of the smell of the burning wood. It was new to her, sharp and sweet at the same time. She liked it.

"That's mesquite wood," Dede explained over the chatter and the fire's pops and cracks. "We use it for cooking, too. I hope you're still with us when we get to Lone Star, so you can chow down on some genuine Texas barbeque."

The campfire turned out to be like a party. Bottles of beer (and orange juice for Wanda) were brought out. Wanda had tried beer once, when Jan had snuck a bottle from home; she hadn't liked the sour taste at all. Dede showed her how to toast marshmallows by holding them on a skewer near the fire. They were just about the best things she had ever eaten, charred crispy on the outside, gooey sweet on the inside.

A crew member started playing a guitar. Soon everybody was singing along, pre-War songs by famous cowboys like Gene Autrey and Roy Rogers. Wanda only knew the words to a few of them, but she didn't mind just listening. The rich, strong melodies built a cocoon of sound around her. The lyrics sometimes almost seemed to be about life in a windrider.

When Wanda started yawning, Dede said to Jim, "Time to call it a night, don't you reckon?"

"I do indeed—sun comes up early. Ready to spread your bedroll, young'un?"

Wanda nodded. She was having a wonderful time, but she could hardly keep her eyes open. They got up and headed for the park escalator. The fire and the party were still going strong behind them.

The trip back to the apartment was a vague half-dream to Wanda. Dede helped her get ready for bed, and tucked her in. When the glow panels went out and the door closed, she expected to fall right to sleep.

But suddenly she started crying. Tears ran down her cheeks like water from a faucet, and sobs shook her. She had no idea why, but she felt totally miserable. She plowed her head into her pillow, so Dede and Jim wouldn't hear. She didn't want them to see her like this.

Curled into a fetal ball, she cried herself to sleep.

CHAPTER SIXTEEN

Wanda was awakened early by Jim's imitation of a rooster. She remembered her crying jag and still couldn't explain it, but she felt normal again. Her burns now hardly bothered her at all.

She put on old clothes in anticipation of a hard day's work. Then she joined Dede and Jim at the dining room table for breakfast. Dede was wearing shorts and a T-shirt like Wanda, and had her hair pinned up. Jim's coveralls and bandana were fresh, but his boots and battered hat were the same ones he had been working in yesterday. Dawn was starting to paint the darkness outside the window wall with purple and red. There was enough light to see a solid cloud cover below. The clouds and the thin air told Wanda that Lone Star Five had been climbing.

She yawned between bites of the omelet and gulps of the milk Dede had served. "You folks sure get up early," she said.

"That's an aggie's life for you," Jim replied. "Sweat from first light to last, and still don't get it all done."

"You can catch a few more winks after breakfast, honey," Dede told her. "I've got to do some chores, then I'm off to work, too. Got to catch up on what I didn't do yesterday. You'll have to fend for yourself until suppertime. I'd stay out of Vic Jarman's way if I were you—otherwise you've pretty much got the run of the place. There's lunch for you in the fridge."

But Wanda didn't have time to play. She had to convince the shakedown crew, even Mister Jarman, that she would make a useful addition to Lone Star Five. "I want to help both of you with your work. Can I? Please?"

"You don't have to earn your keep," Jim assured her. "You're a guest."

"I really want to."

Dede and Jim looked at each other. Then Dede said, "That's mighty nice of you, honey. You can help me with the decon mechs after lunch."

"I reckon the farm can always use another hand." Jim was sipping the last of his coffee. "If you're set on helping out, you can come topside with me now."

"I am."

"Then we better get to it."

Jim and Wanda did the dishes, while Dede collected dirty clothes for a trip to the laundry room. Before the two of them left, Dede gave them each a kiss and a box lunch. Then they headed for the escalator.

They had the radial corridor to themselves; eighty-one townsfolk weren't a lot when spread out through a windrider. Wanda found the empty, deserted feeling a bit creepy.

"So you want to be an aggie, at least for a few hours," Jim said cheerfully. "Know anything about farming?"

"Not much," she admitted. "What's there to know? You stick seeds in the ground, water them, then pick the crops, right?"

Jim's laughter was loud and booming; it echoed in the corridor. "I surely wish! I spent three years studying what they call sustainable farming—organic, biological, natural, biodynamic, ecological and regenerative methods, plus things like permaculture, agroecology and agroforestry. And that's just the disk learning. I got my green thumb apprenticing under Raf Holman—that old man could grow crops in a holopic of dirt."

Wanda noticed that when Jim talked about his work, he sounded less like an old cowboy vid and more like Mom or Dad. "Why, it's almost as hard as becoming a windrider engineer, isn't it?"

Jim nodded. "Just as important, too. No point in staying aloft if you starve to death. We aggies have to feed six hundred folks from a truck patch not much bigger than a tic's ear. Oh, we can squeeze in two, three crops a year thanks to bio-engineered strains. We can fake a quick winter for plants that need it by tenting them and letting in some cold outside air. But we still have to work our dirt for all it's worth without killing it."

"Killing dirt?" Wanda didn't understand. "Isn't dirt already dead?"

"Don't you believe it. I spent some time in a Pemex Under factory watching ours being made. Country rock ground up fine, organic material, anaerobic bacteria, earthworms and so on, all mixed as carefully as Dede mixes a cake batter. Everything you need to grow crops, nothing you don't want. Better than natural surface dirt, which we can't use anyway thanks to the War."

When they got off the escalator at the ground level, the sky was crisply blue. They followed a walkway through hard dried mud and over irrigation ditches toward the middle.

The farm buildings were on the other side of the lake from the park. The pens and coops were empty. Wanda figured the stock would come from the rest of Lone Star, as soon as the farm could support it. The coldhouses for plants needing temp and/or moisture control were long, low blocks of clear plastic. Everything was clustered around the big red barn.

About a dozen men and women were standing in front of the barn's open doors. Jim and Wanda joined them, getting a loud welcome.

"Howdy, Jimbo!" yelled a husky man with a black beard even longer and thicker than Dad's. "So this is the young'un who kicked up all the fuss. Pleased to meet you, ma'am. I'm Craig Parmalee, the foreman."

"Thanks," she replied. The faces looking at her seemed friendly, and that was a good sign. "Please call me Wanda, everybody. I'd like to help you with the farm."

Craig stroked his beard thoughtfully. "Well, we're going to be turning ground today, and that's no job for a greenhorn." Then he brightened. "But if you really want to throw in with us, you can clean the mud off the buildings."

Wanda didn't like the sound of that. "I want to do something important, Mister Parmalee, not just make-work."

"It is important," Jim cut in. "Besides keeping things in trim, remember what I told you about our dirt. We need every speck of it where it belongs."

Mollified, Wanda said, "I'm sorry. I'll be glad to do it."

So, while the other aggies were inside the barn charging the batteries of the four tractors and hooking up plows to them, Jim brought a backpack-like gadget out to Wanda. A thin piece of pipe was connected by flexible tubing to one side.

"This here is a power sprayer," he explained as he helped Wanda put it on. "Hold the wand—the controls are there on the handle. To fill the tank, just stick the wand in the lake or a ditch and push the load button. Got it?"

"I think so."

"If you need anything, holler."

Wanda filled the tank with water at an irrigation ditch, then set out to clean up the ground level. The rain had washed the mud off of the inside of the shell, otherwise the job would have taken a week. But a lot of brown still stuck to places where it didn't belong.

She started with the farm. At first waving the wand and watching the water wash mud down building sides and off fences and walkways was fun. She pretended it was a real magic wand. The battery-powered pump buzzed softly as it launched a hard narrow spray. The aggies were driving the tractors or swinging hoes in the walkway-defined checkerboard of fields. Every now and then Jim or somebody else nearby would wave to her.

But as the sun rose higher, the heat started to get to her. She drank often from the tap water fountains, and splashed herself when she refilled the sprayer. She wished she had a bandana like the aggies to wipe the sweat away. The sprayer kept getting heavier as she finished the farm and the freight elevator entrance, then trudged around the lake to do the park. Her arms and back ached, sweat stung her eyes, and she was breathing hard. She had to take more and longer rest breaks. Jim and Craig both told her to stop when she got tired, but she wasn't about to quit.

She had to show everybody that she could do an adult's share of the work.

The sun was overhead when she finally finished the last escalator entrance. She headed back to the barn, too worn out to even admire her work. She sat with her back to the barn, and enjoyed the wonderful feeling of doing nothing.

A few minutes later Jim came over. "You look rode hard and put away wet," he said seriously. "You okay?"

She struggled to her feet. "I'm fine. I cleaned the mud off everything."

Jim grinned. "You surely did. Mighty nice job, too. Here, I'll put the sprayer away."

"Thanks." The news that she had done the cleanup right took away some of her tiredness.

Jim helped her get the sprayer off her back, and carried it into the barn. Squinting from the sun, she looked around. The fields were deserted; the tractors were parked, the hoes were leaning against fences. "Where is everybody?" she asked when Jim came back.

"Over by the lake. It's chow time—fetch your box and come on."

The aggies were sitting by the lake on dried mud that would soon be park lawn, eating and drinking their lunches. Craig complimented her on her job. She pounced hungrily on the sandwiches, fruit and apple cider that Dede had packed. Feeling better, she tried to make some sense out of the farm talk going on around her.

The aggies let their lunches digest awhile, then started back to the fields. Jim talked to Dede over his pocket com. Turning to Wanda he said, "Dede is waiting on you back at the apartment. Hate to lose you—you've got the grit for aggie work—but fair is fair. Dede would tongue-hide me for sure if I tried to hog you. Better mosey."

"Okay. Can I help out again tomorrow?"

"I reckon. See you later."

"Wide sky."

Wanda was tired, sore and sticky as she rode down the escalator, but she felt pretty good. Things were looking up. Maybe she could stay in Lone Star Five by becoming an aggie.

Dede was waiting for her in the apartment's hallway.

Dede stared, then shook her head in mock unhappiness. "Just look at you! Now I've got a pair of mud hens to clean up after. If you still hanker to help me, you better shower and change clothes pronto."

"Yes, ma'am." Wanda rushed into the bathroom, her room, and back to the bathroom. Then she rejoined Dede.

"There, you look like a little lady again," Dede said, grinning. "Did you have fun topside?"

"I was working," Wanda corrected her primly. "I cleaned mud off the buildings."

"And got it all on yourself. Well, tech work may be dull as dishwater, but at least it's clean. Coming?"

"You bet." The shower had recharged Wanda's batteries; she was ready and eager to do more work.

They rode the park escalator down into the engineering levels. The engineers and techs they met were busy, but Dede managed a few friendly words with most of them. Wanda envied her popularity and her easy way with words.

Getting off on the work level, they headed for the work crew station. Wanda realized she was retracing yesterday's desperate trip, but the corridor looked different with its glow panels on. Anyway, she didn't remember much about those last few minutes before she had passed out.

The work crew station was like the one back home, but cluttered with boxes and other supplies. Every now and then somebody came in, grabbed something and left; otherwise they had the big pie-slice room to themselves.

Dede led Wanda over to four stacks of five boxes each. "Here they are," Dede said, patting a box affectionately, "Hitachi SM-7B's. Nothing but the best for Lone Star. How about unpacking a dozen of them, honey, and looking them over for defects? The rest are spares—they can wait. I'm going to load a diagnostic program."

"Okay," Wanda replied eagerly.

Opening a box, she lifted out the decon mech. It looked like a fat flying saucer two feet across, made out of bright yellow plastic. It was lighter than she had expected. The top was smooth except for the round airscoop in the middle; on the bottom the ultrasonic emitter was surrounded by blower holes and six evenly spaced recesses near the rim. She had watched decon mechs in action, but this was the first time she had ever been this close to one.

She knew how important it was, so she handled it very carefully. Remembering the terrible heat she asked, "Couldn't the mechs have been damaged during the launching?"

Dede, working at an electronics bench, laughed. "These crabs are built to work outside weeks at a time. They ought to be tough enough to take a little heat."

Soon twelve mechs were sitting on the white floor. Dede brought over two hand computers, and gave one to Wanda. "They all look fine," Wanda told her.

"Glad to hear it. Now we'll check their innards—watch how I make the connection." Dede opened a small access hatch on the top of the nearest mech, and jacked in a lead from her computer. "You try one, honey."

Wanda opened the hatch on another mech, and stuck the jack in the right hole. "Got it."

"Now hit the run button on your computer. Ignore the spinach you'll see on the screen—just let me know if it says nominal."

Wanda touched the button. She stared at line after line of confusing tech stuff, until she spotted the word she was looking for. "Nominal!"

"Same here," Dede said as she unjacked her lead. "Let's check the rest."

A few minutes later eleven of the mechs had been cleared, one had been shelved for repairs, and another one had been unpacked and cleared. Dede took the computers back to the electronics bench, then returned with a control unit.

"Time to get these crabs on the job," she told Wanda. "The shell picked up plenty of fallout during the launching. Have you done any outside work?"

Wanda winced, remembering how she had gone outside to patch the breach in the shell back home. She didn't want to talk about that, especially about Miguel rescuing her. "Once," she admitted warily. "I know the drill."

"Let's see if we can find something to fit you." Dede led her over to the outside suit alcove. She wondered which of the neatly hanging silver suits was the one that had saved her life. They were arranged by size; Dede went to the small end and eyed the last one. "Good thing you're strapping for a young'un. We Lone Star folks tend that way ourselves."

Dede held the suit in front of Wanda, as if they were dress shopping. "This here should do," Dede said. "Let's suit up."

Wanda climbed into the suit, while Dede picked out and put on another one. They carried the helmets back to the decon mechs.

"All right." Dede thickened her drawl. "Let's head them up and move them out." She tapped buttons on the control unit. Each of the mechs rose a few inches as spindly legs with bulbous feet emerged from the underside recesses. Dede headed for the corridor doorway, and the mechs followed single-file. "Bring up the rear," Dede said over her shoulder. "If you spot any glitches, holler."

"Okay." Wanda fell in behind the last mech as it waddled along the radial corridor. Dede was busy keying instructions. Two crew members wheeling a laser welder past them toward the station dissolved into knee-slapping laughter. Wanda's nose went up; didn't they know how important decon mechs were to a windrider?

The procession stopped in front of the freight elevator entrance, while Dede summoned the car. They all rode topside together. Squinting in the ground-level sunshine, Wanda watched Dede march the mechs out of the elevator. Dede tapped in more instructions. Three of the mechs followed her on a walkway toward the rim, and Wanda followed them.

She spotted Jim on one of the tractors plowing a field. Dede yelled, "Yo, Jim!" and he waved his hat.

Wanda looked at the dusty brown fields that would someday be covered with crops, the coldhouse sides she had cleaned, the mechs waddling in front of her. The shakedown crew was working hard to turn Lone Star Five into a real windrider. And she was helping. Not a whole lot, admittedly, but even so it gave her a warm feeling of doing something special.

They came to one of the four topside air locks, a brick-shaped box big enough to hold a cargo cart. Dede opened the inner hatch, then led the mechs and Wanda inside. The hatch closed behind them, sealing them in the white, glow panel lit compartment.

Dede touched buttons on her suit's com. "Bridge?"

"Yo, pardner." The voice came from the neck ring speaker. "Lefty here. That you, Dede?"

"Yep. I'm in Lock G1 with decon mechs six, nineteen and twenty. How about a telemetry check?"

"On it . . . got them."

"Stand by. I'm going to stick them outside, then they're all yours." Dede turned to Wanda. "Let's get to it. Helmet on, suit check, and hook your lines to the mid-wall clamps."

Soon Wanda was looking out her bowl helmet, and listening to Dede's instructions over her suit's com. When she told Dede she was ready, Dede cycled the air lock. Wanda heard the hissing air through her sound pickup as the pressure in the airlock dropped a fraction of a PSI. The outer hatch swung open.

Wanda stared at the sky, feeling a bit queasy because there wasn't anything between it and her. The suit's heating system kicked in to keep her warm despite the near-zero outside temperature. She knew better than to look down. She had taken the Long Drop once, and didn't ever want to again.

Dede's gloved hand awkwardly tapped the control unit. "Okay, honey, pass me number six."

Wanda, in the middle of the air lock, carefully carried the mech to Dede, who was using her lines to brace herself in the outer hatchway. Dede placed the mech's feet against the outside of the shell. It started waddling up the outward-slanting surface, clinging to the slick plastic composite by vac-traction. The other two mechs quickly joined it.

Dede talked to the bridge again, then closed the outer hatch and cycled the air lock. When the inner hatch opened, Dede and Wanda unclipped their lines and left the air lock. Taking off their helmets, they watched as the mechs spread out across the shell. By now the mechs were busy scrubbing away dangerous fallout and dirt that would cut down the greenhouse effect.

Dede patted Wanda's arm. "You did good. Not everybody can keep reined in that close to the Long Drop."

"Thanks. It wasn't bad."

They repeated the routine at the other three topside air locks, and didn't have any trouble. Wanda learned a lot about the mechs, the shell and Lone Star Five's electronics. Even so, she was glad when the last outer hatch closed behind her. The sun was a red ball hanging low in the west.

On the walkway Dede told her to take off her outside suit. She did, gratefully, and Dede took it. "I've got to go debug that downed crab," Dede said. "You can't help me with that, so you're off-shift as of now. You can take a dip in the lake, if you like. Should be quite a crowd there cooling off after the day's work."

"But I didn't bring a swimsuit."

Dede laughed. "Don't reckon anybody did. But you're wearing undies, aren't you?"

Wanda looked down, hoping to hide her blush. Some Lone Star ways were going to take getting used to. "I, uh . . . don't want to go swimming right now, thanks. I think I'll look around until dinner time."

"Wish I could join you. Well, have fun."

"Wide sky."

Dede headed for the park escalator. Wanda didn't have anything particular in mind, so she set out along the rim walkway. The setting sun was turning the horizon purple and red. Gaps in the cloud-land below showed dark green mountains. She had hardly ever noticed the surface before visiting Pemex Under, but now she did, and wondered about it.

The gray plastic floor of the ground level curled up about four feet at the rim to meet the shell, a safety measure to prevent accidental breaches. Every hundred yards the walkway crossed the beginning of an irrigation ditch, fed by a wide stream of water spilling down the shell. Looking across the ground level, she was reminded that it was actually a slight bowl to make the ditch water flow toward the lake. The aggies and their equipment were gone from the fields. She could see a group of crew members splashing around in the lake. She was tempted to join them, but she just couldn't. Instead she kept walking, enjoying the sights as well as being by herself.

Her mind wandered. She saw Dede, the mechs and herself marching along the corridor the way the two crew members must have. She laughed, something she hadn't done in a long time. It felt good.

Suddenly she heard/felt a familiar voice/presence. At first she thought she was imagining it, because she yearned for Puff so much. But it was too strong, too real. She looked up.

A ball of pale blue light was gliding down from the sky, following the curve of the shell. It darted through a fancy geometric pattern, then hovered about a hundred feet outside the plastic composite. A brilliant white flash came from its core.

"Puff! Puff, you're wonderful! I'm so glad you're here. But how in the sky did you find me?" She didn't expect an answer, of course, but she was so thrilled that she couldn't help babbling. Had Puff followed her here? She hadn't sensed Puff's presence since leaving home. Maybe Puff had finished eating sunshine in the ionosphere, and found her by turning in on her mind somehow.

It didn't really matter. She and Puff were synched, and that was what counted. Puff's joy wrapped around her like a warm hug. Her love spoke/reached out to Puff.

Sitting cross-legged on the ground to get comfortable, she noticed that some of the swimmers were looking at Puff. But they just saw an ordinary fireball, and they quickly lost interest.

Puff turned her core into a pulsating heart of green fire, a trick Wanda really liked. Wanda stared at the hypnotically beautiful light show, and heard/felt an echo of Puff's total freedom.

Puff was a great listener, the only one Wanda could trust with her terrible secret. "Puff, we're on our own now," she said haltingly. "I've run away."

Puff fidgeted from the pain in Wanda's mind.

"I guess I better tell you the whole story, or you won't understand." It was all built up inside Wanda, aching to burst out. "It started at dinner, the day you put on your show for the teachers. Mom told us she was going on a supply run to Pemex Under . . ."

CHAPTER SEVENTEEN

Linda stared out the lounge's long port at the surface terrain unfolding under a cloudy mid-morning sky. The *Mayan Princess* was less than five hundred feet up, descending gradually and shedding speed. The plain below had once been fenced cropland; now it was a barren brown expanse with patches of feral growth. Rows of unhealthy-looking trees formed windbreaks beside fields, and lined roads leading to ruined farmhouses. The zep was following the dry bed of Putah Creek northwest.

She wasn't alone. The other scavengers had gathered in the lounge to watch the landing. They were from Pemex Under, and usually worked the ruins near the enclave. By reputation they were every bit as good as windrider scavengers. There were twenty of them, plus Rico Ortiz, the laser expert, and herself.

The bulkhead speaker woke. "Your attention, please, all passengers and crew. This is Captain Ramirez. We're about to land on the outskirts of scenic Davis, California. Surface drill will begin upon landing."

The three-day cruise northwest had brought about another metamorphosis in Linda. She was still terribly worried about Wanda, especially since the proctors hadn't yet found any trace of her. But the worry couldn't keep burning hot without fresh fuel to feed it. Gradually it had moved into the back of her mind, and she had become more involved in the details of the expedition. She had studied the background material, attended planning sessions, checked equipment and gotten to know the other scavengers.

As for Captain Ramirez, it hadn't been possible to avoid him under the circumstances. But she had kept their contacts minimal and strictly proper. His romantic manner seemed impervious to rejection. If only she could be as impervious to him. Despite everything that had happened, her dreams kept teasing her with possibilities.

The town of Davis hadn't been a military target, so it and the land around it hadn't been directly scarred by the War. But to the east she could make out a dark circle, the bomb crater and surrounding ruins where the city of Sacramento had been. Beyond the foothills to the west there was supposed to be another crater marking the grave of Travis Air Force Base. She was glad that the *Mayan Princess's* course hadn't taken it fifty miles west, over the slagged hills and ocean which were all that remained of the San Francisco Bay area.

She stared down at the sparse vegetation, feeling the familiar sadness from her scavenging days. With nearby blast sites in addition to the upper-atmosphere fallout, the local radiation level was almost too high for outside suit work. Yet even here the healing process was at work. Some hardy plants and animals had managed to survive, and life was returning to the land as its memory of the War faded. But it would be centuries before folks could live here again.

The vid's nose-camera view showed that the *Mayan Princess* was nearing a ribbon of cracked concrete and collapsed overpasses which had once been a highway. Beyond it a medium-sized town lay like a child's play set on the brown plain. Linda spotted the four round water towers which were the main aerial landmarks for Davis. Residential areas encircled a business district, except to the south where the buildings of the University of California were clustered.

The *Mayan Princess* was descending toward a field to the east of the campus. It had probably been used for

University agricultural research, but now it was empty
except for some patches of weeds. As the town swelled in
the vid screen, Linda saw that it was in bad shape. She
wasn't surprised. Even though it hadn't been bombed,
decades of fires, weather and earthquakes had reduced it
to semi-ruins.

Captain Ramirez demonstrated his piloting skill with
another gentle landing. As soon as the *Mayan Princess* was
resting solidly on its landing pads, Hector Lopez, the chief
scavenger, rose from his chair. His stooped shoulders,
white-fringed hair and tired yet alert eyes befitted someone who had been at his difficult, dangerous work for a
long time. He spoke to everyone in the lounge.

"Before we go out, a few reminders. First, safety. You
don't need a lecture or you wouldn't be here. But this isn't
Mexico—this is where the War was actually fought. It's
like an unshielded reactor outside, and rads are only one
worry. There may still be active toxins. Some bio-bugs
have survived in animals while waiting for their favorite
hosts—us. So watch your suit integrity, and don't touch
anything that's questionable.

"As for what to salvage, remember the briefings. Rare
metals, chemicals, machine tools, electronic components,
specialized equipment, usable supplies and so on. The
steel fabricating plant and the bio-engineering companies
that Research reported will be priority sites. Check with
the shipboard computer for ID and/or market value. The
university libraries may hold some salable information—
Professor Ortiz and Señora Calhoun will be looking into
that. Any questions?"

There were no questions, but a few knowing smiles
aimed at Linda and the young man sitting next to her. The
veteran scavengers had realized early on that Davis was
too small to justify the expense of a zep expedition. She
and Rico had dutifully dropped a few hints; Señor Cardenas'
myth about agricultural genetic engineering secrets was
now common knowledge among them.

"Then let's suit up and get on the job," Hector finished.
"We're burning golden time."

The scavengers hurried out of the lounge toward the

cargo hold. Linda and Rico were at the rear of the pack. She had spent much of the cruise in his company, because of the secret they shared. He was lanky and dark, and introverted except when talking about lasers. An instructor at Pemex Under's University, he had been picked for the expedition because of his experience doing surface research.

"Well, Rico, this is it," she said, her Spanish crumbling somewhat. She always suffered from stage fright before going outside. "For me it has been a while. I hope I remember everything."

"You do. In case you didn't notice, Señor Lopez kept an extremely close eye on both of us during the suit drills. If we weren't ready for outside work, we would have heard from him."

"I noticed." Still, it was reassuring to hear Rico say it.

In the cargo hold the flight engineer and a crewman were checking the big decon air lock which had been installed in Pemex Under. The *Mayan Princess*'s crew had been trimmed to twenty-three, barely enough to fly it, to help lighten it so it could carry the scavengers, their equipment and hopefully a full load of salvage. Linda had done some familiar housekeeping chores along with the other scavengers, since the "hotel staff" had been left behind.

The scavengers went to the lockers and began putting on their outside suits. Ignoring the loud banter around her, Linda pulled the bulky silver suit over her ship's coveralls. It looked like a work-crew suit, but there were important differences. It was heavier due to its thick anti-rad lining, and it held extra air on its back instead of a para-pack. She strapped on the tool belt, then methodically ran through the suit's checklist. It would be the only thing between her and the killzone for the next few hours. One mistake, and she would never see Wanda again.

"Your attention, please, in the cargo hold. This is Captain Ramirez." His speaker voice came faintly through her helmet, until she switched on the sound pickup. "I wish I could come there to see you off personally, but I have to make sure the wind doesn't turn the *Princess* into a tumbleweed."

She was glad that he was staying in the bridge; the last thing she needed right now was to be distracted. She wondered if he knew that.

"Remember, the *Princess* must sail by four. Don't be late. In case of an emergency, I'm as close as com channel six."

His casual tone cushioned the chilling reminder. The *Mayan Princess* couldn't safely remain long in this radiation hot spot, so every night it would have to climb above the killzone. There it would fly into the wind to remove fallout from the hull, flush the air lock, refill the air tanks, and swing out over the ocean for a water pickup.

Even if it meant leaving a scavenger behind.

"Now, my friends, I'll let you get on with your work. I hope to carry home a cargo that will shame my fellow captains. May good fortune go with you."

"In this miserable excuse for a town?" a scavenger yelled. "How's the market for concrete?" Everybody laughed.

The crawler was being maneuvered into the air lock. It resembled a cargo cart: all aluminum and gray plastic, sixteen feet long, seven wide, with an open cab seating two and a long flat bed. But instead of a cart's fat tires it had two sets of caterpillar tread on each side. As soon as it was inside the air lock, the other scavengers squeezed in. Decon used up a lot of air, so cyclings were kept to a minimum.

Linda felt a twinge of claustrophobia as the inner hatch closed, sealing the scavengers and crawler inside the cramped white compartment. A few seconds later the outer hatch swung out and down. She was the last one to walk down the short ramp to the surface. The crawler lumbered down, then the outer hatch swung back into the hull. She heard the muted howl of bad air being flushed from the air lock.

The bare ground provided uneven footing. Linda looked around at the dirt and weeds, the University buildings to the west, and the long looming curve of the *Mayan Princess*. Her breath rasped over the hiss of the suit's air system. A light breeze was kicking up dust, but of course she couldn't feel it.

She checked the wrist readouts. All of the suit's systems were green, but the radmeter reading made her sweat despite the temp control. The suit couldn't keep all of that radiation out. Radiation caused cancers and genetic damage, and destroyed bodily systems. A dose of three hundred and fifty REM killed half the time; one thousand REM killed every time. The effects of radiation exposure were cumulative. A body could repair some of the damage, and cell-regen drugs could do more. But she decided that exceeding the outside work schedule would be extremely unwise.

"*Mayan Princess* to scavengers." Linda recognized the com voice as Teresa's. "Key your telemetry, please."

Linda touched the button on her wrist, as did the others. "All telemetry on line," Teresa reported. "Good luck."

Linda felt better knowing that the shipboard computer would be keeping an eye on her, monitoring the suit's and her own functions. Support was an important word in a scavenger's vocabulary.

"Partner up," Hector ordered over the common channel. Linda walked over to Rico. As the two-man scouting teams sorted themselves out, Hector waved to the men in the crawler. "Juan, Diego, be ready to roll when we start calling in for salvage pickups."

"No problem, chief," one of them replied.

"All right. Scouts, let's go."

A car-strewn parking lot and the creek bed lay between the field and the edge of the campus. The business district was to the northwest, beyond the campus. (Linda didn't need to check the maps in the flatscreen clipped to her belt; she had memorized them.) The teams spread out in an arc as they headed for their pre-assigned scouting sectors. Linda and Rico were at the western end of the arc.

The University of California had once been a beautiful place: impressive buildings with plenty of landscaping between them, connected by a network of asphalt streets, sidewalks and bicycle paths. Linda never failed to be amazed at the mammoth scale of surface construction. And Davis wasn't even a city.

As she and Rico crossed the creek bed, she looked at

the five-story concrete block in front of her, and the smaller brown building beyond it. "That should be the Admin Center in front of the Law School," she said to Rico over the team channel. "You check me?"

"I do. The open space south of the Admin Center appears to be the beginning of the fairway."

By unspoken consensus they angled left through low brush toward the fairway. Professor Fuentes' report had stated that the Project Rainmaker headquarters was located in the basement of Wickson Hall, and the company research department had been able to furnish a map of the campus. The rest was up to them.

Her wrist readouts were all still green. The suit was wearing lightly so far, as her workouts paid an unexpected dividend.

The fairway was a wide strip of dirt and cracked asphalt running straight to the center of the campus. The buildings on both sides ranged from more big concrete blocks to Quonset huts to structures of mostly shattered white glass which had been nurseries. There were some oak and smaller trees, but few of them had survived the killzone as well as the end of irrigation. Patches of weeds and tall field grass now grew on what had once been lawns.

Occasionally Linda spotted other scavengers at work in the distance, but for the most part the two of them were overwhelmingly alone. Moldering bicycles were mute testimony to the panic and flight which had occurred here when the A-bombs exploded. The hissing breeze scattered leaves and bits of debris. Barely seen things flitted through the air and scurried amid the ruins. The small animals which had survived in the killzone were no threat to someone wearing an outside suit, but they still made her nervous. Too many horror vids.

The clatter of the scouting tools on her belt reminded her of her ugly task. She wished that she was an actual scavenger doing actual scouting. Instead she was searching through this monument of the dead for the means to kill more.

"Does it bother you, Rico?" she asked.

"I beg your pardon?"

"What we're doing. I mean, if we find the information we're looking for, does it bother you what they plan to do with it?"

Rico was quiet for a few seconds. "I suppose so, when I think about it, which I try not to. I prefer to think about working with the most sophisticated laser technology ever developed."

"I envy you your professional detachment."

He shook his head. "Don't. It's fear of such things that keeps this," he made a sweeping gesture, "from happening to us."

They had followed the fairway almost a half mile, when they came to a rectangle of open space on the right between two big buildings. "The Quad, the Library and the Student Union," she identified them aloud. Her gaze swung to the building on the left across from the Student Union. "So that must be Wickson Hall."

It was a four-story shoe box of tan-colored concrete, aluminum and broken glass, running north/south. Remains of sun awnings hung over the rows of tiny windows. Parts of the upper stories had collapsed; a dish antenna which had risen from the flat roof now hung over the edge.

"That," Rico pointed, "was a laser transceiver antenna of the sort used to communicate with orbiting satellites."

"Bingo. But that building is a structural engineer's nightmare—one good sneeze could bring it the rest of the way down."

"The basement might be undamaged."

"But will we be able to say the same if we go in?" Linda shrugged. As long as there was any chance at all, they had to try. "I don't see an unblocked entrance on this side. Let's circle around."

They walked around Wickson Hall, skirting wreckage and brush. They finally stopped at the main entrance which was on the west side. Rubble was piled up against the double doors, but they seemed passable with some work.

"Looks like we're going to have to put our backs into it," she said. "Unless you have a better idea."

Rico shook his head. "The other entrances were even

worse, and scrambling through a window would be a good
way to hole our suits. Where do we start?"

During her scavenging days Linda had acquired a keen
eye for balances and stresses. She walked around the pile,
studying the chunks of concrete and plaster. She nudged a
few experimentally, and did some rough calculating in her
head. Finally she pointed to a thick concrete slab near the
bottom. "That seems to be a keystone. If we can pull it
out, the pile should shift enough so we can get by."

Rico stared at the slab dubiously. "It looks extremely
heavy, not to mention well wedged in. Maybe we should
request some help."

"Only if we have to—they would want to know what
we're after. I think we can handle it."

"You're the engineer."

Linda tried to wrap the line from her belt around the
slab, so they could free it from a safe distance. But she
couldn't get the line around the slab's buried end. "I'm
afraid we're going to have to do this hands-on," she told
him nervously.

She and Rico squatted beside the exposed end of the
slab, took good holds on it, and braced their legs. "On the
count of three," she said. "And when it gives, back away
fast! Okay?"

"Yes."

"One . . . two . . . three!"

Linda pulled. Not the sudden jerking which dislocated
shoulders, but a steadily increasing pressure. The slab
didn't even twitch. She moaned through clenched teeth as
her tortured muscles neared their peak effort. Next to her
Rico was rigid with strain, his face gray and sweaty.

The slab moved toward them.

The pile rumbled, began to slide. Linda hopped to
regain her balance. She was about to jump backwards,
when Rico fell into her.

The ground trembled. Dust and gravel raced ahead of
the bigger chunks, battering her. There wasn't time to run
or jump. She grabbed Rico, who was futilely trying to get
up, and rolled away from the pile.

The shower of concrete and plaster thickened. Every

millisecond she expected a big chunk to find her, tearing her suit open, crushing flesh and bones. A fitting reward for carelessness. Then they rolled out of the dust cloud.

"Rico, are you all right?" she gasped.

"I seem to be. Thank you for saving my life."

"It was the least I could do, since I was the one who almost got you killed."

"Hey, what's going on out there!" Teresa demanded from the *Mayan Princess*. "Both of your telemetries just blipped off the scales!"

Linda checked her readouts, then she switched to the zep channel. "Just a minor accident. Everything is green now."

"I confirm that, but please try to be more careful."

Linda and Rico climbed awkwardly to their feet. She felt as if she had been run through a food processor.

"There's our way in," Rico said dryly, "if you're still in an adventurous mood."

The dust was settling, revealing a lower, wider pile. The steps leading up to the entrance were still mostly buried, but she could see the metal and reinforced-glass panel doors. Simple block lettering over them read WICKSON HALL.

Linda's blood was up, an exhilarating sensation that she hadn't known (except with Captain Ramirez) for much too long. She raised Teresa. "We're going inside a building. We shouldn't be out of com for more than a half hour."

"I copy."

"Ready?" Linda asked Rico. He nodded. "Then let's go."

They carefully climbed over the remaining pile. The doors had been mangled and shoved inward when the upper stories collapsed. Linda maneuvered between them into the lobby, and Rico followed her.

The lobby was a square area with corridors running right and left. By the wan light from the entrance and the empty windows she could see that it was basically intact, albeit with plenty of minor damage. Display cases along the walls held the remains of bottles, maps and pictures. There was a directory on the wall, but it was illegible.

While Linda checked the ceiling for signs of imminent collapse, Rico peered into each corridor. "There seems to be a stairwell door at the end of this one," he said, pointing left.

"The structural damage doesn't look too bad down here, but we better watch our step."

"Sound advice."

They started along the left corridor. The only light came from occasional open doors, so they switched on their helmet lamps. The linoleum floor, white plaster walls and overhead fluorescent light fixtures ran straight for about a hundred and fifty feet to the stairwell wall. The open doors revealed classrooms in various states of disrepair.

The insides of surface buildings always gave Linda the creeps, particularly when they were as undamaged as this corridor. She could almost see the students rushing to their classes, hear their happy chatter. They were long gone, but their ghosts remained. . . .

She shook her head sharply. Some scavengers cracked up; others lost their concentration and made fatal mistakes. But she wasn't going to do either.

Cautiously opening the stairwell door, she peeked in. There was an ominous blockage above the second-floor landing, but the stairway down looked clear. "We're going to have to take this part very smoothly," she told Rico. He nodded.

The stairway was narrow, and it doubled back halfway to the basement. Linda pretended that she was walking on a souffle. Their lamps warned them of rubble on the steps to be avoided. The soft scuffing of their traction heels echoed hollowly off the unfinished concrete walls.

The basement door wouldn't open. "I hope it's just stuck," she whispered. "Try to force it—gently—while I listen for trouble. If I do this," she held up her left hand, "freeze."

"As you say."

She touched her sound pickup to the wall. No vibrations; so far so good. Rico wrapped both hands around the door knob and began to pull.

For a few seconds nothing happened. Then there was a startlingly loud crack, and the door creaked open.

When Linda started breathing again, she listened intently. Still no vibrations, much to her surprise and relief. "Nicely done, Rico. In we go."

She stepped into the basement, followed quickly by Rico. The view in their lamp beams was so unlike what she had been expecting that she felt ill. "Something wrong here," she whispered urgently. "This certainly isn't Project Rainmaker."

The basement was long, and so broad that it had to extend beyond the building. Rows of square pillars supported the floors above. The damp concrete surfaces were dappled with cobwebs and patches of mold which she automatically avoided. Rows of tall wooden racks covered with wire mesh held bottles on their sides. There were antique machines, tables covered with the remains of chemistry lab glassware, and dozens of big barrels. Her imagination added a musty rotting smell.

Many of the racks had been knocked over, and chunks of the ceiling had fallen. But the most disquieting sights were the gaping fractures in the walls and pillars.

"Have we stumbled across Baron Frankenstein's laboratory?" Rico asked in a confused/disappointed/nervous tone.

Linda laughed softly. "Only if he dabbled in viticulture and enology on the side. This is a teaching winery."

"Oh. But it isn't what we're looking for. Could your information source be wrong?"

"How should I know?" Some of her own concern came out in her voice. "If he is, we've come a long way for nothing. Let's look around," she suggested because she didn't know what else to do.

They started across the cavernous room. Linda didn't like the way things seemed to be lurking in the darkness just beyond her helmet beam. She thought she heard faint chittering noises. She was about to attribute them to nerves, when she spotted a pair of tiny close-set eyes near the floor. "I don't think we're alone in here," she told Rico.

"I was hoping I was imagining that."

She saw more eyes as they went. Then Rico managed to

catch a pair with his beam; they got a momentary look at
the owner before it disappeared.

"A rat," she muttered in disgust. "I wonder why the
most worthless creatures turned out to be the best
survivors."

"That . . . creature was over a foot and a half long!" Rico
gasped. "I always thought the notion of mutant monsters
was foolish, but . . ."

"According to the background material, they grew that
big around here before the War. Sounds like it has plenty
of friends. I hope they keep on being afraid of us—they
can't gnaw through our suits, but I can still do without
their company."

They reached the far wall without encountering anything more unpleasant than beady eyes. It was lined with
racks and barrels, but there were no doors.

They had come to the end of the trail.

"None of this makes any sense," Rico objected. "Project
Rainmaker wasn't a military project, but it was operating a
laser satellite, so there would have been some effort at
security. You wouldn't be able to just walk in the way we
did. This can't be the right building."

Linda was thinking the same thing. She was about ready
to call it quits, her disappointment tinged with relief. Then
her engineering sense twitched.

"Do you recall how long the building is?" she asked, her
voice rising in excitement.

"Roughly."

"This basement isn't even half as long. Does that suggest anything to you?"

"More basement beyond the wall?" Rico looked thoughtful for several seconds. "It makes sense. Wall off half of
the basement, put in a private entrance—the one at the
building's south end—and you have unobtrusive security.
Excavating that entrance is going to be a major job."

"It might not be necessary." Moving along the wall,
Linda found what she remembered seeing on the way
over. A long, widening crack in the concrete disappeared
behind one of the racks. "Help me move this rack, please."

They manhandled it away from the wall. Behind it, as

she had hoped, the crack became wide enough for them to climb through. "Shall we?" she suggested.

"Ladies first."

She carefully squeezed through the crack, ending up on a broken linoleum floor. She helped Rico through.

"Well, we're somewhere," she said. "But where?"

They moved their beams around. They found themselves in a white corridor with doors along the far wall. The damage was extensive, but the corridor seemed to be navigable and reasonably safe. Linda aimed her lamp at the nearest door.

It had a nameplate, tarnished but still readable. Under the big STAFF LOUNGE she was able to make out in smaller lettering PROJECT RAINMAKER.

She smiled. "Double bingo."

CHAPTER EIGHTEEN

Sergeant West of B Platoon's second squad wasn't a happy man. After the Tokyo Four sortie Patterson's Plunderers had been due for some R-and-R. He should have been blowing his action bonus in Alpha's red-light level; instead he was here.

His surface combat suit, a liberated scavenging outfit overlaid with camouflage-colored plastic armor, weighed a few megatons. Sweat stung his eyes despite the cooling system, he needed to scratch all over, and his muscles ached from hours of cramped immobility. Worst of all, he didn't like what his wrist readouts were telling him about the radiation level. Somebody was going to pay for this.

Probably the two civvies out there trying to uncover Wickson Hall's main entrance.

Sergeant West was a squat slab of muscle, with thick arms and legs and virtually no neck. He shaved his head as part of his tough image, and had picked up some sword scars plus a broken nose living up to it. He and PFC Williams were crouched below the sill of a blown-out window on the first floor of the Student Union. The rest of the second squad was staked out in pairs on the other sides of Wickson Hall. His orders called for a covert recon. Why, he didn't know and didn't care. Orders were orders.

He grinned when the civvies almost brought the rubble

piled against the entrance down on themselves. PFC Williams laughed (they were wire-jacked for com silent communications) and said, "Shit, those two are gonna do themselves before we get the chance."

"Keep your eyes open and that wound under your nose shut," Sergeant West snapped. Sergeants didn't socialize with grunts.

"Sure, Sarge."

They watched the civvies get up and go into the building. "Now what, Sarge?" PFC Williams asked.

"Now you stay put and on the bounce, while I report to HQ."

Sergeant West unjacked, made sure his sword was ready for quick use, and crawled away from the window before standing up. He worked his way through the half-collapsed corridors to a back exit. Outside under the cloudy sky he took a deep breath; he had been expecting the whole damned place to fall on him.

He set out north across the campus. Having been on surface patrols before, he hadn't been spooked like some of the greenies. His suit wasn't built for stealth, but he did the best he could, bending low and using the available cover. He didn't spot any civvies or other aircavs, just wind-blown trash and a few small animals. The civvies weren't supposed to know they had company until the right time.

Then they would find out the hardest way.

Coming to a low building in better shape than most, he waved in the direction of the unseen sentries and went inside. One of the doors across the lobby was open. He headed for it.

Portable lamps lit a big room which had been some sort of lab. Its good condition, lack of windows and still-usable metal furniture had caused Captain Patterson to pick it for the company's field HQ. A Platoon's first squad was busy taking reports from runners, working at mapscreens (not easy in combat suits), and passing on summaries to Captain Patterson in his partitioned office. The tech sergeant was sitting in front of a radio linked to an antenna hidden on the roof.

The *Shenandoah* had landed the company here at dawn,

before withdrawing east out of visual range of the approaching Pemex Under zep. A platoon had set up the HQ, B Platoon's second squad had surrounded Wickson Hall, and the rest of the company had staked out the likeliest landing sites for a zep. According to the battle plan, C and D Platoons were now shadowing the scavenging teams, while B Platoon's first squad was keeping an eye on the Pemex Under zep.

Sergeant West went straight to the pretty-boy lieutenant and saluted. "Sir!" he said on the com, which was safe to use now that he was well indoors.

"Report, Sergeant."

He crisply described the activities of the two civvies. When he finished the lieutenant said, "Wait here, Sergeant," and disappeared into Captain Patterson's office.

He didn't have to wonder what was up for long. Captain Patterson came out from behind the plastic partition like a cruise missile. The aircav commander wasn't particularly big, strong or tough-looking, but he had something which Sergeant West could only vaguely define as style. He was an aircav's aircav.

They exchanged salutes, then Captain Patterson spoke in his rock-crusher voice. "You say only two civvies went into Wickson Hall?"

"Yes, sir."

Captain Patterson looked pleased. "Our friendly told us that Pemex Under was trying to keep its search secret. So much the better for us. Come with me, Sergeant. The show is about to start, and you're going to play a big role."

Confused but warmed by the implied praise, Sergeant West followed Captain Patterson over to the radio. Captain Patterson caught the radio operator's eye and said, "Encode a message for *Shenandoah*."

"Yes, sir."

"Captain Patterson to Colonel McCrarey. Two civvies, probably the ones referred to in our friendly's report, went into Wickson Hall at eleven oh five hours. Nine scavenging teams and a crawler are spread out across the campus and the business district, and the Pemex Under zep is still in landing mode. No signs of detection. My men are in position. Out."

The radio operator touched two buttons on the radio's panel. "Encoded and sent, sir." Messages between the field HQ and the *Shenandoah* were a necessary risk, and a very small one. Before the Pemex Under zep's radioman could identify them as anything but static, it would be too late.

They waited. Captain Patterson stood perfectly still, watching nothing and everything, while Sergeant West shifted his weight restlessly from leg to leg. Around them the HQ kept working, but they were definitely the center of a lot of attention.

A couple of long minutes later a green light flashed on the radio's panel. The radio operator touched another button, and Sergeant West straightened instinctively as Colonel McCrarey's voice came from his helmet speaker.

"Colonel McCrarey to Captain Patterson. The *Shenandoah* will commence its attack run on the Pemex Under zep at twelve ten hours. You'll commence your surface action at the same time. Eliminate the scavenging teams, but take the civvies in Wickson Hall alive. Remember, the whole point of your action is to get them to do the dirty work for us—don't kill the goose until we find out if it has any golden eggs for us. When the Pemex Under zep tries to escape, the *Shenandoah* will burn it out of the sky. Good hunting, Captain. Out."

Captain Patterson turned to Sergeant West. "Have you got the picture now, Sergeant?"

"Uh . . . not all of it, sir."

"This mission has two objectives. One is to eliminate the Pemex Under expedition—you heard how we're going to handle that. The second is to get certain information about a Project Rainmaker which operated out of the basement of Wickson Hall."

Sergeant West figured asking what sort of information they were after would be a bad move. So he worded his question carefully. "May I ask what form the information will be in?"

"That's why we let Pemex Under carry the ball this far. Nobody knows. At twelve ten hours you'll take half of your squad inside Wickson Hall, leaving the other half on perimeter guard. Capture the civvies as intact as possible, and take particular care with any salvage in their possession. Secure the Project Rainmaker site. When the *Shenandoah* lands, the civvies will be taken aboard for interrogation and a tech team will go over the site. Any questions?"

"No, sir."

Captain Patterson put a hand on his shoulder. "I'm sure I picked the right man for the job, Sergeant."

"Thank you, sir."

Captain Patterson walked to the middle of the HQ. "Men," he said loudly, and everybody froze, "we jump off at twelve ten hours. I expect every one of you to be on the bounce. Runners, get the word to your units. Move out!"

The HQ erupted into excited noise and activity. Sergeant West felt his ambition stirring as he headed for the doorway with the other runners. Something big was going on, and this mysterious information was the key. Why should the officers make all the points? If he could come up with the information, he might be wearing lieutenant's bars by Christmas.

Even if it meant bending his orders as well as the two civvies.

CHAPTER NINETEEN

Hector Lopez swept his helmet lamp around the windowless darkness of the back room of Feldman's TV and Stereo Emporium. Looting, weather and earthquakes had all but eliminated the salvage value of the showroom. But here stock was piled on the still-standing shelves along the cracked plaster walls, or lay on the faded linoleum floor, surrounded by bits of the packing materials.

Unclipping the pick from his belt and unfolding it, he started attacking the TV sets, stereos and VCR's. He hacked out the circuit boards and tossed them into the plastic sack which he had spread open on the floor. His technique put speed ahead of delicacy; the semi-conductors and so on were destined for materials recycling rather than reuse.

"Hey, chief, watch where you're swinging that thing!" Geraldo Santos yelled on the team channel as he carried an armload of replacement parts past Hector to his own sack.

Hector shrugged and said nothing. During their fourteen years of scavenging together he had learned to ignore his partner's incessant complaining. Geraldo knew his job, which was all that mattered.

Hector's thoughts were never far from Carmen. His beloved, beautiful Carmen, waiting at home for him to return and worrying about his safety. Scavenging was dangerous work, but she never complained. She accepted that it was what he did. Raising their children by herself during his long trips was difficult; she never complained about that either. Rico and Innocencia were filled with her wisdom, energy and love. The three of them were the joy at the center of his world.

"What's the matter? Are you dazzled by this veritable cornucopia of prime salvage?" Geraldo snorted.

Hector understood how his partner felt. University lab supplies, a few steel fabricating tools, books about farming, miscellaneous items from stores and distributors: the cargo was going to be a joke. He hoped Professor Ortiz and Señora Calhoun found whatever they were hunting for; otherwise the expedition would be a total fiasco.

Fortunately the company had put up a high guarantee to recruit scavengers for the expedition (high enough to trigger his suspicions). The pay would let him postpone his next trip for a few months, so he could spend more time with Carmen and the children. For that he had accepted whatever mystery came with the expedition. But he planned to be even more careful than usual.

"Full up," Geraldo announced.

Hector sealed his sack. "Same here. Let's haul them outside."

They dragged the sacks through the ruined showroom out onto the asphalt sidewalk in front of the car-littered street. Several other bulging sacks lined both sides of the street. All salvage went into radtight sacks, so it could be safely handled until it was deconned.

Hector called the *Mayan Princess*. "Lopez here. How are the other teams doing?"

"Sixteen telemetries are reading green," the radioman replied. "Four are out of com but not overdue, and they were reading green at the last contact."

"Thanks. By the way, we're ready for a pickup."

"Who isn't? Right now the crawler is bringing in a load of chemical fertilizers. I'll put you on the list—ETA twenty minutes."

"We'll be here," Hector sighed, and switched back to the team channel.

"That fertilizer might actually be worth something if it hasn't decomposed," Geraldo said. "What next, chief?"

Hector looked around, at the partly wrecked storefronts, the dead and dying maple trees, the wind-stirred dust, and the openness without end. The surface was a treasure trove, but he hated and feared it. He wished that he was back in Pemex Under with Carmen bustling around the apartment and his children in his lap. Yet a man did what he had to do.

The sound of heavy boots on asphalt caught his attention. He turned, and Geraldo did too.

Three strangers had appeared around the corner of the block. Their scavenging suits were covered with brown and green plastic plates like fish scales, a feature which he had never heard of and didn't understand. A long, sheathed cutter hung from each belt instead of the usual selection of tools. Through their helmets he saw that they were anglos.

He was surprised. The surface was a big place, and the odds were very high against two expeditions scavenging the same site at the same time, especially such a worthless prize as Davis. He switched to the common channel and spoke in English. "Welcome, gentlemen. I'm Hector Lopez, the chief scavenger of this Pemex Under expedition. And you are?"

The strangers didn't answer. They were about fifty feet away, walking briskly toward them.

"Hey, there's no reason to be upset," Geraldo told them. "There's plenty of nothing here for everyone. If we both want the same item, we can flip a coin."

More silence. They were thirty feet away now, and it seemed to Hector that they were grinning.

His soul turned cold. Their muteness, bizarre outfits, unvarying pace: it was as if they had emerged from some dark Aztec legend. He blinked, but they were still there. He felt an inexplicable urge to run, even as he tried to figure out what in the ground was going on.

They were ten feet away now. They pulled out their cutters, and the glistening strips of metal looked more like ancient weapons than scavenging tools. Geraldo was staring open-mouthed.

Hector could make out the nature of their grins, the set

of their eyes. He had never seen such expressions before. But the blood of his ancestors recognized them. His right hand reached for the pick on his belt, his left switched his com to the zep channel. "We're—"

Too late. One of the cutters swung at his neck. He ducked, and it was deflected jarringly by his suit's neck ring. He staggered. In a moment of surreal horror he watched Geraldo's helmet and head bounce on the sidewalk.

The strangers closed in on him, their murderous lust blotting out the world. Something sharp and very cold pierced his suit, his coveralls, his chest.

A pain greater than all other pains tore him apart. He screamed bubblingly. Clinging to that which was nearest and dearest, he slid down into the final darkness.

Carmen . . .

CHAPTER TWENTY

In the *Mayan Princess*'s bridge Captain Miguel Ramirez was sitting back in his chair, feet up on the edge of his console, whistling softly. At times like this it wasn't easy for him to project a relaxed attitude. But if the captain looked worried, his crew would assume he had good reason to, and they would worry too. Worry interfered with efficiency. So he had made an art of seeming unconcerned.

Appearances to the contrary, he had quite a bit to occupy his mind. First, he was unobtrusively keeping track of all that went on around him. The cloud cover was still thick over the fields and ruins beyond the windscreen. Elena was concentrating on her flight controls, poised to act upon a moment's notice. Jose was unhappily studying his weather displays. Teresa was taking pickup calls and monitoring the telemetries which rolled up her console's main screen. He listened to their reports, and periodically checked the displays in front of him to reinforce his intuitive feel for the *Princess*'s well-being.

Then there was the constant awareness of his command responsibilities, which on this trip were even more demanding than usual. One landed zep, twenty-two scavengers at their dangerous work, a secret mission of vital importance to Pemex Under: the burden would have crushed an ordinary man. The last two matters were out of his hands for the moment. All he could do was wish the scavengers well, and make sure they had a serviceable zep to return to.

It was a galling situation for a man of action.

"Captain, the wind is gusting up to eleven MPH," Jose reported, "still out of the west."

Miguel turned to Elena. "What would you do if you were me?"

"I would retire and let younger talent move up. Or I would use the motors to offset the gusts, distributing some of the strain on the frame."

Miguel laughed. Their friendship had endured beyond their romance, a rarity for him. She was a treasure, and she was going to make a fine zep captain someday. "Go ahead, my pretty pilot. Mind the power drain."

"Aye aye, great hawk of the sky."

He heard and felt motors waking as he turned to Jose. "If the wind reaches sixteen MPH," he told the navigator, "we'll have to call in the scavengers and cast off. How does the short-range forecast look?"

"The wind should hold below sixteen through the rest of the afternoon. The overcast will stay, but no rain."

All immediate decisions made, the romantic side of his nature returned to the problem which had been on his mind for days. Linda. Lovely, troubled, yearning Linda. He had been fascinated by her since their first meeting. Now he knew he loved her with the great passion a man held for a woman once in a lifetime. That she was married was unfortunate, but not an insurmountable obstacle. He was determined to win her. He would explode like Krakatoa if the love inside him remained unrequited.

Somehow, despite exquisite orchestration, his initial campaign had failed. Now she was preoccupied with her role in the expedition and her missing daughter, just as he was with his responsibilities. But when the *Princess* returned to Pemex Under, and mother and daughter were happily reunited, he would again lay his heart at her feet. This time he would succeed.

A very personal worry stood out among his professional concerns. Linda had been out of com for over twenty minutes, after reporting that she and Professor Ortiz were entering Wickson Hall. His imagination conjured various accidents which might have befallen her there. He wished he could have gone with her, to help and protect her. But a captain was a prisoner of duty.

He pushed the uncharcteristically bleak line of thought from his mind. Linda was an experienced scavenger; she knew the dangers of surface work, and how to avoid them.

"Oh my God!" Teresa shrieked.

Miguel kicked his chair around. A moment later he was standing behind her. "What is it?" he demanded.

She was frantically slapping buttons and twisting dials. Her face had turned ashen, and the roll of fat around her middle was actually trembling. He followed her eyes to the telemetry screen. The data lines glowed greenly. But where many of them should have been, there were only flashing bars.

When telemetry flatlined, it meant a life had ended.

Miguel struggled to keep the shock out of his voice. "Are you sure there isn't a flaw in the system?"

"That's what I've been checking! There's no mistake!"

Please, he begged, not Linda. "Who was it? And what happened?"

"Who! Thirteen—no, fourteen so far! Sudden, severe trauma and loss of suit integrity! No explanation or warning!"

Fourteen scavengers dead. Fourteen. This was a disaster beyond his experience, almost beyond belief. What in the sky was going on out there? He was aware of Elena's and Jose's horror echoing his own. "Teresa, raise one of the remaining scavengers," he said as calmly as he could manage. "Anyone."

Her hands moved quickly over the suit com panel. The bulkhead speaker crackled, then a scared voice yelled, "—need help!" The words became a scream which ended with ghastly suddenness.

She thumbed a button. Another voice croaked, "—strange men cut Carlos's head off . . . chasing me . . . no, don't!" The transmission stopped.

"Sixteen telemetries flatlined!" she choked.

Somebody was killing the scavengers. It made no sense, it wasn't possible, yet it was happening. Then a lightning bolt of understanding came to him. Could the attackers be the hostile force that destroyed zeps and windriders? It fit. Somehow they had learned about this supposedly secret mission, and they were here to keep Pemex Under from learning how to build laser weapons.

His suspicions flared up into white-hot rage. "Keep the con," he told Elena over his shoulder as he headed for the door. "Stand by to cast off if I order it, or if I drop out of com."

"Where are you going?"

"Outside. I'm taking a party to rescue any survivors and retrieve the dead."

He started to open the door, but a slim arm held it shut. He spun. Elena had violated regs by leaving her controls. "Get back to your station," he snapped.

Her frightened, determined face was inches away from his. "You heard the scavengers!" she almost shouted. "They're being butchered! If you lead some crewmen out there like an avenging angel, you'll just be supplying more victims! I know you! You want to punish whoever is doing this, and you don't care if you die trying! But you don't have the right!"

He mastered his anger at the insistence of her dark eyes, and thought. It sounded like the attackers were using swords, while there wasn't anything even resembling a weapon aboard the *Princess*. Could a handful of unarmed zepmen hope to accomplish anything? Just the end Elena had described. But if not that, then what could he do?

What was next on the attackers' agenda?

Zep captains were well paid. They wore impressive uniforms, they enjoyed many privileges, and beautiful ladies admired them. They also got to make the sort of decisions which shamed a man for life.

"Thanks, Elena," he said softly. He walked back to his chair, forcing every step. Elena returned to her duties without a word.

"Twenty telemetries flatlined," Teresa reported dully. "Professor Ortiz and Señora Calhoun are still out of com."

Miguel steeled himself against his outraged heart. Linda was surely dead too, her small, soft body lying in a bloody puddle somewhere inside Wickson Hall. He almost hoped so. Otherwise he would be the one killing her.

Switching his com to the all-ship channel, he composed himself before speaking. "Your attention, please, all crew. This is Captain Ramirez. Emergency drill. I repeat, emergency drill. The scavenging party has been attacked by an unidentified group—there are no survivors. I must assume the *Princess* will be the next target. Prepare to cast off."

He could almost feel the shock spreading through the zep. But his crew was the finest in the fleet; they would do their duty.

"Teresa," he said, "can you set up a radio relay to Pemex Under?"

She typed on her keyboard and checked the computer screen. "None of our zeps are in relay position, but I should be able to set one up through a windrider."

"Please do."

Teresa went to work, while Miguel considered how to word his report so he wouldn't sound mad. Suddenly she yelped, tore her headset off, and rubbed her ears. Displays were flashing red on her radio panel.

"What now?" Miguel sighed.

Teresa punched up the radio's diagnostic program and studied the readout before answering. "A few seconds after I started sending, a powerful incoming signal burned out every circuit in the transmitter. We're out of com."

"How is that possible?"

"Ask a com engineer—I'm just a radioman. But I read that before the War the military had a way to do it using a focused electromagnetic pulse."

"Can you fix the transmitter?"

"There's nothing left to fix! Both the on-line and the backup chips are fused, and we don't have another in stores because the company is too cheap!"

Miguel had an ominous feeling that this had happened to other zep captains. He couldn't call for help, couldn't even warn anyone about the attack. He wondered what other military equipment the attackers had. The windscreen, monitor screens and radar still showed images of serenity, but he knew how deceptive they were. Was the *Princess* about to become the next unexplained loss?

Not if he could prevent it.

"Still no word from Señora Calhoun or Professor Ortiz?" he asked Teresa levelly.

"Nothing."

He took back the con from Elena, then reopened the all-ship channel. "Your attention, please, all crew. This is Captain Ramirez. We're about to cast off. Brace for maneuvering."

Trying to ignore the hazel eyes, blond hair and elfin face of the ghost who was already haunting him, he turned all of his attention to his flight controls.

CHAPTER TWENTY-ONE

Linda led the way along the rubble-strewn corridor. It was pitch-black except where their lamp beams fell. In places the ceiling had collapsed, creating mounds of concrete and plaster which they had to climb over. She moved slowly, carefully, watching for structural weak points to be avoided. This part of the basement was even more of a deathtrap than the stairwell. Her nerves were wound tight, and the bruises from her fall were throbbing.

They checked each door they came to, either by managing to read the faded nameplate or by opening the door and looking inside. She avoided the second approach as much as possible, because disturbing stress vectors here was risky. She hoped that they would come across a readable directory.

They found the room they were looking for first.

The plate on the metal door read SATELLITE OPERATIONS. "Triple bingo!" she announced. "This must be where they worked with the laser satellite."

"And where we should find some sort of operating manual." Rico sounded as if he was licking his lips.

Linda tried gently to open the door. It was locked or stuck. Rico added his strength, to no avail.

"I could give it a kick," he suggested.

"You could also bring the whole building down on top of us. Let's try melting our way in."

She cut three lengths of thermite cord from the spool in her belt pouch, treating them with the instinctive respect that townsfolk felt for things highly combustible, and wrapped them around the door's hinges. She touched the igniter to them, then quickly stepped back. When they stopped sizzling and spitting white flames, she and Rico were able to pull the door out of its frame and lean it against the wall.

Linda looked around carefully, making sure the thermite hadn't started any fires. She took advantage of the pause to suck some water from her helmet's nipple. Then she stepped through the doorway, and Rico followed her.

They moved their beams around to get an overview of the room. Linda's excitement quantum-jumped when she saw that there wasn't any major damage. The room was narrow and filled with electronic equipment; it looked very much like a windrider's bridge. Consoles and overhead monitor screens lined the long walls, while computers, memory units and cabinets were clustered at the far end. The flourescent light tubes were painted red.

"Well," Rico said somewhat helplessly, "where should we begin?"

That was a very good question. She peered around more thoroughly, trying to sort out what had been done where. The electronic equipment was primitive but mostly recognizable. One row of consoles seemed to be the satellite's telemetry; the other was apparently for weather analysis, communications, computing and systems monitoring. The gray cabinets were more electronics, while the glass-fronted ones contained memory disks, videotape cassettes, printed material in various stages of decomposition, and supplies.

There was so much here to fascinate Linda, to distract her from the search. Had Project Rainmaker succeeded? Could weather patterns actually be changed by laser satellites? Irrelevant now, of course, but she knew that the ghosts hovering around her would be pleased if their work could become part of the human database.

She idly thumbed the power switch on a console, but nothing happened. She laughed at herself. The salvage value roused her scavenging instinct. She would have to tell Hector about it, after she and Rico found what they had come for.

"It's all so . . . tidy," Rico commented softly. "They didn't panic and run. They shut down by the numbers, put everything away, and locked up behind them. As if they expected to come back."

Linda shook her head. "They would have known better. But they might have hoped somebody would come back, someday. And here we are."

"We could begin by checking titles," Rico suggested. He took a book out of one of the cabinets. It crumbled in his gloved hand.

"If the satellite manual is on paper," Rico said as dust fell through his fingers, "we have a serious problem."

"Too true. But I don't think it is."

"May I ask why not?"

"Convenience and security. The manual would be easier to use in disk format, and limiting access to it would be easier too."

"That sounds like wishful thinking to me."

"Part of every scavenger's kit," Linda admitted. "Let's check the disks, and hope for the best."

They walked over to the pair of tall disk storage cabinets. Each held five rows of twelve inch metal disks in upright slots. Linda opened a glass door, and pulled out a disk to examine it. Her lamp beam slid over the smooth surface, breaking up into iridescence.

"Laser disk technology certainly has come a long way since these monsters." Rico shook his head. "The bytes might as well have been carved on granite blocks."

Linda peered below the slots, looking for some sort of identification system. Three-digit numbers were pressed into metal strips; the filler, if any, was long gone. "Now all we need is the directory."

Rico's beam swept down to scraps of paper on the floors of the cabinets.

Linda sighed. "I suppose we could take all the disks."

"That would require several trips, during any one of which the ceiling could collapse on us. I would feel better about risking it if we knew for sure that the manual is among them. We might end up with nothing more than a few thousand hours of experimental data."

"We can't read them here," she snapped, irritated because he was echoing her own doubts. Something felt wrong. She mentally reran her examination of the room until she came to opening the cabinet door, at which point she screeched to a stop. "You're right, Rico."

"I am?"

"We're going about this the wrong way. If the manual contains the sort of information we're after, it would have been guarded. They wouldn't have kept it in an unlocked cabinet. Since there aren't any disks in the memory units, it must be wherever it was stored when not in use. In a safe place."

"Maybe it's in a senior official's office," Rico offered.

Linda shook her head. "I think not. It would be kept here for convenience. Please check that side of the room," pointed arbitrarily to her right, "while I check this side. We're looking for something which should be fairly easy to spot."

"And that is?"

"A lock."

They started searching. The doors of the electronics cabinets were locked, but they were only protecting circuitry. The locked panels on the consoles and other equipment also turned out to be for access. Linda was beginning to wonder if there was a flaw in her reasoning, when Rico shouted, "Over here!"

One of the telemetry consoles had a square door in the right side of its base, and the door was locked. "It could be a cabinet for special material," he said eagerly.

"Or just another access panel." But she could feel her pulse and respiration speeding up. "Let's find out."

Even with two scavenging picks at work, the door took a good deal of prying before it popped open. Linda stooped so that her beam illuminated the inside.

It was a single-shelf cabinet. Spiral rings were almost all that remained of several notebooks. Beside them lay a handgun in a rotting leather holster.

There was also a red-painted metal box of the right size to hold two memory disks.

She pulled the box out with trembling hands. It was definitely a disk holder. On the front faded letters read GOES-NINETEEN, SECURITY CLASSIFICATION SIX.

"GOES," she said shakily, "was the series designation for the Unites States weather observation satellites. Nineteen was the Project Rainmaker satellite. They pretended it was an observation satellite for security reasons."

Opening the holder, she tipped it and two glistening disks slid halfway out. They looked intact.

Suddenly she wished that she could look into the future, and see what would come from this discovery. Would taking the satellite manual back to Pemex Under lead to a safer sky? Or would it be better to trample the disks under her boots here and now? Unfortunately she didn't have a crystal ball. She could only do what seemed right.

"Aren't you going to say quadruple bingo?" Rico asked, staring hungrily at the disks.

"I'm not so sure this is a moment we'll remember with pride." She took a deep breath. "Anyway, we found what we came for. Let's get out of here. We're closing in on our out-of-com time limit, and the sooner we put more protection between us and the killzone the better."

"I agree," Rico said absently. Most of his mind seemed to be pondering the contents of the manual.

She sealed the holder in a decon sack, and clipped it to her belt. Then they headed for the doorway. She led the way into the corridor.

"All right, you two, stay right where you are!" a strange voice growled in English on the common channel. Lamp beams struck them from both sides. Momentarily dazzled, she froze. She sensed Rico beside her, also still.

When her eyes cleared she saw that two men in bizarre scavenging suits were standing ten feet along the corridor to her right, and two more to her left. Their grins didn't seem very pleasant.

Each one was holding a long cutter pointed at her and Rico.

CHAPTER TWENTY-TWO

Linda's first reaction was to laugh. The threatening poses were overly melodramatic, and the suits looked like something out of Wanda's school plays. Or so it seemed for a moment. Then she remembered the windrider eater.

The laughter died in her throat.

"Who are you?" Rico asked on the common channel. "Please put those cutters away before you hurt someone."

One of the men, wide and bald, took a step forward. "We'll ask the questions, civvie! You'll answer up fast and straight, if you want to keep breathing. What did you find in there?"

"I don't see that it's any of your business, whoever you are." Irritation entered Rico's voice. "We scavenged this site first, so anything we found is ours. Now please get out of our way."

Horrified, Linda realized that Rico thought the men were rival scavengers. She had no such illusion. Only one thing could explain the presence of these violent strangers here and now. They had to be part of the windrider eater. Somehow it had learned about the plan to build military lasers, and sent them to keep any laser information from reaching Pemex Under.

How were they going to do that? Men who routinely killed thousands, including children, certainly wouldn't hesitate to kill two more.

"What's that, bitch?" The bald man pointed his cutter at the decon sack hanging from Linda's belt.

She couldn't speak. Her mind was filled with death: her own, personal, ultimate end. Life after death was religious wishful thinking. Windrider townsfolk weren't squeamish about dying. They faced it squarely, as they had to face everything in their microcosms. It was always there, sometimes waiting patiently in the background, sometimes stepping forward. She had seen it in many of its ugliest forms. It had taken away folks whom she had known, liked and loved, and she had felt its nearness herself several times. She had always thought that she would be able to accept it when her time came.

She had been wrong. She was terrified. Her body shook, wave after wave of nausea swept through her, and her bowels were moving. She wasn't ready to die. Not yet, not with everything in such disarray. Not while Wanda was lost and hating her. She had to find Wanda, put things right between them. Then, maybe then she could face the endless night. But not now!

The bald man's cutter waved in front of her face. "You better answer me, bitch, or you aren't going to like what happens next."

"Stop that!" Rico shouted. "You could put a hole in her suit!"

The bald man laughed. "Wake up, civvie. Like the bitch here—she knows the drill." The point of his cutter came to rest touching Linda's suit over her heart. "Talk to me, bitch."

"You're going to kill us no matter what," she managed to reply despite a constricted chest and pounding heart. "You can't let us return home—as they say in old books, we know too much. So why should I answer your questions?"

"Because there's another way to go. Answer up, and we'll take both of you back to Alpha to be slaves. Our whores live pretty good. You look like you could heat up a bunk."

Linda's shaking increased. A moment ago she had feared death more than anything else; now it might be the best option left to her. What in the sky was the windrider eater, that it could create a man like this? Even confronted by his undeniable reality, she could scarcely believe he existed. What kind of a mind actually enjoyed causing pain, degradation and death? She wanted to ask him, so she could at least understand, but she sensed a gulf between them too wide for meaningful communication.

Now that it was too late, now that the satellite manual would never reach Pemex Under, she realized what a disaster that would be. The towns and zeps would continue to be helpless against the windrider eater. This . . . disease would go on killing and destroying, incurable.

"Last chance, bitch," the bald man snarled. The point of his cutter pushed slightly against her suit.

"No!" Rico shouted. He threw himself at the bald man. The bald man's free arm swung like a club, knocking Rico to the floor. Linda was relieved to see that Rico's helmet hadn't cracked. He struggled awkwardly to his feet.

The bald man said something on another com channel, and two of the other men closed in on Rico. Grabbing him, they held him with his arms twisted behind him.

The bald man walked over to him, grinning thinly. "I only need one of you to answer questions, tough guy. You just bought yourself the losing ticket. Maybe watching you choke on your own blood will smarten up the bitch." His cutter rose toward Rico's chest. Rico struggled futilely, his face flushed, his eyes angry slits.

Linda had to stop it. There wasn't any point in keeping the secret now; they would find out all about the manual when they took it from her and ran it. All her stubbornness would accomplish was to get Rico killed. "It's an operating manual," she said levelly.

The bald man looked at her. "Say what?"

"You wanted to know what I have in the decon sack. Two ROM disks, an operating manual for the Project Rainmaker satellite."

"That's it?" The bald man looked puzzled.

"Yes! Now let Rico go!"

"You need a lesson in manners, bitch." The bald man's cutter pierced Rico's suit twice, quickly but deeply, entering his body over each lung. Rico screamed. Bright red blood gushed from his mouth, splashing across the inside of his helmet.

The sheer monstrousness of the act paralyzed Linda for a moment. She felt as if she had been stabbed too. Then she stepped toward Rico, out of instinct rather than any real hope of helping him. But the bald man's reddened cutter tip touched her chest. She stopped.

Rico took a long time to die. He coughed bubblingly; soon she couldn't see his gray face through the blood. Red was also seeping out of the two cuts in his suit. His struggles became weaker, and finally stopped. He hung limply in the grip of the two men. At a gesture from the bald man they let him slide to the floor.

"You didn't have to kill him," Linda whispered, looking up from the ghastly corpse at four grins which were even ghastlier.

"He came at me, bitch. Any hostile does that, I do him. Or her."

Adjusting (or becoming numb) to the horror of the situation, Linda found that she could think analytically again. She glanced at the corridor's walls and ceiling, and spotted the thing she remembered from earlier. It offered a very small chance for escape, a much bigger one for a clean death.

"Give me that sack," the bald man told her.

She backed away from him, toward a certain part of the wall. She didn't have to fake a helpless, terrified expression. "Why do you want it?" she asked to stall him.

"None of your business, bitch. You do what you're told, or you'll die a lot slower than your pal did." He moved toward her, holding his free hand out.

Linda's hands were behind her. Hopefully shielded from view, she felt across the plaster for the sheared concrete support with its upper section sitting precariously on the edge of the lower. She found it as the bald man flicked his cutter in front of her face.

She shoved the upper section sideways with all the strength she could manage in the awkward pose. Desperation channeled every bit of her energy into the effort.

The upper section gave, and dropped with a thunderous crack.

The bald man's expression flickered through surprise to anger. She expected to die then, and anticipated the sensation of the cold piercing metal. But the bald man only reached for her.

She dove under his arm, sliding across the linoleum. All four men spun and lunged at her.

A loud, ominous groaning from overhead distracted them. They looked up. She didn't have to; she knew what it was. She crawled as fast as she could.

The ceiling came down.

The false ceiling, fiberboard panels and fluorescent light fixtures in a metal framework, sagged and buckled. Slabs of concrete tore through it, crashing to the floor. A rain of smaller chunks pounded her flat. The cracking and rumbling overloaded her sound pickup, almost deafening her even through her helmet. Dust rose in a cloud that swallowed the corridor.

A big slab cratered the linoleum a few inches to her left. For a moment she was afraid that she had triggered a major collapse, then the noise level began to subside. Behind her she heard a groan of pain and angry yells. She was alive, but so were at least some of the windrider eater's men. She kept moving.

She emerged from the dust cloud, jumped to her feet, and ran. Her lamp beam lurched wildly as she scrambled over rubble piles and around corners, turning the corridors into a strobe nightmare. Sobs mingled with her gasping for air. Adrenalin brushed aside her tiredness and put a sharp edge on all her senses. The new bruises on her back and legs throbbed painfully. Her suit readouts, surprisingly, were still green. But rad sickness was now the least of her worries.

She heard echoes of her own boots pounding on linoleum coming from behind her. Chasing her.

Her first thought was to switch off her lamp and hide. In the pitch-black labyrinth of Project Rainmaker she should be able to find a safe place. But then all the men would have to do was guard the one exit. When her suit's air ran out, she would either have to give up or die. No, her only hope was to outrun them.

She wasn't going to let them recapture her. She had a small cutter in her belt, sharp enough to slit a wrist through her suit if necessary.

Retracing her route and avoiding accidents weren't easy under the circumstances, but she managed to reach the crack in the wall ahead of her pursuers. She climbed through. She thought about pushing the nearest bottle rack in front of the crack, decided that it would slow her down more than them, and started across the wine cellar. She maneuvered as quickly as possible through the racks, tables and barrels.

Was there anywhere to escape to? Linda had no idea what was going on topside, but the man's presence didn't bode well for the rest of the scavengers or the *Mayan Princess*. She made herself stop thinking about it.

"Damned tricky, bitch!" Her heart almost jumped through her chest as the bald man's laboring voice came from her helmet speaker. She looked over her shoulder, and was reassured to see that the men were just coming through the wall crack. "You got Lou, and Al's suit is holed. But you aren't going anywhere. Give up, or it'll go harder on you."

She didn't answer. She was close to the exit, but she could hear the three men racing across the wine cellar after her.

"Now don't be that way," he continued, sweetening his tone. "I want you in one piece. But if you make me mad, I just might forget my good intentions."

The com voice made her think. If the men had a signal tracker, her suit telemetry would act like a homing beacon. There was only one thing she could do about that without stopping. It would also put her out of com, but at least she wouldn't have to listen to the bald man anymore. She used her cutter to slice through the com's battery leads.

Remembering the condition of the stairwell, she slowed down before going through the doorway. She took the steps as carefully as she had coming down. It wasn't easy with the pounding boots growing louder over her shoulder.

The idea was so foreign to her training and nature that it didn't occur to her until she reached the ground-floor landing. She hated it. But she knew that she couldn't outrun the men all the way back to the *Mayan Princess*. She had to slow them down.

She could hear them coming up the stairs.

She spent a precious second figuring out the surest way to accomplish what she wanted to do. Then she began kicking the stairway to the second floor, as hard and fast as she could.

Her fourth kick turned the second floor blockage into an avalanche. She jumped through the doorway an instant before falling concrete tore away the stairs and landing. The terrible sounds drowned out the fate of the windrider eater's men, for which she was grateful. She fled along the corridor and out the main entrance.

She scrambled over the rubble pile in front of the entrance. The sky was still cloudy, but the light of day made her squint. After the horrors in the basement darkness, even the endless expanse of ruined buildings, cars, debris and unhealthy vegetation was reassuringly familiar. Everything seemed to be as she remembered it. The only dangers were the ones a scavenger was trained to face. The events in Wickson Hall might have been nothing more than a ghastly nightmare.

But she knew better.

She felt utterly alone and vulnerable. Briefly she wished for a working com, so she could hear the sound of a friendly voice. But a transmission might have brought her something else too. She huddled against the side of Wickson Hall until she was sure no one was in sight. Then she walked wearily around the north end of the building. Leaving the cracked sidewalk for the hard-packed dirt of the fairway, she headed east toward the hoped-for safety of the *Mayan Princess*.

Rubble clattered to her left. She looked, and saw one of the windrider eater's men charging toward her from the Student Union. Another one was closing in across the open space to her right. She forced her aching legs back to running.

When she glanced over her shoulder a handful of seconds later, the two men were on the fairway fifty yards behind her. Worse, two more men were a hundred yards behind them. All four were running hard and gaining on her. If anyone was watching, she imagined that it looked like a bizarre lumbering track race.

A race that she didn't dare lose.

The closer pair of men was only thirty yards back. Her adrenalin used up, Linda dug deep for her last reserves of strength. Each stride was an agony of burning muscles, tortured lungs and dizzying exhaustion. The suit now wore like a slab of concrete. Sweat poured out of her, stinging her eyes.

Her hand curled around the hilt of her small cutter. If it was going to end anyway in a few more minutes, why not stop now and rest? A long, deep, infinitely welcome release from pain and horror. But the image of Wanda which she kept inside her, as she kept all of her family, wouldn't let her. She could give up on herself, but not on her responsibilities. Hopeless or not, she hardened herself to keep going.

Nearing a street which intersected with the fairway, she glanced left and right. She was afraid that her pursuers might have called in more of the windrider eater's men to head her off. She didn't see any of the strange green and brown suits. But she spotted something which caused her heart to miss a beat.

The crawler.

It was stopped a half block north of the fairway, in front of a fire-gutted wooden structure. It sat askew on a sidewalk pile of rubble, as if it had rolled there out of control. Some of the drums in the back had spilled into the street.

She ran toward the crawler, desperately hoping that it was still operational. She wondered what had happened to it and where its crew was. When she got closer she found out; two of the "drums" in the street were actually silver-suited bodies with helmets and heads severed. Two more murder victims. But she didn't have time to mourn them or Rico. She would do that later, if there was a later for her.

She climbed up into the driver's seat. Please start, she pleaded silently as she pushed the power button. The two men were less than twenty yards away and closing in fast. They had their cutters in their hands. One of them was yelling something into his com, probably meant for her.

Relief surged through her as the motor woke. She hadn't driven a crawler in over fifteen years, but the controls

were simple and she had a good memory. She frantically
backed the crawler off the rubble, into the street. The
men angled toward her.

She floored the accelerator, and the crawler started
toward the fairway. Unfortunately it was designed for cargo
capacity rather than speed. It rumbled ahead on its tread,
building up speed with agonizing slowness.

The men were in front of the crawler, but they veered
left out of its path. Their plan was obvious. The crawler
wouldn't be moving very fast when it passed them. They
would climb into the cab and kill her. The same way
others of their kind must have murdered its crew.

Killing and death! Rico, the man named Lou, the crawler's crew, and who knew how many more. She had seen
too much, suffered too much. Right, wrong, her entire
moral sense crumbled under an irresistible onslaught of
rage, and primeval instincts took over. She didn't want to
die. The two men wouldn't be able to kill her, if she killed
them first.

The crawler's speed was up to ten MPH. The men
swung around and ran beside it. They edged closer until
they were just a few inches away, reaching for handholds.

If they loved death so much, she would give it to them.
Her trembling hands jerked the wheel over hard.

The crawler swerved to the left. One of the men managed to jump on the running board; the other was knocked
down by it. The tread rolled toward him. His scream came
clearly through her sound pickup, until it was cut off by a
loud crunching sound. The crawler kept moving, ignoring
the slight bump.

The other man was perched on the running board in
front of her, clinging to the corner of the windshield with
one hand. He had his cutter in the other hand, but he was
too busy keeping his balance to use it on her. For the
moment. She steered the crawler sharply back to the
middle of the street, barely missing a wrecked car, but the
man didn't fall off.

She leaned forward and hit his windshield-gripping hand
as hard as she could. He grunted, but held on. She hit it
again. He swung the cutter at her arm. She struck her last

blow, and he fell. Spinning the wheel again, she heard and felt another crunch.

Shame and regret were emotions too mild for the person she had become. She was overwhelmingly glad to be alive.

Sobbing, she concentrated on driving and watching for more of the windrider eater's men. She didn't look back, but her imagination furnished an unsought image of two flattened suits in spreading red puddles.

She reached the fairway and turned left. The crawler was rolling at its maximum speed of twenty-four MPH. She could have increased its speed somewhat by unloading the cargo, but she wasn't about to stop for anything short of the *Mayan Princess*.

The second pair of pursuers was almost at the intersection when she made the turn. They came after her. But, while the crawler wasn't very fast, it was faster than suited men who had already run a long way. It steadily pulled away from them.

She wasn't worried about them. But she was worried about whomever they might have alerted by com between her and the *Mayan Princess*.

The crawler gave her a fragile sense of security and power. She drove along the fairway, between the partly ruined buildings, like a queen parading through her realm. Wind-swirled leaves and small debris were the only signs of movement. Spotting two more indisputably dead scavengers near a building entrance, she noted the fact as she would a detail of an engineering problem, but she felt nothing.

She kept looking around, hoping to find living scavengers or someone from the *Mayan Princess*, fearing to find more of the windrider eater's men. What if they had already captured or destroyed the zep? What would she do then?

At last she saw the Admin Center and the Law School up ahead, marking the end of the fairway. And in the distant field she could make out the *Mayan Princess*. It looked undamaged and free of the windrider eater's men. But her brief hope died. Ballast was splashing on the ground under the hull, and through the noise of the crawler she heard its motors revving. A thin line of sunlight appeared below the landing pads.

The *Mayan Princess* was leaving.

Linda screamed at it to wait, a futile act without a working com. She wanted to jump, wave, do something to attract the bridge's attention. But the crawler was more visible than anything she could think of. Her only hope was to keep going.

She did. The crawler neared the end of the fairway, while the *Mayan Princess* rose a few feet and swung ponderously into the wind. Piles of decon sacks lay where they had been waiting to be taken aboard. She groaned. Of course Captain Ramirez had to get his zep away from the danger. But to have tried so hard, come through so much, only to arrive seconds late. She couldn't stand it.

She kept going anyway, because there was nothing else to do. Eight more of the windrider eater's men stood between the creek and the parking lot, cutters in hand, blocking her way. She didn't care. She bore down on the middle of their line, zigzagging so hard that more drums fell out of the back. The two men in the crawler's path dove aside barely in time. Others tried to jump aboard, but the crawler was moving too fast. One of them slipped under the right front tread, leaving a sizeable red stain on it.

Then the crawler was past the line. Linda wove through the parking lot, banging into several cars, and drove onto the field. The surviving men chased her.

The crawler bounced and jolted over the rough ground, tearing up patches of weeds. But where was she fleeing? There was nothing within the crawler's range except more killzone. Soon, very soon at this rate of drain, the batteries would run down. Then she would have to use the cutter.

Even sooner than that, it seemed. More of the windrider eater's men were climbing out of holes at the far end of the field. Linda was trapped between those ahead and those behind. With the crawler's speed reduced by the irregular terrain, she knew that she wouldn't be able to escape again.

A dark shadow swallowed her.

Looking up, she saw a long curve of white hull less than thirty feet overhead, matching her course. Captain Ramirez had spotted her, and come back for her. More than that, he was risking the *Mayan Princess* in a fantastically dangerous maneuver to save her. But what in the sky did he have in mind? Landing wouldn't help; the men would be upon her before she could reach the air lock. And there was no telling what they might be able to do to the landed zep.

Then, through moist eyes, she noticed the dark hole in the hull's underside which was the open decon airlock. A rope ladder with plastic rungs unwound almost to the ground.

Transferring in her outside suit would take some tricky acrobatics and an unlikely amount of luck. But the alternative was even less attractive. She steered over to the flapping ladder, reached out with her free hand, and grabbed it. Taking a deep breath, she locked the crawler's controls and waited for the right combination of motions.

Now! She stepped onto a rung, and clung for dear life. The crawler bounced up into her, knocking her feet off of the ladder. She hung by her screaming arms until her feet found the rung again.

The *Mayan Princess* climbed, leaving the field, the wandering crawler and many frustrated men below. The wind buffeted her, and she could feel the motor vibration through the ladder. As carefully as she could she started up the rungs.

She hadn't done this sort of thing in a long time, and she was wretchedly weary. But she was relieved to find that she still possessed some of her old agility. She moved slowly but surely, not looking downward. An eternity later she reached the top of the ladder. Gloved hands reached down from the lip of the air lock to help her scramble inside.

She lay gasping on the air lock's deck, while the two crewmen reeled in the ladder and sealed the outer hatch. Only then did she give in to the shakes.

CHAPTER TWENTY-THREE

"The target is taking off, sir," the navigation officer reported. "Preliminary course due west and climbing."

Colonel McCrarey nodded, then sat back in his command chair. Even lit by muted sunshine from the windscreen, the atmosphere in the OCC was somber, sanctified. The *Shenandoah* was at battle stations; he could feel it functioning at peak efficiency.

This time the target was a zep, a fast one with an able captain, according to the friendly. By now the captain had some idea of the danger he faced. All of which made the zep as worthy an enemy as Colonel McCrarey was ever likely to fight. Pre-engagement excitement coursed through him, an intoxication which sharpened rather than dulled his wits.

He swiveled his chair. "Pilot, commence attack run."

"Yes, sir."

The tempo of activity around Colonel McCrarey jumped a notch. He tasted impending victory, and he was pleased. The Pemex Under zep was destined to crash and burn.

So far everything had followed the optimum scenario. The Pemex Under zep had landed where he had figured it would. The two scavengers had done all the hard work for him; Captain Patterson's men might even now be relieving them of the prize. The com officer had burned out the zep's long-range transmitter on schedule. Anticipating that the zep would flee west for a water pickup, Colonel McCrarey had ordered the *Shenandoah* to a position twenty miles northwest of Davis. The attack would take place when the zep reached the *Shenandoah*'s four thousand feet. He didn't want to risk combat maneuvering any lower.

"ETA at target sixteen minutes, sir," the navigation officer reported.

"Picking up any other traffic?" Colonel McCrarey asked the pilot.

"Nothing in radar range, sir."

Through the windscreen Colonel McCrarey saw that the *Shenandoah* was sandwiched between dark clouds and the surface. It was cruising south over brown fields, crumbling roads, ruined farmhouses and dead or dying trees: an enduring monument to mankind's powers of destruction. There were low hills to the west and farther away to the east, while in the distance straight ahead he thought he could make out a river.

No sign yet of the Pemex Under zep.

"Gunner," he said, "is the laser powered up?"

"Hot and ready, sir," the weapons officer reported cheerfully. "All that hydrogen should make a pretty fireball."

"Colonel," the com officer cut in, "message incoming from Captain Patterson."

"I'll take it here." He clamped down on his surging excitement. The surface operation was ultimately important to him, for a reason which had nothing to do with the mission. He put on his headset for privacy, then slapped a button on his armrest. "Colonel McCrarey here."

"Phase Two objectives attained, Colonel," the gravelly voice began. "The Pemex Under scavenging teams have been eliminated. Wickson Hall has been secured. Four dead, two seriously wounded."

Colonel McCrarey heard what wasn't said as well as what was, and didn't like either. Six casualties in an operation which should have gone down without a scratch? But more importantly . . . "What about the two scavengers who were searching for Project Rainmaker's laser data? Did they find anything?"

Captain Patterson paused; when he resumed, his voice was stiff. "Sergeant West and three men from B Platoon's second squad entered Wickson Hall. They tracked the scavengers to Project Rainmaker, and attempted to capture them—"

"Attempted?" Colonel McCrarey demanded.

"Part of the ceiling collapsed. One of ours was killed, and one caught a dose of rads. One of the hostile was killed trying to escape. The other did escape—a stairwell collapsed, preventing pursuit. Sergeant West only just dug his way out and reported. Other units reported that a single hostile reached the Pemex Under zep just as it was taking off."

Colonel McCrarey took a deep breath, and managed to keep control. Barely. "An unarmed civvie escaped from four of your aircavs? Captain, that's a damned miserable excuse for soldiering. Hold a summary court martial for Sergeant West—I expect to see him in a body bag."

"Yes, sir." The stiffness in Captain Patterson's voice increased. "I'm afraid there's more bad news. According to Sergeant West's report, the hostile who escaped claimed to be carrying a satellite operating manual salvaged from Project Rainmaker."

Colonel McCrarey's fist slammed down on the armrest, and heads turned his way. He could hardly believe it. His scheme, his entire future, shot down in flames by inept subordinates. He felt the frustration familiar to commanders throughout history, of events unraveling beyond his control. "Go on," he rapped.

"I have my men packing up the field HQ, collecting bodies and gear, and policing the site. When we pull out, there won't be anything to tell a rescue expedition what happened here. Just another unexplained zep loss."

"The site better be clean, Captain. I've had all the incompetence I'll tolerate on this mission."

"Yes, sir. What should I do about Wickson Hall?"

Colonel McCrarey thought hard and fast. His scheme was badly riddled, but maybe he could patch it up and keep it in the air. "Forget Wickson Hall. What we're after isn't there anymore—it's aboard the Pemex Under zep.

But we're still going to get it. Be ready to pull out as soon as the *Shenandoah* lands."

"Yes, sir. Out."

Colonel McCrarey swiveled to face the pilot. "Abort attack run."

"Sir?"

"You heard me. Get us back to Davis ASAP. When the aircavs are aboard, we'll be going after the Pemex Under zep. So be damned sure you don't lose it on radar."

"Yes, sir." The pilot looked puzzled, and he wasn't the only one. But the OCC officers knew better than to ask questions.

"Gunner," Colonel McCrarey said crisply, "lock down the laser. For now."

Leaning back, he tried to decompress. He heard the growl of the motors change pitch, and felt the *Shenandoah* coming around to the new course. The activity in the OCC lost some of its intensity.

Having taken care of the immediate damage control, he considered what his next move should be.

He had risen as high in Alpha's chain of command as he was going to playing by the rules; General Armbruster had made that abundantly clear by passing him over for promotion four times. Good enough to command a zep, but not Alpha. He intended to show the general just how wrong that was.

But the amazing possibility which fate had shown him required the satellite manual. He intended to get it. Acquiring laser data was a mission objective, so he could justify pursuing the Pemex Under zep. Then what? Attacking the zep would destroy the manual. If he threatened to attack and demanded the zep's surrender, the captain might call his bluff. No, he needed something foolproof.

Most of the anger had seeped out of him; he was feeling confident again. Stern chases were usually long ones. He would have plenty of time to come up with an approach.

CHAPTER TWENTY-FOUR

One of the crewmen helped Linda to her feet. Swaying from exhaustion, she grabbed a bulkhead handhold for support. The decon air lock was shoebox-shaped; its white surfaces were covered with handholds, glow panels, ultrasonic emitters, radmeter sensors, controls, vents, and the big hatches at each end. The artificial light seemed dim after daylight. The crewman was saying something to her. She pointed to her com and shook her head.

The tilt of the deck and the motor vibration told her that the *Mayan Princess* was climbing away from Davis. She was glad; she wanted to put as many miles between her and the town as possible. The ready light over the inner hatch turned bright orange. She and the two crewmen braced themselves.

The light turned red. A breeze began blowing through the air lock, from the vents at one end to the vents at the other. It quickly grew into a strong wind. Linda felt the bone-deep tingling which meant ultrasonic scrubbers were at work. She barely managed to stay upright as she exposed every part of her suit (even the boot soles) to the wind. A few minutes later, when the radmeter readings dropped below the safety level, the wind died. The ready light turned green.

Linda's weakened fingers had trouble removing her suit.

The crewmen quickly shed theirs and helped her. She remembered to unclip the decon sack from her belt, then the three of them hurried to the inner hatch. The suits would stay in the air lock, awaiting more decon and servicing. The hatch opened just long enough to let them out.

The cargo hold was empty except for a crewman operating the air lock controls, and Dr. Santos in his neat white suit. The crewman was talking into the com on the control panel. Dr. Santos came over to them, looking professionally concerned.

"Thank you," she said wearily but sincerely to the crewmen beside her. "You saved my life."

"It was nothing," one of them said politely but soberly. Everyone in the cargo hold looked like ambulatory shock victims trapped in a nightmare they couldn't understand or wake up from. She sympathized. She knew that her face wore the same expression.

The absence of any other suits in the air lock had already told her the terrible answer, but she had to ask. "How many others made it back?"

The crewman just shook his head. Linda tried to accept it, but couldn't. Twenty-one human beings. Husbands, fathers, folks who had places in the world. What right did she have to survive when they hadn't?

Dr. Santos was running a hand radmeter over the three of them. When he finished he said, "All of you are clean. Cesar, Ramon, you may return to your duties."

They nodded and headed aft. Dr. Santos turned to Linda. "Please come with me for your checkup, Señora."

"But I have to tell Captain Ramirez what happened," she objected weakly.

"All in good time. Your health comes first. Your suit telemetry was interrupted, and you were exposed to the killzone longer than is good for you."

She docilely went forward with the doctor, still clutching the decon sack. In the passageway she saw more crewmen. They looked worried and confused, but they were going briskly about their duties. Under other circumstances she would have been impressed.

The sickbay wasn't much bigger than a cabin, a compact arangement of state-of-the-art medical equipment. Beige and light brown had been used to creating a comforting environment. At Santos's instructions she stripped, put her arm in the blood/tissue sampler, then stepped into the upright cylinder that was the body scan unit. She shivered from more than the cool air as he studied the diagnostic readouts.

The post-surface checkup routine was familiar to her from her scavenging days, but medical advances since then had speeded it up. Less than a minute later Santos said, "I find no sign of nerve toxins or BW viruses. The radiation cell damage is well below the danger level. A regen shot and some rest are all you need."

"The rest will have to wait," Linda almost yawned, "until after I see Captain Ramirez."

"Then I'll give you a stimulant too, if you promise to rest afterwards."

Linda nodded. Santos loaded two cartridges into an injector, and gave her the shot. Then he treated her collection of minor scrapes and bruises.

As she pulled her sweat-soaked coveralls back on, Dr. Santos coughed discreetly. "I hope you won't take offense, Señora. But before you call on the captain, you may wish to, ah, refresh yourself."

Linda grinned wanly. "No offense taken. A shower and a change of clothes are definitely in order." She shook his hand. "Thank you, Doctor."

"You're welcome." He paused. "I've only heard sketchy reports as to what happened to the scavenging party, and I'm not sure I want to know more. But I'm glad you've returned unharmed. Good day."

The stimulant began to take hold as she walked to her cabin. Her head cleared, her back straightened, and some strength returned to her muscles. But she was still emotionally numb. She wondered if she would ever feel again.

Her cabin was identical to the one which she and Wanda had occupied on the trip to Pemex Under. The lower bunk tempted her to lie down, pull the blanket over her head, and forget everything. But she couldn't. Responsibilities kept her going; they were all that kept her going.

She paused by the port. The *Mayan Princess* had climbed above the dreary surface, and was cruising over a patchy plain of white clouds. The canopy of clean blue sky lifted her spirits somewhat. According to the early afternoon sun, the zep was heading west.

Collecting her bathroom kit and fresh clothes, she hurried to the communal shower. She had the cramped fake-tile compartment to herself. Her dirty clothes went into the hamper. She ran the water as hot as she could bear, and tried to scrub herself raw. After the blow-dry cycle she dressed, combed her hair, and nerved herself up to face the world again.

She went back to her cabin to call Captain Ramirez, but as she entered she saw the com's message light flashing. She touched the play button.

"My compliments on your safe return, Señora." There was an undercurrent of tension in Captain Ramirez's casual tone. "Would you please come to my quarters at your earliest convenience for a debriefing."

Linda wondered if that last part was a typically outrageous pun or an innocent choice of words, and decided that there was nothing innocent about him. But she was too worn out to take offense. Fetching the decon sack from the upper bunk, she left for his cabin.

He opened the door at her first knock and gestured her inside. "You seem none the worse for your ordeal," he said warmly, but his smile looked frayed around the edges. "Dr. Santos assures me you're in perfect health."

"I . . . want to thank you and your crew," she told him. "You risked your zep coming back for me."

"Standard *Mayan Princess* service, my lovely lady. You're booked for the round trip."

They were in the captain's office. The thick ivory carpet, brass fixtures, and fake-mahogany bulkheads and furniture were stylish bordering on ostentatious. Holopics of zeps covered the bulkheads; the built-in shelves and desktop held bookdisks as well as aviation mementos. The door in the forward bulkhead presumably led to the private quarters. Ramirez guided Linda to a comfortable chair, then went over to the non-automated bar shelf. "Would you care for something to restore the inner woman?" he asked.

She rarely drank anything stronger than a glass of wine

with dinner, but in this case it would be medicinal. "Please. A Scotch and water, with ice."

Captain Ramirez made a production of filling two glasses and transferring cubes from the ice bucket. He brought her drink to her, and sipped his own while she quickly emptied half her glass. "Is it satisfactory?" he asked.

The ethanol glow spread through her, smoothing the jagged edges and distancing her from her pain. "Yes, thank you."

"I'm surprised to find you here," she added. "Shouldn't you be on the bridge at a time like this?"

Captain Ramirez sat on the corner of the desk closest to her. "The immediate crisis has passed, so I ended the emergency drill and turned the con over to Elena. After our meeting I'm going to inspect the ship, and otherwise resume my normal routine."

"But . . ." How could he stand to be away from the bridge, in case trouble arose? "But what if something happens?"

"Then Elena will either handle it or yell for my help. At the moment my most important task is to restore the crew's sense of order. Haunting the bridge would be pointless and bad for morale."

"Is the crisis really over?" Linda asked softly.

Ramirez nodded. "We're heading out to sea for a water pickup, then back to Pemex Under. Teresa assures me that the sky is empty as far as radar can see."

Linda dropped the decon sack on the desk next to him. "Would you please turn this over to Señor Gutierrez when we get back? I don't want to have anything more to do with it."

"Certainly." He ran a hand over the slick gray sack. "May I ask what's inside?"

"The operating manual for the Project Rainmaker satellite."

His smile broadened. "You found it! Congratulations! Today's events have convinced me that we desperately need war lasers."

"I don't want to think about that. I just want to find Wanda and go home."

Captain Ramirez was quiet for a moment. "I regret

having to ask you to relive such an unpleasant experience, but as the expedition's commander I must know what happened to you." He pushed a button on the desk's control panel, presumably activating a recorder.

So she told him everything from leaving the *Mayan Princess* to her return, in as much detail as she could drag from her memory. Somehow putting it into words, as if telling a story, made it easier to bear. Even so, by the time she finished she felt ill.

Captain Ramirez shook his head in wonder. "I said it before, and I'll say it again. You're a most remarkable woman."

She thought bitterly how wrong he was, but said nothing.

Captain Ramirez shut off the recorder. "Now I imagine you have questions about the rest of the expedition. So do I, but I'll tell you what I know." He gave her a synopsis of the events on the bridge.

"Fortunately," he finished, "the crewman in the aft observation room spotted you and your pursuers. I formulated a rescue plan which didn't violate more than a dozen regs, and the rest is aviation history."

After another silence Linda said, "Those men must have been sent by the windrider eater—anything else would be an impossible coincidence."

"My thinking exactly."

"The one who . . . who killed Rico said they were from a place called Alpha. I've never heard of a town or enclave by that name. Have you?"

Captain Ramirez shook his head. "But let's check the ship's database." He typed on the control panel's keyboard, and glanced at the tiny screen. "No windrider town, enclave or zep with that name, past or present. Maybe the mysterious Señor Cardenas will be able to make something of it."

Linda let the subject drop. Her mind shied away from trying to envision the environment which could nurture such violence.

She gulped down the last of her drink. Then she stood up, and the deck swayed in a way which had nothing to do with rough air. She unobtrusively held the bar shelf for support.

Captain Ramirez came over to her. Putting a hand on her shoulder he said, "You must be exhausted after your ordeal. May I suggest that you return to your cabin and rest."

She automatically reached up to remove his hand. She didn't feel tired. She was still emotionally numb, but not empty. The horror and desperate effort had built up a tremendous pressure inside her, unnameable, seeking release. Every cell in her body seemed intensely alive.

Her hand touching his acted like the throwing of a main power switch. The surge burned away all reason, all self-control, as if they had never been. It was animalistic and purely sexual. She ached for him to overwhelm her, to use her brutally and entirely. She hungered for oblivion.

She all but threw herself at him. Before he could react, her arms wrapped vise-like around him. Her mouth found his. Gasping and moaning, she ground rhythmically into him.

He tried to pull away, but she wasn't having any of that. She started to tug at his uniform shirt. His hand moved up her back, and pulled the top of her coveralls away from her neck.

Suddenly an incredible coldness/wetness spilled down her spine. Trapped between her skin and the loose-fitting coveralls, it rounded her rear end and poured down both legs.

Her entire body spasmed violently. She spun, trying to free herself of the freezing sensation. Captain Ramirez and her lust were forgotten as she shook like a zock dancer. Ice cubes tumbled out of the bottom of the coveralls' legs, joining a puddle of water on the carpet.

When she regained control of herself, she whipped to face Ramirez. She was as cold as the ice. "Well, really!"

Captain Ramirez returned the empty ice bucket to the bar shelf and tucked his shirt back in. His knowing smile was like a slap across her face.

"You bastard!" she snarled. "After your big macho act, you won't respond to me when I need you! Damn you! What is it—don't you want a woman if she makes the first move?"

"I sincerely apologize for the indignity," he replied gently, "but it was necessary for two reasons. First of all, I'm on duty. A zep captain on duty must be a paragon of virtue, to avoid distraction and as an example to this crew. But more importantly, I love you too much to be the tool for your self-destruction."

"I beg your pardon?" she demanded frostily.

"Don't mistake what you were feeling for desire. Today you were forced to do things which went against your most deeply held beliefs. They sickened you, made you hate yourself. Subconsciously you decided to complete the destruction of your conscience, so it would stop tormenting you. You set out to thoroughly degrade yourself. Not very flattering to me, I might add."

She tried to tell him how stupid that was, and how much she despised amateur psychiatry. But she couldn't speak.

"In time you'll forgive yourself," he went on. "The evil isn't in violence itself—it's part of our animal nature—but rather in what causes one to be violent. You acted to defend yourself. You're still decent and good, no less so for also being strong."

All the sights/sounds/emotions from her waking nightmare whirled through her mind, even the sick-joyous feeling when she crushed the men under the crawler's tread.

Captain Ramirez's tone lightened. "As for not responding to you, my lovely lady, you underestimate yourself. I'm sure your keen powers of observation will note that I'm not entirely unaffected."

She saw what he meant. The next thing she knew she was laughing: loud, total, lung-emptying laughter that spewed all the poison out of her. She doubled over and almost fell, but Captain Ramirez steadied her.

He helped her back to her chair, and gave her his handkerchief to wipe her eyes. "May I inquire what's so amusing?" he asked.

Her laughter subsided. "Oh my . . ." she gasped. "What I must have looked like . . . trying to eat you . . . and your poor carpet . . . I'm so sorry."

"Don't be. The carpet will dry, and that was the only damage done. Would you like another drink?"

"I don't think . . . that would be a very good idea. As soon as I catch my breath, I better go back to my ca—"

The desk's com beeped.

He touched a button on it. "This is Captain Ramirez."

"Teresa, Captain," the speaker voice identified itself. "Is Señora Calhoun with you?"

"Yes. Why do you ask?"

"I just got around to checking the last transmission relayed from Pemex Under, the one you had me store because we were about to land. In addition to the usual garbage, there's a message for Señora Calhoun."

Captain Ramirez looked at Linda. "Teresa can read it to you, if you like. I'll step outside."

"You can stay." She hoped that it wasn't another worried gram from Jack.

Captain Ramirez turned back to the com. "Teresa, the lady is listening. Please read it to her."

"As you say. Message begins. From Proctor-in-chief Felix Guerrero, to Señora Linda Calhoun. We have received notification of a stowaway aboard Lone Star Five, the windrider which was launched the same day you reported you daughter missing. The stowaway refused to identify herself, but her description matches that of your daughter. She is in good health and being looked after. Lone Star Five is presently near the mouth of the Mississippi River, traveling northwest to join its town. Position and course figures follow. If we can be of any assistance in arranging her return, please let me know. Message ends, followed by those figures."

"Thanks, Teresa." Captain Ramirez thumbed the off button.

Linda's light-headedness returned, but this time for a much happier reason. The news was like sunshine breaking through the clouds which had been surrounding her. Soon she would be taking Wanda home. More than anything else in the world she yearned to hug Wanda close and never let her go.

"That is indeed wonderful news," Captain Ramirez said, looking somewhat surprised. "Stowing away in a windrider during its launching is supposed to be impossible. Still, if anyone could do it, it would be your audacious daughter.

I'll have to check the schedules, but I imagine a Pemex Under zep will be docking at Lone Star before too long."

His comment and her need gave birth to a highly irregular idea, one she would never have suggested to him under normal circumstances. "Captain, changing course to dock at Lone Star Five wouldn't add much time to our return trip. I realize it's a lot to ask, but for Wanda's sake as well as mine . . . please?"

"I wish I could," he said regretfully, "but you know the seriousness of our mission more than anyone. I would be derelict in my duty if I let personal considerations delay our return by even a moment. I'm sorry."

Linda thought frantically. "You're right, of course. You must report what happened at Davis to Señor Gutierrez as soon as possible. But with the long-range transmitter out, that won't be until we reach Pemex Under. Wouldn't it be quicker to dock at a windrider en route, and use its radio to make a preliminary report?"

Captain Ramirez's smile returned. "An excellent point." His hand moved back to the com. "Jose, are you sleeping on duty again?"

"No, I'm not," came the irritated reply. "I'm trying to plot a safe course without WeatherNet updates."

"I hope you haven't put too much work into it. I want you to plot a new one, a rendezvous with windrider Lone Star Five. Teresa can give you its position and course."

"As you wish." The com clicked off.

Linda squeezed Captain Ramirez's hand. "Thank you. For everything."

"For you I could do no less."

CHAPTER TWENTY-FIVE

Colonel McCrarey was eating dinner in the *Shenandoah*'s wardroom. He was alone, holding to the old maxim that the commander has no friends. Besides, he had a lot on his mind. The plain gray bulkheads and utilitarian furniture suited his grim mood as he tried to come up with a way to salvage his scheme. The ports looked out on a blood-red sunset and the Pacific Ocean far below. Beethoven's Fifth Piano Concerto came softly from the bulkhead speaker.

He sipped his coffee while the steward removed the dishes, and reviewed the current situation. The *Shenandoah* was still trailing the Pemex Under zep. It had, as expected, flown west over deep ocean and carried out a water pickup. The *Shenandoah* had used the delay to do the same. Then the pursuit had resumed in a new direction: southeast. After the night watch had come on duty, he had left the OCC for his first sit-down meal since the beginning of the Davis fiasco.

Maybe he should mix more with the officers. If his scheme fully developed, he was going to need their support; especially that of Captain Patterson and Lieutenant Ford, the day watch com officer. He didn't dare sound anyone out yet, since General Armbruster took a very dim view of treason. But it wouldn't hurt to lay some groundwork.

"OCC calling Colonel McCrarey." The music was interrupted by the voice of Major Santee, the night watch commander.

Colonel McCrarey went over to the bulkhead com and tapped buttons. "Colonel McCrarey here. What is it, Major?"

"Sorry to interrupt your dinner, but I thought you would want to know about this right away. We've plotted the target's new course. It lies well to the north of Pemex Under."

"You're sure of that " Colonel McCrarey demanded.

"Absolutely. The course will take the target across the southern United States."

"Do you have an explanation?"

"None. There isn't any bad weather to go around, and there are no enclaves along the new course."

Colonel McCrarey hated things which didn't make sense. "I'm on my way. Out."

He went forward, automatically returning the salutes of passing crewmen. Where the hell was the Pemex Under zep going? Would the new course give him more time or less to get his hands on the satellite manual? He might just have to resort to direct action after all, and hope for the best.

The OCC was bathed in bloody sunlight from the windscreen, a sight which always stimulated him. He acknowledged the "Commander on deck" anouncement and settled into his chair. (Major Santee had tactfully already vacated it.) A quick survey assured him that the night watch had everything under control.

"The target is crossing the central California coastline," Major Santee reported from behind the pilot. "We're twenty miles astern and hanging tight. No sign of detection."

"Excellent." Colonel McCrarey swiveled to the navigation officer. "Show me the bad news."

"Yes, sir." An outline map of North America appeared on one of the monitor screens. A blue line indicating the Pemex Under zep's projected course ran from California to Florida and on into the Atlantic Ocean. None of the black squares representing enclaves were anywhere near the line.

"Beats the hell out of me," he muttered to himself. Turning to the com officer he asked, "Any recent transmissions to or from the target?"

The com officer typed on his keyboard and glanced at a screen. "None, sir. Its transmitter must still be out. Nothing incoming in file since the relay we intercepted just before it landed at Davis."

That started Colonel McCrarey thinking. He hadn't had time to scan that last intercept, and the Pemex Under zep's Captain had been equally busy. If the captain had just gotten around to looking at it, something in it might explain the course change. "Let me see that intercept."

"Yes, sir."

Messages started rolling up the monitor screen. Colonel McCrarey studied them carefully. The official business didn't tell him anything, but when the first personal message came up he muttered, "So that's it. How touchingly humanitarian."

He had the com officer freeze the message on screen, and reread it twice. Then he told the pilot, "The target's destination is windrider Lone Star Five. Get the coordinates and course off the screen. Now that we know where it's heading, I expect you not to lose it."

"Yes, sir."

Colonel McCrarey leaned back in his chair. The new destination imposed a time limit; he would have to act before the Pemex Under zep's captain could use the windrider's radio to report to Pemex Under. But it also suggested a course of action, and offered an unexpected bonus which would fit very nicely into his scheme. Best of all, he knew how to sell the course of action to General Armbruster without triggering any suspicion.

"Can you set up a two-way with Alpha through the satellite?" he asked the com officer.

If the com officer was surprised at breaking com silence, he didn't show it. "Our position is okay. If the satellite isn't being temperamental, yes."

"Do it. I want to speak directly to General Armbruster."

"Yes, sir."

Colonel McCrarey took advantage of the delay to plan what he was going to say. General Armbruster was a canny old warbird; outwitting him was going to be no easy job. Colonel McCrarey unobtrusively took a few deep breaths.

Finally the com officer said, "Colonel, I have General Armbruster for you."

Colonel McCrarey slipped on his headset. "Colonel McCrarey here, General."

"Colonel, you better have a damned good reason for breaking com silence!" The voice crackled and wavered, but it was definitely General Armbruster's deep growl.

"I do." Colonel McCrarey gave a brief summary of the mission to date.

After he finished there were long seconds of crackling. Then General Armbruster spoke, and his voice trembled with suppressed rage. "We'll discuss the botch you've made out of a simple operation when you get back. What I want to know is why are you playing tag with that zep? It's crew knows 'way too much about us to live. Burn it out of the sky, and shag ass back here."

"I beg your pardon," Colonel McCrarey said more calmly than he felt. "One of the mission objectives is to acquire information about Project Rainmaker's laser satellite. The satellite manual is aboard that zep—I'm in the process of acquiring it."

"By allowing the zep to dock at a windrider?" General Armbruster asked acidly. "The risk of revealing our existence is unacceptable."

"The risk is minimal. When the zep docks at Lone Star Five, I plan to use our usual tactics to capture both of them. The windrider is traveling alone, so burning out its long-range transmitter will effectively isolate it."

"You want to conduct a full-scale raid just to retrieve the manual?"

That was a line of thought which General Armbruster had to be carefully steered away from. "Of course not," Colonel McCrarey said quickly. "I broke com silence to propose an additional mission objective. This combination of events has created an opportunity which I don't believe we should let pass."

"Spit it out, colonel."

"I understand that the General Staff has been considering whether we should acquire a new windrider to replace

Alpha. Transferring everything would be a major operation. But Alpha is near the end of its service life—we'll have to replace it sooner or later. Why not now? According to the Intelligence files Lone Star Five is state-of-the-art, fresh from the yard. Give the order, and I'll bring back our new Alpha as well as the satellite manual."

General Armbruster was silent even longer this time. Finally he said, "I don't like the idea of another windrider loss so soon after Tokyo Four, not with Pemex Under and Calgary already suspicious. But your proposal has merit, definite merit. Proceed under the assumption that you have a go for the raid. I'll call a meeting of the General staff, and get back to you by twenty-two hundered hours."

"Thank you, General."

"Initiative is a fine quality in an officer, Colonel. But remember, it doesn't make up for botched operations."

"I understand," Colonel McCrarey said through gritted teeth. "Out."

But as soon as his headset went dead, excitement pushed his irritation aside. Let the old warbird chirp. The raid was going to be approved, and that was all that mattered. If his scheme fully developed, he would have his revenge. General Armbruster would realize how skillfully he had been tricked. Then he would be executed, by order of General McCrarey, the new commander of Alpha.

Taking off the headset, Colonel McCrarey concentrated on enjoying the last of the crimson sunset. Fortuitous events and an omen in the sky. They warmed him like fine Kentucky sipping whiskey.

CHAPTER TWENTY-SIX

"Yo, unidentified zep, this is Lone Star Five. You're in our airspace. Please identify yourself pronto." The voice from the bulkhead speaker sounded exasperated. It had every right to; it had been repeating its message for the past twenty minutes, ever since the *Mayan Princess* must have first appeared on the windrider's radar.

Linda sat unobtrusively in an observation seat, while Captain Ramirez and the others busily tended their flight stations. Captain Ramirez had invited her to watch the docking from the bridge. She was grateful. Watching from the lounge would have painfully reminded her that she was the only passenger, and why.

The windscreen revealed a panoramic view of the young night. The moon hadn't risen yet, and the surface was lost in the darkness, but a myriad of stars were sprayed across the sky. Lone Star Five floated straight ahead, a ball of ghostly iridescence punctuated by brighter lights from the levels. It looked so much like home that it brought dampness to her eyes.

"We're six miles from the dock," Elena reported, "closing at twenty-four MPH. Altitude sixteen thousand feet."

Jose's rendezvous calculations had been inexact, due to the lack of updated information on Lone Star Five's position and the vagaries of the wind. But they had brought

233

the *Mayan Princess* close enough to pick up the windrider's transponder. The zep had homed in on it. Fortunately Lone Star Five was below the zep's ceiling; otherwise Ramirez would have had to ask the windrider to descend.

"I think we're in com range now," Teresa told Captain Ramirez. She had spent much of the two-day flight from Davis adapting the suit com system's short-range transmitter so that it could be used to contact Lone Star Five.

"Let's find out." Ramirez didn't look away from his piloting. "If your haywire creation doesn't work, you'll have to grow wings and deliver my message in person."

Teresa worked her com controls, spoke softly into her headset mike, and listened. Then she said aloud, "We're in the com, Captain. Lone Star Five's chief engineer, a Señor Jarman, wants very much to speak to you."

Sighing theatrically, Captain Ramirez switched on his com. "Señor Jarman," he said in English, "this is Captain Ramirez of the Pemex Under zep *Mayan Princess*. I apologize for our unannounced intrusion in your airspace. Our radio is down—we're using our com transmitter. I request permission to dock."

"Vic Jarman here, Captain," a drawling voice replied. "Permission granted. Approach from one six five, and set your guidance to channel D. Need anything else?"

"A local weather report would be helpful."

"One WeatherNet summary coming up. I'm switching your call to our weather board. See you soon, Captain."

Captain Ramirez had Jose take the summary so that he could concentrate on the tricky docking maneuver. The *Mayan Princess* swung wide to approach the belly of Lone Star Five on the assigned heading. The dimly luminescent shell swelled, until the curve of the levels loomed overhead. Linda stared. Even shrouded by night the windrider was an awesome sight, a triumph of art as well as engineering.

Floodlights came on, illuminating the girders and pads of the dock. "We're on the beam," Elena reported.

Captain Ramirez switched com channels. "Your attention, please, all crew. We're about to dock at Lone Star Five. Brace for maneuvering. A word to the wise is sufficient."

The *Mayan Princess* slowed as it closed in on the dock. Captain Ramirez had juggled the watch schedule so that his best folks would be on duty, and it showed in the calm skill of the bridge crew's work. He handled the flight controls, his gaze darting back and forth between the windscreen and his displays. Elena fed him a steady stream of information, and held herself ready to take the con if necessary. Jose was scanning the incoming weather summary for danger signs, while Teresa tended the laser guidance system and the radio link to Lone Star Five.

The *Mayan Princess*'s motion became irregular and the motor vibration kept changing as Captain Ramirez maneuvered the zep's back into the dock. Linda, who had docked blimps in blimp bay cradles, admired his technique. He acted without hesitation or uncertainty, yet he had a gentle hand, never overcorrecting.

Much like his technique with women.

He had been a perfect gentleman since saving her from herself in his office. At first the memory of her bizarre behavior had made her uncomfortable around him, but his casual attitude (and discretion) had soon dissipated the feeling. Why did he have to be such a fascinating, capable, basically decent man? He was making it very hard for her not to fall in love with him.

The slight bump of the *Mayan Princess* settling into the dock broke her reverie. The magnetic clamps took hold, and the motors shut down.

"Entryway deploying," Teresa passed along the message from Lone Star Five's bridge. Moments later a second bump told Linda that it was in place.

Captain Ramirez made sure that all the shipboard systems were green, then he turned over the con to Elena. "Señora Calhoun and I will be going aboard the windrider," he told her. "We won't be long. Don't go away."

"Aye, aye, great hawk of the sky," she said merrily.

Captain Ramirez stopped at Jose's station on his way to Linda. "Plot us a homeward course—we cast off at dawn. I'll try to wangle a replacement chip for our transmitter, so we can tie back into WeatherNet."

"That would be helpful," Jose replied.

Linda went with Captain Ramirez back to the cargo

hold, and they rode the elevator platform up to the top-side hatch. Since there was no cargo to transfer, and therefore no need to match the cargo hold's air pressure to Lone Star Five's, they used the topside hatch's air lock. Soon they were walking up the entryway's ramp.

"I imagine the shakedown crew hasn't had time to get the ramp moving," Captain Ramirez puffed as they climbed the thirty-degree slope. "Unfortunately for us."

Linda was glad to be free of the *Mayan Princess*'s thick, cool air. "At least they set up the dock. We could be shinnying up a mooring line."

Captain Ramirez laughed as best he could.

An undersized man in a cowboy outfit—jeans, a maroon shirt with a black yoke, tooled leather boots and a black Stetson—was waiting for them in the busy, noisy blimp bay. "Señor Jarman, I presume?" Captain Ramirez asked him.

"Vic Jarman," the man drawled, doffing his hat. "Welcome to Lone Star Five, Captain, ma'am."

"Captain Miguel Ramirez, at your service. This lovely lady is Señora Linda Calhoun from Calgary."

"I'm pleased to meet you," Linda said.

After a round of handshakes Mister Jarman turned to Linda. "Miz Calhoun? Now I know what brings you all to these parts. We got a message from the Pemex Under proctors that our stowaway most likely answers to the handle Wanda Grigg, and that her ma would be in touch about retrieving her. I'm mighty glad to see you."

Linda's impending reunion with Wanda stirred a number of emotions inside her, but the predominant one was relief. "Is she well?"

"Fit as a fiddle, according to our sawbones and the folks who are looking after her."

"I sincerely apologize for Wanda's actions. When you add up the trouble she has caused you monetarily, I'll be happy to pay—"

"That wouldn't be very neighborly of us, now would it?" Jarman's sour expression softened. "She earned her keep by helping out around here. She's a good young'un, smart and spunky. But she needs a hiding for the fool stunt she pulled."

Neither Linda nor Jack believed in corporal punishment, but in this instance she was tempted to agree.

"With Calhoun for a handle, you must surely have some Texan blood running in your veins," Mister Jarman changed the subject.

"I suppose it's possible," she replied politely. She thought that identification with nations and other pre-War factions was an unhealthy anachronism. "Our family records don't go back before the War, so there is no telling."

Jarman's attire and speaking style didn't surprise Linda; she had seen such deliberate cultural regression in other towns and enclaves. According to sociologists, it was a byproduct of the isolation of post-War communities. Lone Star's Old West motif was no odder than the Montreal enclave's return to French colonial days.

Jarman turned back to Captain Ramirez. "I don't mean to pry—much—but the message didn't say that a zep would be sent."

"The *Mayan Princess* is on a special assignment. When we received the good news about Señora Calhoun's wayward daughter, I decided to detour here on our homeward flight. But I must confess to an ulterior motive. While Señora Calhoun is attending to her business, perhaps we could adjourn to a more private place," Captain Ramirez glanced at the townsfolk working around the blimp bay, "and discuss it."

"Surely. Miz Calhoun, your young'un is staying with Jim and Dede Polk on the ninth level, rim apartment sixteen. If you want to find Captain Ramirez and me later, we'll be in my office."

"Thank you, Mr. Jarman," she said. "If you gentlemen will excuse me, I want to go get Wanda."

"Of course," Ramirez replied, and Jarman nodded.

Linda walked quickly to the park escalator, and rode the moving ramps up through the levels of Lone Star Five. Her engineer's eye noted some interesting new developments in windrider construction. She was impressed by how much the shakedown crew had already accomplished; even at this hour they were hard at work. The townsfolk she passed looked at her curiously and greeted her pleasantly.

She focused on the external to avoid her growing nervousness. What in the sky was she going to say to Wanda? The situation was so strange and delicate that nothing in her experience covered it. She had spent hours trying to come up with the right words, to no avail. Finally she had decided to wing it. She wiped damp palms on her scavenger coveralls.

Deboarding the escalator at the ninth level, she checked the wall map, then took the east radial corridor and turned left at the rim circum. (Directions in a windrider were fixed relative to the windrider itself, rather than compass points, for convenience.) She stopped in front of the apartment marked sixteen. After staring at the door for long seconds, she touched the chime button.

Moments later the door opened, and she found herself facing a tall, lanky young man. He grinned. "Howdy, ma'am. Can I help you?" Curiosity entered his expression, probably because he didn't recognize her.

"Please excuse the intrusion, but are you Jim Polk?"

"Sure am."

"My name is Linda Calhoun. I believe you've been taking care of my daughter, Wanda?"

Surprise and sadness flashed across his face before the grin returned. "Right the first time. I'm mighty pleased to meet you, Miz Calhoun. Come on in."

He ushered her into a furnished but undecorated living room. Starlight from beyond the window wall added to the soft illumination of the glow panels. "Set a spell," Jim suggested. "Wanda is in the kitchen helping Dede—that's my wife—with the dishes. I'll go fetch her."

"Thank you." Despite his friendliness, his gaze made her uncomfortable. She wondered what Wanda had told him and his wife about why she had run away.

Linda was too nervous to sit down. Jim disappeared through the kitchen doorway. The cleaning-up sounds stopped, and low voices rumbled. Then Jim and a young woman with a spectacular head of red hair emerged, guiding an unwilling Wanda between them.

Everyone froze, staring at each other.

"I've come to take you home, dear," Linda told Wanda softly.

"I won't go!" Wanda blurted out. "I hate you!"

Linda had broken a hip in a loading accident, and both of her deliveries had been difficult. But Wanda's words hurt her worse than all three put together. The Polks stepped back.

"We'll discuss that later. Go get your things. We'll sleep aboard the *Mayan Princess* tonight. I came in it, and it sails for Pemex Under in the morning. From there we'll take passage on the next zep home."

"Calgary isn't my home anymore!"

"You don't meant that," Linda said soothingly. "Calgary is where you belong. It's where your relatives and friends are. Your father misses you very much."

The last part was fighting dirty, and Linda regretted it the moment it left her lips. The blood drained from Wanda's face. When she spoke, her voice trembled. "You don't care about me! All you care about is . . . you know!"

Linda did, but she certainly didn't intend to discuss it in front of strangers. "I've been worried sick about you ever since you ran away. Why do you think I'm here? Because I love you."

"Leave me alone! This is where I live now! I have friends here, and I'm working to pay my way! I don't need you!"

Linda was beginning to lose her temper. Wanda had always been respectful and obedient; this open rebellion was as uncharacteristic as it was hard to deal with. "I can't leave you here. I'm your mother—I'm responsible for your welfare. When you turn eighteen, you can move here or anywhere else you please. Until then your place is with your family. Now go get your things."

"No!" Wanda almost shouted. Her face had gone from pale to flushed. "I won't pretend we're a family! We aren't! You don't love Dad or me!"

It was Linda's turn to shudder from a low blow. "I said we'll discuss that later. In private."

But Wanda was out of control. Venom spewed out of her mouth. "I saw you in Miguel's room! You two were making love!"

Linda struggled to hang onto a remnant of her own control. The Polks were trying to blend into the wall.

"Whatever you saw, or thought you saw, you misunderstood it. I admit I almost made a terrible mistake. But I didn't."

"You were hugging and kissing him, and you had your dress off—!"

Linda lurched forward. Her open hand swung half the distance to Wanda's face before she could stop it.

"Liar!" Wanda exploded. Whirling, she fled to one of the bedrooms and slammed the door behind her.

The Polks studiously avoided Linda's eyes. As her temper subsided below the boiling point, she fervently wished that she could erase the entire meeting and try again. She had thoroughly botched it. The Mother's Handbook was a well-worn joke; for the first time she really wished one existed.

Now she didn't seem to have any choice. As sickening as the thought was, she would have to go into the bedroom and drag Wanda to the *Mayan Princess* by main force. But as she took the first step, Dede moved into her path. "I wouldn't do that if I were you, Miz Calhoun."

Linda had been tried beyond the limits of politeness. "Are you going to try to stop me?"

"Nope. You all are family—it wouldn't be right for us to interfere. But I'd like to suggest something, if you don't mind."

"Go ahead."

"Both of you all are mighty worked up right now. If you try to take her with you, I reckon you'll have a fight on your hands. One both of you will regret for a long time."

"I can't leave her here."

"Of course not. But you said your zep isn't going to leave until morning. Why not let it be for now, and come back around sunup to fetch her? She'll have some time to get used to the notion, and you'll be steadier."

The suggestion appealed to Linda; not just for the reasons stated, but because it would let her put off the ugly task for a few hours. "That makes sense. I'll return then."

The Polks walked Linda to the front door. Pausing, she turned to face them. "I apologize for airing our dirty linen in your home."

The Polks still looked embarrassed, but Jim managed a

grin. "That's what friends are for. We're Wanda's friends, and we'd like to be yours too."

"I'm honored." Linda smiled back. "Thank you very much for taking care of Wanda. You've made a difficult time easier for both of us."

"Our pleasure. Wanda is a mighty fine young 'un—we're going to miss her."

"I'll see you in the morning. Good night."

"So long."

Linda was lost in a whirl of thought and emotion as she walked back to the park escalator and rode up to the fifth level. The relative emptiness and silence of Lone Star Five added to her sense of unreality.

She had no idea what she was going to do about Wanda. Getting Wanda back to Calgary Three was only a physical solution. She had to explain about Captain Ramirez in a way that Wanda would understand. Otherwise Wanda's disillusionment and hate would not only tear the family apart; it would cripple Wanda's ability to trust, to love. But how to explain, when she didn't understand fully herself, was a poser.

She checked a wall map and headed for the office of the chief engineer. By the time she arrived, she had pushed the troubling dilemma into the back of her mind.

The chief engineer's office was next to the mayor's. She knocked on the door, and moments later Mr. Jarman let her in. The office, like its counterpart in Calgary Three, was designed for both administrative and technical functions. Built-in shelves and monitor screens shared the walls, while the furnishings were dominated by an enormous desk/console. But Jarman's hat sitting on a shelf was the only relief from the stark whiteness. Decorating Lone Star Five would have to wait until the more important work was done.

Captain Ramirez had been seated, but he sprang to his feet as Linda entered. "How is Wanda! Did your reunion go well?"

Linda shrugged. "She's healthy. The reunion went as well as could be expected. She's going to spend the night with the Polks—I'll pick her up before we leave."

"I see," Captain Ramirez said sympathetically. "Don't despair. Injuries to the heart heal too."

Linda took the chair next to Ramirez as they sat down, Mister Jarman settled behind the desk/console. "I'm glad you dropped by, Miz Calhoun," the chief engineer said, looking even grimmer than he had in the blimp bay. "Captain Ramirez here has been spinning a mighty tall yarn, and I'd like to hear your version. If you don't mind."

"I've been telling Señor Jarman about Alpha and our adventure in Davis," Captain Ramirez explained.

Linda was surprised. "We're supposed to be keeping all that secret."

Some steel entered Captain Ramirez's smile. "Señor Cardenas will probably be unhappy with me, but I've decided the time for secrecy is past. Alpha already knows what we're up to—a fact which will certainly interest him—so I'm warning the world of the danger, starting here. Unfortunately, Señor Jarman thinks I'm deranged."

So Linda told her story, beginning with the meeting in Mayor Keith's office. The events in Davis came out of her slowly, painfully. When she finished she felt drained and somewhat embarrassed.

Jarman looked dubious. "I don't know what to say. Or think, come to that. If what you all have told me is so, it's the worst danger we've faced since the War—"

"If you keep calling Señora Calhoun and myself liars, you're going to make me angry." There was steel in Captain Ramirez's voice.

"Sorry, don't mean to be rude. But you must admit it's a lot to swallow, particularly without any proof. What could make folks act that ornery? And how could they lie so low that nobody has ever heard tell of them?"

"I can't answer your questions," Linda said softly. "I don't want Alpha to exist either. But wishing won't make it go away."

Jarman didn't believe them. She could see it in his eyes.

So did Captain Ramirez. Sighing, he said to Jarman, "Events will take their course. May I use your radio to report to Pemex Under?"

"Surely." Jarman seemed relieved to be leaving the subject. "Let's mosey on down to the bridge."

He led them back to the park escalator, and they rode down to the blimp bay. Nobody spoke during the trip. Linda's mind was on Wanda, while the two men also looked thoughtful. They descended the short stairway to the bridge. Jarman's hand on the ident-plate opened the door; they went in.

The bridge was softly lit, a muted background against which the colorful screens and displays stood out. The transparent floor revealed darkness relieved only by faint moonlight reflecting from the clouds below. As was usual on a normal shift, only three of the stations were occupied; routine bridge operations were almost entirely automated. Jarman made the introductions. Lefty Adams, a rawboned extrovert in a cowboy outfit which made Jarman's seem tame, was the shift chief. Catlin Rogers was dark-haired and intense, while Gary Tanner was very attractive in an overendowed way.

"Everything green?" Mister Jarman asked Lefty.

"Like the wide open prairie. What brings you all around? Trouble?"

"Could be, but we'll get to that later. Right now Captain Ramirez here wants to use our radio to chew the fat with Pemex Under. Can we oblige him?"

"How about it?" Lefty asked Gray.

She moved over to the com station and went to work. A minute later she looked up. "Atmospheric conditions are good. Ought to be able to get through without a relay."

"Go to it."

While her hands moved over the radio board, Jarman gestured to three of the empty station chairs. "Let's hunker down," he suggested to Linda and Captain Ramirez. "This could take a spell."

They sat down. Captain Ramirez was sounding out Jarman about buying some current for the *Mayan Princess*'s batteries, and Linda was admiring the latest word in bridge equipment, when Gray yanked off her headset and said something very unladylike.

"Something wrong?" Lefty asked laconically.

"Damn near took my head off," she muttered as she rubbed her ears. "Some kind of power surge—never heard anything like it." She was frowning at the radio displays, some of which were glowing red. "The transmitter is down."

"How long you reckon it'll take to fix?"

"Can't rightly say—I'm running the diagnostic now. Want me to switch in the backup?"

"I wouldn't do that, if I were you," Captain Ramirez interrupted. He was staring at the radio board. His smile had hardened again, and there was a haunted look in his eyes.

Lefty swiveled to face him. "Why not?"

"Because your transmitter's backup chip will be burned out too. Just as ours was."

Lefty looked at him with curiosity and dawning suspicion. But before he could speak, Jarman said, "I'm taking the reins, Lefty."

"I knew it. Trouble." The two men exchanged stations.

Jarman looked as if he had just found half a worm in his apple. "Captain, that yarn you told me about that attack on your zep—"

"Exactly."

Linda was gazing into the darkness below the floor. The night no longer seemed empty and safe. She couldn't see anything, but she knew it was out there. The windrider eater.

"Remember the unexplained windrider losses?" she managed to ask Mr. Jarman through gathering fear and sickness. "Whatever happened to them . . . is about to happen to us."

CHAPTER TWENTY-SEVEN

Wanda lay huddled on her bed, crying.

The bedroom was pitch black, but not nearly as dark as her heart. The anger that had held her together through the terrible ordeal with Mom had given way to utter misery. She wanted to die. She wanted to jump off the shell, preferably with Mom watching, and fall and fall and fall until she hit the surface.

Then she wouldn't have to feel like this anymore.

There was a soft but insistent knocking on the door. She tried to ignore it, but it wouldn't stop. Finally she unburied her head from the pillow and yelled, "I won't go back with you! I won't! Leave me alone!"

"It's me, Wanda." Dede's muffled voice came from beyond the door. "Are you okay?"

Wanda managed to speak through her sniffling. "Yes. Where's Mom?"

"She's gone. She went back to her zep, I reckon. May I come in?"

Wanda didn't answer. She didn't want to be rude to Dede, but she wanted to be alone.

"Please, Wanda? I reckon you must feel lower than a snake's belly right now, but we really ought to talk. How about it?"

"Okay," Wanda gave in wanly.

The door opened, and a moment later the glow panels turned the room from black to gray. An adult body settled on the side of the bed. Wanda looked up suspiciously, but Dede was alone. She had closed the door behind her.

"Poor child," she said as she wiped Wanda's eyes with a handkerchief. "You've had a mighty rough time of it."

"Please let me stay here with you and Jim," Wanda begged. "Don't let Mom take me back. I'll be good, work hard, do all the chores—anything you say. I really like it here. I like you and Jim a lot."

Dede was quiet for a long time, and her comforting look turned sad. "I'm as sorry as a body can be, honey," she finally said, "but we can't rightly do that."

"Please! This isn't Calgary—she can't make you do anything."

"It's not that simple. Your ma would say we stole you, raise a big fuss. That would cause trouble between Lone Star and Calgary. Vic Jarman wouldn't sit still for that, particularly since we'd be in the wrong. He'd put you on the zep himself."

Wanda felt tears welling up again. "But I *can't* go back. I can't live with Mom. She . . . you heard . . ."

Dede was quiet even longer this time. "I heard, Wanda, but I'm not about to say who's right or who's wrong. It's not my place."

"She was with Miguel—that's Captain Ramirez, you remember him—in his room. They were—"

"Whatever they did, she's still your ma. And a mighty good one too, or you wouldn't have turned out so well. Think about how much she has meant to you—one night oughtn't to wipe all that out. One more thing, and I'll stop preaching. She loves you. She wouldn't have looked the way she did when you turned tail, if she didn't."

Wanda lay helplessly while feelings pushed and pulled at her. Finally stubbornness won. "I won't go back."

Dede sighed. "Can't be helped, honey. Your ma is going to come for you tomorrow at sunup. I surely hope you all work out your trouble."

Wanda didn't say anything.

"So much for my two cents." Dede stood up. "I better

mosey, so you can hit the hay. If you need anything at all, you know where to find me. Sleep tight."

"Good night," Wanda said meekly. "I'm sorry for being so much trouble."

"You've been a pure joy." Dede kissed her on the forehead, and left.

Wanda lay on her back, staring at the gray ceiling. Images of folks from home flashed in her mind: Dad, Cheryl, Grandma and Grandpa Calhoun, Jan, Lori, Jeff and many more. She missed them so much. But home could never be home again. Because if she went back, she would have to pretend Mom was still Mom. She would have to keep Mom's filthy secret, so Dad wouldn't be hurt. She couldn't stand the thought of that.

She wasn't going to let Mom take her back.

Running away had worked once. Hopefully it would work again. She had been all over Lone Star Five, and she knew where the best hidey holes were. If she disappeared long enough, the *Mayan Princess* would have to leave and Mom would have to go with it. Then she could come back to live with Dede and Jim.

Wiping her eyes, she went to the closet and got out her suitcase. She put in some clothes and personal items, including her flatscreen and romance bookdisks. Then she held her ear to the door. The apartment was quiet. Like Jim said, aggies were early to bed, early to rise.

Opening the door a crack, Wanda saw that the apartment was darkened except for a line of light under the door to Dede's and Jim's bedroom. Her nervousness quantum-jumped. She was tempted to wait until they were asleep. But she figured going now would be safer; their pre-bed preparations would cover any noises she made.

Slowly and as quietly as possible, she felt her way into the kitchen. She used the fridge's light to find some food she could eat cold and stuff it into her suitcase. She felt bad about stealing from Dede and Jim, not to mention taking off without so much as a note. But she promised herself she would make up for both things later.

She went to the front door. Her heart pounding, she peered out into the corridor. It was empty. It probably didn't matter if anybody saw her leaving, but she was being as careful as possible.

She followed the circum corridor to the east radial, then went inboard to the east escalator. She was glad that there were so few folks in Lone Star Five, and that most of them were asleep or working somewhere else. She didn't see anybody until she was riding the escalator down. A pair of crew members passed her going up. Swallowing her nervousness (which was easier this time thanks to experience), she made sure her suitcase sitting on the moving steps was out of sight. Then she smiled and waved like she always did. They waved back.

The escalator ended at the bottom residential level. She started down the stairway into the engineering levels. Now she had to be very careful, because anybody who spotted her would wonder what she was doing here so late, particularly with a suitcase. She moved quickly but quietly. Twice she ducked into corridors to avoid crew members. Thanks to a combination of sneakiness and luck she reached the level just above the work level unnoticed.

This level was all one big open space, over a half mile across, and over a hundred feet from the aluminum-reinforced plastic floor to the glow panels in the ceiling. There were some box-like offices and unassembled equipment clustered around the dark escalator; otherwise the cubic was empty except for scattered structural girders, vents, pipes, conduits and the four stairways. A few of the glow panels were on, dimly lighting the level, while the window wall surrounded Wanda with a ring of starry night. She was all alone.

She knew from overheard conversations that this level was going to be a petrochemical plant, Lone Star Five's contribution to the town business. Plastics and plastic composites designed for strength, lightness, durability, anti-rad, insulation and other special qualities were very important to modern civilization. Windriders couldn't exist without them. She figured this was the best place to hide, because crew members hardly ever came here. The plant wouldn't be set up until they reached Lone Star and the rest of the plant's equipment (and the townsfolk) were transferred. Also, there was a bathroom in the offices she could use if she was careful.

She walked over to one of the offices. It was small, and it didn't have any furniture, but the carpet looked inviting now that her excitement was giving way to sleepiness. The ceiling and the upper half of the walls were clear, so she would be able to spot anybody who came into the level. If anybody did come, there was a closet where she could hide herself and her stuff.

It would do, she decided. Opening the suitcase, she started to get ready for "bed."

She was in the bathroom brushing her teeth, when the crash siren went off. Her heart jumped. What was going on? On a shakedown cruise it wouldn't be a drill. Was Lone Star Five about to fall out of the sky?

She started to run out of the bathroom, then stopped as she answered her own questions. There couldn't be anything wrong with Lone Star Five, since it was brand new. The siren had to be for her. Dede and Jim must have found out she was gone, and Mister Jarman was organizing a search for her. She ran back to the office, scooped up the suitcase, and almost dove into the closet.

The cramped darkness frightened her for a moment, reminding her of the mall-level closet where she had almost baked to death. When the siren stopped, she listened hard. But all she could hear was her own nervous panting.

Finally she got tired of waiting for something to happen. Using a wad of clothes for a pillow, she curled up on the closet's floor and let the sleepiness take her away.

CHAPTER TWENTY-EIGHT

Jarman slapped a button on the console in front of him. The bridge reverberated with the piercing crash siren for a few seconds, until he cut the feed to the bridge. To Linda the sudden return of silence seemed even louder.

"You sure you want to get everybody stirred up?" Lefty asked dubiously. "Could just be transmitter trouble."

"Or something a lot worse," Jarman replied. "I'd rather look like a jackass than be one. Let's get to it."

The bridge crew concentrated on the complex task of putting Lone Star Five on emergency alert, while Linda and Captain Ramirez watched silently. Linda imagined the frantic activity throughout the windrider: off-shift townsfolk roused from sleep hurrying to their stations, department heads organizing and reporting to the bridge, emergency systems being brought on line. Jarman and Lefty were busy with their coms, while Catlin was running a tight-beam radar scan and Gray was still trying to diagnose the problem with the transmitter. One by one the rest of the bridge crew rushed in, until all nine stations were manned and Linda and Captain Ramirez were standing behind Jarman.

Linda wanted to run to the Polks' apartment, which would be Wanda's emergency station, take her and flee. But there was no safe haven from what she feared was about to happen. If anything could be done to protect Wanda, it would be done here. She had to stay. Ignoring her deepest instinct, she watched and listened and hoped.

Jarman was trying to explain the situation to the bridge crew, when the woman who had taken Catlin's place at the flight station reported, "I've got something on radar."

"Something?" Jarman demanded.

The woman looked puzzled. "Could be a zep. Bearing two six ought, range two point five miles and closing, relative altitude zero."

"Two and half miles out, and it just showed up on our scope?"

"The blip is just barely there now. Beats hell out of me—maybe it's a ghost."

Jarman looked questioningly at Captain Ramirez.

"I've never heard of any way to shield a zep from radar," Ramirez said calmly. "But I imagine it would be a useful trick in a war, and these Alphans seem to have access to sophisticated military equi—"

"Incoming call," Gray interrupted. "I reckon it's from Sara Jane's ghost zep."

Linda saw worry dawning in the Lone Star Five faces around her. She sympathized, knowing how much worse was yet to come.

"I'll take it," Jarman said sharply.

Gray routed the call to his station. "You're on."

Jarman switched on his mike. "This is windrider Lone Star Five, chief engineer Vic Jarman here. You all are in our airspace. Identify yourselves."

A tense handful of seconds passed. Then a thin, cold, totally self-assured voice came from the wall speaker. "This is Colonel McCrarey," commander of the zep *Shenandoah* attached to Alpha Command. "You'll surrender your windrider to me at once, or suffer the consequences."

Linda groaned inaudibly as her worst fear was confirmed. Death had followed her across the sky; she had led it to Wanda.

"You all are *attacking* us?" Mister Jarman asked incredulously.

"A crude but adequate description. Technically we're

commandeering your bubble for military operations, all very proper under the articles of war."

"But there isn't any war!"

"Guess again. Now we can do this the easy way or the hard way—hard on you. The choice is yours."

Jarman cut off his mike and turned to Gray. "Got all this recorded?"

"Yep."

"Throw in our position and course, pack it into a tight pulse, and squirt it out on the WeatherNet frequency. Ought to do for a Mayday as well as a warning."

Gray went to work at her radio board. But when she touched the transmit button, she yelped and yanked off her headset again. "So much for the backup," she muttered, rubbing her ears.

"That was a futile and wasteful gesture." Colonel McCrarey's voice sounded smug. "Are you ready to surrender now?"

"Range one mile and holding," Sara Jane reported.

"I've got an outside camera hunting your track with full computer enhancement," Lefty told her. "Something is blocking stars, but I can't see hide nor hair of it. Its hull must be black as sin."

"This has to be somebody's notion of a joke," the man at the computer station said rather desperately.

"Can you get me through to that ranny?" Jarman asked Gray, his anger barely under control.

"The zep ought to be in range of the com system's transmitter." She touched buttons on her com board, then added, "Go ahead."

"Colonel McCrarey, you can take your tricks and your articles of war and clear out!" Jarman seethed into his mike.

"Admirable bravado, but not a very responsible attitude for a leader. Under normal circumstances I would send a boarding party over to eliminate you and your crew and take what I want. But I would prefer to have your cooperation. In case you doubt either my ability to crash your windrider or my willingness to do so, maybe this will convince you. Out."

An alarm sounded. Red lights woke all over Lefty's systems station.

"Breach!" he yelled. His eyes and hands moved quickly over his console.

The word, usually the most terrifying in a windrider engineer's vocabulary, had little effect on Linda. At this point, what did one more disaster matter?

The rest of the bridge crew was either busy at their own stations or watching Lefty. Nobody asked him any questions; they knew better than to distract him.

"Puncture near the equator," he said a few seconds later, sounding somewhat relieved but not slowing in his work. "Lateral one eight six degrees by vertical zero nine three degrees. Mean diameter fourteen inches. No main cable damage."

"Radical depressurization point zero zero four two PSI/seconds," Catlin reported from the environment station. "Auto-responses in effect—pumps and heaters at max."

Sara Jane punched up a display. "We're going down. Relative altitude negative twenty feet, delta vee building slowly but surely."

"I've got a shell deflation stress projection," Lefty added. "Red-line in fourteen minutes fifty seconds."

Jarman switched on his com. "Yo, Swede. How about patching this breach, before we turn inside out?"

Linda assumed that the gruff speaker voice belonged to the chief of the work crew. "We're on it, Vic. Sandy and Dallas lit out as soon as Lefty fed us the site coordinates. ET for the patch seven minutes, thereabouts. No time to chew the fat—got them on another channel." The com clicked off.

"Vid coming up," Lefty announced. The big monitor screen over his head filled with an inside view of a section of the shell, faintly lit by the topside lamps. A small round hole was centered. Its melted rim suggested that extreme heat had caused it. Air was blowing out, creating what looked like a mini-whirlwind. The breach was serious, Linda decided, but controllable if the work crew did its job.

The camera panned left and zoomed out to take in more of an access belt. Two figures in outside suits were just jumping from the rising belt onto a work platform. One of them grabbed a patch kit and clipped it to his/her belt. Then they began moving sideways across the vertical shell, wall-walking while clipping their waist lines to a succession of the clamps set in the shell. Linda was impressed by the speed they made without sacrificing safety.

Minutes dragged by, punctuated by terse reports and low-voiced com conversations. All the attention that could be spared from work was focused on the screen. To Linda it seemed that the bridge crew almost welcomed the breach as something they could understand and deal with. Meanwhile, according to Sara Jane, the Alphan zep was quietly circling Lone Star Five.

The work crew members reached the hole in the shell. The one with the kit assembled a patch out of interconnecting aluminum plates, while the other filed down the rim of the hole. Then both of them fought the whirlwind to position the patch over the hole. Superadhesive edges held it there and formed an airtight seal with the shell. Catlin's report, "Pressure holding steady," brought a measure of relief to the bridge.

Jarman was collecting status reports when Gray broke in. "Incoming call from the *Shenandoah*."

"I'll take it." Jarman switched on his com, and when Gray gave the go-ahead he spoke grimly. "Jarman here. What in the blue blazes did you all hit us with?"

"Now that you've had time to recover from my little demonstration," Colonel McCrarey replied, "let's get back to business. The weapon we 'hit you with' is called a free-electron laser. It can just as easly burn a twenty-foot hole in your shell—one too big to patch. I intend to give the order to do just that, unless you surrender at once."

Jarman's anger had evolved into something else, a reaction that Linda recognized and empathized with from her own encounter in Davis: shock. Events had pushed him out of the light of the world he knew into the darkness beyond. He had nothing to guide him: no training, no experience, no rule book. When he answered, his voice lacked its familiar drive. "I can't just hand Lone Star Five over to you all like a loaf of bread. We need some time to think, to talk it over—"

"You have five minutes. I hope you use them wisely—the wrong decision will cost you your lives as well as your windrider. Out."

Switching off the com, Jarman looked around the bridge helplessly. But the rest of the bridge crew had nothing to say. They seemed equally in shock.

"I hope you aren't seriously considering surrendering," Captain Ramirez said, all the casualness gone from his voice.

Jarman swiveled to face him. "I surely don't hanker to, but what other choice have I got?"

"You can resist."

"Resist! How? We don't have any weapons—wouldn't know what to do with them if we did. Meanwhile we're a mighty fat floating target for that hogleg the Alphan zep is packing."

There was a light of excitement in Captain Ramirez's eyes which normally would have outraged Linda; now it gave her a faint hope.

"Recharging the laser must require a certain amount of time," he explained. "We can make use of that. I'll launch the *Mayan Princess*, unmanned under auto-con, to try to ram the Alphan zep. That should at least attract its attention. Meanwhile Lone Star Five will climb above its flight ceiling, where it won't be able to attack us."

To Linda it was a solution as desperate as the situation. The only way a windrider could climb that high at night, without the greenhouse effect, would be to jettison almost all of its water. Even then the rate of climb would be slow. Depending on how long it took to recharge the laser weapon, the Alphan zep might be able to crash both the *Mayan Princess* and Lone Star Five.

Jarman must have been thinking the same thing. "You're plumb loco! Hightail it in your zep, if you all are set on dying. But I've got eighty-nine folks to look after. I'm going to do everything I can to keep them alive. I reckon we can work things out with this Colonel McCrarey."

"That is exactly the reaction McCrarey wants to create," Linda said softly.

"What in the blue blazes do you mean by that?" Jarman demanded.

Linda shuddered from her memories of Davis. "You've seen and heard, but you don't understand. You're trying to judge how these Alphans will act by our standards. But they aren't like us. They hurt, kill and destroy, not just to get what they want, but because they *enjoy* hurting, killing and destroying. In their eyes we're nothing more than prey to be hunted and exploited."

The bridge crew faces staring at her showed disbelief; even now it was too black a picture for them to accept. But she had to keep trying. "No one wants to die. But the crashing of Lone Star Five might not be the worst possible outcome."

A grim silence followed her words. When Jarman spoke, he let out some of his anger and frustration. "Things are bad enough as is—we don't need you making them sound worse than they are! Colonel McCrarey said he hankers for our cooperation. If we cooperate, he won't have any cause to get riled." He seemed to be trying to convince himself as well as everyone else.

"You're wrong," Linda replied. "But I'm terribly afraid you won't find that out until it's too late."

"Who in the blue blazes are you to tell me my job! You and Captain Ramirez here brought this trouble down on us. Least you all can do is keep still while we handle it."

Captain Ramirez stood up, radiating a forceful dignity which reminded Linda of Señor Gutierrez. "Señor Jarman," he said stiffly, "I assure you I didn't know the Alphan zep was trailing us, as apparently it was. I had no intention of putting Lone Star Five in danger. I would lead the danger away, if I could. But all of us are caught in the same trap now. I suggest we stop bickering and pool our efforts."

"Don't make the mistake of thinking that this isn't your trouble too," Linda added. "The Alphans have crashed twenty-three windriders."

Jarman stared at his boots. The rest of the bridge crew tended their stations automatically, fending off com calls from worried department heads, while they watched and waited. Finally he looked up at them. "Any opinions?"

Nobody spoke.

He shrugged. "Well, I hankered to ramrod this outfit,

so here it is. We can't fight, we can't run, and we can't holler for help. We have to surrender."

Linda felt an icy hand grip her heart. Glancing around the bridge, she saw that everyone except Captain Ramirez shared her reaction. No one questioned Jarman's right to make the decision; the chief engineer on a shakedown cruise had the same authority as a zep captain.

Mr. Jarman turned to Ramirez. "You all can hightail it or not. But if you stay, you all will do as you are told. Got that?"

"I suspect our dear Colonel McCrarey has the *Mayan Princess* in his targeting scope at this very moment." Captain Ramirez was his relaxed, smiling self again. "Therefore on behalf of my crew I accept your gracious invitation."

"Your five minutes are up," Colonel McCrarey's voice came from the speaker. "I'll have your answer now."

Jarman switched his com back on. "We surrender," he muttered.

"Excellent." But Colonel McCrarey sounded vaguely disappointed. "As of now Lone Star Five is under occupation martial law. In case you're unfamiliar with the term, it means that you and your personnel will obey our orders to the letter. Failure to do so will be punished severely. Is that clear?"

"Yep," Jarman replied through gritted teeth.

"Here are your first orders. Don't try to send any radio messages or launch a blimp. Remove the crew from the Pemex Under zep. The *Shenandoah* will dock in thirty minutes—you have that long to move the Pemex Under zep to an auxiliary berth. Assemble all personnel except those with essential duties in your town hall, and have the rest listen in by com. I'll be addressing you upon my arrival. Any questions?"

"Nope."

"Apparently you're unfamiliar with military courtesy. You'll address my officers and myself by our ranks, or by the honorific 'sir.' One more thing. The Pemex Under zep is carrying an item of salvage from its scavenging expedition: a set of memory disks. I want it waiting for me in your blip bay when I come aboard. Out."

Jarman swiveled his chair to face Lefty. "Get Swede to

work jacking the *Mayan Princess* over to Berth B. Bolt it in for long-term mooring, and slave it to our systems."

"On it." Lefty went to work at his console.

"Captain Ramirez," Mister Jarman said, "you'll coordinate with Lefty on this. Head your crew up and move them out to the town hall—and don't forget those disks Colonel McCrarey hankers for. You heard the deadline. Get to it."

Captain Ramirez bowed. "As you wish."

"Vic," Gray cut in, "com calls are piling up. Everybody wants to know what's going on."

"They just reckon they do." Jarman turned with visible reluctance to his com. Ramirez headed for the door; Linda followed him.

The blimp bay was busier than when they had arrived. Several crew members near the dock air lock were donning outside suits while others prepared the jacks, pumps, flexpipes and cables which would enable Lone Star Five to operate and maintain the unmanned *Mayan Princess*. Slaving would let the windrider change altitude without losing the zep. But even with the zep's hydrogen cells fully inflated, the crew removed, and all the ballast upped into the windrider, the windrider's flight ceiling would be reduced by the zep to approximately twenty-four thousand feet.

Linda and Ramirez didn't say anything until they reached the top of the enteryway ramp. Then she stopped. "Please excuse me, Captain. I have to go fetch Wanda."

Ramirez turned to her. "May I ask why?"

"Why!" Linda hadn't bothered to think about reasons. She just knew that, in the face of this terrible danger, Wanda's place was with her. Their argument now seemed small and unimportant. They would endure the Alphan occupation together, so she could protect Wanda.

"Don't misunderstand me," Captain Ramirez said soothingly. "Of course the two of you should be reunited as quickly as possible. But why waste time and effort hunting for her, when you know precisely where to find her in thirty minutes? At the town hall."

Ramirez's suggestion didn't ease the aching emptiness under her breast, but it was logical. She tried to clear her mind so she could think productively, come up with some way to keep Wanda safe.

"The satellite manual," she mused half to herself as they started down to the *Mayan Princess*. "The *Shenandoah* must have been hiding near Davis—the men who attacked us must have come from it. Then it followed us here. But why? Is the satellite manual that important to Alpha?"

Captain Ramirez looked dubious. "Alpha already knows about war lasers. I could understand McCrarey pursuing us to prevent the satellite manual and news of what happened in Davis from reaching Pemex Under. But that would only require a momentary use of his zep's laser, whereas he seems to be planning on an extended stay. We must be missing some of the puzzle's pieces."

"What could Alpha want with a windrider?"

"A good question, and one I imagine we'll learn the answer to eventually. At the moment all we can do is survive, study our opponents, and watch for an opportunity to undo them."

That suggestion was just as reasonable and unsatisfying as his other. "What about the satellite manual? Should we give it to Colonel McCrarey? Maybe we should hide it, or drop it out an air lock?"

Captain Ramirez shook his head. "Too little to gain, too much to lose. Neither action would help Pemex Under to build war lasers. But from what I've observed of Colonel McCrarey's mood, I suspect not turning over the manual would be a fatal mistake."

"I suppose you're right," Linda admitted. Hopelessness was thickening around her, but she couldn't give in to it.

For Wanda's sake.

CHAPTER TWENTY-NINE

Colonel McCrarey was at the head of the boarding party as it marched up the entryway ramp of the captured windrider. His long-unused combat suit felt hot, cumbersome, and exciting. Behind him the beats of pounding boots and slapping scabbards echoed hollowly off the plastic tube, while orders crackled on the com's common channel.

He was taking a calculated risk. With the *Shenandoah* docked, rendering the laser useless, but the occupation not yet in place, this was an unavoidable window of vulnerability. An ambush in the blimps bay could decimate his force, while a bomb dropped from an airlock or one of the blimp hatches could wreck the *Shenandoah*. But he understood these gutless civvies. They wouldn't even think of such violent tactics until it was too late. The risk of leading the boarding party was slight compared to the advantage of immediately asserting his authority.

The back of his neck itched as he stepped out into the blimp bay, but there wasn't any ambush or explosion. The cluttered expanse of gray deck was deserted except for three civvies standing together near the entryway. He ignored them for the moment. While Lieutenant Ford and A Platoon's first squad fell in behind him, he watched the rest of the aircav company deploy through the blimp bay at a dead run. After a few minutes of note-so-tidy reconnaissance Captain Patterson reported, "All secure, Colonel."

"Excellent. Proceed with Phase Two."

"Sir!"

Captain Patterson led B, C and D Platoons up the park escalator. Their objectives were to reconnoiter and to mount guard over key positions in the upper reaches of the windrider, while A Platoon's second squad did the same in the blimp bay and the bridge.

Satisfied that the boarding was well in hand, Colonel McCrarey gestured for the three civvies to join him. He removed his helmet. "I'm Colonel McCrarey," he said before any of them could speak, to establish control. "Identify yourselves."

"Vic Jarman," the man in the ridiculous cowboy outfit muttered, returning Colonel McCrarey's appraising stare with an angry one. But Colonel McCrarey read what he had expected to find: the windrider's leader was hamstrung by his concern for the safety of his people.

"Captain Miguel Ramirez of the Pemex Under zep *Mayan Princess*, at your service." The dark dagger of a man bowed slightly, but his relaxed grin ran about one micron deep. Colonel McCrarey made a mental note to keep an eye on him.

"I'm Linda Calhoun from Calgary," the attractive woman said hiding her fear well. Colonel McCrarey recognized the name from the friendly's report and the intercepted radio message. She had been a prime mover in bringing him to his destiny; it was fitting that she should be here. She was holding a small decon sack under one arm.

"Is that the Project Rainmaker satellite manual?" he asked her curtly. When she nodded he added, "Give it here."

She handed the decon sack to him without a word. The chief engineer started to say something, but he turned and gave the sack to Lieutenant Ford. "These are the disks we discussed. Have them deconned, then see what you can do with them. Top priority."

"Yes, sir." The com officer looked like a big dumb kid, but his blond crewcut covered a substantial amount of ability and ambition. He saluted, spun smartly, and jogged back to the entryway.

The chief engineer moved around in front of Colonel McCrarey. "Now, Colonel, there's no call for all this high-handedness. If you'll just tell me what you all hanker for—"

Colonel McCrarey's gloved fist slammed into the chief engineer's gut, doubling him over. He moaned, the woman paled, and the Pemex Under zep captain took a step forward before regaining control of himself.

"What I want, and will get, is obedience," Colonel McCrarey rapped. "You have nothing to negotiate with. Have all my orders been carried out?"

The chief engineer managed to straighten up and answer, "Yep . . . Colonel." He looked more surprised than hurt or angry.

A Platoon's first squad was still standing at attention behind Colonel McCrarey. He turned to the sergeant. "Burney, we're moving out for the town hall. Bring these civvies along, and stay on the bounce for trouble."

"Yes, sir."

Sergeant Burney took the point, while the rest of the squad was strung out behind him in patrol formation with Colonel McCrarey in the middle and the civvies near the rear. They rode up the park escalator through the levels of the windrider. Colonel McCrarey admired the modern features of his prize, and thought about how much more civilized life would be in it than in cramped Alpha. If this scheme fully developed, the new Alpha would combine the best of the military and civvie worlds. The idea of shaping it to his will was exhilarating.

They deboarded on the fourth level, which held the big public facilities. The entrance to the town hall was across the central rotunda from the escalator landing. Colonel McCrarey noted with satisfaction that four aircavs were on guard duty in front of the row of doors. They followed his group inside.

The so-called town hall was actually a multi-purpose facility. Big enough to hold all of a windrider's six hundred or so townfolk, it could be used for sports events, pubvids, dances and so on as well as town meetings. It was a hatbox-shaped cubic four hundred feet in diameter, and so tall that it reached into the second level. Its surfaces were plain and white. There weren't any bleachers, chairs, stage, podium or other fixtures yet, just stacks of crates by the walls. A crowd of townsfolk and zep crewmen were milling around in the middle of the floor. Their loud, confused babble died as McCrarey's group entered the hall.

He spotted a wall com panel which also accessed the hall's loudspeaker system, and went over to it. Sergeant Burney deployed his squad plus the four guards around the perimeter of the crowd. Thirteen against eighty might not have seemed like good odds, but Colonel McCrarey had no doubt that thirteen armed and armored aircavs could handle these sheep. The three civvies with him were shoved into the crowd.

He switched on the com's common channel as well as the loudspeaker system. "Attention, all personnel," he said, and his voice boomed from the overhead speakers. The townfolk and zep crewmen turned to face him. The aircavs kept watching them, hands on hilts.

Colonel McCrarey studied the faces staring at him, and was pleased by the emotions he saw. During his Academy days he had done some reading on how to control a civvie population. Since he didn't have enough aircavs to watch everyone every second, he had to destroy their will to resist. Break down their sense of community, of self; eliminate their ordered reality and impose his own. As Nidal had put it in his book on terrorism, make them afraid.

"Attention, all personnel. I'm Colonel McCrarey of Alpha Command. In case Mr. Jarman hasn't informed you, this windrider is now under military occupation. You'll continue to put it in order, and carry out all orders given to you by myself or my men. Any disobedience will be considered treason, punishable by death."

The fear in the faces was growing, but many of the civvies were still insulated by disbelief. Anger was also appearing here and there. Colonel McCrarey glanced at Sergeant Burney, whom he had assigned to identify and target potential troublemakers for the demonstration. The sergeant nodded.

"You might be tempted to be less than cooperative," Colonel McCrarey continued. "You might want to send a radio message for help, or launch the Pemex Under zep or a blimp, or carry out acts of sabotage, or hinder our operations by giving less than your best effort. You might even want to rebel against us. But you won't. Because the lives of the women among you will be pledged to your good behavior."

He raised his voice to crush a rising angry rumble from the crowd. "When I dismiss the men, the women will remain here under guard. The women presently on duty will report here within the hour. They will be provided with food, bedding and other necessary items. There are lavatories here. They will be safe and reasonably comfortable—so long as the men cooperate."

The chief engineer pushed his way to the front of the stunned civvies. "You can't do that, Colonel! You can't just lock folks up like they were bandits!"

"I can do anything I please. I suggest you remember that."

"But if you lock up half my crew, how are we going to keep Lone Star Five aloft, let alone put it in trim? We've got a heap of work to do."

"You'll have the male personnel from the Pemex Under zep to help you. Beyond that, I'm confident you'll find a way to carry on, considering the alternative. You might think of the detention as protective custody. My men have been without female companionship for some time. They have orders not to abuse your women, but men will be men."

His last comment struck a nerve. Noisy anger spread throught the civvies from several sources, building to the point which would turn the crowd into a mob. He watched the reaction like a cook judging the right moment to add an ingredient.

It came. He nodded to Sergeant Burney, who began rapping orders into his com. Five of the aircavs knifed into the crowd, threw armored punches, and dragged out five partly conscious civvies; three townsfolk—one a woman— and two zep crewmen. He was vaguely disappointed that the zep captain wasn't among them. The action was carried out so quickly and surgically that there wasn't time for the rest of the crowd to react. They just stared. Sheep!

"I warned you about the penalty for disobedience,"

Colonel McCrarey addressed the crowd as the five civvies were frog-marched to where he was standing. "That includes inciting disobedience, as these five were doing. Don't expect any legal formalities. I have the authority to act as judge, jury and executioner."

Colonel McCrarey walked over to the five civvies. They were being held up from behind by the aircavs. They were still dazed from the blows, their eyes glazed and their muscles jellied. He doubted that they were aware of what was happening. That would blunt some of his anticipated pleasure, but the demonstration wasn't for their benefit.

He drew his sword. He had personally sharpened the too-long-unused blade for this occasion; it gleamed like a silver flame. He was aware of the intensity of the crowd's attention focused on him.

He swung the sword in a flat arc. Once. Twice. Five times. Five heads tumbled from their necks to the white plastic floor. Bright arterial blood spurted from the stumps, but he knew from experience where to stand to avoid being splashed. The moan from the crowd was that of a single wounded animal.

Each death sent orgasmic tremors up his sword arm and through his entire being. To end in a moment everything which a lifetime had created, that was power. That was meaning.

As the aircavs let the five bodies join their heads on the floor, Colonel McCrarey turned back to the crowd. The civvies were quiet, motionless, staring at the bloody corpses. All the fight had gone out of them. They were clay, ready to be molded as he saw fit.

"You have you orders," he told them coldly. "Carry them out, or there will be more executions."

He smiled as the male civvies filed slowly out of the hall and the female civvies huddled closer together. Their movements were listless; their eyes were wide and unseeing.

Make them afraid.

CHAPTER THIRTY

Wanda isn't here!

The realization was a voice screaming at Linda, drowning everything else out. She pushed through the cluster of stunned women, as heedless of her rudeness as those that she bumped and shoved, searching for the beloved golden locks. But she couldn't find Wanda anywhere. She was close to total, out-of-control panic, even closer than she had been in Davis. Then only *her* life had been endangered.

She had expected to find Wanda among the others when she was brought to the hall. She hadn't, but that hadn't worried her too much at first; Wanda could have been easily swallowed up among so many tall folks. She had left Captain Ramirez and Mr. Jarman to search through the crowd. Colonel McCrarey's speech and the ghastly climax had held her attention irresistably, but then she had resumed her hunt.

Now the cavernous town hall was empty except for about thirty-five women gathered together for mutual comfort, as far from the five corpses as possible. The male townsfolk and *Mayan Princess* crewmen had left after a few pitifully futile words of encouragement to female friends/lovers/wives. Everyone was in a state of shock which Linda remembered all too well, except for Captain Ramirez, who had flashed her a grin and a covert thumbs-up on his way out. Colonel McCrarey had ordered his soldiers to disable the hall's com units; then they had all marched out of the hall. It was a relief not to have to look at them, but Linda knew that some of them were on guard outside the locked doors.

The women were milling around aimlessly. Some of them were talking to each other, their low voices echoing hollowly off the distant walls. Others were trapped inside themselves by the horror. Linda spotted Elena, and started toward her to ask if she had seen Wanda. But as Linda drew closer she realized that Elena was struggling to hold back tears. The slight chance that Elena knew something didn't justify intruding on such grief, and she couldn't spare any time for comfort, so she veered away.

She wasn't indifferent to the five murders or the grim future which Colonel McCrarey had described. They had hit her just as hard as anyone else. But her experience in Davis had acted like a vaccination, enabling her to better resist this second onslaught. She was learning a hard lesson in human adaptability.

"Yo, Linda!" a voice drawled behind her. She spun, and saw Dede Polk coming toward her.

She all but ran to close the gap. Grabbing Dede by the shoulders, she demanded, "Where is Wanda? Please!" She looked around frantically, but Dede was alone.

Dede seemed to be emerging from the worst of the shock. "I don't know. I'm as sorry as a body can be, honey, but I just don't know."

"What do you mean?" Linda shook the larger woman. "Didn't you bring her here?"

"Nope. I tucked her in at bedtime, but when the crash siren went off she was gone. She had lit out with her suitcase full of clothes and food from the kitchen. No note, no warning."

"She ran away again?" Dede's words didn't make any sense; they just bounced around inside Linda's head. "Why?"

Dede forced Linda's arms back to her side. "Get a hitch on yourself." Dede paused. "You know Wanda wasn't too set on the notion of going home with you. She must have reckoned that if she dug a hole and pulled it in after her, you'd go away and leave her be."

Linda's fear for Wanda's safety quantum-jumped. "If she's hiding out there somewhere . . . and those soldiers find her . . ."

"You shouldn't think such things," Dede said reassuringly. "Remember what that Colonel McCrarey fellow said about his folks leaving us alone—even those rannies wouldn't hurt a young'un. Besides, they have to catch the rabbit first. In a game of hide-and-seek my money is on Wanda."

Linda wasn't convinced. "Maybe I should tell Colonel McCrarey, so he'll know she's not deliberately disobeying him."

"I reckon that would be a mighty bad mistake," Dede said softly.

Linda's eyes turned to the five headless corpses. The smells of blood and sweat were a reek in the hall, despite the best efforts of the air system. She shuddered. "I do too." She tried to think, to figure out some way to help Wanda. But everything seemed utterly hopeless. Her long downhill slide had finally reached the bottom.

"Al Beaumont had a wife and a new baby waiting for him back at Lone Star."

Dede's words confused Linda. Then she realized that Dede was staring at the corpses too, and that her eyes were damp.

"Can't say as I knew Sally Raintree too well," Dede went on, mostly to herself. "But Craig . . . poor Craig Parmalee. He was Jim's foreman, and a finer human being never walked the sky. . . ."

"I'm sorry," Linda told her softly. "I must seem terribly self-involved—"

"No more than any hen with a missing chick." Dede forced her face into a wan smile. "Enough moping—time to start showing some backbone."

Linda felt tired and helpless. There wasn't anything she could do to protect Wanda, herself, anyone. She wanted to curl up in a dark corner and slip into oblivion. "Why bother? We're trapped here, and the men have to do as they are told. To the rest of the world we'll just be another unexplained windrider and zep loss. We don't exist anymore."

Dede squeezed her arm. "Don't count us out just yet, honey," she whispered. "You don't know about Texans. I admit we're mighty spooked right now, but that's not the same as being yellow. Jim, Vic Jarman and the rest of the menfolk are going to come up with some way to fix these rannies' wagon."

"What do you think they will do?" Linda whispered back. A flicker of reviving hope struggled against the fear that resistance would just make things worse.

"Beats me. But when they make their play, we'll be ready to back it."

CHAPTER THIRTY-ONE

Colonel McCrarey spent the remaining hours of the night in the bridge of the captured windrider. While the tamed civvies worked at their stations, and a pair of aircavs watched them just in case, he turned his attention to the next steps in the occupation.

First, because it was most important, he arranged for the windrider to escape detection. He knew that a nearby zep would be sent to search its last known position as soon as it was out of com for six hours. So he had it descend into a stiff west wind at fourteen thousand feet. The radical course change would take it clear of the search area, after which it would head north to rendezvous with Alpha. He used the *Shenandoah*'s radio to report the successful capture to General Armbruster, and to arrange for weather updates from Alpha's covert WeatherNet tap.

The male Pemex Under zep crewmen were reassigned to suitable duties replacing female townsfolk. They were taken aboard the zep under guard to pick up their belongings, and installed in residential-level quarters in the windrider. The zep captain, now a member of the windrider's bridge crew, was very helpful in making the transition a smooth one. Colonel McCrarey found the zep captain's cheerful attitude pleasantly, but suspiciously, at odds with the sullenness of the other civvies.

As the zep crewmen took their places, the female towns-folk on duty reported to the detention area. Getting all the women under wraps was a top priority; Colonel McCrarey didn't want any incidents that might arouse the civvies. The women were taken to their quarters under guard to pick up their personal items. Meanwhile a work party delivered food and bedding to the detention area and removed the five corpses.

An entire residential level was cleared for the officers and crew of the *Shenandoah* and the aircav company. They transferred their belongings to their new quarters, and the *Shenandoah* was slaved to the windrider's sys-tems. The guards in the blimp bay would keep the civvies from developing any unhealthy ideas about the zeps or the still—crated blimps. Captain Patterson set up his Com-pany HQ in an apartment between his officers' quarters and the "barracks" of his men. Colonel McCrarey left the details of guard schedules, reconnaissance sweeps and sur-veillance to Captain Patterson. The incoming reports indi-cated that the windrider was locked down tight and resistance was nonexistent.

As dawn turned the eastern sky red and lit the rolling hills below, the immediate situation was under control. Colonel McCrarey went up to the big outside apartment in "officer's country" which Major Santee had picked out for him. It had been prepared for his habitation with items from the *Shenandoah* and the windrider's stores, and his belongings had been transferred. He ate a light meal, then enjoyed the rare luxury of a bath before sacking out for a few hours.

Upon waking he checked in with Major Santee and Captain Patterson. Everything was green, so he collected a work party and converted the unoccupied mayor's office into his own. The other *Shenandoah* officers, now dou-bling as his occupation staff, were setting up in the smaller offices nearby. The *Shenandoah* crewmen were assigned occupation and zep maintenance duties.

The captured windrider sailed east, then north. The

bridge crew plotted a course which would bring it to Alpha in five days. During the second day and much of the third it rode a wind at thirty-one thousand feet, while the two zeps followed at their flight ceiling manned by *Shenandoah* skeleton crews. At no time did any windrider or other zep come within radar range. Several radio messages were intercepted about the futile search for the "missing" Lone Star Five and *Mayan Princess*.

The civvies cooperated efficiently if not enthusiastically, while Colonel McCrarey and his men settled into the novel routines of occupation work. He spent much of his time studying the windrider and the Pemex Under zep. The more he learned about the windrider, the more convinced he became that it would make a worthy new Alpha. He also determined that the Pemex Under zep could be refitted for raiding if the *Valley Forge* didn't survive General Armbruster's "retirement."

Among all the mundane details of the occupation, his thoughts kept returning to the work that Lieutenant Ford was doing with the Project Rainmaker satellite manual. He didn't insist on updates, knowing that Lieutenant Ford would report when there was something to report. Still, as the hours became days, he chafed with growing impatience. Finally, on the morning of the third day, Lieutenant Ford called and requested a meeting. McCrarey told him to come right up.

Colonel McCrarey was doing screenwork at his desk, when Lieutenant Ford arrived. Holopics, raid souvenirs, bookdisks and other personal items from the *Shenandoah* partly offset the sterile whiteness of the walls and furniture. The big telescreen was showing a belly-camera view of fluffy clouds floating above the dark blue North Atlantic Ocean. The *Shenandoah* crewman doubling as Colonel McCrarey's office staff buzzed Lieutenant Ford in.

Lieutenant Ford looked as if he had missed some sleep lately, but he was grinning as they exchanged salutes. "I'm glad to see you, Lieutenant," Colonel McCrarey said affably. "Have a seat. How about some coffee, so you won't nod off in the middle of your report?"

"I'd appreciate it, sir," Lieutenant Ford sat down across the desk from him.

He called the outer office; a minute later the crewman brought in two steaming cups. When the two of them were alone again, he said, "I gather you have some progress to report. Let's hear it."

"I deconned the disks myself," Lieutenant Ford began. "They're both in good condition. Then I set up the portable computer and memory unit which you told me I'd find in the *Shenandoah*'s stores. They were indeed compatible with the disks. A curious thing—they aren't regulation zep equipment, and I couldn't find either one listed on the inventory."

McCrarey knew what Ford was saying. The lieutenant wasn't stupid; he had realized that the mission orders wouldn't call for the satellite manual to be investigated in the field. "Have you kept a tight security lid on?"

"As you requested. I did all the work myself, in my quarters, and I haven't discussed it with anyone except you. I've spent the past two days studying the satellite manual plus the Alpha library information you told me I'd find in the *Shenandoah*'s computer."

"And?"

"The Project Rainmaker satellite was originally an SA-7B weapon platform armed with a twelve-megawatt free-electron laser. The beam's wavelength and focal point were modified for the satellite's mission, heating the atmosphere to create low-pressure areas for weather modification experiments."

"Would that make the laser useless as a weapon?" Colonel McCrarey demanded urgently.

"No, sir. The programming allowed it to be tuned and focused from the downlink. The satellite was launched into a pole-to-pole orbit twenty-two hundred miles up, high enough to avoid significant decay."

"Was it destroyed during the War?"

"I don't think so. Our intelligence on the other side's ASAT assignments was pretty good. They targeted—and blew away—all of our laser satellites. But the Project Rainmaker satellite wasn't on the list."

"Then," Colonel McCrarey drove the key question home like a sword thrust, "could it still be operational?"

For the first time Lieutenant Ford seemed uncertain. "Seven decades is a long time. But the SA-7's were solar-powered and built to be durable. If it was shut down with its solar collectors retracted, it wouldn't have presented much of a target for meteoroids. The exposed collector would have provided enough current for housekeeping. All I can tell you is that it's possible."

Colonel McCrarey felt excitement bubbling through his blood stream. It *was* still up there, and still operational; he sensed it. His destiny wouldn't be denied. But now, so close to victory, he had to be even more careful. "Lieutenant, you've done an excellent job. Your talents are being wasted as a mere com officer."

"I was hoping you might notice that, sir."

"I want you to move your equipment to the windrider's radio room. I'll arrange with Captain Patterson to post guards to keep it off-limits to everyone but you and me. In the *Shanandoah*'s stores you'll find another item not listed on the inventory—like the others—I acquired it from Alpha's stores through somewhat unofficial channels. It's one of the satellite-relay transceivers we supply the friendlies. Would your abilities extend to cobbling together a downlink for the Project Rainmaker satellite?"

"I believe so." Lieutenant Ford's voice was carefully neutral, but Colonel McCrarey could read him like a flatscreen. He was finally realizing the full scope of Colonel McCrarey's scheme, and it worried him.

Colonel McCrarey knew the cure for that. "I'm sure I can rely on your discretion, Lieutenant. If the satellite turns out to be non-operational, I'll return the equipment the same way I acquired it, and deliver the satellite manual to General Armbruster per my orders. Everything will be green."

Lieutenant Ford looked relieved. It didn't occur to him that, in that eventuality, Colonel McCrarey didn't intend to leave anyone with knowledge of his scheme walking around.

"But if the satellite is operational," he continued in a smooth, tempting tone, "I anticipate some major changes in Alpha's chain of command. I know for a fact that a zep command will be available. How does Colonel Ford sound to you?"

"It sounds very good, sir."

"Then get to work. I need results before we reach Alpha. Remember, no guts, no glory."

Lieutenant Ford rose, saluted and left. Colonel McCrarey leaned back in his chair, thinking pleasant thoughts.

CHAPTER THIRTY-TWO

Wanda stayed in hiding for three days.

There were a few tense times, when crew members visited the petrochemical plant level. But she always heard them coming, and reached the closet without being spotted. She curled up in the darkness, trying to breathe quietly, hoping she hadn't left anything outside. The visit the first night, probably part of a search for her, was the closest call; heavy feet even walked through the office outside the closet door. But each time the crew members finally left without finding her.

The rest of the three days was pretty boring. She ate cold food, drank tap water, read each of her bookdisks a dozen times, and even did some exercises when she got too antsy. She played with Puff, until Puff took off somewhere during the second night. She thoroughly explored the level, such as it was. But a lot of the time she just sat by the window wall, watching clouds and stars and the colors of the sky, wishing everything would be okay again.

She couldn't see the dock, and she hadn't noticed the *Mayan Princess* leaving, but she figured after three days it was probably gone. And hopefully Mom with it. So, after eating her meager breakfast on the fourth morning, she decided to sneak out. If she could make it up to the farm, Jim would tell her what was going on. He wouldn't give her away.

She started up the west stairway. She was an experienced sneak thanks to childhood hide-and-seek and tag games; the secret was listening really hard and not being in a hurry. She had been all over Lone Star Five, so she knew where crew members went least and where the best cover was. Having so few crew members in the windrider would help too. The thrill of the game mixed with her fear of being caught and turned over to Mom.

Bending low, she took the stairs quickly but quietly. At the water level she heard footsteps coming down. She jumped over the railing, landed lightly, and ducked into the shadow of a noisy pump until the tech was well past. Making sure none of the crew members working in the level were looking her way, she continued up the stairs.

When they reached the residential levels and turned into an escalator, she became even more careful. Twice she hid under ramps, and once in an empty apartment; the last time she had to wait for over ten minutes before she was sure the coast was clear. Her eyes and ears kept busy. Finally she reached the top of the last ramp, and the sunny ground level.

She was happy to be topside again after so long. The hissing breeze blew (as always) toward the lake. The air smelled like dust instead of greenery, but she liked it anyway. The irrigation ditches gurgled. She crouched behind the top of the ramp, squinting and blinking until her eyes adjusted. Then she carefully peered over the ramp.

The ground level was really coming along. The farm fields were almost all plowed. Saplings stood in rows in the orchard, and green grass covered the park lawn. The aggies were spread out across the farm, driving the tractors and swinging hand tools.

She was looking at the aggies, trying to find Jim, when she noticed the black men. There were four of them, two standing near the park escalator, the other two walking around the fields. They seemed to be watching the aggies. They were all dressed the same: weird black outside suits made from solid plastic parts, bowl helmets, parapacks and belts holding what looked like overgrown cutter sheaths. The aggies frowned at them from time to time, but mostly ignored them.

They weren't shakedown crew members or from the *Mayan Princess*, that was for sure. She had never seen or heard of anybody like them. She couldn't figure out where they came from or what they were doing, but for some reason the sight of them sent cold shivers down her back. Just what she needed: something else to worry about.

She wanted to talk to Jim more than ever. But as she peered at aggie after aggie, she noticed another puzzling thing. None of the women were there. Instead she saw some strangers who looked like *Mayan Princess* crewmen.

Finally she spotted Jim. He was working alone, testing field drainage a quarter of the way around the rim.

Sneaking across the open ground level in broad daylight would be a lot harder than coming up through the levels, particularly with the black men watching. But she had a plan. Taking off her sandals and sticking them in the back pockets of her shorts, she waited until everybody was looking somewhere else. Then she scuttled on hands and knees across the plowed furrows toward him. Ten yards from the escalator entrance she dropped into the nearest irrigation ditch.

Nobody yelled or ran toward her, so she figured she had gotten away with it.

She stood on the shallow plastic bottom of the ditch, hunched over to use the banks as a shield. Her bracing hands touched small holes in the sides under the water line: the mouths of pipes that irrigated the fields. The cold rushing water came up to her knees. It felt ultra, and she wished it was safe to take a bath. Instead she crept along the ditch.

The ditches meandered but pretty much ran radially, so Wanda had to move from ditch to ditch. The short scurries across the ground were the riskiest part of the sneak. But she was extra-patient, watching and waiting for just the right moment to go. Then she went low, fast and quietly. Nobody spotted her; adults weren't very observant. The ditch water rinsed the mud from her arms and legs, so she was wet but reasonably clean when she finally reached Jim.

She peeked over the inboard bank. Jim was about twenty feet away. A thin pole was stuck in the ground, and he was frowning at a tiny display screen on top of it. The nearest aggie was a hundred yards away, the nearest black man even farther. Nobody was looking her way.

"Jim!" she whispered urgently, just loud enough to reach him. "It's me! Wanda!"

He looked around, then shook his head. Wiping his face with his bandana, he turned back to the pole.

"I'm over here, Jim! In the ditch!"

This time he looked right at her. His frown turned into wide-eyed surprise. He was frozen like that for a second, then he winked. Casually he pulled up the pole, walked toward her, and stuck it in the ground beside the ditch. Pretending to read the display screen, he said softly, "You spooked me out of three year's growth, popping up like that. Are you okay?"

"Sure. Why wouldn't I be? I'm sorry I had to run away without telling you or anything. But I won't go back. I won't! I want to stay with you and Dede. Has Mom gone home?"

Jim didn't answer right away. "No, she's still here. She's locked up with the rest of the womenfolk."

"Huh?"

"After you lit out, a pack of rannies from someplace called Alpha showed up in a zep. They're soldiers left over from the War, real bad medicine. They've taken over. We have to do like we're told, or else."

"Or else what?" Wanda asked, totally confused by Jim's news.

He took his time answering again. "Or else they'll kill the womenfolk," he finally said, sounding grim. "But don't fret—your ma is just fine, and she's going to stay that way."

"I want to see her!" Wanda had no idea why she said that, considering how much she hated Mom. It had just come blurting out. Jim's story didn't make much sense to her, but she understood enough to feel scared. She peered at the nearest black man. He looked like she had always imagined a soldier would look, only worse.

"You can't do that just yet," Jim said. "If the soldiers catch you outside the hall, there's no telling what they might do. Look, it's not safe for you to be here. Where were you hiding out?"

"In the petro plant level."

"Smart—no wonder they didn't find you. Can you mosey on back without getting caught?"

"Sure," she answered confidently.

"I want you to lie low again, and don't come out no matter what. There are going to be some bad doings this afternoon. I'll come and fetch you as soon as it's safe." A moment later he added, "Or somebody will."

"But—"

"Get going! I have to move this meter now, before the rannies get curious. Be mighty careful."

"Okay."

Ducking down in the ditch, Wanda started back the way she had come. She was even sneakier. It was hard for her to believe that real soldiers had come out of the vids and history bookdisks to threaten her, but Jim wouldn't lie. He had sounded strange, like something wound tight inside him was about to snap.

She found herself wishing that she and Mom were back home, and pushed the thought away. Jim had said something was going to happen this afternoon. She wondered what. Maybe the shakedown crew and the *Mayan Princess* crewmen were gong to fight the soldiers! But the soldiers had those suits of armor, and probably weapons too. How could you fight them?

Part of her wanted to watch and see. But most of her wanted to get back to her hidey hole as fast as possible.

She recrossed the fields without being spotted. A quick peek behind her showed that Jim was doing his testing farther away. She had to huddle against the side of the last ditch, while the two soldiers walked by not ten yards away. Then she scuttled across the ground and down the escalator.

Luckily, she didn't run into anybody coming up. Her eyes adjusted to the gloom, and she went on as carefully as she could. She didn't see or hear anybody, until she reached the residential levels. She ducked into a corridor, while a group of soldiers in black and silver uniforms came out of another corridor and rode the escalator up. She wiped some sweat from her face. Dangerous or not, this was the best game of hide-and-seek she had ever played. When the soldiers were gone, she started down again. On the bottom residential level she walked around the last corridor ramp toward the stairway.

A uniformed soldier was sitting on the top step less than five feet in front of her, drinking something from a bottle.

She froze for an instant. Then she turned to run to the up ramp, but the soldier jumped to his feet and grabbed her arm. "Well, what have we here?" he chuckled, jerking her around painfully.

She looked up at him, angry, scared and curious all at once. The soldier was as big and strong as Dad. His brown hair was cut really short, and his face would have been good looking except for the mean eyes and a long scar down his left cheek. One of the overgrown sheaths hung from his uniform's belt.

"Let me go!" she demanded. She tried to twist out of his grip, but his fingers were like machine clamps. He laughed.

"Relax, girl. I don't want to hurt you." His friendly grin didn't fool her. "What's your name?"

"Wanda. Wanda Grigg."

"You don't look old enough to be part of the crew here. What are you—some sort of mascot?"

"I'm an aggie," she replied stiffly.

"Then you should be in detention with the rest of the female civvies. What are you doing on the loose?"

She didn't want to get Jim in trouble, so she didn't say anything.

"Do you know the penalty for escaping detention, Wanda? It's death."

She shivered.

The soldier looked around, and lowered his voice. "If I was a bad sort, I'd turn you in. But I'm not. I'll take care of you. Come on."

She didn't trust him, and she particularly didn't like the way he was looking at her. There was something ugly hiding behind his friendly manner. But she really needed to find Mom, and it sounded like the soldier was going to put her in the town hall where they were keeping all the

women. So, as he pulled her into the radial corridor, she
didn't try to get away.

He kept looking around nervously. They were alone in
the corridor, and that suddenly frightened Wanda even
more. He stopped in front of an apartment door. Opening
it, he yanked her inside and closed it quietly behind them.

"Why did you bring me here?" she asked, but she was
afraid she knew why. He kept staring hungrily at her legs
and chest, and he was breathing faster.

Tossing his empty bottle aside, he grabbed her other
arm and jerked her up against him. "You're a very pretty
girl, Wanda. Are you a virgin?" His breath smelled sour.

"Y . . . y . . . yes," she quavered.

"Then you don't know what you've been missing," he
said in a hoarse, eager whisper. One arm went around her
back, while the other stroked her face. She flinched from
the rough, unwanted handling. "There's a nice comfy bed
in the bedroom. I'm going to teach you a game that's more
fun than any you've ever played, the game men and women
play. Don't be afraid—it won't hurt. In fact it's the best
thing about being a woman. You'll see."

Wanda was really scared now. "I don't want to! You
better let me go, or you'll be in big trouble!"

He laughed, a loud cruel sound that hurt her. His hand
moved from her face to her breasts. She tried to squirm
out of his grip, but he was too strong.

"You're the one in trouble, you little bitch. If you won't
be a good girl, I'll have to teach you some manners too.
You won't like that."

Grabbing her hair, he yanked her head back so hard
that she opened her mouth to scream. But before she
could, his lips covered hers in a brutal, irresistible kiss.

CHAPTER THIRTY-THREE

Wanda's first reaction was disbelief. Boys did get out of hand at times, and you had to know how to handle it. But rape was something she and Jan and Lori had whispered about, only half believing in it despite the well-worn stories they had heard. It was one of the transportable crimes, but nobody back home had been sent down to the surface for it in years.

But it was really happening. The soldier's disgusting mouth was grinding into hers. His arm around her was crushing her, while his other hand was pulling up her T-shirt. She didn't feel happy or sexy or any of the other things you were supposed to feel when you were making love. It was all wrong. She felt sick in her stomach. Twisting her mouth free, she yelled, "Let me go! I don't want to!"

"You will," he laughed. "Quit fighting it."

"No!" Remembering how he had looked around to make sure they were alone, she added, "I'll yell for help! I'll get you in trouble!"

"Try it, you little bitch, and I'll beat you to a bloody pulp. Then I'll fuck you anyway. All the same to me, but a lot worse for you." He squeezed even harder, so she could hardly breathe.

It was hopeless. He was going to rape her; he was too

strong for her to stop him. Instead of the wonderful experience she had dreamed of, she would have to carry an ugly, painful memory in her head forever. Her imagination tortured her with images of the things that were going to happen next. She felt like she was about to throw up.

Suddenly she remembered Mom teaching her how to cool off overeager boys. Of course the soldier wasn't a boy, but it might work anyway. Especially if he wasn't expecting it.

"Okay," she said as sweetly as she could. "I'll do what you want. Please don't squeeze me so hard." She stroked his back the way she had learned from vid love scenes.

"Good girl." Grinning widely, he loosened his grip so there was enough room between them for him to slide his free hand under her T-shirt. He kissed her again, and she let him.

She tried to ignore everything except getting in the right position. Moving carefully so as not to warn him, she slid sideways until her right knee was in front of his partly spread legs. Mom had taught her to do it gently, to discourage rather than hurt. But she didn't care if she hurt the soldier. She just wanted to stop him.

She brought her knee up as hard as she could.

She could tell by the softness that her aim had been perfect. Her kneecap hurt from the impact, but not nearly as much as the soldier did. He made a horrible moaning sound, and fell slowly to the carpet. Curling almost into a ball, with both hands between his legs, he glared up at her. "You little bitch!" he gasped. "I'm going to kill you . . . cut your fucking heart out!"

The rage in his words and eyes convinced Wanda that he meant it. She backed away from him, toward the door, tucking her T-shirt back in and wiping her mouth with her hand. "I'm sorry I had to do that," she told him in a shaking voice, "but you made me. I hope you'll be okay."

The soldier started to uncurl. "You're dead meat!" His face was as white as the walls, twisted by pain and rage. But Wanda figured he was going to be back on his feet soon.

She fled from the apartment.

The corridor was still empty. She started to sneak back

to the stairway, hoping to get away before the soldier could come after her. All she wanted was to reach her hidey hole without being caught. She wouldn't come out again until all the soldiers were gone. She had a bad case of the shakes, and the sickness in her stomach wasn't going away.

She had only gotten about a hundred yards from the apartment when she heard a door slam behind her. Glancing over her shoulder she saw the soldier running after her. He had the long cutter from his belt sheath in his hand.

Wanda did a lot of thinking in a hurry. The soldier was probably slowed down by his injury, but he was still running faster than she could. He would follow her down to the petrochemical plant level, and by the time she got there he would be too close for her to hide. She didn't want to think about what would happen to her then. What could she do? Hiding was out, the crew members couldn't help her, Mom was locked up, and the other soldiers would kill her too for not being in the town hall. She wished she was Puff, so she could just fly away.

Fly away? She couldn't do that, but maybe she could get away from the soldier by teaching him one of *her* favorite games: tag. There was one place where her smallness and lightness would give her the advantage. She knew from painful experience how dangerous it would be, but it certainly beat the alternatives.

She ran to the stairs and down them as fast as she could, not worrying about being seen or heard. At this point she wouldn't be any worse off with a bunch of soldiers chasing her, and speed was the only thing that could save her. But now that it didn't matter, the two of them seemed to have Lone Star Five all to themselves.

Reaching the work level, she took the circum corridor toward the work crew station. She was sweating a lot and gasping for breath. Her stride was getting ragged; she knew she was slowing down. She didn't make it any worse by looking back, but the soldier's pounding boots were much closer. She tried to run harder.

She would have given anything to find Mr. Hansen and his whole crew in the work crew station. They would know how to stop the soldier. But it was empty, like it usually was when there was work to do. She was still on her own. She grabbed her outside suit from the alcove and put it on in about ten seconds. Then she ran over to the window wall and the access belt.

The other three belts started on the ground level, but this one started here to get work crews topside in a hurry. They weren't really belts. The track, eighteen inches wide and six inches thick, climbed straight up the inside of the shell. Motor boxes of the sides moved the individual rungs when the belt was on, which it wasn't. Grabbing a control unit from the rack next to the belt, she stepped on the bottom rung and clipped her suit's waist lines to a higher one.

"Don't go away, you little bitch! I have something here for you!" The soldier's yell came sharply through her suit's sound pickup, as he burst into the work crew station. He ran toward her, waving the sharp-pointed cutter in front of him.

She froze for a moment. Then she frantically pushed the control unit's UP button.

The tiny electric motors buzzed like bees, as the rungs started to climb the track and folded ones came down the back. The plastic strips were narrow for standing on, but Wanda hung onto a higher one with her free hand and easily kept her balance. The belt lifted her up the outward-slanting window wall. It moved slowly at first, and she stared in wide-eyed terror as the soldier closed in on her. But by the time he reached the foot of the belt, she was just beyond the swinging cutter.

He glared up at her and laughed. "You don't get rid of me that easy!" He headed for the outside suit alcove.

A hole in the ceiling swallowed Wanda, and she found herself in a shaft not much bigger than she was. The strip of window wall let in plenty of sunlight, showing that the other three sides were plain white plastic except for some hatches and emergency lights. She had never been in the shaft here or back home, but she knew it had been built to let the belt rise through the levels.

The fright she had gotten in the work crew station passed enough for her to start thinking again. She set the control unit to stop the belt from being reversed, even though she didn't figure the soldier knew to try it. He was probably putting on an outside suit right now to keep chasing her. That reminded her to check her own suit, doing all the things she had skipped in her hurry. The suit felt bulky and awkward, but the soldier would have the same problem. She would need the suit, if she had to play the game to the end.

The belt slowed and stopped for a moment, then it started up again. Wanda knew what that meant. The soldier had boarded. At least she had a pretty good lead, and he wouldn't be able to get any closer until the end of the ride.

Suddenly the shaft disappeared from around her, and she was rising above the ground level. This part of the ride was familiar from her flying. Going up the belt had scared her when she was a novice flier, but she had gotten used to it. Any other time she would have enjoyed the wonderful view, the sensation of being lifted over the world.

But the bright morning sky, cloud streaks and ocean outside the shell seemed like a bad joke now. The aggies were still working in the farm, and the armored soldiers were still watching them. She tried to pick up Jim, but everybody was too far away. Except for a few glances nobody paid any attention to her; she must have looked like a work crew member on the way to do something in the top of the shell.

She kept looking down nervously. When she was about five hundred feet above ground level, somebody in an outside suit rode the belt up out of the shaft. She couldn't see who it was at that distance, but she was sure it was the soldier. Finding the right size suit and putting it on had slowed him down, but not nearly enough to make her feel better.

The belt followed the curve of the shell until it was climbing straight up at the equator. As Wanda passed the work platform, she considered jumping off and using the suit's parapack to glide down to the ground level. But the soldier would do the same, and she wouldn't be any better off. She kept going.

Now came the tricky part of the ride, where the shell

curved over her. The rungs stayed level, so she didn't have any trouble with her footing, but she had to lean in more and more. The waist lines kept her from falling. The ground level shrank below her, turning into a brown and green plate with the blue lake in the middle. It was warmer in the upper part of the shell; the suit's cooling system kicked in automatically.

Wanda was grateful for a few minutes of rest to catch her breath and get her strength back. She would need both when she reached the top of the shell. It also gave her time to do some planning. She had only been to the top a few times, and had never played tag there. But she had some notions on how to lead the soldier a merry chase. They were pretty wild; she didn't dare lose this game.

She was really leaning in, as she neared the top. The heels of her suit boots were made to hook on the lip of the rungs, but it was still an awkward pose. If her feet slipped off the rung, which had happened a lot when she was a novice flier, she would dangle from her lines in an even more awkward position.

She was ready with the control unit just in case, but the belt slowed and stopped automatically as she came to its upper end. Her feet were level with the edge of a radial catwalk. Unhooking heels from the rung one at a time, she carefully stepped across the two-foot gap. When she was solidly planted on the catwalk, gripping a handrail, she unclipped both lines. The belt started moving again.

Wanda looked down at the approaching soldier, and figured he would reach the catwalk in less than a minute. She tried to stop the belt with the control unit, but he had set his anti-override too.

She turned and looked around. The solar cell panels and catwalks followed the curve of the top of the shell, dangling from support rods hooked to it. They looked like a weird floating hill. The solar cell panels were laid out in a closely spaced circular grid about half a mile across and seven feet under the shell. Each panel was a thin twelve-foot square, sky blue on the bottom, dark and glittering from the thousands of tiny solar cells on top. A web of wires ran from the panels to electrical boxes on the shell, from which conduits ran down to the ground level. The radial and concentric circum catwalks were laid out among the panels. The narrow walkways with waist-high handrails looked flimsier than they were. The shell was an endless crystal ceiling between her and the sky, while the ground level over three thousand feet below looked like an art-class model.

She lost a few precious seconds staring at the spectacular sights. A quick look back told her the soldier was almost up to the catwalk. She ran for her life, inboard and up. The catwalk swayed precariously under her, so she slid both hands along the railing for balance. Falls were why outside suits had parapacks.

The soldier was getting ready to dismount, and not looking her way. She turned right onto a circum catwalk, then inboard again on the next radial. When she heard the belt stop, she dropped flat on the walkway and squirmed around.

She was about a hundred yards from the soldier, hidden from him by the curve of the catwalks and panels. Hopefully, facing a search of the whole top, he would give up and go away. Scrunching as flat as she could, she waited and hoped. The silence filled up with tension. She thought about using the suit's com, but there wasn't anybody to call for help, and she definitely didn't want to hear anything the soldier had to say.

She lifted her head for a quick peek, and got a fright like an electrical shock. The soldier was walking quickly toward her, following her exact path. He was just turning onto her radial. For a moment she couldn't figure it out, then she did. The catwalks kept swaying awhile after somebody walked on them. All he had to do was look for moving ones.

She jumped up and ran the other way. She heard the boots behind her start running, and the catwalk's swaying got worse. Glancing over her shoulder, she saw the soldier about twenty yards back and gaining on her. He was waving the cutter in front of him.

The distraction cost her dearly. She misstepped, slipped, and slid off the catwalk.

But on her way over the edge she managed to grab a

support rod. Going into a flier's maneuver, she swung down, around, and back up on to the catwalk. Scrambling to her feet, she kept running. The soldier was even closer now.

She knew she couldn't outrun him. Her legs were tightening up, and she couldn't get enough air in her lungs. She would have to outmaneuver him. There was something she had never tried, but work crew members did it to fix panels, so she figured she could pull it off.

Taking the next circum catwalk, she ran to the midpoint between two radials. To her left there were two panels, one after the other, then the next inboard circum. The gaps were about four feet wide.

Licking her dry lips, she ducked under the handrail. Then she jumped as hard as she could.

A moment of dizzying flight later she landed on the edge of the first panel. The suit threw her balance off. Instead of the graceful maneuver she had planned, she staggered forward. The slick plastic protecting the solar cells tried to slide out from under her. But she managed to recover before she fell off. Hanging onto support rods when they were handy, she moved carefully to the far edge.

When the panel's swaying brought it closest to the second one, she jumped across. She had the hang of panel-walking now. A few seconds later she was standing safely on the other catwalk.

It would take the soldier *minutes* to reach her the long way around. Relieved, she looked back to see which radial he would take. And got another bad shock. He was crossing the first panel the same way she had, with a lot more agility than adults usually showed.

Wanda ran. She heard and felt the soldier land on the catwalk behind her. Then he was chasing her again.

She headed inboard and up. Desperate now, she tried anything she could think of. She sprinted. She dodged from catwalk to catwalk. She tried panel-walking again. But nothing worked. The soldier kept getting closer, while her batteries were definitely running low. Sweat stung her eyes, her breathing was ragged, and the suit weighed like metal.

There was only one thing left to try. She would have to go outside, on the shell. It was off-limits to most folks, because it was so dangerous. But she had been there once, when she had patched the hole in the shell back home. She might have an advantage.

Of course, she had almost been killed that time.

There were access air locks scattered all over the shell, but the one Wanda wanted to use was at the very top. She had been heading in that direction, just in case. Now she ran for it with all the speed she had left. The soldier was so close behind her that she could hear the swinging cutter as well as his pounding boots.

Up ahead, all the radial catwalks met at the top of the "hill." The round platform held some girl-high boxes around the rim; power and com equipment, she figured. But her eyes were locked on the white cylinder hanging over the middle of the platform, its top end set in the shell. It looked barely big enough to hold an adult in an outside suit.

Skidding to a stop under the air lock, she slapped the hatch button. The bottom end of the cylinder swung down. The inside was a cramped space dimly lit by glow panels, with control panels and a ladder set in the side. She grabbed the bottom rung of the ladder and scurried up. As soon as she could reach it, she pushed the CYCLE button. The bottom hatch started to close.

The soldier appeared under the hatch, looking up at her as it eclipsed him, grinning his ugly grin. He tried to stick his cutter into the airlock, but the hatch clicked shut first.

Something, the cutter or his gloved fist, banged on the hatch. It startled her and almost knocked her off the ladder. But the air lock was built to be tough; he couldn't get at her that way. And it wouldn't let him open the bottom hatch until it finished the cycle.

A few seconds after the bottom hatch sealed, the top hatch started to swing up. The pressure difference between inside and outside wasn't enough for Wanda to notice the drop. She blinked up at the bright blueness.

Not having the shell between her and the sky made her feel strange. Suddenly she didn't like her plan as much as she had. But she climbed out of the air lock, because the danger behind her was worse than that ahead. Instinctively she checked her suit's readouts as she went. The heating and air systems were green, protecting her from the unbreathably cold and thin outside air.

She stood up carefully on the shell. The hatch started to close. She wished there was some way to stop the air lock from cycling again, but she couldn't think of anything that wouldn't damage it, and of course that was out.

The top of Lone Star Five looked like a smooth plain for hundreds of yards all around, glistening with reflected sunshine. Spidery radio and radar antennas, plus a newly installed one she didn't recognize, were spaced around the air lock. She could make out more hatches and a waddling decon mech in the distance. The sky surrounded her more spectacularly than it could anywhere inside. She could hear a light breeze blowing across the shell (inertia kept the windrider from fully matching the wind's speed), but she couldn't feel it through the suit. For a moment it seemed as if she was alone on an empty planet.

Then she remembered she wasn't alone. She stared down through the shell at the platform. The greenhouse tint made everything dim and vague, but she could tell that the soldier wasn't there, and that the air lock's bottom hatch was sealed.

The top hatch started to rise again.

Wanda had to get going. Her plan was to walk to one of the nearest air locks, about two hundred yards away. To travel on the shell you were supposed to clip your lines to a succession of the clamps set in the plastic composite. It was safe, but slow. She figured she could put a lot of distance between her and the soldier by not using her lines. The shell was really slick, but it was almost flat here at the top, and her suit boots had traction soles. She was desperate enough to try it.

Taking short, careful steps, she started walking. She kept her eyes on her feet. She didn't think about what she was doing; she just did it.

Glancing over her shoulder, she saw the soldier climbing out of the air lock. She walked a bit faster.

Everything went okay until she looked up to make sure she was still heading toward the air lock hatch. She saw the shell curving down, steeper and steeper, disappearing into the endless sky. . . .

Her eyelids slammed shut, and the memories came rushing back.

She had finished patching the hole. There was an access air lock thirty yards down the shell. She unclipped one line to start the clamp-by-clamp crawl to the air lock. Either she hadn't attached the other line properly, or something was wrong with it. As she leaned on it, it gave. She scrambled for traction, but the plastic composite was slick as glass. She grabbed for clamps and missed. Faster and faster she slid down the increasing slope. She had a moment to regret her stupidity and everything she was going to miss. Then she hit the rim of the air lock helmet-first. The pain was followed instantly by nothingness.

She had fallen off the shell. True, she had woken up in midair and used her suits' paraglider to soar above the killzone until the *Mayan Princess* had rescued her. But she knew she could never be that lucky twice.

She couldn't move. She tried as hard as she could, so that sweat ran down her face and she whimpered from the effort. But her feet refused to take another step.

She could sense the soldier closing in to kill her. Twisting her feet an inch at a time, she managed to turn around. Making her eyes open was even harder, but she did that too.

The soldier wasn't bothering with lines either. He was about twenty feet away, walking the same slow, bent-kneed, short-stepping way she had. He was staring right at her, and his grin was even uglier. He held the cutter casually in his right hand.

Wanda was more scared than she had ever been, and had the wet panties to prove it. Her imagination jumped ahead to what it would feel like when he stuck the cutter into her. But she still couldn't move.

Now the soldier was only fifteen feet away.

Images flickered between her and the sky. Mom cooking in the kitchen. Dad napping on the sofa. Cheryl crying. Puff playing. Jan and Lori. Jeff. Flying. Swimming. Chores. Homework. Shopping. . . .

Ten feet.

Was it more imagination, or was she really hearing/feeling Puff? It was Puff! She wished she could fly off with Puff, away from everything. But at least she could say goodbye.

Five feet.

Puff appeared above and behind the soldier, a bright dot diving out of the sun. She got bigger. Wanda had never seen Puff fly so fast. She could hear/feel that Puff wanted to play, but there wouldn't be any more playing, ever.

The soldier stopped in front of Wanda and casually swung the cutter across her waist. She barely managed to lean back out of its way. He lifted the cutter over his head, getting ready for a second swing that would slice her in two. She screamed.

Puff passed about forty feet overhead. A wave of heat washed over Wanda, and she heard/felt Puff's confusion. The pass startled the soldier, delaying his swing momentarily. Wanda made a last all-or-nothing effort to get away. But the terrified paralysis had spread to her whole body.

The cutter swung down.

Puff must have banked sharply. She hurtled back across the shell, even lower. Love and reassurance poured into Wanda's mind. Puff's fire blazed dazzlingly white, as she touched the cutter and the soldier.

The soldier blew up.

CHAPTER THIRTY-FOUR

The soldier's suit ruptured along all its seams, spewing out a thick pink cloud. Wanda winced from the loud bang, and the force of the blast made her stagger backwards. She almost slipped and fell. The cutter slid across the shell, while the shredded, half-melted suit collapsed as if nobody was in it.

Puff kept going as if nothing had happened, except that her color faded to an almost invisible blue.

Wanda had been all set to die. Still being alive was a shock, particularly the way it had happened. It took her a few seconds to stop shaking and start thinking again. Then she felt tremendously happy. The soldier's death didn't bother her. He had been some kind of evil monster from the past, and he had gotten what he deserved.

"Thanks, Puff!" Wanda gasped. "I don't know how you did it, but you saved me!" Relief filled her thoughts, and she heard/felt Puff echoing it.

Either the explosion or the end of the soldier's threat had freed Wanda from the paralysis. The front of her suit was covered with wet pink stuff; she figured it was part of the soldier. Wiping her helmet so she could see better, she peered at the pink-stained shell around the soldier's suit.

Checking for breaches was an instinctive reaction. She

295

didn't see any damage or telltale mistiness; the suit must have shielded the shell from the worst of the explosion. She was glad, since she had no idea how she could have fixed a breach without a patching kit. Then she made sure her own suit was okay.

Puff soared into a series of fancy maneuvers a hundered feet overhead. Craning her neck, Wanda enjoyed the show for a few seconds. Then she said, "Sorry, Puff, but I've got to go right now. The bridge must have picked up the explosion through the sensor web. Some soldiers might come here to see what happened—I can't let them find me."

Breaking off her play, Puff dropped a bit and hovered. Wanda heard/felt her disappointment, and shared it.

"I don't want to leave," Wanda insisted. "I wish I could tell you all the weird things that are going on. But I've got to get back to my hidey hole fast."

Puff spiralled away into the sky. When she disappeared, Wanda turned regretfully and walked back to the airlock at the top of the windrider. She avoided looking at the soldier's suit as she passed it. She figured a work crew would come and clean up the mess.

She peered through the shell to see if anybody was waiting for her on the platform or catwalks. But they were empty as far as she could see. Opening the hatch, she got into the air lock and cycled it. When the bottom hatch swung down, she stooped and looked out. The coast was clear. She dropped to the platform, and pushed the CLOSE button before going on. Even townsfolk in a big hurry didn't leave air lock hatches open

She walked down the sloping radial catwalk toward the access belt she had ridden up. The top of the shell looked normal again, not scary like it had when the soldier was chasing her through it. The ground level looked the same. The folks way down there wouldn't have noticed her trouble with the soldier. Fortunately Puff had.

Wanda heard/felt a faint reaction to her last thought. So: Puff hadn't gone away after all. She was hanging around nearby, the big worrywart. Not that she could do anything now that Wanda was inside. Yet somehow it made Wanda feel better.

Wanda worried that the belt might already be in use, bringing more soldiers up. But as she got close to the end of the catwalk, she saw it wasn't moving.

She clipped her lines to a belt rung. Then she stepped out onto the rung across from the walkway and grabbed a higher one for balance. Fetching the control unit from the pocket she had stuck it in, she pushed a button. The belt started down.

During the long ride she had time to think. She wondered a lot about how Puff had made the soldier explode. No fireball had ever done anything like it, so far as she knew, or even come that close to a windrider. But they were made out of some kind of energy, and she remembered the proverbial tale of the cat in the micro-oven. With enough energy you could probably do the same thing to a soldier.

She tried to look like a work crew member coming down from the top of the shell. It must have worked, because the soldiers on the ground level ignored her. She tried to spot Jim, but the aggies were too far away for her to recognize anybody. The belt carried her down to the ground level and into the mouth of the shaft.

When she reached the work crew station, she would sneak back to her hidey hole. She would be really careful this time. Nobody would see her. She would curl up in the closet, in the dark, keeping as still and quiet as she could. She would be safe there, until all the soldiers were gone.

If they ever *were* gone. After her experience with the soldier, she didn't see how the shakedown crew and the *Mayan Princess* crewmen could possibly beat the soldiers in a fight. What if they tried and lost? What would she do then? She couldn't hide forever. And what would happen to Mom, Dede, Jim and everybody else?

Wanda descended from the shaft into the work crew station. Looking down, she saw two uniformed soldiers standing by the bottom of the belt.

Her heart almost stopped from the fright. Desperately she pushed buttons on the control unit, but the anti-override she had set up kept her from stopping or reversing the belt. It was taking her right to them. They had been watching the bottom of the shaft, but they looked as surprised to see her as she was to see them.

The rung she was standing on reached the bottom of the belt and stopped. Unclipping her lines, she tried to dodge sideways. But the closer soldier was too quick for her. He caught her by the arm, almost yanking it out of its shoulder socket. She whimpered.

"Hey, Steve, we caught ourselves a frisky one," the soldier holding her said to the other. "It ain't our AWOL, but it should be worth a few points."

Steve stepped in front of Wanda. He was shorter than the soldier holding her, but they both had the same short hair and mean eyes. He took off her helmet.

"I'm Wanda Grigg," she said as bravely as she could. She had learned there wasn't any point in demanding to be let go, so she didn't bother. She hoped the soldier holding her would loosen his grip, so she could squirm free and run.

"What are you doing outside detention?"

She looked at her suit's boots, and didn't say anything.

"Quit wasting time, Steve," the soldier holding her muttered. "We're supposed to be hunting for Frank, remember? You better call the captain, tell him the unauthorized belt use the bridge reported turned out to be a clear miss."

"You think so?" Steve casually scraped some of the dried pink stuff from the front of Wanda's suit with a fingernail, and looked closely at it.

"What's that?" the soldier holding her asked.

"About what you'd get if you fed somebody into a blender."

"The hell you say!"

Steve glared at Wanda so hard that she cringed. "How did that stain get there, civvie?" he demanded.

She figured telling them about the soldier's death would make them really mad, so she didn't answer.

The soldier holding her jerked her arms up behind her. It hurt so much that she screamed.

"Cut it out," Steve told him.

"Why?"

"It's my guess she took Frank somehow. The captain

will want to know about that. He may decide to interrogate her personally, and he won't like it if she's already damaged."

The terrible twisting of Wanda's arms eased. She tried not to whimper.

"Get her out of that suit, while I report in," Steve said. He walked a few steps away and spoke softly into his com. The soldier holding Wanda started to unzip her suit.

She wanted to get out of it too; besides being heavy and awkward, the pink stuff made it smell like a butchered hog. So she didn't try to stop him. When the suit was a pile at her feet, he twisted her arms behind her again and held her.

Steve came back. "Better not bend her."

"Why not?"

"The captain passed the word up. For some reason this kid is hotter than a nuke. We're to take her to the colonel's office, immediately if not sooner. Come on."

Wanda didn't like the sound of that at all.

CHAPTER THIRTY-FIVE

The soldier opened the door to what was supposed to be the mayor's private office and pushed Linda inside. He closed the door behind her without coming in.

Her eyes sought to avoid the man seated behind the desk by taking in the rest of the office. Its walls, carpet, and furniture were unstylized white, a stark setting appropriate for the occasion. A few personal items had been spread around to lend it some personality. The wall telescreen held a view of the icebergs and ocean below Lone Star Five.

Colonel McCrarey rose slowly from his chair, like a powerful but geared-down engine. His eyes found hers, and she felt the same repellant intensity she remembered all too well from her first encounter with him. She had spent many of the empty hours in the town hall trying to figure out how anyone could do so much evil, actually *enjoy* doing it. Now, the object of his dark attention, she finally understood. Alphans didn't see non-Alphans as people. It was as simple and insane as that.

But understanding Colonel McCrarey didn't make her any less afraid of him. Especially if he knew about Alamo.

"It's good to see you again, Linda." The pretense of friendliness in his voice made her skin crawl. She stepped backwards, so that her back was against the door. Her hand felt behind her for the knob.

"Don't try it," he said in the same tone. "Your escort is waiting just outside."

She moved away from the door. It hadn't been much of an idea anyway.

"I'm glad to see you're feeling energetic." Colonel McCrarey began to circle her slowly, tracing an intangible cage. "Detention seems to agree with you."

Actually it didn't. Stress and boredom had worn her down; she hadn't slept more than a handful of hours since the arrival of the Alphans. Despite sponge baths she felt as grubby as her scavenger coveralls. Adrenalin gave her senses a sharp, brittle edge.

"I had you brought here," Colonel McCrarey went on, "to assign you to a work detail. One of my men, Lieutenant Ford, is installing some special equipment in the radio room. He's coming up against a deadline, so you're going to help him."

She did her best to hide her relief. She wasn't going to be tortured to find out what she knew about Alamo (which wasn't much anyway). But she certainly didn't like the thought of working for the Alphans. "Why me?" she asked.

"The male civvies are fully occupied with their duties. You're a windrider engineer, which makes you one of the female civvies best qualified to help Lieutenant Ford. So you will."

She had no idea what the "special equipment" might be. But if it was important to the Alphans, it probably meant trouble for the rest of the world. "No, I won't," she said levelly.

Colonel McCrarey's reaction surprised her; he almost seemed pleased. "You know the penalty for disobedience."

She did, but she didn't much care anymore. "Killing me won't change my mind."

"Stubborn, eh?" He stopped in front of her, and stroked her cheek before she could pull away. "Strong-willed, attractive, intelligent—and at the very peak of your female power. That's a rare combination of qualities among you spineless civvies, and I treasure it."

Linda shivered. "If you try to rape me, I'll do anything I can to stop you."

"Rape is a primitive vice—my tastes are somewhat more sophisticated. Beneath your elaborate facade of civilization and self-worth there's a weak, helpless animal. I intend to strip away the facade, break you to my will. Pleasing me will become the sole purpose of your existence. You'll do tricks you never imagined in your worst nightmares. But you'll remember when you were a person, and suffer excruciatingly."

Linda stared at the . . . the *thing* pretending to be a human being. "You're as sick as you are crazy. You can hurt me, but you can't hurt me enough to . . . to break me, as you put it."

"Ah, the courage of ignorance." Without warning Colonel McCrarey punched her in the face, knocking her back against the wall. A strong arm held her up by her hair, while the fist slammed into her face three more times. Pain as terrible as labor ripped through her, and polychromatic flashes blinded her eyes. Groaning, only vaguely conscious, she slid down the wall into a crumpled heap. Blood-wetness ran down her face.

Colonel McCrarey lifted her, and slapped her until the bursts of pain cleared her head somewhat. When he let her go, she managed to stand on her own.

"That was a minor demonstration," he said mildly, rubbing his knuckles. "Are you still sure pain can't tame you?"

"Yes," she mumbled through bruised lips.

"Excellent. The greater the resistance, the sweeter the victory. It's a crude technique anyway—sacrificing your beauty would be a shame. No, the best techniques are those that only mark the soul. Leverage, for example. Fate has handed me the perfect tool to control you. It's why I picked you to help Lieutenant Ford. After you've done that, I'll teach you other ways to serve me."

Colonel McCrarey went over to the desk and whispered into the com. Linda used her sleeve to wipe the blood from her face. Her head felt terrible; she was glad the office didn't have a mirror. Waves of dizziness wracked her. She watched his smug smile, wondering what new ugliness inspired it.

The door behind her opened. Turning, she saw a soldier dragging Wanda into the office.

Linda's and Wanda's eyes met. Linda tried desperately to hide her horror. Wanda's clothes were mud-stained and her hair was matted, but she seemed unharmed. She looked as stunned as Linda felt. Linda remembered their last bitter meeting in the Polks' apartment. A small thing in the middle of this nightmare, but the hate in Wanda's eyes had hurt her more than anything before or since—because she knew she deserved it. How could she possibly hope to win Wanda's forgiveness now, when a clean death was the best future either of them could hope for?

The tears which hadn't come during Colonel McCrarey's beating ran down her cheeks.

She realized that Wanda was staring at her battered face, wide-eyed and pale. Suddenly Wanda jerked free from the soldier's grip. She ran to Linda and hugged her with frantic strength. "Mom!" Wanda's voice was muffled by Linda's shoulder. "They hurt you! I'm sorry—it's all my fault!"

Linda gently wrapped her arms around her daughter. "No it's not, dear. Don't worry. It's not as bad as it looks. I'll be all right." Despite everything, Linda felt a warm wonderful glow. They were together again.

The soldier hurried over to retrieve Wanda, but Colonel McCrarey waved him back. Then McCrarey stepped behind Wanda. His expression suggested that he was enjoying the tableau, but in a way no healthy mind could imagine.

"Now do you understand?" he asked Linda.

Cold hopelessness returned to crush her momentary joy. She did understand. To protect Wanda, she would do anything this monster told her to do. Anything. She couldn't even take the Long Drop. She would have to endure whatever he put her through, become whatever he intended to turn her into.

He ran his hand gently down Wanda's golden hair. "She's a very pretty girl. It would be a shame if I had to damage her to convince you of my sincerity. Or give her to my men—she would find the experience educational but not pleasant."

Tearing free from Linda's arms, Wanda whirled and tried to kick Colonel McCrarey in the crotch. But his reflexes were too quick for her. He stepped back, so that her kick went wild and threw her off balance. She fell hard on her rear end, letting out a loud, "Oof!"

"That's a very old trick," Colonel McCrarey told her smugly. "Try it again, and I'll break your leg."

"You folks better leave Mom alone!" Wanda screamed. "If you hurt her any more, I'll kill you! I'll . . . I'll . . . !"

"Hush, dear," Linda whispered urgently as she helped Wanda up. Colonel McCrarey seemed more amused by the outburst than anything else, but she was deathly afraid for Wanda's safety.

She looked Colonel McCrarey in the eye. "I'll do whatever you want, as long as you don't hurt Wanda."

"Your daughter's treatment depends on the degree of your cooperation. I'm sending her along to help you, and as a reminder." Colonel McCrarey turned to the soldier. "Take these two to Lieutenant Ford in the radio room."

"Yes, sir." The soldier drew his cutter. "Out, civvies," he said crisply, and prodded Linda in the back with a sharp point.

"Come on, dear," she told Wanda, who was barely holding in her red-faced anger. "It's all right."

The soldier herded them through the outer office and into the corridor. Wanda turned to Linda. "What are we—"

"Shut up!" the soldier snapped. "No talking, either of you. March!"

Taking Wanda's hand to comfort as well as guide her, Linda put a warning finger to her lips. Wanda nodded. They set out for the park escalator, with the soldier bringing up the rear.

Linda's head was throbbing fiercely; drops of blood were running down her face and falling from her chin. The shakedown crew members and *Mayan Princess* crewmen they passed stared at her, then looked away to hide their reactions. They seemed to be thoroughly cowed. But that had to be a pose, if Alamo meant what she and the rest of the women fervently hoped it did.

It was approximately ten A.M., so Alamo was scheduled to begin five hours from now. But now more than ever she didn't see how the men could possibly defeat the Alphans in a fight. Not only did the Alphans have cutters, body armor, training and experience on their side; they also had a bestial savagery that no townsman or stockholder could match. She knew that the men would try bravely. She also knew that they would fail. And die.

She couldn't do anything about it. Her world had focused down to keeping Wanda safe, and she would be incredibly fortunate to manage that.

They rode the escalator down to the work level and followed a radial corridor into electronics country. A soldier wearing body armor was standing in front of the radio room door. He exchanged crude greetings with their guard, then knocked on the door. A few seconds later it opened.

The young man holding the knob was wearing a rumpled uniform; he looked as if he had been going with little sleep for several days. For a moment his almost boyish features gave Linda some hope. Then their eyes met, and she knew better. He was another monster.

Their guard saluted him. "Colonel McCrarey said to bring you these civvies, Lieutenant."

"I know," Lieutenant Ford replied. "I'll take them—no need for you to come in. Carry on."

"Yes, sir." Their guard prodded Linda and Wanda through the doorway, and Lieutenant Ford closed the door.

The radio room, a modest name for a windrider's communications center, was almost identical to the one Linda knew so well in Calgary Three. Tall cabinets and monitor panels lined the walls; consoles, work benches, and large pieces of equipment were laid out in an open grid across the eighty-foot-square floorspace. There wasn't any window wall, but glow-panel light reflecting from the white surfaces made the room sunshine-bright. Faint hums and tones came from the electronics, and the wall vents sighed as they kept the air cool, dry, and dust-free. Here, operating automatically and unobtrusively, were Lone Star Five's radio, com, vid, and radar systems.

Lieutenant Ford lifted Linda's chin to look at her face. She flinched, but didn't try to pull away. "I see Colonel McCrarey has marked you for his own." Lieutenant Ford's knowing grin cut her like a knife. "RHIP. But right now you two are going to help me finish this job. I expect complete cooperation, and I'm just as capable as Colonel McCrarey of making sure I get it." He put a hand on the hilt of his sheathed cutter for emphasis.

Determined not to give way to either anger or fear, Linda asked levelly, "What do you want us to do?"

Lieutenant Ford led them over to two adjoining benches holding a bizarre collection of equipment. The pair of mottled green metal boxes looked like pre-War military radio components. The portable computer and memory unit seemed to be of the same vintage. Surrounding them were transformers, amplifiers, adapters, and other items from the supply cabinets. Sloppy wiring linked everything, and cables ran to several consoles and wall sockets.

"Mrs. Calhoun," Lieutenant Ford said. "I understand you found the satellite manual. Since you made this project possible, it's appropriate that you should help complete it. A new day is dawning for Alpha Command and the world."

"What are you talking about?" Wanda asked.

"I've been studying the manual." Lieutenant Ford kept talking to Linda, ignoring Wanda's question. "Once I knew where to look, I modified the windrider's radar and searched for the Project Rainmaker satellite. It's still up there. I've set up this downlink to bring it to operational status."

It took Linda a moment to realize what he was saying. Then her blood turned to liquid nitrogen. If the Alphans added a laser satellite to their weaponry, nobody would ever be safe from them. They wouldn't have to hide and limit their attacks. They would be able to dominate the towns, or destroy them. In her mind's eye she saw Calgary Three falling out of the sky, taking Jack and Cheryl and so many others to a terrible death.

The throbbing in her head became even worse. Somehow she would have to stop Lieutenant Ford. But if he caught her at it, she knew Wanda would pay the price.

"I'm just about ready to establish contact with the satellite," Lieutenant Ford went on. "But first this rig has to be interfaced with the windrider's computer and radar. You're a windrider engineer, so you know the layout here, right?"

Linda nodded.

"Sit down." He pointed to a chair in front of the portable computer. "I'm going to show you what I've done so far, and the functions that have to be interfaced. Then we'll get started on the hardwiring and programming. The kid can do the scut work."

Giving Wanda's hand a quick reassuring squeeze, Linda sat down.

CHAPTER THIRTY-SIX

Two fifty-seven P.M. Three minutes to Alamo.

Vic Jarman cleared the time check and continued scanning his station's displays, trying to look casual. He hoped Lefty and Jose, the *Mayan Princess* navigator, were doing the same. They were going to need every bit of surprise they could get.

He didn't dare look around, but he was acutely aware of the bridge behind him. Jose was at the weather station two chairs to his right, Lefty was at the systems station beyond Jose, Colonel McCrarey was pacing in the middle of the floor, and the soldier in body armor (but fortunately no helmet) was standing by the door. The monitor screens and the floor were showing different shades of blue; Lone Star Five was sailing twenty-two thousand feet above the North Atlantic Ocean, all systems green. He was glad to have the altitude. The windrider might need plenty of room to drop in case of breaches.

"What's our ETA at Alpha?" Colonel McCrarey demanded.

Vic glanced at his flight displays. "If the wind pattern holds, I reckon we'll be there in about twenty-one hours."

"High noon. Very symbolic. Plan on standing off a hundred miles—I may have to do some negotiating which will be safer at a distance."

"On it." Vic figured the order had something to do with

the secret work going on in the radio room, but he didn't have time to wonder about it.

The murders in the town hall had convinced him that the Alphans were every bit as bad they acted. He hadn't been able to find out what was in store for his and Captain Ramirez's crews when they reached Alpha, but he figured more slavery was the best they could hope for. More likely they would all be killed, except the pretty ladies. His frustrated anger had turned into grim determination. Texans didn't go meekly like sheep to the slaughter. The notion of killing folks, even these rannies, had turned his stomach. But it had to be done; they were beyond law or reason. The department heads and Captain Ramirez had asked around, and everybody agreed.

The Alphans had confiscated the few obviously dangerous tools like laser welders, but otherwise they had become fairly relaxed in their guarding, confident that the hostages would keep everybody reined in. Even so, Vic had known that the menfolk didn't have a chance of winning a fair fight. So he had decided to make it as unfair as possible. They were going to use their skills and knowledge of Lone Star Five against the Alphans, in a desperate experiment in applied engineering that Lefty had named *Alamo*. Plotting had been kept to a minimum for secrecy's sake. He didn't even know what the department heads and Captain Ramirez were planning to do. He had told them the edge he was going to give them, what they had to get done, and when. The rest was up to them.

He felt as shaky as a newborn colt, and he had to work not to show it. He wasn't afraid for himself. He knew the odds were long against them, but he was ready to do his damnedest and take what came. It was what he was about to do to Lone Star Five that scared him silly.

During the past two days, under a variety of pretexts, he had arranged for supplies throughout Lone Star Five to be shifted to the north side. The trim system was just barely keeping the windrider level. In another fifteen seconds the instruction he had secretly fed into the computer would run, and Alamo would be on.

"Yo, pardner," Lefty said to Jose. "Time for the hourly course check."

"As you say." Jose got up to walk over to the flight station.

The crash siren wailed. Red displays flashed on the trim board. Vic felt the distant throbbing of hundreds of tons of water being pumped at high pressure from the south tanks into the north ones, as the trim system ran in reverse. The bridge started to move south and up.

"What in the name of—" Colonel McCrarey broke off his startled yell to concentrate on his balance, spreading his legs and reaching for the back of Vic's chair. The soldier, at the south end of the bridge, had instinctively grabbed the doorknob behind him. He was busy trying to switch hands on the knob, draw his cutter, and stay on his feet at the same time.

Vic reached down and gripped the kitchen knife taped to his leg. Then he went around the chair in the move he had been planning ever since Colonel McCrarey had showed up to inspect the bridge. Out of the corner of his eye he saw Lefty and Jose scrambling toward the soldier. The plan was for him to cut Colonel McCrarey's throat while the Alphan ramrod was off balance, and they would do the same for the soldier. An old-fashiond Indian massacre.

The plan lasted about two seconds.

Vic swung his knife just south of Colonel McCrarey's anger-twisted face, but the Alphan ramrod lurched back out of range. His hand grabbed for his cutter. Vic staggered after him.

Something big, black and hard slid into Vic, taking his legs out from under him. He fell on top of it. Colonel McCrarey's cutter whistled through the space his head had occupied the moment before.

Sliding down the listing floor, he had time to realize that the soldier must have escaped Lefty and Jose by falling past them, either deliberately or accidentally. Then he and the soldier came up hard against the front of the computer station's console.

Vic heard a gut-shredding scream and a yell from the upper end of the bridge, where Lefty and Jose were going after Colonel McCrarey.

The soldier had dropped his cutter in the collision, but he was big and strong, and he undoubtedly knew plenty of ways to kill with his gloved hands. So Vic wouldn't give him the chance. Vic's knife stabbed at the soldiers leathery throat.

The soldier caught Vic's knife arm. His free hand tried to claw Vic's face, but Vic grabbed the wrist. Pushing both of his arms to the limit, Vic just barely managed not to lose ground. He and the soldier were locked in a gasping, straining, rigid pose.

The floor had been listing slowly but steadily. Now it lurched several degrees at once, and another alarm sounded. The low, distant groan of flexing structure scared Vic more than the soldier did. His calculations had shown that Lone Star Five could, probably, survive what was happening topside. Even so, he half expected the windrider to turn inside out. But it didn't.

"Drop the blade, little man!" the soldier growled. He twisted Vic's knife arm savagely.

That was exactly the wrong thing to say to Vic Jarman. A lifetime of rage at his size boiled up inside of him. Tearing his knife arm from the soldier's grip, he buried the knife to its handle in the soldier's right eye.

The soldier looked utterly surprised. His body spasmed twice, then went limp. His chest settled.

Postponing the soul-searching over what he had done, Vic staggered to his feet. The listing had stopped at thirty degrees, the maximum possible. He started up the floor to help Lefty and Jose, but that was all over.

Lefty was sprawled on the floor, blood spurting from a cutter wound in his chest. Jose was futilely trying to stop the flow with direct pressure. Colonel McCrarey was gone.

Grabbing the first-aid kit from under his chair, Vic lurched over to Lefty. Lefty's face was sheet-white, but his grin was as wide as ever. "Ranny . . . too slick for us," he gasped over the alarms, ". . . got away . . ." He coughed up blood.

"Just temporarily. Hang on—I'm going to patch you up—"

"Don't waste time . . I've had it . . . Happy trails, pardner. . . ."

The blood stopped spurting. Vic closed Lefty's eyes.

"He jumped in front of me to save me," Jose said in a

dazed voice. "I put my knife in Colonel McCrarey's arm, but he escaped."

With an effort Vic turned away from the corpse of one of the finest folks he had ever had the honor of knowing. Lone Star Five came ahead of anybody, himself included.

"Lock that door," he told Jose, "and take Lefty's systems station. See what you can do about all those red-lines on the boards. Won't do us much good to clean out the Alphans if we crash. I'm going to get on the com and find out how we're doing."

If the news was bad Vic would get to blow the vents in the heat-exchange system and crash Lone Star Five himself. Everybody had agreed on that too. Just like at the real Alamo, there would be no surrender.

CHAPTER THIRTY-SEVEN

The hot afternoon sun beat down on the back of Jim Polk's neck. Having shoved the drainage meter into the hard-packed dirt, he leaned on the metal rod and caught his breath. He pushed his hat back and used his bandana to wipe sweat from his face.

Through heat-shimmers he looked around at the plowed fields, green park lawn, scrawny saplings, glistening buildings and walkways, all surrounding the cool blue of the lake. The other aggies, including the *Mayan Princess* replacements, were spread out across the farm plowing and hoeing. Two of the soldiers were walking through the west fields, while the other two were keeping an eye on everything from the central location of the park escalator entrance.

Jim glanced at his watch, then pretended to check the drainage meter readings. Less than two minutes to go. He wiped his face again; not all of the sweat came from the heat.

Luck of the draw had brought the walking pair of soldiers closest to Red and Tomas, so they would get to set the trap. Jim couldn't honestly say if he was disappointed or relieved. But he had volunteered to work in the north fields, and that would be almost as dangerous. Pulling up the drainage meter, he trudged toward the nearest water fountain as if he wanted a drink.

The crash siren went off, shrieking hollowly all through the topside. The ground level began to list north-down.

That was the starter's whistle for Red and Tomas. Yelling "Remember the Alamo!" and "Viva Mexico!" respectively, they ran over to the soldiers on the walkway. The soldiers, startled by the siren and the listing, didn't react until the aggies hooked their hoes around armored legs and yanked. Both soldiers fell down.

Dropping their hoes, Red and Tomas took off for the north fields as fast as they could. Seconds later the two soldiers were up and hot on their heels. Jim tossed the drainage meter aside and ran to the fountain. Jock and Emilio, who were also working in the north fields, were both dashing for the nearest well-anchored structures. The rest of the aggies were closing in on the park escalator entrance, just in case. But the soldiers there obligingly joined the chase after Red and Tomas.

By the time Jim reached the fountain, he was having trouble keeping his balance. A deep, vast groaning sound rose through the siren's noise. His hat blew off in the stiffening breeze. With fumbling fingers he unbuckled his belt, pulled it tight around the base of the fountain, and rebuckled it. Wrapping his arms around the base too, he nerved himself up to look south.

The ground level wasn't level. It climbed hundreds of feet above him like the side of a mountain. The running aggies and soldiers had slowed down to keep their balance. Almost everything loose was rolling down the slope. Dust clouds bellied and swirled.

But he scarcely noticed any of that. His horrified gaze was held by the man-high wall of churning, frothing brown water which was hurtling down at him. Most of the lake had spilled over the bank, picking up dirt and anything else in its path. The roaring noise was almost deafening.

Jim turned his back to the onrushing wave and clung to the fountain for dear life. The water hit him like a framework girder swung by a giant. It hammered him into the fountain, knocking the air from his lungs. His belt almost cut him in two as the wave tried to drag him along. That pressure eased, then eddies bounced him around. The water was cold and slimy. He opened his eyes, but still couldn't see anything. He desperately needed to breathe.

The water level dropped quickly, until he found himself sprawled in mud at the foot of the fountain. He coughed up some water and gratefully filled his lungs with air. His body felt like one big bruise. Unbuckling his belt, he staggered to his feet on the listing walkway.

He looked around, and wished that he hadn't. What had happened to the ground level hurt worse than anything that could have been done to him. He felt like dropping back down in the mud and having a good cry.

The water had cut a swath over a hundred yards wide from the lake almost to the north rim. Jim supposed he should be grateful that the hundreds of tons of water hadn't hit the shell. But the actual damage was just about as bad. The lake was mud-fouled and almost empty; Lone Star Five would have to make do with the water in the tap and trim system tanks for awhile. Coldhouses and stock pens had been flattened. Near the lake the soil had been stripped away right down to the plastic composite floor, leaving twisted irrigation pipes and brown pools.

Near the rim the water had finally been soaked up. The fields were a waterland of mud banks and puddles. The irrigation ditches were clogged; water from the shell as well as the lake was starting to collect at the rim. Bits of plastic, grass, branches and tools were scattered everywhere. Twenty yards away the tires of a tractor stuck up from a mud mound. Jim didn't want to think about how much precious soil had gone down the north escalator well. The east, west and south fields also showed some erosion from overflowing irrigation ditches.

Jim's aching back remembered all the work the aggies had put into the farm and park. Now they would have to start over. If Alamo gave them a chance.

"Yo, Jimbo! You okay?"

The yell from Wes Barnes, who had taken Craig's place as foreman, dragged Jim back to the here-and-now. Looking toward the lake, he spotted Wes and five other aggies coming around it. They had left their hoes behind; now they were holding scythes, pitchforks and other sharp tools.

"Banged up a bit," Jim yelled back, "but nothing to fret about."

Wes turned his attention to Jock and Emilio. They were climbing to their feet, mud-covered and looking as if they had been ridden hard. Jim laughed bitterly as he realized he must look just as bad. They yelled that they were okay.

"Hey, gringo, remember us?" Two rising mounds of mud near the north rim became Tomas helping Red get up. Jim joined in the aggies' cheering. Although the plan had called for the baiters to outrun the water as well as the soldiers, there had been so many question marks that he honestly hadn't expected them to make it. He had been wrong before, but never so happily.

"That wild horse tried to plow a furrow with me!" Red yelled through gritted teeth. "I think my arm is busted!"

"Tomas," Wes shouted back, "get him over to the barn! There's a first-aid kit there—do what you can for him!"

"As you say!"

Wes's group was entering the north fields. "Listen up, you all!" he yelled loudly enough for everybody to hear him. "Spread out and find the soldiers! And watch out—in those suits they might still be alive and kicking!"

Jim hadn't seen any sign of the soldiers since the wave hit him. He set out along the walkway toward the north rim, looking carefully at the fields on either side.

"Got one here!" Roy yelled. He was pulling a black-suited body out of a mud bank. The two nearest aggies ran over to help him deal with the soldier one way or the other.

Just as somebody else announced a find, Jim spotted a suited figure floating face-down in a pool. "Check off another one!" he shouted to Wes. Since everybody else looked busy he added, "I reckon I can handle him myself!"

"Holler if you need help, Jimbo!"

Jim circled the soldier warily, looking for signs of life and finding none. The cutter sheath was empty. Grabbing the hard plastic boots, Jim put his back into it and managed to drag the soldier up onto the walkway. He rolled the limp body over and took off the cracked, mud-smeared helmet.

The soldier was almost a young'un, not even twenty, Jim

guessed. The clean-cut, pale face was topped with short
sandy hair. The soldier was unconscious but coming around.
Jim couldn't tell what was wrong with him.

The soldier coughed, and his eyes blinked open. He
looked up vaguely at Jim. "Help . . . medic," he croaked.
"God, it hurts. . . ."

Either he thought Jim was a fellow soldier, or he was
too far gone to care. Reluctantly Jim pulled the skinning
knife from his boot. He stared at the razor-sharp edge.

The soldier saw it too. "Christ, no!" he gasped. "It's not
. . . that bad! Get a medic . . . please!" He tried to reach
for Jim's knife hand, but all he could manage was a feeble
twitching of his arms.

Jim looked into the scared blue eyes; tears were welling
up in them. The soldier reminded him a lot of himself a
few years back, on the outside. The soldier hadn't asked to
be born in Alpha. If he had been raised anywhere else, he
probably would have turned out okay. All the soldiers
would have.

The soldier finally recognized him. "Please, civvie . . .
don't! Whatever you say . . . I'll do it! I don't want to die!"

But blameless or not, the soldier was what he was: a
killing machine, a danger to Dede and every other decent
man, woman, or child. Lock him up, and he might escape.
Send him away, and he might come back. Rehabilitate
him, and he might backslide. The only sure way to end
the danger was the one Vic had called for.

"I'm mighty sorry," Jim told the soldier. "I'm not doing
you a favor dragging it out like this. But some things a
man has to work himself up to."

Ignoring the knot in his stomach, Jim rolled the soldier
over and straddled his back. Jim yanked the soldier's head
back by the hair. The soldier's scream turned into a bubbling sigh as Jim ripped his knife across the taut throat.
Jim let the head drop limply into the widening puddle of
blood, and lurched quickly to his feet.

Just like butchering a hog, he tried to tell himself. As
compost the soldier would have his finest hour.

"How's it going, Jimbo?" Wes yelled from behind him.
He wiped wetness from his eyes, and turned. All the

aggies except Rod and Tomas were heading for the park escalator entrance.

"All finished here!" Jim's voice broke.

"Then it's a clean sweep! Come on—there's more work to do downstairs!" Wes waved a soldier's cutter, and Jim noticed a red stain on the edge.

Jim remembered Dede and the rest of the womenfolk in the town hall, and poor Wanda hiding in the petrochemical plant level. "I'm on my way!"

As he ran to join the other aggies, he wished the soldier hadn't lost his cutter.

CHAPTER THIRTY-EIGHT

Dede Polk had long since decided that the worst part of being locked up was not knowing what was going on.

She hadn't seen or heard from Jim since the menfolk had been ordered out of the town hall three days ago. Wanda had never been brought in. Linda had been taken away that morning and hadn't returned. The food deliveries were the only contact the womenfolk had with the rest of Lone Star Five, and soldiers came in with the men to make sure there was no conversation. It was as if they weren't part of the world anymore.

The mattresses, blankets, clothes and everything else which had been scattered across the floor were now piled against the walls. The womenfolk were standing in a ragged, nervously chattering row facing the entrance doors. They were talking about everything except Alamo, in case the soldiers on guard outside were eavesdropping. Dede was between Sara Jane Austin, who had taken charge in the hall, and Doc Starnes. She felt as scared and determined as the faces around her looked. Everybody was holding two-foot-long aluminum rods, braces they had found in the bleachers' crates. Hers felt cold in her hand. They didn't know if the thin rods would dent the soldiers' armor, but if it came to that they surely intended to find out.

Yesterday they had discovered two liquid-filled tubes hidden in a ration pak, with a word and a time written on one of them. The word was Alamo. The time was three o'clock this afternoon, just a few minutes away.

They had spent a lot of time trying to figure out what Alamo would be. They hadn't come up with anything that didn't sound suicidal. But whatever it turned out to be, Dede knew the Alphans weren't going to like it. The womenfolk were all set to do their part.

Sara Jane held up a finger to warn everybody that the countdown had reached one minute. The chatter faded. Dede should have been worrying about herself, but her thoughts kept jumping back to Jim. If anything happened to the big galoot . . .

The crash siren went off.

Dede almost jumped out of her hide. There were a few screams, quickly stifled, and somebody dropped her rod. "Tighten your cinches!" Sara Jane snapped. "I reckon that's just to let everybody know Alamo is on."

"What's happening to the floor?" a shrill voice demanded. Dede realized with growing shock that the floor was listing.

"We really are going to crash!" somebody yelled.

"We are not!" Sara Jane shouted everybody down. "I know just about everything that can go wrong with a windrider, and this isn't on the list. I'll bet you all a month of sewage-plant chores that Vic Jarman is doing it on purpose."

Several women looked like they were about to disagree, when one of the doors rattled. Everybody froze.

Dede's grip on her rod tightened. The rest of the womenfolk were getting themselves ready too. If the soldiers made it through the doors, they were going to get a big surprise.

The floor kept listing. Other doors rattled, but none of them opened. Armored fists pounded on them; boots kicked them. They still didn't open.

"It's going to work!" Sara Jane yelled. The super-adhesive created by mixing the contents of the tubes had effectively turned the entrance into a solid wall.

The cheering that went up had an hysterical edge. It was

quickly shut off by harsh scraping sounds from the out-
sides of four of the doors.

"What's that?"

"It sounds like the soldiers' cutters! They're chopping
holes in the doors so they can get in!"

Sara Jane turned to Catlin Rogers. "Structural proper-
ties are in your line. Can they cut through?"

Catlin couldn't meet her eyes. "The composite is tough,
but not tough enough to stop steel-alloy blades."

The tip of the cutters were coming through the doors,
scoring them. Dede felt hopelessness spreading through
her like poison. Steel cut plastic. The Alphans were the
steel; they were the plastic.

"The rannies will be through in a few minutes," Sara
Jane said grimly. "You all know what we have to do then."

CHAPTER THIRTY-NINE

Colonel McCrarey leaned against the stairway wall outside the bridge. Finishing the job the civvie's knife had started, he tore off the left sleeve of his uniform shirt. He used a strip of it to bandage his arm. The wound burned like hell, and he felt a bit dizzy; otherwise he was physically intact.

But mentally he was seething with rage and shame. The sensation of the knife blade tearing through his skin and muscle and bouncing off the bone had been so intense, so self-involving that it had pushed everything else out of his mind. Forgetting four decades of discipline and training, he had fled from a pair of civvies armed with kitchen knives while he still had a sword and the ability to use it. He glared at the locked door to the bridge. Too late now to undo his momentary cowardice. But he would make the civvies pay bitterly for it.

He was thinking like a soldier again, and he didn't like what he was thinking one bit. The windrider's listing and the attack had clearly been planned. Just killing him and a guard wouldn't get the civvies anything except some bloody retribution, so this had to be part of a general rebellion. He had misread the signs; they weren't as thoroughly beaten down as they had seemed. But they would be. A second, more forceful lesson in terror was called for.

He was reaching for his com when he noticed a breeze in the stairway, cool and strong. It was ominously unnatural. Drawing his sword, he crept quietly to the top of the crazily tilting stairway.

The blimp bay looked cavernous and empty without blimps. The unassembled parts were collected at what was now the lowest point in the bay—no coincidence, he realized. The floor should have been a smooth white expanse; instead there was a deepening trench over six hundred feet long and two hundred feet wide near the blimp parts. The sides were flat, and the bottom was a deep but widening strip of blue. Colonel McCrarey felt as well as heard a deep motor rumbling. The air had all but stopped whistling past him toward the trench, but it was cold and getting colder.

The civvies were opening one of the blimp docking hatches.

The sight of the huge breach shocked him. He looked up, and was relieved to see that the escalator and stairway well hatches were sealed. The civvies hadn't gone completely insane. They might have been conducting an unannounced test of the docking equipment, but he didn't think so.

He was gasping for breath as well as shivering, as the warm enriched air in the bay was diluted by the thin frigid air from outside. He had gone through enough high-altitude drills to know that he could only take it for a few minutes. He looked around for the two aircavs who had been on guard duty. They were gone, and it wasn't hard to figure out where. If the docking hatch had started to open when the floor listed, anybody in the middle of the bay would have been blown out the hatch by the sudden decompression. They were probably still falling.

The only people in the bay were two civvies wearing outside suits. They were at the high end, doing something to the clamps which held a helium tank to the floor. The tank was a rounded cylinder of aluminum-reinforced plastic forty feet long and half as wide, mounted horizontally.

Colonel McCrarey wondered what they were up to. He glanced back at the widening gap in the floor, and saw a curved black shape appearing below the hatch.

The *Shenandoah*. The civvies were going to roll the tank down the floor and out the hatch, onto the zep. The tank was big and heavy enough, and would be traveling fast enough, to break the zep's back.

The hell they were! Yelling inarticulately, he charged up the floor toward them. Both the floor and his boots were designed to give traction; even so he almost fell several times. If he fell, he would join the two aircavs.

The civvies either heard or saw him. One said something to the other by com, then grabbed a crowbar from the tool kit on the floor and stood up. The other civvie frantically resumed his work on the clamp.

Colonel McCrarey took on the crowbar-wielder first. Contemptuous of the crude weapon in unskilled hands, he closed in on the civvie. The civvie swung the crowbar at his head. He parried with the edge of his sword, then thrust the point through the civvie's helmet and startled face. The crowbar fell from lifeless fingers. He yanked the sword free. The civvie collapsed and started rolling down to the hatch.

Colonel McCrarey had to wait for a wave of dizziness to pass before he could go on. The air was more of a danger to him than the civvies, particularly when he exerted himself.

Four clamps held the tank down. The civvie was unbolting the third one, when Colonel McCrarey staggered over to him. He jumped up and tried to hit Colonel McCrarey with his heavy wrench. Colonel McCrarey put a stop to that by amputating the wrench-swinging arm near the shoulder. Writhing, blood spurting from the stump, the civvie followed his companion down the floor and out.

A few seconds of examination assured Colonel McCrarey that the remaining clamps would hold the tank in place. Then he staggered over to the control console next to the escalator landing. The crash siren died, leaving the bay quiet except for the motor rumble and the hissing breeze below the hatch. He reversed the docking cycle, and the hatch started to close. It would take a few minutes to seal. Then warm enriched air would be pumped into the bay, and the well hatches would open. His shivering had gotten worse, and he was so weak that he could barely stand or think. But now that he wasn't fighting, he knew he would be able to hang on.

The glow panels went out and the hatch motors stopped for a couple of seconds. What in God's name was happening in the rest of the windrider? He couldn't wait for warmth and oxygen. He was the commander, and his command was under attack.

Holding his com with numbed fingers, he managed to key Major Santee's channel. No response. He tried Captain Patterson, and was somewhat relieved when he heard the gravelly voice acknowledge.

"Captain, Colonel McCrarey here," he gasped. "Report your status."

"Are you okay, sir?"

"Better than the other guys. But the civvies are holding the bridge—I'm in the blimp bay. I assume the rebellion is general?"

"General and damnably effective." Bleakness leaked around the edges of Captain Patterson's crisp professionalism. "We were caught with our pants down."

"How bad is it?" Colonel McCrarey asked, sure that he wasn't going to like the answer.

"The topside, air level, water level, power level, work level, blimp bay and bridge guards are all out of com and presumed MIA. Lieutenant Montana and two crewmen are on their way here from the base offices, but Major Santee and everybody else on duty bought it. The hostages have somehow barricaded themselves in the detention area. The guards are cutting through the doors—ET four minutes. Lieutenant Ford reports no hostile action at the radio room. I've set up temporary HQ in the mall level at Circum Three, Radial F. I have eight of my men here, plus three ship's officers and seven crewmen—all that made it out of the barracks and quarters alive. We aren't currently under attack."

Twenty-nine men. Twenty-nine men remaining out of

an occupation force of almost a hundred. It was more than a defeat; it was the worst disaster in Alpha's history. Colonel McCrarey looked at the closing hatch. All he had to do was walk over and jump, leave his failed dream and disgraced career behind. . . .

No! He had blundered badly, but he still had resources at his command. As long as he did, he would fight. He was a soldier, not some spineless civvie.

"What's your opinion of the tactical situation, Captain?"

Patterson paused before answering. "The civvies outnumber us three to one, and they have captured swords and combat suits. But they aren't actually engaging us. They're using tricks, traps. I mean—"

"I know what you mean," Colonel McCrarey cut in ruefully.

"Yes, sir. My opinion is that with our reduced force we can't defeat the civvies by engaging them. I suggest that we secure the detention area, and use the hostages for leverage."

It was a tempting idea revenge-wise, but fundamentally flawed. "No good. The civvies must be expecting that—we wouldn't last long enough to reach the hostages."

"What then?"

"Order all personnel to fall back to the *Shenandoah*. Your men will have to do crew duty, but we'll be able to fly and fight. Then we'll have some real leverage."

"I see." Some enthusiasm returned to Captain Patterson's voice.

"Then get on it. Out."

Colonel McCrarey called Lieutenant Ford. "Lieutenant, Colonel McCrarey here. Still all clear at your end?"

"Yes, sir. There was some breakage when the room listed, but the downlink wasn't damaged."

"We're pulling out temporarily. I want you to execute the civvies, then shag ass to the *Shennandoah* with the satellite manual."

"Uh . . . yes, sir." Lieutenant Ford sounded puzzled.

"I'm counting on you, Lieutenant. Out."

Colonel McCrarey put away his com. The docking hatch was sealed, and he could feel a warm breeze. His head was clearing as more oxygen reached it. The worst was over.

If the *Shenandoah*'s laser convinced the civvies to give up, all well and good. He wouldn't make the mistake of leaving the men alive to rebel twice. If not, he would burn the windrider out of the sky. The satellite manual was important enough to salvage his career despite this debacle, and knowledge of his contemplated treason would die with Lieutenant Ford.

Either way he would have his revenge on these damned civvies.

CHAPTER FORTY

The words "Execute the civvies" echoed over and over in Linda's mind, drowning out the end of Lieutenant Ford's com conversation with Colonel McCrarey.

She was standing against the radio room wall, with one arm around a wide-eyed and quiet Wanda. They had been ordered there by Lieutenant Ford when the crash siren sounded and the radio room began to list. The listing had elated rather than worried her; it meant that Alamo was not only under way, but more imaginative than she had expected. Then, as minutes passed without any further developments, her hope had faded. Now it died completely.

The floor was littered with small items, but none of the room's equipment seemed damaged. Unfortunately, that included the satellite downlink. Lieutenant Ford was standing a few feet in front of Linda and Wanda, his cutter drawn and pointing in their direction. Taking the satellite manual disks from the memory unit, he put them in the holder and tucked it under his arm. His eyes never left Linda long enough for her to reach anything heavy enough to hurt him.

He tapped his com. "Any trouble?"

"Still all clear, sir," the guard outside the door answered crisply.

Lieutenant Ford unlocked the door. "Get in here."

The guard looked inhuman and invulnerable in his black

armor, but there was uncertainty as well as grim ferocity
in his expression. He was also holding his cutter.

Lieutenant Ford seemed as relaxed as ever. "Ladies,"
he said in a mocking tone, "I'm sorry to have to cut our
brief association short, so to speak. Fortunes of war. But
rest assured that our departure is only a temporary setback—
the Project Rainmaker satellite will be burning our enemies out of the sky soon enough. Too bad you two won't
be around to see it."

Linda made herself look into his eyes. "Wanda is only a
child . . . sir. She can't possibly cause Alpha any harm.
I'll . . . go with you and do anything you want, if you'll
leave her here alive. Please."

"No!" Wanda yelled, squirming violently. "Don't go
with him!"

"A tempting offer," Lieutenant Ford replied. "But time
is short, and I have my orders." He turned to the guard.
"Execute them. I don't want to get bloodstains on my
uniform."

"Yes, sir."

The guard lumbered awkwardly across the listing floor
toward Linda and Wanda, while Lieutenant Ford backed
away. Linda's muscles tensed for a desperate, futile dash
to escape with Wanda.

The door exploded inward, springing its lock, under the
force of a big hurtling body in a brown uniform.

Off balance, the *Mayan Princess* crewman fell to his
knees. Three more men surged past him into the room,
waving scavenging picks and yelling, "Viva Mexico!" Captain Ramirez was at the head of the pack.

The guard turned quickly to confront them. He stabbed
his cutter at Captain Ramirez, but Captain Ramirez managed to knock it aside with his pick. The other two crewmen closed in on the guard from the sides, swinging their
picks at his helmet and chest armor. The plastic cracked
but didn't give way. The three men fell in a writhing pile
of bodies and weapons.

Lieutenant Ford had backed away cautiously from the
onslaught. Now, seeing Captain Ramirez alone, he tossed
the satellite manual on a bench and advanced cutter-first.

One of the crewmen in the pile screamed and rolled

away, his hands slowing the flow of blood from a slice in his side. The two remaining foes were wrestling for possession of the guard's cutter. Then the big crewman got up and staggered over. He swung his pick in a broad overhead arc ending on the guard's helmet. The helmet and the head inside it shattered in a horrible mix of plastic, blood and brains.

Linda and Wanda had been watching the scene in sick fascination. Now past exposure enabled Linda to snap out of it. The floor between them and the door was too full of fighting men to be crossed safely. So she darted to a nearby tool cabinet, and pulled out the largest screwdriver. Returning to Wanda, she pushed Wanda behind her. She didn't know how Alamo was going throughout Lone Star Five, or even who would win the fight in front of her. All she knew was that any Alphan who tried to touch Wanda was going to have the screwdriver shoved in his eye.

Captain Ramirez was falling back toward the door, fending off Lieutenant Ford's cutter with his pick. But it was an awkward tool for the job. Linda feared that each stab or slice would be the one which reached its goal.

"Captain!" the big crewman shouted. "Here!"

The crewman tossed the guard's cutter toward Captain Ramirez. Ramirez threw the pick aside and caught the cutter in one smooth motion. "Remind me to put you in for a bonus," Captain Ramirez told him.

Captain Ramirez and Lieutenant Ford faced each other with weaving cutters. The two uninjured crewmen started forward, but Captain Ramirez waved them back. "See to the ladies and Jorge."

Captain Ramirez's eyes lingered for a moment on Linda's damaged face before returning to Lieutenant Ford. "This would be an affair of honor," he said to the Alphan, his thin smile becoming even thinner, "if you had any."

"It takes more than a sword to make a swordsman, civvie."

Having seen the soldiers use their cutters, Linda knew that Lieutenant Ford was right. Captain Ramirez's misguided gallantry was going to get him killed. She felt ill.

"Let me show you what I mean," Lieutenant Ford added as he advanced.

Wearing a contemptuous expression, he swung his cutter at Captain Ramirez's neck. But at his first motion Captain Ramirez stepped back into a strange, awkward pose: turned sideways, legs spread, cutter arm out front and free arm raised behind his head. His cutter barely seemed to twitch, but Lieutenant Ford's was knocked aside.

Lieutenant Ford looked surprised, then his grin returned. "I see. You aren't quite as ignorant as the rest of these civvies."

Captain Ramirez glanced at his own cutter. "This meat cleaver is too heavy and poorly balance for delicate work—I prefer the foil. But it will serve. On guard!"

Lieutenant Ford assumed a similar pose. Lunging forward, he stabbed at Captain Ramirez's heart. Captain Ramirez knocked the cutter aside again, then thrust his own at Lieutenant Ford so quickly that the Alphan barely managed to lean out of its way.

A thrill of hope ran down Linda's spine. The martial arts were as taboo as weapons, but somehow, somewhere, Captain Ramirez had learned how to fight with a cutter.

Steel rang against steel. The two men moved with grace and blurring speed across the listing floor, their cutters weaving intricate patterns. Time after time a cutter would seek some vital part of the opponent's body, only to be stopped short, knocked away or avoided. Linda couldn't follow every movement, so she stared in fearful amazement at the overall ebb and flow. She wasn't alone. Wanda and the crewmen, even the injured one, were watching raptly.

Lieutenant Ford was bigger and his arms were longer, but Captain Ramirez was quicker. They seemed evenly matched. Lieutenant Ford tried to force Captain Ramirez back against the wall by the door. But Ramirez ducked under a slice and sprang past the other into the open floor. Spinning, Lieutenant Ford reengaged him.

Five throats yelled warnings as Captain Ramirez stepped back on a fallen chip board. Too late. His legs went out from under him, and he fell on his back.

Lieutenant Ford swung his cutter at Captain Ramirez's head in a two-handed chop, as if he were splitting a log.

But Captain Ramirez rolled sideways down the sloping floor. The cutter buried itself several inches in the white plastic. By the time Lieutenant Ford yanked it free, Captain Ramirez was back in his fighting pose.

Sweat was flying from both faces. Captain Ramirez had been sliced across his upper cutter arm, while Lieutenant Ford had a stab wound in his shoulder; red stains were spreading from them. But the men's eyes shined with exhilaration.

Lieutenant Ford drove Captain Ramirez back against an empty bench. Maneuvering his cutter in a corkscrew pattern, he sent Ramirez's clattering across the floor.

"I've wasted enough time on you!" Lieutenant Ford gasped. Both men were breathing hard. He stabbed at Captain Ramirez's chest.

At the last moment Captain Ramirez jumped up on the tilting bench. Lieutenant Ford tried to slice his legs off, but he hurdled the swinging cutter. Then he leaped head-first over Lieutenant Ford's surprised face. He landed in a gymnast's forward roll, retrieved his cutter, and sprang to his feet.

Just in time. The aerial escape had finally broken through Lieutenant Ford's self-control. Snarling, red-faced, he charged Captain Ramirez like a mad bull. His two-handed slashes almost knocked Ramirez over. But the zep captain held his ground, warding off blow after blow. Then exhaustion began to weaken Lieutenant Ford's arm. His attack slowed down, became erratic.

Finally Captain Ramirez must have spotted a window of opportunity. He lunged forward, stretching his body in a straight line from his back foot to the point of his cutter. The point drove completely through Lieutenant Ford.

All expression left the lieutenant's face. He jerked violently, then slid off the cutter to the floor. Arterial blood spurted from the entry wound in his chest, ebbed, and stopped.

Linda pulled Wanda close so she wouldn't see, but it was too late. Too late for both of them.

The crewmen yelled enthusiastic congratulations. Captain Ramirez cleaned his cutter using the corpse's sleeve, and bowed graciously. Then he raised his hand for silence. "Jorge, how seriously are you hurt?" he asked the injured crewman.

"I feel like a torn piece of network cording, Captain," Jorge replied in a weak voice. He was holding a folded piece of his shirt over his wound, and the big crewman was helping him up. "But you won't need to sign on a replacement."

"I'm very glad to hear it. The company has gone to a great deal of trouble to make you a master rigger—it would be selfish of you to die." Turning to the other two crewmen, he added, "Escort Jorge to the hospital. Take the other swords with you, but try to avoid any disagreements."

"Your whim is our command, Captain." They picked up the cutter and a pick, and helped their injured companion out the doorway.

Captain Ramirez looked concerned as he stepped over the corpse and approached Linda and Wanda. "I apologize for ignoring you ladies for even a moment, but a captain has to look after his crew."

Wanda hung back, frowning at Captain Ramirez, so Linda went over to meet him alone. As she reached him, the accumulated shocks of the past few hours caught up with her. Her world spun, and she started to fall. Captain Ramirez caught her in his bloodstained arms.

She lifted her head to look into his dark eyes. A lust for him stronger than any she had ever experienced surged through her. It was a primitive, physical response to the man who had fought and killed to save her. To win her. As strong as it was, though, she was now stronger. She understood the hunger, even reveled in it, but she wasn't about to give in to it. Ever. She gently disengaged from him and stepped back.

"Thank you," she said, "for both of us."

"You're most welcome. I see you need medical attention too. But since your need is less urgent, it would be best to remain here until the danger is past."

Linda nodded. "How did you and your crewmen happen to arrive in the proverbial nick of time?"

Captain Ramirez kept glancing at the doorway, and his hand still held the cutter. "Alas, I can't take credit for that. Our task was only to deal with the Alphans here. When I saw you and Wanda, my heart nearly stopped. But fate has been kind to us."

"Where did you learn to use a cutter like that?" she whispered.

Captain Ramirez looked sheepish. "Now you know one of my darkest secrets. Fencing was a highly respected art in old Mexico. I belong to a very private club which keeps the art alive—purely for sport, you understand. I never expected to put it to martial use."

Linda should have been disgusted, but she wasn't, and she no longer saw any reason to pretend otherwise. "I'm very glad you did. I've never seen anything so frightening and fascinating at the same time."

"I do have a gift for it," Captain Ramirez admitted modestly. He stared through her eyes into her soul, and read what was written there for him. "I love you now and always," he breathed softly so that Wanda wouldn't overhear.

"I love it that you love me," Linda whispered back. "It makes me feel . . . very special. If I were free to return your love, I would."

Sighing, Captain Ramirez kissed her on the forehead. She knew it for what it was: a gracious acceptance. "I'm pleased to see that your heart is no longer empty, my dear lady. I can only wish that I was filling it. If I'm ever fortunate enough to meet another lady of your quality, one who is available, I intend to marry her on the spot and trade my roaming life for one of domestic bliss."

Linda laughed at the image. "No woman who truly loves you would ever do that to you."

Captain Ramirez joined in her laughter. Then he said, "If you'll excuse me, I'll check in with the bridge and find out how Alamo—an offensive name, I suggested Cinco de Mayo—is coming along."

He brought out his com, and Linda went back to Wanda.

CHAPTER FORTY-ONE

"Hell and damnation!"

When Vic Jarman's expletive faded, silence returned to the bridge except for the muted sounds of the equipment. The sharp smell of blood hung in the air. He sagged back in his chair. Jose was still busy at systems station two, offsetting as much of the Alamo-caused damage as he could. Not that there was much point now.

Vic glared up at the monitor screen which showed the Alphan zep backing out of the dock. The long black hull was only a few hundred feet away, and moving at a slow crawl. But it might have been a million miles away as far as Lone Star Five's ability to do anything about it.

They had given it one hell of a try. The first com reports had been good news. The aggies had arranged for the lake overflow to take care of their soldiers. The womenfolk had used the super-adhesive he had sent them to keep their soldiers out of town hall. In the air level's fractional distillation plant the soldiers had been frozen by a spray of liquid nitrogen. The power-level gang had rigged a cattle prod with enough kick to melt plastic armor and incinerate bodies, which it did. Pecos Smith and Rowdy Grange, who usually placed one-two in the roping events at every rodeo, had lassoed the soldiers in the water level and yanked them off catwalks forty feet above the floor. The

work-level soldiers had been caught in the traps set up by
Swede and his crew: monomolecular filaments strung at
neck height across corridors and microwave-weakened sections of floor. Captain Ramirez's team had killed the soldiers in the radio room, and the ones in the blimp bay had
been sent on the Long Drop.

Unfortunately, the most important parts of Alamo hadn't
gone as well. While normally the notion of releasing a
poisonous gas in a windrider would have been as incon-
ceivable as setting off explosives or starting a fire, there
was one which could be safely used, and it was available in
quantity from the fractional distillation plant. The Alphan
offices and living quarters had been flooded with pure
oxygen. But some of the rannies had caught on too soon,
and escaped.

They had gathered in the blimp bay, where the plan to
wreck their zep had also failed. They had stayed there for
a few minutes, as if waiting for something. Only when
they had spotted the work crew moving down the outside
of the shell toward the dock's anchoring clamps did they
rush aboard their zep and fly.

Somebody pounded on the bridge's door. "Who is it?"
Vic yelled, reaching for the cutter on the floor beside his
chair.

"The rest of your crew, Vic." Sara Jane's voice came
through the door. "Reckoned you could use some help."

"Come on in!" Now that Alamo was over, everybody
was getting back to their regular jobs. Swede had freed
the womenfolk from the town hall with a power saw. Vic
shut off the door's lock, and Sara Jane and the others
headed for their stations. There were sobs and groans as
they saw Lefty.

Even with Jose taking Lefty's place, there was still an
empty chair: Frank McCullough's.

Lefty, Frank, how many more? Then Vic remembered
that there wasn't any point counting the dead. They were
all going to take the Long Drop soon enough.

Why had he ever hankered to be a chief engineer?

Around him the bridge crew got to work. Eyes scanned
displays, hands moved over controls, low voices spoke into
coms. Once again the bridge was the fully functioning

brain of Lone Star Five. He automatically absorbed much
of the information they were gathering.

Lone Star Five was hurt. It had dropped to nineteen
thousand feet. It was listing thirty-two degrees now, and
the water collecting in the north rim of the ground level
was threatening to tip it even further. But its structure
remained sound. The aggies were setting up portable pumps
and lines to spread the north rim water over the south
fields; the ground would soak it up. Throughout the levels
weight was being shifted back where it belonged. The
flight and life-support systems were all at least marginally
operational, and the most urgent repairs were already
underway.

Only Vic seemed to realize how futile all their efforts
were. But he didn't say anything. They were Lone Star
Five's shakedown crew, and they would keep on doing
their job as long as they could.

He switched his screen to another outside camera as the
Alphan zep started to swing around a half mile out. It
moved with the slow inevitability of a monster from one of
his childhood nightmares. When its nose was pointing at
Lone Star Five, it came to a stop.

"Incoming call from the *Shenandoah!*" Gray reported.
The activity in the bridge faltered as the crew members
realized that the Alphan danger wasn't over. All eyes
turned to stare at Vic's screen.

"I'll take it," he said in a tired voice, and switched on
his com. "Lone Star Five, Vic Jarman here."

"This is Colonel McCrarey." The speaker voice sounded
as smug as ever. Vic cursed himself for letting the Alphan
ramrod get out of the bridge alive. "I congratulate you on
your ingenious rebellion. I should have expected such
cowardly tricks from civvies. But you've had your turn—
now it's mine. You know the *Shenandoah*'s laser can burn
you out of the sky. Surrender or die."

"Hold on a minute," Vic replied, not really giving a
damn whether Colonel McCrarey did or not, and switched
his com to the common channel. "Yo, everybody, this is
Vic Jarman. Listen up. Some of the Alphans got away in
their zep. Now they're threatening to crash Lone Star
Five with the zep's laser unless we give up. The way I

figure it, I'd rather take the Long Drop than be a slave or whatever else they have in mind for us. If any of you all feel differently, holler. Otherwise I'll tell them what Jim Bowie told General Santa Anna."

Vic looked around the bridge. He saw some fear, anger and sorrow in the faces, but no surrender. The com was quiet.

"Can't we do anything?" Catlin asked him.

"I'm open to suggestions," Vic replied sourly. "We can't launch the *Mayan Princess*—fixing it up would take too long. Same for climbing above the Alphan zep's ceiling. It's too far away to throw rocks at."

Catlin and the others looked thoughtful, but nobody spoke up.

Shrugging, Vic switched back to the Alphan zep's channel. "Yo, Colonel."

"I'm waiting for your answer," Colonel McCrarey replied.

"Your answer is, go straight to hell!"

Colonel McCrarey didn't say anything right away. Vic braced himself for the breach, but second after second passed and nothing happened. The waiting made him mad. Too mad to be afraid.

"I applaud your courage." Colonel McCrarey's voice took on a soothing tone. "Maybe we can settle this disagreement short of violence. Do you recall the set of memory disks that Mrs. Calhoun turned over to me? I inadvertently left it behind in your radio room during our hasty departure. If you return it to me, I'll go my way and let you live. Meaningless slaughter is as abhorrent to me as it is to you."

Resisting the temptation to laugh, Vic said, "Hold on a minute," and called the radio room.

"Captain Ramirez, at your service," came the com reply. "Has doomsday been delayed?"

"Seems like. Colonel McCrarey wants to make a swap. Put Miz Calhoun on."

A moment later an uncertain female voice replaced Captain Ramirez's. "You want to speak to me, Mister Jarman?"

"Colonel McCrarey is offering not to crash us," Vic told her, "if I hand over that satellite manual you scavenged in Davis. Any notion why he hankers for it so much?"

"You can't give it to him! The Project Rainmaker laser satellite is still in orbit, and it might still be operational. The Alphans built a downlink here in the radio room, so they could use the laser as a weapon. With the manual they could do it again."

A laser satellite. Vic whistled. "Can you bring the satellite on line and use it to crash the Alphan zep?"

"I'm afraid it would take hours, if it can be done at all. The Alphans hadn't even made contact with the satellite yet. Besides, it's near the south pole now. I'm sorry."

Vic's momentary hope died. "We all are. Don't fret—I'm not about to hand the Alphans something like that. Colonel McCrarey would crash us anyway, after he got it. Just for fun."

Vic switched back to the Alphan zep's channel. "I see why you hanker for that manual, Colonel. We found your satellite downlink, and we're about to build a mighty hot fire under you. If I were you, I'd turn tail and run."

Colonel McCrarey laughed. "That bluff is very weak. I know the stage Lieutenant Ford reached in his work. Are you going to turn over the manual?"

"Nope!"

Colonel McCrarey's voice sharpened. "Then you've lived long enough. Into the ocean you go."

Vic felt a slight, distant tremor. The crash siren went off again, and red lights flashed on the shell monitoring board. "Breach in level three," reported Ringo Cade, who had replaced Jose at systems station two. "Lateral two three eight degrees by vertical one four six degrees."

"How bad?" Vic demanded.

Ringo was studying his displays. "Circular—roughly fourteen inches across. No main cable damage."

Vic figured the Alphan zep's laser could burn a bigger hole than that. Colonel McCrarey must be playing a cat-and-mouse game. The bridge crew was handling the breach drill quickly and effectively; Texans didn't quit, not while they were still breathing. Vic punched up the work-crew channel on his com. "Yo, Swede. I hope you've got some of your roughnecks patching this hole."

"On it, Vic."

"Better drop everything else, and get ready for more patch jobs."

"I reckoned as much. We're all saddled up and ready to ride."

Vic felt another tremor, and Ringo reported another small breach. The bridge and work crews got right on it.

Vic glanced around the bridge at the busy crew members. He saw a lot more anger and determination than fear. Almost everybody in Lone Star Five knew what was going on, but there were no panicky com calls. He was proud of each and every one of them. If he had to die, he couldn't ask for better company.

"Now that you've had a taste of extinction, maybe you're ready to be reasonable." Colonel McCrarey's voice had turned savage. "You have ten seconds to agree to turn over the manual. If you don't, the next shot will be the last one."

CHAPTER FORTY-TWO

Mom came back from talking to Miguel, and lifted Wanda's chin with her fingers the way she did. Their eyes met. "Are you all right, dear?" Mom asked.

Wanda couldn't bear to see the terrible cuts, purple bruises and dried blood on Mom's face. She looked down. "I'm sorry, Mom. It's all my fault."

"No, it's not."

"If I hadn't run away, you wouldn't be here. You wouldn't be hurt."

Mom pulled her close and hugged her. She was surprised to find that she was as tall as Mom. "We'll talk about your running away later," Mom said softly, stroking her hair. "But none of this was your fault. You didn't want it to happen, and you didn't make it happen."

Wanda started sniffling. She knew she was being childish, but she couldn't help it.

Mom wiped her eyes with a sleeve. "Excuse me a moment, dear. I'm going to find out what is happening in the rest of the windrider. As soon as it's safe, we'll go up to the hospital."

"Okay," Wanda said. She was all right except for the

341

queasy feeling in her stomach, but Mom looked like she was trying to hide how much she hurt.

Mom sat down at the monitor system console. It faced banks of wall-mounted screens, small ones surrounding a big one. She started working the console's controls.

Wanda wandered closer to the console, to get a better look at the screens and to get farther away from the dead bodies. She had avoided looking at them since the fight, but she could smell them, and that was bad enough.

Miguel finished his com call and came over to watch what Mom was doing. Wanda didn't know how to feel about him. She had cheered him on in her mind during the amazing fight. But since she didn't blame Mom anymore for their making love, she figured it had to have been his fault. He had tricked Mom, just like he had tricked her. She decided to keep on hating him.

Mom was tapping into the bridge transmissions. The views on the main screen came from the fixed cameras and portable ones carried by crew members. The views changed quickly, as she jumped from channel to channel.

Wanda saw that Lone Star Five was a mess, especially the ground level. But the shakedown crew and the *Mayan Princess* crewmen were working like high-speed mechs. They were moving things out of the low parts of the levels, laying pipes across the farm, patching holes in floors, taking down wires in corridors, and checking, repairing, and replacing equipment. They were also dragging dead soldiers topside to the composting machines, but she looked away when those views appeared.

Then the screen showed an outside camera view, and Mom kept it there. A zep was floating motionlessly about a half mile away, its nose facing the camera. It was so black that it looked like a zep-shaped hole in the sky. It certainly wasn't the *Mayan Princess*, so Wanda figured it had to be the soldiers' zep.

"The surviving Alphans may be fleeing for home," Miguel said to Mom, "but somehow I doubt it."

Mom nodded, her face pale. She was about to say something when Mr. Jarman's sour voice came out of the wall speaker.

Wanda listened to his speech in growing fright. When he finished, Mom and Miguel looked at each other. Wanda figured they were deciding if they wanted to surrender. Part of Wanda tried to scream that she didn't want to die, but she made it shut up. Instead she went over and squeezed Mom's hand. A grateful smile flickered across the terrible sadness in Mom's face.

"A captain is supposed to go down with his zep," Miguel said, "but I imagine this is an acceptable alternative. I apologize to both of you dear ladies for my inadequate job of rescuing. At least I won't have to bear the shame for long."

"You did the best you could," Mom told him, "and that was very good indeed." She took his hand too.

The room's com buzzed. Miguel went over to the com system console and took the call. Moments later he said, "Linda, Señor Jarman wishes to speak to you."

"I'll be right back, dear," Mom told Wanda. Then she joined Miguel at the com console. Wanda kept watching the black zep and wallowing in her misery.

When Mom and Miguel came back, they looked even more unhappy than before. "I was wondering what you ladies were doing here," Miguel said. "It's a cruel fate that places the means of defending ourselves in our hands," he gestured to the satellite manual and the downlink, "but won't let us use it."

Mom didn't say anything. She put her arm around Wanda, and they all stared at the zep.

"Simply waiting here to be killed like so many rats in a trap is galling, to say the least." Miguel looked like he wanted to go somewhere and do something.

Mom smiled wanly. "If you have a miraculous last-second notion to save the day, don't let us keep you."

"Alas, the cupboard is bare."

Wanda felt the floor shake slightly, and the crash siren went off again.

"What was that?" she asked, even though she was pretty sure she knew.

"The Alphan zep has a laser weapon which can melt holes in the shell," Mom explained in a low, hoarse voice.

She quickly sat down again at the monitor console, and her hands moved over it. Shell-integrity data glowed greenly in one of the small screens. "I'm afraid we can't do anything to stop it, and the *Mayan Princess* is disabled."

Before today Wanda wouldn't have believed that anybody could be so bad that they would kill a windrider. But now she did.

Mom looked puzzled. "The breach is only fourteen inches across—not nearly big enough to crash us."

"Maybe that was a warning shot," Miguel suggested.

"What's it like to die?" Wanda asked, her voice squeaking. If it had to happen, she wished it would hurry up and happen.

"Try not to think about it, dear. It's . . . like falling asleep. When we start to break up, just hug me tight and remember that."

"I will. I love you, Mom."

"I love you too."

It made a crazy kind of sense to Wanda that Lone Star Five was about to fall apart around her, sending her on the Long Drop. So many other things that she had thought were solid and real had fallen apart too. All she had left (or again) was Mom. Mom would stay with her to the very end.

She stared at the black zep. Her mouth was dust-dry, her stomach was burning, and she could hardly breathe. She was even more afraid than when the soldier had chased her to the top of the shell and Puff had . . .

Puff!

Wanda still wasn't sure what Puff had done to the soldier, but maybe she could do it to the zep too. If Wanda could find her and get her to try. Wanda hadn't heard/felt her since being captured by the soldiers in the work-crew station. Puff could be far away by now, eating sunshine up in the ionosphere or playing somewhere else.

But Wanda didn't really think Puff would desert her at a time like this. Pushing everything else out of her mind, she called/reached out as hard as she could. She felt her face scrunching up from the effort. But, as second after second went by without an answer, she started to lose hope. The way Mom and Miguel were acting, Lone Star Five was going to crash any minute now. There just wasn't time.

Then she heard/felt Puff's beloved voice/presence, faint but getting stronger fast. Puff was coming at top speed.

Wanda and Teacher Ware had been experimenting with a way to talk to Puff with pictures. She hadn't been able to get Puff to understand anything complicated, but maybe this would be simple enough. She stared at the screen, trying to see the zep as clearly and sharply as possible. She let the fear build up inside her, until she was shaking like a blimp's motor gondola; not just fear for herself, but for Mom and everybody else. She hardly noticed Mom comforting her. If Puff would just connect the zep and her fear, the way she had with the soldier. . . .

Wanda could hear/feel that Puff was upset by her fear, but she could also hear/feel Puff's confusion. She wasn't getting through.

She felt the floor twitch again. This is it, she thought, and her heart tried to jump out of her chest. But Mom looked at the shell-integrity readouts and shook her head. "Another small breach."

"Colonel McCrarey is having his little game with us," Miguel said grimly. "When he tires of it, we die."

Wanda frantically tried another way to make Puff understand. Closing her eyes, she visualized the soldier exploding as vividly as she could remember it. Then she visualized the black zep. The soldier again. The zep. . . .

Puff reacted, but not the way Wanda had hoped she would. At first Wanda thought Puff was just echoing her own fear. Then she realized it was something she had never heard/felt before. Puff was afraid, terribly afraid. Wanda couldn't stand to hear/feel Puff's suffering. She closed her mind.

"What in the—I do believe that's a fireball out there," Miguel said in a surprised tone. Wanda opened her eyes and looked at the main screen. A dot of pulsing red light was soaring between the zep and Lone Star Five. Her heart went out to Puff one last time.

"It picked a remarkably poor time and place to frolic,"

Miguel said. "One should at least be able to have some dignity at one's funeral."

Puff was flying around the zep in short, jagged maneuvers. Wanda could tell by that and Puff's color that something was very wrong with her.

"I've never seen a fireball act like that." Mom sounded like most of her mind was somewhere else.

"I doubt Colonel McCrarey is enjoying the performance," Miguel replied. He was watching the screens curiously as if he wasn't about to die. "If the fireball keeps playing tag with the zep, it may become the laser's next target."

"That's Puff," Wanda admitted miserably. "I tried to get her to explode the zep, but she won't. She's afraid."

Miguel started to say something, but Mom cut him off. "You know fireballs never come close to windriders or zeps," she said gently to Wanda. "And they've never shown any ability or willingness to cause damage. I'm afraid Puff can't help us."

Wanda remembered what Teacher Ware had told her about metal being dangerous to Puff's fields of force. Mom was right; Puff couldn't save them. And Puff was in danger too.

Fly away! Wanda yelled/pushed desperately. The zep can hurt you! Hurry! I love you!

Puff's answering love filled Wanda with warmth. She urged Puff on. Puff soared and banked through a really fancy maneuver, then climbed like a rocket.

But Puff wasn't leaving. "No!" Wanda yelled as Puff made a tight one-eighty and dove at the zep.

The view of the zep zoomed in to a close-up. The zep's props spun, trying to move it aside.

Too late. Puff hit the top of the hull right in the middle. When she hit, she blazed through the spectrum to a white brighter than the sun. The camera's filter kicked in, but even so Puff's brilliance filled the sky. Then, almost as quickly, it faded and went out.

The black zep was still there, but it looked to be in bad shape. A hole at least fifty feet wide had been melted in the top of the hull. The zep was listing about ten degrees to port, its tail was dipping, and the hull seemed bent at the hole. The props were slowing down. And the zep was falling slowly; auto-tracking kept it centered on the screen.

"Its back is broken!" Miguel yelled. "By all the gods of aeronautics, it's done for!"

Yells, cheering, and excited questions from all over Lone Star Five poured out of the wall speaker. The bridge must have set up the com's party line. Miguel looked happy and fierce as he watched the screen. Mom gathered Wanda in her arms and hugged her.

But for Wanda being saved was worse than dying. When Puff had melted the hole in the zep and filled the sky with light, her voice/presence had disappeared. She was gone. And this time Wanda knew she would never come back.

Clinging to Mom, Wanda cried.

CHAPTER FORTY-THREE

Wiping blood from his eyes, Colonel McCrarey lifted himself on his good elbow and looked around. He groaned as his broken arm objected to the move. Each breath hurt like hell; he must have cracked some ribs too. At least he wasn't coughing up blood.

The OCC was listing to port and tail-down. Everything electrical was dead, even the emergency lamps. A few small wiring fires were burning themselves out. The keel cubic still had pressure, but the smoke-laden air was just barely breathable. Colonel McCrarey could feel as well as hear the *Shenandoah* buckling. The night-watch navigation officer and the aircav tech sergeant manning the weapons station had also been thrown from their chairs, but they were coming around.

Colonel McCrarey wasn't sure exactly what had happened. When the fireball had started to dive, he had sensed that it was an attack despite their innocuous reputation. But his evasive maneuver had been too little too late. Something like a legendary nuke had blasted the top of the hull. What had exploded? Not the hydrogen in the cells; there wasn't enough oxygen at this altitude to sustain combustion. It must have been the insane fireball. *How* and *why* were two questions he wanted answered, but he had more immediate matters to attend to.

He glared out the windscreen at the windrider receding into the sky, and bit off a savage curse. It mocked him, floating askew but intact, while his mighty *Shenandoah* had been reduced to wreckage. If he hadn't drawn out the pleasure of his revenge, the windrider would have been crashing into the ocean now, and the *Shenandoah* would have been safely on course for Alpha. The damned civvies had been his undoing. They were undoubtedly watching and laughing at him. He would have eagerly traded his zep and his life for one more shot from the laser.

But he wasn't defeated. Not while he was still alive. Somehow he would make it to Alpha, and come back in the *Valley Forge*. This time there wouldn't be any games, just the immediate, total destruction of one windrider.

Colonel McCrarey managed to ease his broken arm into the front of his shirt without passing out. The improvised sling held it steady, as he gripped the back of the nearest chair and struggled to his feet. He lurched over to his command chair rather than to the now-useless pilot's station he had been manning before the explosion, and dropped into it.

"Get back to your posts, men!" he rapped in his best tone of command. He coughed, and spat pink. "You're Alpha Command—try to look like it!"

The navigation officer climbed groggily to his feet and slid into his chair. The aircav was in better shape thanks to his helmetless combat suit. Rising, he staggered back to the weapons station as his shocked eyes took in the damage to the OCC.

"We're hurt, men, but we're far from whipped." Colonel McCrarey knew that he had to restore order and authority before his makeshift crew could panic, so he spoke calmly, confidently. "Lieutenant, I want a status report on all the flight systems ASAP."

The navigation officer had been staring dully at the dark, smoking stations. He turned to face Colonel McCrarey and laughed wildly. "Status report! Your fucking status report is we're fucking dead, sir! We just haven't stopped breathing yet!"

Colonel McCrarey paused until he had his anger under control, then spoke levelly. "That will be enough of that kind of talk, Lieutenant. The electronics may be shot, but we can vent and drop ballast manually. We'll fly the *Shenandoah* back to Alpha like a free balloon, if we have to."

"Fly what? The zep's back is broken somewhere amidship! You can feel it! The first rough air we hit is going to snap the zep in half!"

"Then we'll fly half the zep back to Alpha."

The navigation officer laughed again, bitterly this time. "We're falling—or hadn't you noticed? We must have lost four, five cells! How do you plan to fly without lift?"

Colonel McCrarey was thinking fast. "We'll lighten the zep, toss everything we don't absolutely need overboard. Enough discussion—here's what I want you to do. Work your way aft, get damage reports including a count of effective personnel. Tell Captain Patterson to start tossing weight and to send me a couple of runners. Move out."

But the navigation officer just stretched out in his chair. "With all due respect, sir, I'd rather relax and enjoy my last few minutes."

A blood-red haze filled Colonel McCrarey's vision. He jumped out of his chair, drew his sword, and ran it through the navigation officer's heart. The navigation officer tried to scream, but all that came out of his wide-open mouth was a shuddering sigh.

As the corpse slid out of its chair, Colonel McCrarey turned to the gaping aircav. "You heard the orders I gave the lieutenant. You're it now. Move out."

The aircav's tanned face had turned gray. "Yes, sir!" He ran to the door and opened it.

There was a distant tearing sound; the bridge abruptly listed a few more degrees to port. A loud crash from astern was followed by cries for help. The aircav paused, then started through the doorway.

Despite leakage, the keel cubic still held plenty of oxygen. There were electrical fires and other hot spots. Now hydrogen flooded the cubic, either from a ruptured cell or a cracked reserve tank. A solid wall of orange flame and white smoke roared up the passageway toward the OCC. The aircav slammed the door shut, but it, he, and the entire bulkhead were blown in. The windscreen shattered. The inferno swept into the OCC.

Colonel McCrarey had an instant to grasp and appreciate the poetry of his fate. Then the fiery arms of hell embraced him.

CHAPTER FORTY-FOUR

The Alphan zep broke in half, and orange flames spewed from the open ends. Both halves seemed to shrivel. Then they tumbled out of the camera's range on their way to the ocean graveyard.

Unwrapping one of her arms from around Wanda, Linda turned off the screen.

"I doubt any tears will be shed for those gentlemen," Captain Ramirez said softly. "But it's a sad thing when any zep, even that one, comes to the end of its long flight."

Linda was happier (and more surprised) that she and Wanda were still alive than she could possibly put into words or thoughts. The rest of her life would be borrowed time, and she promised herself not to waste a moment of it. Letting tears of joy roll down her cheeks, she hugged Wanda tighter. The sounds of celebration from the wall speaker continued, until Mr. Jarman sharply reminded everyone that Lone Star Five could still crash if they didn't get back to work.

"I'm terribly sorry about Puff," Linda whispered to Wanda.

"I tried to warn her," Wanda sniffled. "I told her to fly away, but she didn't understand me."

Linda sighed. She hadn't realized how tight the bond between the two of them had been. "Puff understood, dear. She sacrificed herself to save you, because she loved you. Because you were worthy of her love. Always remember that."

"I will."

Captain Ramirez coughed for attention. "My dear ladies, now that it's safe to do so, I suggest you go to the hospital for treatment. I would escort you, but I must see how the *Princess* has endured her rough handling."

"You should have that cut on your arm taken care of," Linda suggested.

"This scratch? I've wounded myself more grievously while shaving. If you'll excuse me, I must fly." He bowed and hurried out.

Linda avoided the dead bodies as she guided Wanda out of the radio room. The listing made the trip to the hospital a surreal experience. The escalators were either broken or shut down, so they had to walk up the ramps, an arduous task at which they took their time. The ventilation system was also down; the stagnant air carried faint smells of mud, blood, and ozone. Lone Star Five felt even emptier and more forlorn than it had, but the few folks they encountered were very busy.

Linda and Wanda used the time to bring each other up to date. In relating her own story Linda carefully edited the attack in Davis and the beating by Colonel McCrarey. Wanda's adventures horrified and amazed her, and made her even prouder of her daughter. The subject of running away was ignored by unspoken mutual consent.

The partially set-up hospital was handling more patients than it could handle when they arrived. Dr. Starnes, Dr. Santos from the *Mayan Princess*, and two helpers were running an emergency clinic. Most of the injuries seemed minor, but three beds and both ICU's were occupied. In one room bodies in plastic sacks covered the floor: the Lone Star Five and *Mayan Princess* dead. Unlike the soldiers, the townsfolk would have proper funerals before going to the farm.

Linda and Wanda waited in the examining room. When Dr. Starnes finished with her patient, she came over to them. "I'm mighty happy to see you all alive and kicking," she said, her professional cheerfulness frayed around the edges. "Young'un, you sure had your ma fretting about your disappearing act."

"I'm sorry," Wanda said contritely.

"What happened in the town hall?" Linda asked Dr. Starnes urgently.

"The rannies lit out before they could cut through the doors. Nobody got hurt."

"Are Dede and Jim okay?" Wanda asked.

Dr. Starnes nodded. "I wrapped a cracked rib for Jim not five minutes ago—nothing serious. Both back at work, I reckon. Now let's see about you all."

Wanda's needs turned out to be limited to water, for drinking and for washing her hands and face. While she was attending to the second task in the lavatory, Dr. Starnes examined Linda's face. She was frowning. "I hope whoever did this to you didn't die easy."

Linda remembered the Alphan zep burning as it broke up. "I don't think he did."

Dr. Starnes carefully cleaned Linda's face, sprayed it with a local anesthetic which freed her from the pain she had been enduring, and covered the cuts with artificial skin. Then Dr. Starnes took her over to the scan unit. Finally the frown left the doctor's face. "No concussion, no broken bones. Your face will look like you were stirrup-dragged for a couple of weeks, but it should heal up just fine." Dr. Starnes handed her a vial of pills. "Take one every four hours for the pain, and try to stay off your face."

"Thank you, Doctor," Linda said sincerely, but Starnes was already heading for another patient.

Linda was about to fetch Wanda when the wall com announced, "Bridge paging Miz Linda Calhoun. Bridge paging Miz Linda Calhoun."

Linda went into an unused office and closed the door for privacy as well as quiet. Using its com—the soldiers had taken hers—she called the bridge. "This is Linda Calhoun."

"Vic Jarman here, ma'am," the sour voice of the chief engineer came from the speaker. "Captain Ramirez tells me your young'un was somehow responsible for that fire-ball crashing the Alphan zep. I'll want to chew the fat with you all about that later. If it's true, Lone Star Five owes her a mighty big thank you."

"It's true, and we all do." Linda's voice was heavy with emotion and weariness.

"Right now, though, we've got a problem. We might need to use that laser satellite real soon. Can you get it working?"

An image of another Alphan zep finding and attacking them flashed in Linda's mind, and her terror returned. "I . . . don't know. The downlink is operational, and every function except control is interfaced with Lone Star Five's systems. I learned a lot about it helping Lieutenant Ford, including how to access the manual for information. Maybe—"

"*Maybe* won't get it done. How soon can you know for sure?"

"Absolutely sure? After I activate the laser and see what happens to the target. But if reasonably sure will do, I can try to bring the satellite on line and run its diagnostic program in about—" Linda paused to remember when the satellite would be in com range again—"two hours."

"I'd be obliged if you'd get to it," Mister Jarman said with labored patience. "Will you need any help?"

"If I do, I'll call you. But I think I can handle it."

"I'm going to round up all the department heads and Captain Ramirez in my office at 8 P.M.—that will give you your two hours and then some. Please be there, and bring some good news with you."

"I'll do what I can," Linda promised.

"Much obliged." The com clicked off.

Linda found Wanda waiting outside the lavatory, scrubbed clean except for her matted hair and mud-stained clothes. But Wanda was still clearly depressed over Puff. "Now what, Mom?" she asked wanly.

"I have to do some more work in the radio room," Linda told her. "Why don't you go to the Polks' apartment and take a nap. I'll come there as soon as I can."

Wanda was quiet for a moment. Then she asked, "Are you going to wake up the laser satellite, so you can use it to protect us from any more soldiers?"

Linda nodded.

"Then I want to come along and help you again. Can I?"

After all that had happened, Linda liked the idea of having Wanda in sight. "Okay, dear. Let's go."

The trip down was much easier than the trip up had been. When they reached the radio room, they found that the Alphan corpses had been removed, and that ration packs and a bottle of apple juice had been left on the bench with the satellite manual. Linda saw Captain Ramirez's hand in both courtesies. They wolfed down the cold, bland, but highly appreciated meal. Linda didn't criticize Wanda's table manners, since her own were no better. Then they went over to the downlink.

Linda looked at the haphazard collection of equipment upon which Wanda's and her survival might depend, and the ridiculousness of the situation struck her like a hard wind. Despite Lieutenant Ford's confidence she didn't really believe that this junk could rouse a sleeping weapon of mass destruction. Laser satellites were a legend from the War. Even if they had existed, they didn't any more. If there was a Project Rainmaker satellite orbiting thousands of miles overhead, it had to be either dead or crippled beyond use. The downlink's signals would go unanswered.

But then she hadn't really believed in soldiers or war zeps either.

Loading the manual disks into the memory unit, she switched everything on. She confirmed that the computer could still access Lone Star Five's database, and that Lieutenant Ford hadn't erased his programs.

"What can I do to help?" Wanda asked plaintively.

Linda gestured to the chair facing the auxiliary station. "You're going to be our research department. Your first job is to call up the orbital position program. Do you remember how?"

"I think so." Wanda went to work, concentrating on her keyboard and screen with furrowed-brow seriousness. Linda felt sad that Wanda had had to do so much growing up so fast. Then she sat down in front of the main station.

With Wanda's help she calculated that the satellite would be within com range in fifty-three minutes, and remain within range for eight minutes. She had plenty to do during both periods, so she worked quickly.

First she made sure that the downlink was fully operational. She was worried that the Alamo activities, the listing in particular, might have caused some damage. She eyeballed the equipment, then ran the diagnostic program. Aside from having to realign the antenna, she found everything in order.

Then she studied how to operate the downlink and the Project Rainmaker satellite. Ordinarily she would have needed weeks to educate herself; she knew next to nothing about either. But she had a windrider engineer's education and experience, and Lieutenant Ford had explained the procedures to her in the course of interfacing the downlink with Lone Star Five's systems. She reinforced her brief training with information from the manual and the windrider's database and some practice runs.

For the practice runs she used a file she had discovered while surveying Lieutenant Ford's computer work: calculations for firing the laser at Alpha tomorrow during the scheduled rendezvous. She had wondered about that; maybe he had wanted to test the targeting function. Whatever the reason, it did add a certain evil pleasure to her simulations.

She could have used a great deal more time to prepare, but as the last seconds before the com window ticked away she thought she knew enough to muddle through.

"This is it," she told Wanda. Feeling like Ali Baba, she ran the access code and revival instructions.

The downlink's screen remained dark.

"Now what?" Wanda asked in a disappointed tone, after almost three minutes had gone by.

"Now we keep waiting. If the satellite is operational, its solar collectors are folded up and supplying just enough power for housekeeping. Having received our signal, it should be waking up—unfolding the collectors, recharging its batteries, and running its diagnostic program. Soon it should have enough power to send the diagnostic data down to us."

"You mean like that?" Wanda asked, pointing to Linda's screen.

Green data lines were rolling up it.

"It's actually up there!" Linda yelped, and squeezed Wanda's hand. "Now let's see how operational it is."

Wanda was frowning at the dense blocks of data. "What does all that stuff mean?"

"I have no idea," Linda admitted. "Fortunately I don't have to. The computer is processing it—we'll receive a summary."

The summary was hard enough to understand, and the window was closing quickly. But with Wanda frantically feeding her explanations from the manual and Lone Star Five's database, she managed to find the key information she was looking for. That information was encouraging, so she sent the self-repair instructions that the computer recommended.

"Fifteen seconds," Wanda said, counting down the window.

Linda didn't have time to test-fire the laser at low power so that the diagnostic program could analyze the telemetry. Hoping for the best, she ordered the satellite to begin powering up the laser's capacitors. The screen displayed the acknowledgment as the satellite moved out of range.

Wiping sweat from her forehead with her sleeve, Linda turned to Wanda. "I believe we did it. Thank you for your help, dear—you did very well."

"Can we fire the laser now?" Wanda asked.

"Soon, maybe. I'll know better when we've deciphered the rest of that diagnostic summary."

Linda called the summary back up. Working at a more relaxed pace, they unraveled its meaning entry by entry. By the time Linda had to leave for Mister Jarman's meeting, she was fairly sure that she had the good news he wanted to hear.

"I have to go to a meeting for a while," she told Wanda. "Would you please keep an eye on the downlink while I'm gone? It's very important that nothing happens to it."

"I'll protect it," Wanda promised. "You won't be gone long, will you?"

"Not a moment longer than I have to be, dear."

The park escalator was running again, so Linda had an easier trip up to the public levels than her last. She

noticed that the listing had eased up to approximately
twenty degrees. She took it as a hopeful sign that things
were returning to normal.

She needed the reassurance. Staring up through the
well at the tiny rectangle of topside night, she felt the
reality of the satellite as a vaguely oppressive sensation. It
was beyond reach. It was power without conscience, willing to destroy anything or anyone, evil or good. And like
Pandora, she was letting it out of its box. Was she rein-
venting war?

She wasn't about to return to the radio room and wreck
the downlink; Wanda's safety might depend upon it. But
she was more afraid than ever of what the future would
bring.

CHAPTER FORTY-FIVE

Jarman's office was crowded, but extra chairs had been brought in so that everyone had a seat. The chief engineer was behind his desk/console, and Captain Ramirez had his boots up on the corner of it. There were three other men and two women.

The men rose when Linda entered. "For those of you all who don't know it," Mr. Jarman said, "this lady's handle is Linda Calhoun. She's from Calgary. She came here in the *Mayan Princess*, and the Alphans have had her working on the satellite downlink I told you about."

Captain Ramirez smiled casually, but Linda felt the intensity behind the stares of the others. "I'm pleased to meet you," she told them, the politeness sounding out of place. She settled into a free chair, and the men returned to theirs.

Jarman introduced the department heads to her. Wes Barnes, the aggie foreman, was covered with mud and seemed utterly exhausted. Sandy Baylor, the head of the air crew, had curly blond hair and a spray of freckles which made her look little older than Wanda. Lu Anne Kanelly had been the head of the power crew for less than three hours; she didn't seem comfortable with the responsibility. Pecos Smith from the water level was another vid cowboy, from his tooled leather boots to the Stetson in his

360

lap. Swede Hansen, the work-crew chief, was the biggest person in the room, and appeared the least happy.

"Doc begged off—too busy—so everybody is here," Jarman finished. "I reckon we can get to it."

"Doc isn't the only one too busy to chew the fat," Ms. Kanelly muttered. "What's so important that you had to round us up for an eye-to-eye?"

"We'll get to that. First I need to know how the repair work is going. More specifically, do we need help right away, or can we keep Lone Star Five aloft ourselves?"

That drew some curious looks, including one from Linda. Jarman didn't elaborate. So one by one the department heads gave brief status reports. Mister Jarman passed around a control unit so that they could supplement their words with camera views and computer data on the wall telescreen. Linda listened in growing shock at how extensive and serious the damage had been, and in amazement at how hard the shakedown and *Mayan Princess* crews were working to undo it. Her engineering instinct cried out not just for help from Lone Star, but for a complete refitting at the Pemex Under yard.

Captain Ramirez reported that the *Mayan Princess* had suffered only minor damage from the listing. The motor parts which the Alphans had removed to disable it hadn't been found, but Mister Hansen assured him that replacements could be made in a few days. Captain Ramirez estimated that the *Mayan Princess* could be airworthy as soon as the parts and his crew were made available.

Mr. Jarman took almost a minute to digest the reports behind his poker face. "Could be worse," he said at last, but he wasn't able to keep the pain out of his voice. "We ought to get to Lone Star pronto, no doubt about it. We need supplies and more skilled hands, and Doc has some patients who need a real hospital. About the only good news is that we ought to be back in trim before sunup. But I reckon we can get by on our own for a few more days. We might have to."

Several voices asked why, but Jarman ignored them. Linda had a faintly ominous feeling which she refused to explore.

Mister Jarman turned to her. "Let's hear your report now, Miz Calhoun."

She gathered her thoughts, then began. "The downlink is fully operational, except that the control function hasn't been interfaced with Lone Star Five's computer. That means the downlink can only be operated from the radio room. My daughter and I have made contact with the Project Rainmaker satellite. There has been significant deterioration and some micrometeor damage, but it's marginally operational.

"The free-electron laser is nominal. Targeting will take some time—it'll have to be done by gyro-reorientation, since the fuel for the attitude rockets outgassed a long time ago. Com is tenuous but adequate—the satellite is using a patchwork of surviving gear. Power collection is sixty-eight percent of optimum—one collector won't deploy. Power storage is forty-two percent—"

"Save the details for later," Mister Jarman cut in. "I need to know if you can fire the laser and hit what you're aiming at."

Linda shrugged away her irritation at being interrupted. "I've started the power-up for the laser. In approximately nine hours I'll be able to conduct a full-power test shot, and let you know."

"Can't wait for that," Mister Jarman said sharply. "For what I've got in mind, we'll need the laser on line by tomorrow noon. No time for a second power-up. I need your professional judgment, ma'am. If we need it, can we count on the laser?"

Linda had answered that question to her own satisfaction before leaving the radio room, but now she was reluctant to voice it. What in the sky was Jarman driving at? Whatever it was, she had a very bad feeling about it. But he had asked her for her professional judgment, so she gave it. "Yes."

"You say the laser is under-powered," Mister Hansen spoke up. "Can it do much damage?"

"It was designed to destroy armored rockets and aircraft. Even at forty-two percent power it can crash anything in the sky today. Anything."

There was a long, thoughtful silence.

"You reckon you can figure out how to fire the laser at Alpha before tomorrow noon?" Jarman asked Linda.

She remembered Lieutenant Ford's calculations. "It's probably the only thing I could hit. But we would have to be within radar range for targeting."

Mr. Jarman stood up. "Now for the really bad news, pardners. When we ran the Alphans out, Lone Star Five was on course for Alpha itself. So far I haven't changed that course."

Linda had assumed that they were on their way to Lone Star. Her shock was echoed in the rising babble of objections and demands for an explanation. Jarman waited for the noise level to drop, then went on.

"I've pieced together the little we learned from the rannies about Alpha. It's a windrider that has been lying low here in the Arctic since the War, run by a gang of rustlers still playing soldier. It robs and crashes windriders— the townsfolk who aren't killed are kept as slaves. It has another war zep like the *Shenandoah*. The rustling has to be stopped, and those townsfolk have to be rescued."

Mister Smith's deep voice pushed through the others. "Are you aiming to attack Alpha?"

Mister Jarman nodded. "We've been traveling com-silent, so Alpha probably still reckons Colonel McCrarey is ramrodding us. That gives us the advantage of surprise. We can use the laser satellite to force Alpha to give up."

"How do you aim to do that?"

"By threatening to crash Alpha."

That shock was even worse than the first, and resulted in total silence. Finally Mr. Barnes asked, "What if the Alphans launch that other zep to attack us?"

"I'll tell them that if they start to launch it, we'll crash both of them. But don't fret—it won't come to that. They know better than most what a laser satellite can do. They'll have to give up. We'll make them scuttle the zep and turn over all the townsfolk, then we'll mosey on to Lone Star. Defanged, they won't be much of a danger to anybody. The towns can figure out what else to do about them."

"Why don't we just go straight to Lone Star and let the towns handle the whole thing?" Ms. Kanelly asked, her cheeks flushed. "We don't have any right to start a fight, and we're certainly in no shape for one! We're what's left of a shakedown crew and a zep crew in a windrider that's barely aloft!"

Jarman looked grim. "I don't cotton to it any more than you all do, but we don't have a choice. We're too close to Alpha. If we don't show up tomorrow, that zep will come looking for us, and we won't be too hard to find. Same problem if we rig a long-range transmitter and send out a Mayday—Alpha will pick it up."

"No course leads to safety," Captain Ramirez said calmly. "Since we must deal with Alpha either way, Señor Jarman's plan offers the best hope of success."

"Even if we could hightail it," Jarman continued, "what about Alpha? It'll know the cat is out of the bag, and most likely hide somewhere else. Be mighty hard to track it down then. It'll keep on rustling windriders."

Linda went over his arguments carefully, hoping to find a flaw. She wasn't nearly as confident of the outcome as he was (or sounded), and she hated not being able to take Wanda out of danger. But he was right about there being no choice. And the danger wasn't just to Wanda or Lone Star Five; thousands of mothers would be crying for their dying children, unless Alpha was stopped. She saw reflections of her own trapped feeling in some of the other faces.

"I'm much obliged for your good advice," Mr. Jarman said. "I don't cotton to making this kind of decision, but a shakedown crew can't be a democracy. Any of you all hanker to be chief engineer?"

No one answered, or even met his angry eyes.

"Didn't reckon so. We'll go ahead with my plan then—spread the word. You all will find the details in the computer file on Alpha. We'll meet again tomorrow around 9 A.M. to chew it fine. Any more questions?"

There were none.

"Then let's get back to work. Be a damned shame if we crashed before we even reached Alpha."

Linda was part of the silent group that filed out of Jarman's office. She would have liked to talk to Captain Ramirez, but he had remained behind to say something to Jarman. The group broke up as everyone went his or her own way, and Linda hurried back to the radio room.

When she arrived, she noticed that the door was closed. Not just closed but locked; the door had been repaired. Curious, she knocked and Wanda let her in.

The radio room had been cleaned up. All the fallen items had been picked up, the dislodged equipment was back where it belonged, and even the blood on the floor had been scrubbed away. "What has been going on here?" Linda asked Wanda.

"I got bored," Wanda admitted guiltily. "I didn't touch the downlink, I promise."

"I believe you. But how did you repair the door?"

"Oh, that wasn't hard. The lock was okay—the frame just got twisted. I used a microwave unit to soften the plastic, and a couple of shielding plates to push it back like it should be."

Linda sighed, trying not to think about the various ways Wanda could have hurt herself. But what else should she expect from the daughter of two engineers? "You did a very good job, dear."

Wanda looked a little less depressed.

Linda took her over to a chair, sat her down, and told her about the plan to deal with Alpha. Linda had been worried about her reaction, but she didn't seem to care. All she said was, "Okay." Linda realized that Puff's death had numbed Wanda to any other emotional pain, for which Linda was almost grateful.

Linda was terribly tired, partly from the pain pill she had taken, and Wanda was yawning. "It's bedtime for both of us," Linda told her. "I'll take you to the Polks' apartment, then come back here and keep an eye on the downlink."

"You don't have to do that," Wanda said. "That's why I fixed the door, so you could lock the room up. I called Dede to make sure she and Jim were okay. She said you could use their bedroom, if you want. She said they would be working all night, so it wouldn't put them out."

Linda compared sleeping in a real bed to her plan of fetching some blankets from the town hall. It was no contest. "I think you have two very special friends in the Polks."

They closed up the radio room and headed for the park

escalator. They stopped at the empty townhall so that Linda could collect her belongings. Then they went on to the Polks' apartment.

It was messier than Linda remembered. Unwashed dishes and dirty clothes testified to the three days of occupancy by a dispirited man. The listing had added considerably to the mess, especially in the kitchen. She knew how Dede would feel walking into this after working herself down to a nub. So she turned to Wanda and asked, "Do you feel up to some tidying before we go to bed?"

"Sure." Wanda yawned.

While Wanda picked up and put away, Linda washed the dishes and cleaned the kitchen and bathroom. Linda used the water-conservation techniques that she had learned on scavenging expeditions; water rationing was one of the emergency measures that Mr. Jarman had announced earlier over the com. Then she changed both beds, and Wanda put all the dirty clothes and sheets in the hamper. Washing would have to wait until the water shortage was over.

Linda surveyed the tidy, if not totally clean, apartment while Wanda stared out the living room's window wall at the myriad stars in the black sky. "Now we can call it a night," Linda said.

Wanda looked forlornly at the bathroom door. "I wish I could take a shower. I feel yucky."

"I know exactly what you mean. I think Lone Star Five can spare enough water for two sponge baths."

Wanda looked dubious. "Sponge baths?"

"Come on," Linda said teasingly. "They're not that bad, and they will get us clean."

Normally Linda would have deferred to Wanda's teenage sensibilities about privacy, and let her bathe alone. But Linda wanted to make sure that Wanda hadn't hidden any injuries from Dr. Starnes. So they undressed and went into the bathroom together. Wanda didn't object, and Linda was relieved to find nothing more than minor bruises.

Linda filled the sink with warm soapy water, and they stepped into the bathtub. They used hand towels in lieu of sponges to scrub themselves, helping each other with the hard-to-reach spots. The situation quickly deteriorated from serious to embarrassing to hilarious. They slipped, splashed, got soap where they didn't want it, flicked each other with the towels, and broke into hysterical laughter whenever they tried to say anything. The listing bathroom added the perfect skewed touch.

Refilling the sink with clean water, they used the towels to rinse off the soap. Then they dried off and prepared for bed. Linda went into Wanda's bedroom to tuck her in.

Linda's conscience was nagging her. Wanda hadn't raised the subject, and she seemed to be over her hostility, but Linda had to talk to her about Captain Ramirez. Now. If things went wrong tomorrow, Linda needed to know that she understood.

So Linda gestured for Wanda to sit on her bed, and stood in front of her. "We have to have a talk, dear."

"Can't it wait until morning?" Wanda asked, suddenly wary.

"I'm afraid not." Linda paused. She felt nervous and unprepared. "We have to talk about Captain Ramirez—and you and me."

"I don't want to."

"I don't either. But we can't pretend that it didn't happen. If we try, it'll fester and cause more trouble between us later on. This isn't a mother/daughter talk. It's woman to woman—the first of many we'll be having. So feel free to say anything that is on your mind. I won't hold it against you. Okay?"

"Okay," Wanda agreed sullenly.

Linda paused again. "I can't begin to explain to you how wonderful it is to be a wife and mother—you'll find out for yourself someday. But nothing of value comes cheaply. When I married your father, I made commitments, accepted limitations. I thought the bargain was more than fair, and I still do.

"But seventeen years is a long time. I became bored, and I forgot how important being part of our family is to me. Captain Ramirez is a very exciting man. The night you saw us I came very close to going to bed with him. I'm not going to ask you to believe that I didn't—it would please me, but you have every right not to.

"What I did was bad enough. I was weak and thoughtless, and I hurt you. I owe you an apology. Will you accept it?"

Wanda was squirming uncomfortably, but Linda's eyes held hers and wouldn't let go. Finally Wanda nodded.

"Thank you," Linda said sincerely.

"Are you going to leave us and marry Miguel?" Wanda asked in a fearful whisper.

"Absolutely not. I do love him, the same way you love Lori and Jan because they're special friends. But that doesn't in any way diminish my love for you, your father, or Cheryl. I've learned my lesson the hard way. I'll never do anything to threaten our family again."

"What if I hadn't seen you and run away? Would you have had an affair with Miguel, and pretended nothing was going on?"

Linda writhed inwardly from the ʼpiercing questions. This confession was even harder and more painful than she had expected. "I . . . don't believe so. Do you understand why that would have been wrong? Not because I would have been hurting you or your father, since you wouldn't have known. Because I would have been hurting myself. I would have been breaking the promise I made to your father, and I would have thought less of myself for the rest of my life. Fidelity is part of the price I have to pay to deserve my family."

"But how could you want to make love to Miguel, if you still love Dad?"

"That was something else I forgot for a while." Linda's voice became hoarse, and she could no longer hold back her tears. "No man ever has or ever will mean more to me than your father. He's my perfect partner. We've . . . let our lives become routine, but I plan to do something about that as soon as we return home."

Wanda looked frightened by the tears. Then concern came to the fore, and she reached up tentatively to wipe them from Linda's face.

Linda kissed her, feeling cleansed. "Get some sleep now, dear. And don't worry about tomorrow."

"I won't. Uh, Mom?"

"Yes."

"I don't think Dad would understand. About Miguel, I mean. Maybe we shouldn't tell him."

"If you think that is best, dear," Linda agreed solemnly, keeping the smile from her face. "Good night, dear."

"Good night, Mom."

But as Linda drifted toward sleep in the Polks' big bed, there came a faint knocking on the door. "Come in," she mumbled.

Soft footsteps in the darkness approached the bed. "I'm afraid to sleep," Wanda said in a pitiful little voice.

Linda lifted the corner of her sheet and blanket, and Wanda crawled in the way she used to do when she was a child. Linda held her until she fell asleep, then followed her.

CHAPTER FORTY-SIX

Wanda woke up alone in Dede and Jim's bed, and felt herself turn red with embarrassment. The talk with Mom before bed had been bad enough, but reverting to baby-hood and sleeping with her mother was the ultimate shame. She desperately hoped nobody ever found out about either one. But she had slept well; she was ready to get up and get going.

She heard breakfast sounds coming from the kitchen, so she quickly found some clean clothes in her room, dressed, and wandered into the dining room. A glorious golden sunrise lit the sky outside the window wall. Lone Star Five was sailing over patchy clouds, ocean and ice.

Mom was putting two meager-looking ration-pak breakfasts on the table. "Good morning, dear," she said cheerfully. "I was wondering if you were going to get up today."

"I must have been tired," Wanda admitted. For a moment she couldn't meet Mom's eyes. Then Mom came over and hugged her, and Mom was Mom again.

They ate and watched the sunrise, but they didn't talk much. Wanda was thinking about what Mom had told her last night. Mom had always been perfect, knowing everything, taking care of everything. Then, after seeing her with Miguel, she had become an evil monster. Now Wanda realized she wasn't either one. She was human; she could make mistakes. Wanda felt like she had lost something important last night. But at the same time she felt closer to Mom than she ever had.

It was pretty confusing.

Dede and Jim came home while they were doing the dishes. Jim was a walking mud pile, and they both looked dead tired. Wanda wanted to hear everything that had happened to them since she went into hiding, but she figured it wasn't a good time to ask. They cleaned up, Mom fixed them something to eat, and Wanda took care of their dirty clothes and the mud on the carpet. Then they went into their bedroom for a nap.

"I have to check the downlink and go to a meeting," Mom told Wanda when the dishes were done (again). Mom looked as though she was trying not to look worried. "You can get some more sleep, if you like. But be sure to come to the radio room before noon. I . . . want you to be with me. To help."

"Okay." Wanda remembered what Mom had told her about the plan to capture Alpha, so she understood. If something went wrong and Lone Star Five crashed, she wanted to be with Mom too. "Can I look around until then? I want to see what happened when we . . . Hey, we aren't listing anymore!"

Mom laughed, then turned serious again. "Yes, we're back in trim. As for looking around, very well. But be careful, and be sure to keep out of everyone's way. Is that clear?"

"Yes, Mom. I will, I promise."

They left the apartment together. But when they got to the escalator, Mom went down and Wanda went up. Wanda planned to give Lone Star Five a complete inspection, from topside to the blimp bay. She was tempted to go up to the top of the shell, but she figured tying up an access belt would break the second part of her promise.

Her inspection tour took almost all morning. At first she couldn't tell if any progress was being made on the repairs, despite all the busy folks. Things looked even messier than they had last night, especially the ground level where the swamp had spread into the north, east, and west fields. Then she realized that the messiness was just because the work was being done in a hurry. It was being

done, and it was being done right. In fact, all the really
urgent jobs had already been finished. Now the shakedown crew and the *Mayan Princess* crewmen were taking
care of the slightly less urgent jobs. But it would be a long
time before Lone Star Five was as good as new.

The patched breaches near the shell's equator were
being permanently repaired. Pipes were being laid from
some of the irrigation ditch inflows to the lake's exposed
intakes, channeling shell condensation into the tap water
system before it could be fouled by the swamp. Around 10
A.M. Mr. Jarman announced on the com that water rationing was over. The fractional distillation plant was brought
back on line. The giant compressors throbbed mightily,
cooling outside air so the oxygen could be broken out by
its liquefication temperature. Wherever Wanda went, things
were happening.

She wanted to help. But nobody asked her, and her
promise kept her from offering.

As the morning went by, she noticed everybody was
getting nervous. There were com announcements about
Alpha. The repair work slowed down. She heard low-
voiced, tense conversations, and saw folks between jobs
staring out window walls at the empty sky. She found Jim
keeping Dede company while she worked in the computer
room. Wanda told them about her adventure, and they
told her about theirs. When she said she had to go, they
hugged her tight and Dede's eyes were wet.

In the blimp bay a few *Mayan Princess* crewmen were
going in and out of the dock's entryway, probably fixing
the zep. As she was about to start back up the escalator,
she heard a loud, painfully familiar voice behind her. "A
moment of your time, my friend! Please!"

Turning, she saw Miguel coming toward her across the
big floor. He was the last person she ever wanted to talk
to. She tried to get on the escalator, but a powerful arm
grabbed hers.

She spun angrily to face him. "Let me go!" she snapped.

"I have something important to say to you."

"I don't want to hear it! I hate you! Let me go, or I'll
yell for help!"

He let go of her arm, but his burning eyes pinned her to

the spot. "You have ample cause to hate me," he said in a serious voice. "Feel free to do so, if it eases your pain. But such rudeness reflects poorly not only on you but on your family. All I ask is a few minutes of your time, then I'll never trouble you again."

The comment about her manners stung Wanda. In the coolly polite tone Mom used on folks she didn't like, Wanda said, "Okay."

He guided her into the alcove under the escalator ramp. "Personal matters shouldn't become common gossip," he explained.

She just glared at him. He looked as if he had been up all night. His smile was worn down, and his uniform was a mess.

"I imagine you and your mother have discussed what happened between us, no?"

Wanda nodded.

"Good. Now I too owe you an explanation."

"I don't want to hear it." Wanda's stomach was churning. She would have fled, but his eyes still held her.

"Nevertheless you will. I love your mother, and I hoped to make her love me. I failed. But in the process of trying to win her heart, I hurt you grievously. I beg you to believe that it was unintentional. I would never willingly cause you pain."

"You knew Mom was married! You had no right to make love to her!"

Miguel sighed. "Maybe you're right—I won't debate moral points with you. But I would like to ask you one question. Have you ever done something of which you knew other people would disapprove, because love drove you to it?"

Wanda was about to say no hotly. Then she remembered some of the stupid things she had done chasing Jeff, and her two tries at giving herself to Miguel. She kept her mouth shut.

"I hope that when you're older and wiser in the ways of the world you'll judge me less harshly, and maybe even forgive me."

"I'm not a child!" she almost yelled. Her anger was

getting hotter, fed by something deep inside her that she didn't understand. It frightened her.

"Of course you aren't." Miguel's voice turned soothing. "You're a fine, lovely young lady, and you're very dear to me—"

"Stop lying! You pretended you liked me, but all the time you really wanted Mom! You let me think you . . . I . . . !" Her throat sealed in horror at what she had been about to reveal.

Miguel looked puzzled for a moment. Then understanding flickered in his face, followed by more sadness than Wanda had ever seen there before.

"Of course," he said softly. "That must have been the most bitter wound of all. And it's one for which I don't dare ask your forgiveness. Love should always be recognized and cherished, even when it can't be returned. All I can say in my own defense is that I was blinded by your mother's light. How else could I have missed yours, which shines almost as brightly?"

"I don't . . . feel that way about you anymore." Wanda forced the words out through her embarrassment.

"The fault and the loss are both mine. Still, I thank you for the purest of gifts. Regardless of how you think of me, I wish you well, now and always. If I can ever be of service, I'm yours to command." Miguel glanced at his watch. "Now I'll keep my part of our bargain, and leave you in peace. Good day, my lovely lady."

He walked back toward the dock's entryway. Wanda started to say *wide sky*, then reminded herself that she still hated him. But maybe not as much.

She went up to the petrochemical plant level to get her stuff. The com announcements about Alpha were starting to sound tense, and Lone Star Five seemed even emptier than usual with everybody at their emergency stations. She hauled her stuff back to Dede and Jim's empty apartment.

By then it was twenty minutes before noon, so she hurried down to the radio room.

CHAPTER FORTY-SEVEN

The radio room door was locked. But Mom had set the identi-plate to accept her handprint, so Wanda let herself in quietly instead of knocking.

A good thing too. The room was full of busy folks. They just glanced at Wanda and kept working, except Mom who gestured for Wanda to stand behind her. Wanda went over to the downlink, where Mom was sitting at the main station. Mom squeezed her hand and gave her a quick smile before turning back to what she was doing. Curious but feeling very much out of place, Wanda tried to blend into the background.

Besides Mom there were four other folks in the room. A shakedown crew member Wanda didn't recognize was seated at the downlink's auxiliary station—the job she had done last night but apparently wasn't going to get to do today. Teresa from the *Mayan Princess* was busy over by the com system equipment. Mr. Jarman was sitting in front of the monitor console, and Miguel was standing right behind him. Reports and com calls were being made in low, strained voices. The tension was so thick that Wanda could barely breathe.

For the first time she realized that trying to capture

Alpha was going to be pretty dangerous. Even knowing how strong and bad the soldiers were, she had shared Mom's confidence that the laser satellite would protect them. But now Mom looked worried. Wanda wasn't afraid of dying; she had used up all her fear yesterday. But she wanted the danger to finally be over so that nobody else would be hurt, and she and Mom could go home and be normal again.

"Range forty-two miles," Mr. Jarman reported. He was wearing a headset, so he was probably getting his information from the bridge.

"The laser's firing window will open in six minutes," Mom said in her engineer's voice. "It'll remain open for four minutes and fifty-six seconds. The target is locked in."

Jarman turned to Teresa. "Patch me through to the common channel."

She touched some buttons on a control panel, then said, "Go ahead."

Mr. Jarman spoke into his headset mike. "Yo, everybody. Vic Jarman here. I'm about to call Alpha and tell its ramrod the bad news. The radio will be patched into the common channel from here on out, so you all can hear how it's going." He paused. "If you all have any luck tucked in your saddlebags, now would be a mighty good time to unpack it."

He nodded to Teresa. A moment later she said, "You're off the common channel, and our so-called radio is patched in."

Jarman was listening to his headset. "View of Alpha coming in," he announced. Everybody looked at the main monitor screen.

It filled with the pale-blue sky of Arctic noontime. Clouds were gathering in the distance, but the nearby air was clear except for the windrider. Seen from the side and slightly above, it was floating low over the dazzlingly bright icecap. It was a strange-looking windrider. There was more topside and fewer levels than there should have been. The ground level was empty: no farm, no park, no lake, nothing. The shell around the levels was painted sky blue. The nose of a black zep like the one Puff had destroyed stuck out from the dock.

All windriders were beautiful. But the strangeness made it easier for Wanda to believe that Alpha was as bad as everybody said it was.

The view seemed to be from a couple of miles away. She recognized the unnatural clarity; it was a computer image based on input from the long-range camera and radar.

"According to the database, the windrider is a Goodyear AM2B," the crew member at the auxiliary station reported. "A pre-War military model. Must be a mighty tough old bubble, to have lasted this long."

The color of the sky reminded Wanda of Puff. The terrible pain caused by Puff's death had faded, but the aching emptiness would last forever. There was a Puff-sized hole in her life. Every time she wanted to play with Puff, or tell her something, or just hear/feel her nearby, the ache welled up again. Wanda couldn't bear the thought of a future without Puff.

One of the small monitor screens was showing navigational data. Wanda peered at the maps and numbers, and figured out what was going on. Alpha was forty miles southwest of Lone Star Five, floating in still air fourteen thousand feet above the surface. Lone Star Five had been riding a fast east wind at twenty-three thousand feet, but now it was descending on a course that would bring it to a stop fifteen miles north of Alpha. But there was another course plotted: an emergency climb back into the east wind. All the calculations were estimates, of course, since they depended on the often-fickle winds.

"The laser's window will open in four minutes," Mom reported. "All systems are nominal."

Mr. Jarman turned to Teresa. "Are we close enough to contact Alpha with that transmitter you jury-rigged?"

"Maybe, maybe not," she snapped. "The *Mayan Princess*'s rig wouldn't, but your backup com transmitter has more power. Do you wish me to try?"

"I'd be obliged."

Teresa leaned over a com console and went to work. A

few seconds later she nodded. Mr. Jarman cleared his throat, then spoke into his mike. "Lone Star Five calling Alpha. Do you copy? Lone Star Five calling Alpha. . . ."

He was into his third repetition when the wall speaker crackled. "Alpha here, Lone Star Five," a crisp male voice announced. "What are you doing on this frequency sending in clear? Is your regular gear down? It better be, or the Old Man will have your ass for breaking security regs."

"You're a mite behind the times, ranny," Mr. Jarman said coldly. "The *Shenandoah* is crashed. Colonel McCrarey and his gang have all gone to the last roundup. You all are about to join them, unless I get to speak to your ramrod pronto."

The speaker was quiet for about half a minute. Then a deep, heavy voice said, "General Armbruster here. Who the hell am I talking to, and what's this nonsense about crashing Alpha?"

"I'm Vic Jarman, chief engineer of Lone Star Five. Remember the Project Rainmaker laser satellite? Well, it's operational, and it's aimed right at you all."

"You expect me to believe such a fantastic claim? If what you say is true, prove it. Melt a hole in the icecap." General Armbruster didn't sound very worried.

"So your zep can crash us while the laser is powering up?" Mister Jarman snorted. "I reckon not. But if you need convincing, listen in on the satellite's telemetry." He read a bunch of frequency and direction figures from one of the small screens.

The speaker was quiet. Mr. Jarman switched off his mike and turned to Mom. "You're sure they can't use this information to stop us from firing the laser?"

"Absolutely. The sending frequency is different, and the satellite won't accept any signals without the access code."

General Armbruster's voice came from the speaker. "Okay, you managed to activate the satellite. But it's an extremely sophisticated weapon system—can you hit a target?"

Mister Jarman switched his mike back on. "Yep, thanks

to Colonel McCrarey. He had everything set up and all the calculations done to fire it at Alpha. I reckon he was planning some kind of surprise for you all—you know what they say about honor among thieves."

"The laser's window is open," Mom reported.

"Enough fat-chewing," Mister Jarman said sharply. "You know we've got a mighty powerful hogleg aimed right at Alpha, and we're mad enough to pull the trigger. If you all try to launch your zep, we'll crash Alpha on top of it."

"What do you want?" General Armbruster asked. There were some relieved looks around the room, but Wanda still thought General Armbruster didn't sound worried.

"Your surrender. You all have—" Mister Jarman checked the window countdown flashing on a screen—"four minutes and eighteen seconds to scuttle the zep. Then we'll work out the rest of the details"

"And if I refuse to surrender?"

"We'll crash Alpha."

General Armbruster laughed boomingly. "You actually expect me to believe you gutless civvies would do that? I can hear the trembling in your voice."

"After what Colonel McCrarey did here," Mr. Jarman grated, "we reckon it'll be varmint control, not murder. We aren't going to let you all rustle any more windriders."

"Speaking of murder," General Armbruster replied, "did you know that we have almost three hundred women and children in Alpha? About seventy-five of those are women from your towns. Would you like a list of their names, so you can tell their next of kin whom you killed? Maybe you would like to talk to my granddaughter Cindy. She's a cute little tyke, not quite the monster you think I am."

"The window closes in three minutes." Mom's voice broke.

"If you hanker to save their lives," Mr. Jarman said into his mike, "you better give up." But Wanda could hear the uncertainty in his voice. Everybody in the room looked sick. Suddenly Wanda realized that Mr. Jarman's threat had been a bluff. They weren't going to crash Alpha.

"Alpha will never surrender," General Armbruster said firmly. "Crash us if you can. If you can't, be prepared to surrender or die yourselves. Out." The speaker clicked off.

Mister Jarman tapped buttons on his console's com. "Bridge, Jarman here. Get us out of here, pronto."

"On it," a female voice replied from the speaker.

"Not much point in that," Miguel said calmly. He looked worried, but not as much as the others. "As you well know, a windrider can't outclimb a zep."

"The window closes in two minutes," Mom reported. Her face was pale, and she kept staring at her station's keyboard.

"You have a better notion?" Mr. Jarman asked Miguel.

"We could do what we threatened to do. Crash Alpha."

Everybody looked shocked. "You can't mean that," Mom said in a strained voice. "We would be murdering hundreds of innocent folks."

"Then we're left with General Armbruster's two options—surrender or die."

"We said our piece about giving up yesterday," Jarman said flatly.

"I agree. But if someone has to die, I would rather it be the Alphans." Miguel stepped over to the downlink. "If it'll spare your conscience, my dear lady, tell me how to fire the laser."

Mom wouldn't meet his eyes.

"Get away from there!" Mr. Jarman went over, grabbed Miguel, and yanked him back a step. "We aren't going to sink to the Alphan's level!"

Miguel's eyes were burning again. "You prefer that we let ourselves be killed, when we have the right and the means to defend ourselves?"

"The window closes in one minute," Mom reported miserably.

"The situation isn't hopeless!" Mr. Jarman insisted. "These rannies probably hanker for the satellite too. We can say we'll swap it to them, buy time to pick off their zep with the laser or hightail it in the *Mayan Princess*—"

"If you think General Armbruster will let us live long

enough to accomplish any of that," Miguel cut in, "you're a fool. It's kill or be killed. We're running out of time."

Mom's hand hovered over her station's keyboard for a few seconds, shaking. Finally it dropped to her side. She turned to Wanda. The torn look on her face was one Wanda had never seen before and never wanted to see again. "I'm sorry, dear," Mom whispered. "I can't murder innocent women and children. Not even to save you."

"I understand," Wanda said, even though she didn't.

"Nobody has the right to make that kind of decision!" Mr. Jarman yelled at Miguel.

"A leader can't always be so fastidious."

"That sounds like Colonel McCrarey talking!"

Wanda thought Miguel was going to hit Mr. Jarman. Then everybody was yelling at each other. Wanda squeezed her hands over her ears.

CHAPTER FORTY-EIGHT

General Armbruster slammed his fist down on the console in front of him, cutting off the call and venting some of his rage at the same time. Damn that egocentric idiot McCrarey! Apparently his ambition had finally overreached his ability. Using the Project Rainmaker satellite to usurp Alpha's command was a brilliant strategy, one General Armbruster had never imagined. But somewhere along the line Colonel McCrarey had made a mistake. Because of him Alpha had lost the *Shenandoah*, its crew, and the aircav company, and stood within a sword's edge of losing everything else.

General Armbruster hoped that Colonel McCrarey's death had been a long and painful one.

Alpha's bridge was over twice as big as a civvie windrider's and held over twice as many stations, since it had to direct military as well as flight operations. The rows of consoles faced the wall-mounted monitor screens at one end of the circular room. General Armbruster's command station was in the back, on the elevated observation platform which wrapped around the room. Muted lighting accentuated the screens and console displays.

Less than half of the stations were manned. Alpha's role as part of the Northern Early Warning System had ended with the War. The officers on duty were concentrating on their stations, but General Armbruster knew that they had overheard his conversation with the civvie. He sensed an undercurrent of tension in the bridge. General quarters had been sounded as soon as the civvie identified himself; all of Alpha's personnel were at their duty posts. The noncombatants probably thought it was another drill.

General Armbruster wasn't as confident as he had sounded. The civvies in Lone Star Five could wake up from their insipid pacifism at any time. So, much as he would have liked to add the laser satellite to Alpha's armory, he would have to take immediate, direct action.

He got up and walked around the observation platform to the point overlooking weapons station one. "Gunner, after all these years you finally have a hostile target for your Sparrow batteries. Can you take it out?"

"Yes, sir," the weapons officer said enthusiastically. "Battery C's tubes are loaded, and the birds are hot. At this range it'll be like shooting fish in a barrel."

The Sparrow air-to-air missiles were Alpha's defense against attack by civvies or ambitious zep commanders. Colonel McCrarey would have kept Lone Star Five out of range. Fortunately these ignorant civvies had sailed right in.

"Gunner, you may fire at will."

"Yes, sir." The weapons officer spoke softly into his com.

General Armbruster stared at the main monitor screen. The doomed bubble was floating against a pale-blue background. The com officer was certain that it hadn't sent out any radio warnings, and the radar officer was equally certain that no zep or blimp had been launched. When it crashed and sank into the Arctic Ocean, the secret of Alpha's existence would be safe again. Another zep would have to be captured and refitted, and manpower would have to be built up. But Alpha would endure.

"Countdown to launch," the weapons officer said crisply. "Ten . . . nine . . . eight. . . ."

CHAPTER FORTY-NINE

Wanda tried to shut out all the yelling around her so she could think.

She couldn't understand why Mom and Mr. Jarman didn't want to use the laser satellite to crash Alpha. The soldiers were bad, worse than she had ever thought folks could be. They didn't belong in a properly run world. As long as they existed, nobody would ever be safe.

They were like weeds. (Despite all the precautions, weeds had gone aloft with windriders.) She had done plenty of weeding back home, and she hated it because it was hard, dirty work. But it had to be done. If you didn't get rid of the bad plants, they would spread and kill off all the good plants. So the weeds had to go.

Wanda figured the townsfolk trapped in Alpha would agree with that. She would, if she were one of them. As for the soldier women and children, a weed was a weed. You had to get them all, otherwise they came back.

The last few seconds of the laser's window were counting down. The yelling got louder, but Wanda could tell from the look on Mom's face that she wasn't about to change her mind.

The adults were ignoring Wanda, of course. But for once that was okay. She had watched Mom carefully during the practice runs last night, so she knew what to do.

She moved beside Mom like she did when she needed a hug. Mom absently put an arm around her.

Her hand dove for Mom's keyboard like Puff in flight. It typed six letters and entered them.

The word COMMIT glowed brightly in the middle of the station's screen.

"No!" Mr. Jarman yelled, and yanked Wanda roughly away from the downlink. Mom frantically tried to cancel the instruction, but it was too late. Teresa and the crew member at the auxiliary station were staring at Wanda with horrified expressions on their faces. Even Miguel looked shocked.

Then all eyes turned to the main monitor screen.

Wanda didn't see the laser pulse, since it was invisible. But the air above Alpha shimmered, like it did topside in the heat of the day, only more. In an instant the top of the shell went from clear to brown to black.

Then it disappeared.

Wanda couldn't tell if it had melted, blown out, or just disintegrated. One moment it was there; the next it wasn't. There was a collective groan from the adults. Wanda kept staring silently at the screen. She couldn't believe, didn't want to believe, what she was seeing.

Alpha was falling out of the sky. With all its lift gone, it fell like a rock. The camera and radar were tracking it, so it stayed in the middle of the screen. The zep broke in half. The halves fell up, burning brightly and trailing white smoke. Lots of small things were flying out of the top of Alpha. The sides of the shell were crumpling inward, and the levels were twisting.

Then Alpha hit the icecap. The impact was ike an explosion, spraying ice, water and bits of windrider into the sky. When the clouds cleared, there was a big hole in the ice with wreckage scattered around it.

Alpha was gone forever.

There was a nightmare Wanda used to have when she was a child. She had done something really bad, and no matter how hard she tried she couldn't fix it. That was how she felt now.

"I'm sorry," she whimpered. It was all she could think of to say.

Mom lurched out of her chair and gathered Wanda in her arms. "It's all right, dear. It's all right." But Mom was crying as she spoke.

Mister Jarman shook his head like a dog shaking off water. "I reckon it had to be done," he said weakly. "I'm mighty glad Lone Star Five is still aloft and Alpha isn't, and not the other way around. I ought to have had the gumption to do it myself."

"Fortunately for all of us, Wanda did," Mom said. The fierce pride in her voice did a lot to heal Wanda's hurt.

Mr. Jarman turned to Wanda. "Young'un . . . excuse me, Miz Grigg, I apologize for my ornery words and actions. You have the gratitude of every mother's son and daughter in Lone Star Five. I'd count it an honor if you'd shake my hand."

Wanda did, feeling confused. Miguel caught her eye and winked.

Suddenly an excited voice came from the speaker. "Vic, Sara Jane here! I've got multiple blips on radar, heading our way fast!"

"A parting gift from Alpha," Miguel suggested grimly. The mood of doom that had just lifted came crashing down again. Wanda hugged Mom tighter.

Jarman ran back to the monitor console and slapped com buttons. "Jarman here. Do those blips track like missiles?"

The com voice laughed. "Not unless the Almighty launched them. They're diving out of the sun. Hold on . . . There are six of them, roughly soccer-ball size, flying in a tight formation."

The tension in the room broke. The adults looked puzzled and curious, but Wanda had a pretty good idea what they were. She called/reached out.

"Gray is checking for Em emissions," the com voice went on. "Yep, just like I reckoned—fireballs. The aerial tumbleweeds are playing near the top of the shell. Slim is trying to get a camera on them."

Wanda heard/felt them: a chorus of faint but clear voices/presences so much alike that she had trouble telling them apart. And achingly familiar. Almost like . . . Could it be?

She listened/reached out as hard as she could, with all the love in her.

Mr. Jarman's hands were moving over the monitor console. A new patch of sky filled the main screen, with the filtered sun in the background. The six balls of light in the foreground weren't filtered at all. Scarlet, emerald, orange, turquoise, gold and ghostly white: they blazed brightly as they did a juggling act without the juggler. Up and in, down and out, around and back again. Their maneuvers were so perfectly coordinated that they seemed like parts of a whole. Everybody was watching them, enjoying the show even as they were amazed by it. "That's the damnedest thing I've ever seen," Mr. Jarman breathed.

Wanda recognized the pattern, and knew for sure. All the darkness in her mind went away. A joy as bright and pure as fireball light shined through her. Slipping out of Mom's arms, she jumped up and down and clapped her hands. "They're Puff's babies!" she yelled.

That got her an audience. Apparently the story of how Puff had crashed the soldiers' zep had spread. "They're Puff's babies!" she repeated. "They know me! They came here to play with me!"

Mr. Jarman had a silly expression on his face as he turned to Mom. "Is that possible? I've never heard tell of fireballs reproducing."

"We know so little about them," Mom answered. She was looking at Wanda, her eyes shining. "But Wanda knows more than anyone else."

Wanda ignored the growing babble of life-form-versus-atmospheric-phenomenon arguments. Staring at the screen, she called/reached out to her new pets. She had so much to tell them.

CHAPTER FIFTY

At the end of each scavenging season, before the towns followed the good weather to the other hemisphere, Fairs were held.

Every town which chose to, sent a windrider to represent it. For three days blimps acted like pre-War tugboats, maneuvering the windriders together. Work crews hung bumpers at contact points, shot lines across, winched gaps closed, strung webs of bracing wires, and set up transit tubes between topside air locks. When they were finished, the windriders were joined equator to equator in a great disk. The Fair would run for a week, then the windriders would take three more days to disengage, and rejoin their towns.

Fairs were important events. The towns traded goods, services and information. The Moot resolved disputes. Swaps were arranged for townsfolk who wished to move. Gene pools were enriched formally and informally. Zeps came like bees to clover, deboarding enclave traders and tourists. For Fairs were also the grandest of celebrations, all the world's entertainments brought together in one place.

In mid-April, five months after the crashing of Alpha, seventy-three windriders gathered in calm air over the South Atlantic for the Southern Cross Free Fair.

*   *   *

Wanda stepped off the park escalator into the first night of the Fair.

The Fair had worked its magic on Calgary Two's park, turning it into a fantasy. The lawn was covered with rows of "log and hide" booths. (Calgary's theme this year was Yukon Trading Post.) Beef, leather goods, and other Calgary products were on sale, as well as traditional food and drink. Other booths held games, displays, performances, and demonstrations. The Stampede's rodeo events were starting up in the Quad, and you could take a romantic canoe ride on the lake. Hundreds of folks were enjoying Calgary's part of the Fair, while musicians and singers wandered through the crowds. The maple and spruce trees were aglow with tiny white lights. The air was filled with wonderful sounds and smells.

Most of the folks were wearing period costumes that represented their town or enclave's heritage, a wide and wild variety of styles. For Calgary that could mean anything from pre-War Canadian to early English. Wanda had wanted to make (with a lot of help from Mom) a copy of Queen Victoria's coronation regalia. But Mom had pointed out that in a crowd of fancily dressed folks, simplicity would stand out. Her Fair dress was in the Empire style: white neosilk with just a bit of gold trim, ankle length, with puff sleeves and a Belgian lace collar. She had borrowed Mom's locket (again) because it went perfectly with the dress, and Mom had braided her hair. Strolling along a grassy lane between rows of booths, waving and talking to folks she knew, it didn't take her long to realize that Mom had been right about simplicity.

Wanda was glad to see a lot of folks in Cousin Duncan's booth. She had agreed to help him during the days, and the more leather belts she sold, the more money she would have to spend. But her nights were free. Especially tonight. Mom was off at the Moot, Dad was at work, and Cheryl was with Aunt Margot. Wanda intended to see every cubic inch of the Fair before it ended, but tonight she had a special destination. Lone Star Five had come to the Fair, and Dede and Jim had invited her to a hoedown. She was really looking forward to seeing them and Lone Star Five again.

She worked her way toward the edge of the park away from the lake. Thinking about Lone Star Five reminded her of how things had changed since her adventure. Alpha had been a big deal for a few weeks after she had gotten home; she had been interviewed by the newsnets, and had taken a lot of kidding from her friends. Then everything had returned to almost normal. But like an old dress she had outgrown, her old life didn't fit quite right anymore. Sometimes she saw things in ways her friends didn't. Mom had explained that it was part of growing up, and that the only cure was time.

Wanda joined the group of folks waiting on the walkway where it left the park and went into the farm. The pole lamps in the fields were off; the farm had been darkened to make the park look brighter. The farm buildings, orchard, and fields were shadowy shapes. The Fair's noises and aromas mingled with the night-sounds of the stock and the smell of fertilizer. Beyond the shell she saw the awesome and unnerving panorama of the other windriders surrounding Calgary Two, ghost-reflections dimmed by their greenhouse tints, their faint lights tempting her with exotic excitement. A crescent moon and hundreds of stars stood out from the black night.

The last Fair Wanda had attended had been the Octoberfest a year and a half ago, when she had been too young to really appreciate it. Now she was ready to take advantage of what was a very unexpected windfall. By rights she should have been back home in Calgary Three, since it was Two's turn to go to the Fair. But Mom had been picked to represent Calgary at the Moot, and she had refused to leave her family. So here they all were, living in a vacant apartment.

A gaily decorated New Paris cargo cart arrived. The benches in the back were crowded with happy, noisy folks, some of whom got off and disappeared into Calgary's part of the Fair. Wanda got on with the rest of the folks waiting at the stop and found a seat. The driver welcomed the newcomers and announced the route. Then the cart rumbled toward the north air lock.

Both air lock hatches were open, a sight that normally would have terrified her. But the clear plastic transit tube between the air lock and Jerusalem One's air lock was an extension of the windriders' friendly environment. Over five hundred feet long, it was supported by wires running up to clamps on both shells. The textured white roadway was just wide enough for the cart. She looked down through the tube's wall, but the surface was hidden in the darkness.

Calgary Two was near the middle of the disk, while Lone Star Five, a late arrival, was near the rim. So the cart visited many other windriders first. At each stop the tempting sights, sounds, and smells almost made Wanda jump off the cart and run to them. An Arabian bazaar, the Tivoli amusement park, Masai tribal music, Viennese pastries, the Cairo museum, Osaka ultra-tech, Bogota's emerald market, an Aussieland stock auction, a rug-weaving demonstration in Shanghai, Moscow's New Bolshoi Ballet: it was as if a treasure chest had broken open, spilling its glittering contents at her feet.

During the dull times between stops Wanda kept thinking about the changes in her life. Another one was Mom and Dad. They had had some long private talks right after Alpha, and had gone to some counseling sessions with Dr. Robinson, Calgary's psychiatrist. Since then they had definitely been acting strangely. They talked more, argued more and laughed more. They went out a lot on . . . well, dates. Wanda also suspected, despite their efforts at discretion, that they were making love more often and . . . differently. She wasn't sure she approved. It just wasn't right for parents to be acting like teenagers. But they seemed pretty happy, so she decided not to worry about it.

The windrider from the oldest town at the Fair traditionally hosted the Moot; this time New Hong Kong One was at the center of the disk. Its town hall had been styled to resemble the British Parliament's House of Lords for the occasion. Linda and seventy-two other town reps were seated along the lower tiers, at tables with coms linking each to his or her own windrider. The upper tiers held enclave reps, newsnet casters and other guests. In contrast to the rest of the Fair, the town reps and guests were wearing regular business clothes. Linda's skirt/blouse/bow outfit was the same one which she had worn to the meeting in Mayor Keith's office several lifetimes ago.

A slight, elderly man crossed the well to the podium, and moments later the amplified cracks of his mace cut off the pre-session babble of voices in the hall.

"Welcome to the sixty-second annual Southern Cross Free Fair Moot." His voice sounded like sticks breaking. "I am Phillip Fong, representing New Hong Kong."

One by one the other town reps introduced themselves. When Linda's turn came, she said in her best businesslike manner, "I'm Linda Calhoun, representing Calgary." Dozens of heads turned her way; her role in the Alpha affair was widely known. Cameras turned too. The vid newsnets were replaying the session live around the world: unusually thorough coverage for an unusual Moot.

The sense of anticipation in the hall grew during the opening formalities. Everyone knew that the Project Rainmaker satellite would be the first order of business; the debate over what to do with it had been raging in towns and enclaves for the past five months.

Finally Mr. Fong said, "Now we turn to the new business of the Moot. Several towns have requested to speak, but I suspect we'll pay more attention to other matters if we settle the major piece of business first. But before I call upon Mayor Tyler of Lone Star to speak, I wish to remind all of us of some history.

"The migratory nature of our existence, and our desire to live as we choose, has always kept us from forming larger associations than towns. The few disputes between towns which reasonable folks are unable to resolve themselves are brought before the Moot. But we are purely an advisory body. We have no army or proctors to enforce our recommendations. Generally they are followed, because it is bad for a town's reputation and dealings with other towns to set itself against the common will. At times this has proven to be a less-than-perfect system. But I think we will all agree that it has worked well enough.

"Now Mayor Tyler of Lone Star will address the Moot."

The Lone Star rep walked to the podium. In his old-fashioned vested suit and Stetson he looked like the town banker from a Western vid. His hair was silver, and leathery skin was stretched over his rawboned physique, but his stride was that of a young man.

"Howdy, you all," he drawled expansively. "I'm J. T. Tyler, the mayor of Lone Star. I reckon you all know why I'm up here, but I'll spell it out for the record. The Project Rainmaker satellite is still in orbit, still capable of crashing anything in the sky. The only trigger for this hogleg is the downlink in Lone Star Five's radio room. Seems this makes Lone Star the top dog in the pack."

He paused as an uneasy rumble of voices grew in the hall. Linda felt a chill along her spine. She had been afraid, but not of this.

Then Mayor Tyler laughed, breaking the tense mood. "Don't fret, folks. Ruling the world would be too much like work—it'd take all the fun out of life. I just aimed to show how nervous our having the downlink makes you all feel. Can't say I blame you all—I'd be nervous in your boots too.

"Frankly, we want to get rid of the downlink, before we become as welcome as a polecat at a picnic. But what do we do with it? If we toss it out an air lock, how many of you all will wonder if we have another one hid somewhere? We could give you all copies of the satellite manual, so you all could build your own downlinks, but how easy would any of us sleep then?

"I've got two notions to put on the table. One—the satellite can be made to self-destruct by shorting out its capacitors. It's all powered up, just in case. Two—the Moot can set up some kind of peacekeeping organization, and we'll turn the downlink over to it. Then the satellite can be used to deal with any future Alphas. We'll abide by the will of the Moot either way."

Silence held the hall for several seconds. Then a loud babble of voices erupted, and hands slapped com buttons to call for the floor. Rep after rep walked to the podium to have his or her say. The debate went on for almost two hours, and at times turned into angry shouting matches. No clear consensus emerged. Some towns wanted to eliminate the problem by eliminating the satellite. Others, frightened by what Alpha had been able to do, yearned for protection from any other potential aggressors.

Linda had hoped that she wouldn't have to speak. But the growing acrimony in the hall confirmed her fears. She would have to convince them, just as she had convinced Calgary.

She called for the floor, and Mr. Fong summoned her to speak. She felt the real and artificial eyes following her as she made the long walk to the podium. Looking out at the tiers of town reps and guests, she saw not individuals, but a single enormous creature warped into monstrousness by her stage fright.

"Like all of you," she began, "I thought the War had ended a long time ago." Her voice was stretched taut. "Alpha proved that wasn't so. Now I see the War being fought in this hall, and it frightens me."

Pausing, she felt curiosity, irritation, and nervousness in the attention focused on her.

"For over six decades we haven't wasted any of our limited resources on arms or armies. We've been too busy fighting a hostile environment to fight each other. Now some of you think we need better protection than that. You want to create an organization with folks from every town, to use the Project Rainmaker satellite to prevent aggression.

"But when one person can in less than a second crash anything in the sky, who is going to guard the guardians? You're already arguing about where to keep the downlink, who gets to know the access code, how to decide whether to use the satellite, and so on. If we take this course, won't towns which feel threatened build their own weapons for self-defense? Won't towns with fewer weapons than others build more? Won't towns use their weapons instead of Moots to settle disputes?

"If we revive that cycle of distrust, self-defense, and escalation, we'll finish what the War began: the destruction of the human race.

"We don't need the satellite. It would be naive to hope that we've permanently eliminated war and aggression. But Lone Star Five showed that, as much as we hate violence, we'll fight when we must to defend our homes and loved ones. We'll fight with all the skill and determination which have enabled us to win our fight for survival. The Alphans didn't understand this, and died for it."

Linda paused again. Now the audience-creature was attuned to her, amplifying her own fears and reflecting them back at her. She began to hope.

"You might not believe that we would act the way I've suggested we would if we keep the satellite. If not, reread your pre-War history. I don't have to. I've seen folks who allowed themselves to become less than human. I've seen the face of the enemy. Alpha is a mirror, if we take this course. As a mother, as a human being, I beg you to join me in rejecting it. Thank you."

Before she could leave the podium, town reps and guests were jumping to their feet and applauding. Soon almost everyone in the hall was standing. Mayor Tyler's voice boomed over the commotion. "I call for a vote! I call for a vote!"

The emotional impact staggered Linda for a few moments. Pulling herself together, she walked back to her chair. The applause died down, and Mr. Fong put Lone Star's proposals to a vote.

The vote was fifty-nine to fourteen in favor of destroying the Project Rainmaker satellite.

Mayor Tyler held a quick com conversation, then returned to the podium. "I've been talking to the chief engineer in Lone Star Five. The satellite will be in com range in fifty-eight minutes. I told him to blow it up. Those of you all with an untrusting nature might hanker to watch the sky around altitude eighty degrees, azimuth two hundred and ten degrees."

Mr. Fong brought the session to a close. Linda used her com to report the Moot's decision to Deputy Mayor Oldsmith in Calgary Two; most of the town reps were reporting to their windriders. Then everyone filed into a big room next to the hall, where a lavish buffet and an auto-bar had been set up. The post-session receptions were social events as well as opportunities for town reps and guests to conduct business informally. As soon as Linda could extricate herself from a congratulatory crowd and several newsnet interviewers, she took a glass of white wine and a plate of dim sum to a quiet corner. She felt happy and incredibly relieved, but her batteries were in serious need of recharging.

She was wolfing down the snack when Jack found her. "I got here in time to catch your speech on the outside monitor," he said after he kissed her. He had apparently stopped by their temporary apartment after his shift and put on his gray suit in deference to the occasion. "You really made them understand. Congratulations."

"I'm glad it's over," she replied softly. "All over."

Jack had a teasing light in his eye. "Are you sure you haven't developed a taste for public life? Elections are coming up—how would you like to be mayor?"

"No, thank you! I'm more than ready to slide back into obscurity. I have other interests to pursue. Mutual interests, you might say."

"Like the way you practiced your speech on me in bed last night? I'm glad you were more, um, dignified in the Moot."

They both laughed. There was an awkwardness to their new relationship, as they rediscovered each other. But there were also unexpected delights. She unobtrusively ran a hand over his chest.

"Howdy, Miz Calhoun!" Mayor Tyler popped out of the noisy crowd in front of them. "I've heard plenty about you, and after that speech I just had to look you up."

"I'm pleased to meet you," she replied. "This is my husband, Jack Grigg. Jack, this is Mayor Tyler of Lone Star."

After a round of handshakes Mayor Tyler said, "This hoedown is mighty tame by Lone Star standards. I'm about to mosey back to Five—we're putting on a real foot-stomper tonight. I'd be honored if you all would join me."

"Isn't that the dance Wanda went to?" Jack asked Linda.

She nodded. "I'm pretty tired, but a short visit would be fun. Jack?"

"Sounds good to me. I'd like to see the site of your and Wanda's adventure."

"You all are in for a treat!" Mayor Tyler enthused, and led the way to the door.

* * *

The cart was rumbling through Lone Star Five's farm. Wanda peered into the darkness, amazed. Instead of the swamp, mud banks, and collapsed coldhouses she remembered, she saw a real farm. Some of the fields were fallow, but most held crops in various stages of growth. Water flowed smoothly in the ditches. The rest of Lone Star must have replaced the lost dirt, orchard trees, and so on. She heard the stock in their pens, and smelled the green smell.

The cart stopped on the edge of the park, and Wanda was the first rider to jump down. Dede and Jim were waiting for her. "Howdy there, honey!" Dede yelled as Wanda ran to them. Jim threw his hat high in the air, caught it, and let out a loud, "YAHOO!"

Wanda hugged them as if it had been a lot longer than five months since she had seen them. Then she curtsied and said proper adult hellos. They had picked the American Civil War Period for their costumes. Dede was a Southern belle in her pink hoop-skirted dress with a matching parasol, while Jim was wearing the gray uniform of a Confederate Army officer. They both looked grand.

Wanda stared at Dede's tummy, and her suspicion became a certainty. "You're pregnant!"

Dede pretended to blush behind her parasol, then grinned from ear to ear. "Why, I do believe I am," she admitted in a theatrical drawl. "We're in a neck-and-neck race with the Austins and the Catlows to have Lone Star Five's first baby."

"That's ultra! How far along are you?" Wanda asked eagerly. She wished she was old and married, so she could have a baby.

"Seventeen weeks. If it's a girl, we're going to give her the handle Wanda, and hope she turns out as fine as her namesake."

That made Wanda feel so warm and wonderful that she didn't dare say anything except, "Thanks."

"And if it's a boy," Jim said, "we're going to name him Panhandle Pete after my great-grandfather's horse—"

Dede hit him (gently) with her parasol.

"Lone Star Five looks ultra!" Wanda enthused. "You

folks must have been busy as beavers, ever since Mom and I left."

"We had help from the rest of Lone Star," Dede admitted. "But we worked our tails off too. Lone Star Five is fully on line now, with four hundred and eighty-two folks spreading their bedrolls in her. We'll show you around before the Fair closes, if you like."

"Please! I want to see everything." Then Wanda remembered to ask something she had been wondering about. "How did Lone Star Five get to come to the Fair? Aren't new windriders supposed to start at the end of the line?"

"This is what you might call a special case," Jim replied. "We've got the downlink everybody is fussing over. it could have been moved, of course, but we had a mighty important reason to be here."

"What?"

He laughed. "You'll find out soon enough. So we told Mayor Tyler that if we weren't sent we'd turn outlaw for a few weeks and come anyway. Good thing he didn't call our bluff, because we weren't." A serious tone had crept into his voice. Wanda was totally mystified.

"Let's take a turn around the park on the way to the hoedown," Dede suggested. "There's a lot to see, and we have some catching up to do."

So they set out through Lone Star's part of the Fair. Wanda saw that the park was as on line as the farm. The lawn sparkled with primrose, bluebonnet and Indian paintbrush; the young pecan trees and rose bushes must have been transplanted from the rest of the Lone Star. The lake was full again.

The Fair theme here was the Wild West. "Clapboard," "shingles," and "corral fencing" made the park buildings and booths look like a frontier town. Lone Star's business didn't include retail sales, but there were cowboy clothes, silver belt buckles, lariats, artwork, and souvenirs made by Lone Star craftsmen, plus mechanical bronc riding, a saloon, a wildlife exhibit, and much more. The wandering musicians were playing guitars, harmonicas, and fiddles. A side of beef was being barbequed at the fireplace. Jim bought a plateful for Wanda; it was hot in both senses, but delicious.

Dede and Jim told Wanda about all the hard work that had gone into making Lone Star Five a real home, and their own preparations for the new member of their family. Wanda told them everything that had happened to her since going home. They were particularly glad to hear that she and Mom and Dad were getting along so well.

Wanda noticed a waist-high pillar of white marble standing in the middle of the lawn; it looked un-western and out of place. A lot of folks were stopping to look at it. Dede and Jim were leading her that way.

"It's a gift from Pemex Under," Jim explained while they waited to get a look, "a permanent part of the park. We made one like it but carved from a pecan trunk and gave it to them."

Wanda finally got to step up to it. There was a silver plaque on the slanted top. It read: "In honored memory of those who fell in the Battle of Lone Star Five. They paid the ultimate price for freedom." Below that sixteen names were listed in alphabetical order.

The eleventh name was Puff.

Dede guided her away from the pillar and loaned her a handkerchief to wipe her eyes. "That was really nice," she sniffled. She remembered Puff soaring beautifully across the sky, and had to wipe her eyes again.

"We wouldn't have it any other way," Jim said firmly. "I'm sorry I never got to meet her."

"How are her young'uns doing?" Dede asked.

Thinking about them cheered Wanda up. "They're ultra! They're so cute—you wouldn't believe the things they do. We're getting to understand each other really well. Teacher Ware is going crazy studying them. I wish I could show them to you, but they aren't around right now. They have to spend a lot of time in the ionosphere eating sunshine, so they can grow as big as Puff."

They came finally to Lone Star Five's version of the Quad. It had been decorated to look like an old-fashioned barn. There were tables piled high with refreshments, "hay bales" for sitting, and big red-and-blue flags with white stars in the middle hanging from the "plank" walls. "Alcohol lamps" spread a warm yellow light. A western band was playing on a low loft at the far end of the "pounded dirt" floor. A few hundred folks were eating, drinking, talking, and listening to the music, but nobody was dancing. Almost all of the folks were from Lone Star Five, judging by their cowboy and other Texas period costumes.

But what caught Wanda's eye and made her laugh was the centerpiece tethered over the floor. It was a balloon ten feet across, probably filled with helium, painted like a windrider. It was listing to one side.

"Reckoned you'd like that," Jim said to her. "Lone Star Five has got plenty to be proud of, and we don't mind saying so."

"Poor Vic Jarman," Dede added. "He's a mighty fine chief engineer, but he'll always be the ramrod who stood a windrider on its ear. No wonder he's hiding out in the bridge."

They wandered through the crowd. Wanda got to talk to Doc Starnes, Wes Barnes, and some of her other Lone Star Five friends. A lot of strangers seemed to know her; at least they said hello as she went by. She snacked on food from the farm she had helped start. She was having a really good time, but she got the feeling everybody was waiting for something. She wondered what.

Captain Miguel Ramirez scanned the shifting population of the dance floor with the same keen eye that guided the *Mayan Princess* to gentle landings and dockings. This was a delicate maneuver too, in a different sense, and he intended to bring it off just as deftly. The Lone Star Five fiesta was rather sedate by Fair standards, and certainly by his. As soon as his errand was completed, he intended to take his lady to Rio de Janeiro Four, where any Fair meant Carnival.

"You look thoughtful, great hawk of the sky." Elena was nestled cozily in his encircling arm. In their dress uniforms they more than held their own with the costumed people around them. She looked up at him, her dark eyes merry and tender. "Aren't you having a good time?"

"Merely a lull in a veritable storm of joy," he assured her. Fairs were a cornucopia of delights, as much his natural element as the sky. Having covered himself with glory in the Alpha affair, he had been able to snatch the plum assignment of bringing the Pemex Under traders and tourists here from his envious fellow captains. He was a hero to his crew, all of whom were enjoying the Fair while the *Mayan Princess* was slaved to Mexico City Four's dock. He had a lovely lady on his arm. One more thing, and all would be right with his world.

"Are you having second thoughts about accepting the promotion?" Elena asked him.

He shook his head. After Señor Uribe's scandal-shrouded suicide, he had found himself at the top of the list of possible successors as head of the Zep Service. Being a hero had its advantages. "I'm a zep captain. I have no interest in piloting a desk through the rough air of corporate politics."

"If a certain aging hawk would accept the promotion he richly deserves, an equally deserving subordinate could also move up."

"I see your ploy now, my pretty pilot. Having failed to seduce me out of my command, you hope to promote me out of it. But you won't succeed."

Elena snuggled more closely against him. "I suppose I'll have to go back to my first plan."

"It's worth a try."

Suddenly Miguel spotted Wanda in the crowd. She was talking to a Lone Star Five couple whom he recalled vaguely. He continued forward, until he could see her face while keeping a concealed screen of people between them. Then he stopped.

"Is something wrong?" Elena asked. Her eyes followed his. "Isn't that Wanda Grigg over there?"

"Indeed."

"Let's go over and say hello."

Miguel sighed. "You may, if you wish. But I think it's best that I don't. This night above all should be free of troubling memories for her."

There were certain things a gentleman never discussed, but Elena had seen and heard enough during the Alpha affair to draw her own conclusions. "I understand. If I didn't know you better, Captain, I would suspect that you

were finally growing up. But if you want to avoid her, why
are we here?"

Miguel hardly heard Elena; his attention was focused on
Wanda. He had been invited to this fiesta by Señor Jarman,
and he had come to see if the harm he had done Wanda
was healed. What he read in her face lifted the shadow
from his heart. Children were amazingly resilient. "I wished
to see if all is well with her. Since it is, we can be on our
way." He turned and guided Elena toward the exit.

"You can tell that from fifteen feet away?" she asked.

"Of course. It's a skill one who hopes to become a zep
captain should acquire."

"I bet it only works on ladies."

Miguel laughed. Responsibility was a stern taskmaster,
but for now the sky in front of him was clear. A zepman
asked nothing more.

Mayor Tyler led Linda and Jack into the milling crowd
on the dance floor. Linda had been admiring how well
Lone Star Five had turned out; now she was inundated in
enthusiastic greetings. She remembered some of the townsfolk, particularly women with whom she had been impris-
oned in the town hall. But most of them were new 'steaders.
She managed a steady stream of conversations, while Mayor
Tyler spread the word about the satellite. Jack preferred
to enjoy the show from the background.

Somewhere along the line Mayor Tyler disappeared,
but Linda was too busy to wonder about it. Finally the
cluster around her dwindled away, leaving her and Jack
relatively free. They wandered around the "barn," enjoying the music and looking for Wanda.

"There she is," Jack pointed. "Shall we join her?"

Linda saw that Wanda was talking to the Polks. If she
had been with other teenagers, a parental intrusion would
have embarrassed her. But she was "being adult," so it
should be okay. "Let's."

The Polks welcomed them warmly. Wanda seemed surprised to see them, but she wasn't put out. Linda introduced Jack. He and Jim were soon "discussing" the chances
of the Calgary and Lone Star soccer teams in the World
Cup competition. Linda congratulated Dede on her preg-

nancy, and invited her over to meet Cheryl. Linda would always be grateful for what the Polks had done for Wanda. They were good folks.

Suddenly the band stopped playing. The lamps dimmed. A spotlight followed Mayor Tyler as he walked to the front of the loft. Everybody turned to look; the conversational rumble faded.

"Howdy, you all!" he yelled, and his amplified voice filled the "barn." He waved his hat in the air. "For those of you all who don't know me, I'm J. T. Tyler, the mayor of Lone Star. I hope you all are having as fine a time as I am."

When the cheering and applause died down, he continued. "Now we Lone Star folks don't need much cause to kick up our heels. But tonight we have a mighty special reason to celebrate. Everybody is here, the band is hot, the beer is cold, so let's get to it."

There was more cheering. "The Battle of Lone Star Five will be remembered as long as Lone Star is aloft. We've celebrated our victory and mourned our dead. But the folks who did the most to win the fight got left out of the celebrating, so we're here tonight to show them how we feel about them.

"If it weren't for them, Lone Star Five would be at the bottom of the ocean along with a lot of good men and women. Their courage, wisdom, and love saved the day. In them the best of our new world whipped the worst of the old. So let's shake the shell for a pair of great ladies— and as of tonight honorary citizens of Lone Star—Miz Linda Calhoun and Miz Wanda Grigg!"

This time the yelling, clapping, and boot-stomping were so loud that Linda thought her eardrums would burst. Hats were flying in the air. She could feel her face growing red, as she struggled to keep her self-control. Wanda's mouth was wide open; her eyes were shining with excitement and joy. Their hands found each other. Jack, standing behind them and smiling proudly, wrapped an arm around each of them.

A spotlight found the three of them. The Polks and everyone else were backing away, leaving them alone in the middle of the floor.

"There's plenty more I could tell you all about these ladies," Mayor Tyler went on, when the noise level subsided enough for him to be heard. "But you all will like hearing it better from Rowdy and the Wranglers."

He left the loft, and the spotlights on the band came back up. The lead guitarist, resplendent in his rhinestone-studded white leather outfit, said, "Howdy, folks. We're going to do a song I wrote especially for tonight. Hope you all like it. It's called 'The Ballad of Lone Star Five.'"

The band began playing soft, sweet music evocative of the wind blowing across a wide open prairie or the endless sky. The lead guitarist sang to the silent, intensely attentive audience, while the rest of the band provided harmony.

The verses unfolded, deftly turning the terrible ordeal into an adventure and elevating Linda and Wanda to the stature of folk heroines. Linda looked at Wanda, who was listening too blissfully to notice, and her embarrassment was swept away. She smiled. Out of danger and doubt they had come to this perfect moment, shared with Jack and so many others who cared about them. She would treasure the memory forever.

When the last note of the ballad faded into silence, she joined enthusiastically in the applause.

The band began playing again, and a slow-dance version of "The Yellow Rose of Texas" filled the sweet night air. Jack turned to Linda. In his eyes she saw the deep, enduring love which could come only from a shared lifetime. "May I have this dance?" he asked tenderly.

"And every other." Linda stepped into his waiting arms. Their shapes and weights merging with familiar ease, they moved to the music as one.

Her long journey had brought her home.

Wanda's eyes were misty as she watched Mom and Dad dance away. Dede and Jim and other couples were joining them on the floor. Wanda sighed. Everything about tonight was ultra-wonderful, but she couldn't help wishing she had somebody who loved her the way Dad loved Mom. Or just somebody to dance with. Jeff was back home, probably with Adrienne, and she hadn't known any boy in Two well enough to invite.

Mom caught her eye, winked, and pointed behind her. She turned around.

About twenty boys her age were gathering near the wall. Every single one of them was fantastically gorgeous. They looked adult in their Fair costumes, but they were as frisky as colts. Arguing and shoving each other, they sorted themselves into a ragged line.

The boy at the front of the line—the tallest, most gorgeous one of all—came over to Wanda. He bowed and swept his cowboy hat in front of him. "Howdy, ma'am. I'm Tom Hansen. I'd be much obliged if you'd honor me with this dance."

She curtsied, and said in her best adult manner, "I'd be delighted."

She could feel her heart melting as he took her in his arms and led her away from the line of impatiently waiting boys. What was beyond ultra-wonderful? Whatever it was, she wished it could go on forever.

She noticed that Mom, Dad, and some other folks were looking up at the sky, so she glanced up too. The starry blackness beyond the top of the shell was as beautiful as ever. Suddenly a new star appeared almost overhead. It shined brightly for a few seconds, then faded and went out. She figured it was a meteor.

She quickly made her wish again. Maybe it would come true.

THE MANY WORLDS OF
MELISSA SCOTT

*Winner of the John W. Campbell Award
for Best New Writer, 1986*

THE KINDLY ONES: "An ambitious novel of the world
Orestes. This large, inhabited moon is governed by five
Kinships whose society operates on a code of honor so
strict that transgressors are declared legally 'dead' and
are prevented from having any contact with the 'living.'
. . . Scott is a writer to watch."—*Publishers Weekly*. A
Main Selection of the Science Fiction Book Club.
65351-2 • 384 pp. • $2.95

The "Silence Leigh" Trilogy
FIVE-TWELFTHS OF HEAVEN (Book I): "Melissa Scott
postulates a universe where technology interferes with
magic. . . . The whole plot is one of space ships, space
wars, and alien planets—not a unicorn or a dragon to
be seen anywhere. Scott's space drive and description
of space piloting alone would mark her as an expert in
the melding of the [SF and fantasy] genres; this is the
stuff of which 'sense of wonder' is made."—*Locus*
55952-4 • 352 pp. • $2.95

SILENCE IN SOLITUDE (Book II): "[Scott is] a voice
you should seek out and read at every opportunity."
—*OtherRealms*.
65699-7 • 324 pp. • $2.95

THE EMPRESS OF EARTH (Book III):
65364-4 • 352 pp. • $3.50

A CHOICE OF DESTINIES: "Melissa Scott [is] one of science fiction's most talented newcomers. . . . The greatest delight of all is finding out how she managed to write a historical novel that could legitimately have spaceships on the cover . . . a marvelous gift for any fan."—*Baltimore Sun*   65563-9 • 320 pp. • $2.95

THE GAME BEYOND: "An exciting interstellar empire novel with a great deal of political intrigue and colorful interplanetary travel."—*Locus*
55918-4 • 352 pp. • $2.95

TIMOTHY ZAHN
CREATOR OF NEW WORLDS

"Timothy Zahn's specialty is technological intrigue-international and interstellar," says *The Christian Science Monitor*. Amen! For novels involving hard-edged conflict with alien races, world-building with a strong scientific basis, and storytelling excitement, turn to Hugo Award Winner Timothy Zahn!

WILL *YOU* SURVIVE?

In addition to Dean Ing's powerful science fiction novels—*Systemic Shock, Wild Country, Blood of Eagles* and others—he has written cogently and inventively about the art of survival. **The Chernobyl Syndrome** is the result of his research into life after a possible nuclear exchange . . . because as our civilization gets bigger and better, we become more and more dependent on its products. What would *you* do if the machine stops—or blows up?

Some of the topics Dean Ing covers:
* How to *make* a getaway airplane
* Honing your "crisis skills"
* Fleeing the firestorm: escape tactics for city-dwellers
* How to build a homemade fallout meter
* Civil defense, American style
* "Microfarming"—survival in five acres
  And much, much more.

Also by Dean Ing, available through Baen Books:

ANASAZI
Why did the long-vanished Anasazi Indians retreat from their homes and gardens on the green mesa top to precarious cliffside cities? Were they afraid of someone—or some*thing*? "There's no evidence of warfare in the ruins of their earlier homes . . . but maybe the marauders they feared didn't wage war in the usual way," says Dean Ing. *Anasazi* postulates a race of alien beings who needed human bodies in order to survive on Earth—a race of aliens that *still* exists.

FIREFIGHT 2000
How do you integrate armies supplied with bayonets and ballistic missiles; citizens enjoying Volkswagens and Ferraris; cities drawing power from windmills and nuclear powerplants? Ing takes a look at these dichotomies, and more. This collection of fact and fiction serves as a metaphor for tomorrow: covering terror and hope, right guesses and wrong, high tech and thatched cottages.
